BRIAN JACQUES

High Rhulain

Illustrated by DAVID ELLIOT

PHILOMEL BOOKS

For my friend Alan Ingram,
the guardian at Redwall's gate!

PHILOMEL BOOKS
A division of Penguin Young Readers Group
Published by The Penguin Group
Penguin Group (USA) Inc., 375 Hudson Street, New York, NY 10014, U.S.A.
Penguin Group (Canada), 10 Alcorn Avenue, Toronto, Ontario, Canada M4V 3B2 (a division
of Pearson Penguin Canada Inc.). • Penguin Books Ltd., 80 Strand, London WC2R 0RL,
England. • Penguin Ireland, 25 St. Stephen's Green, Dublin 2, Ireland (a division of Penguin
Books Ltd.). • Penguin Group (Australia), 250 Camberwell Road, Camberwell, Victoria
3124, Australia (a division of Pearson Australia Group Pty Ltd.).
Penguin Books India Pvt Ltd., 11 Community Centre, Panchsheel Park, New Delhi 110
017, India. • Penguin Group (NZ), Cnr Airborne and Rosedale Roads, Albany, Auckland
1310, New Zealand (a division of Pearson New Zealand Ltd.). • Penguin Books (South
Africa) (Pty) Ltd., 24 Sturdee Avenue, Rosebank, Johannesburg 2196, South Africa. •
Penguin Books Ltd. Registered Offices: 80 Strand, London WC2R 0RL, England.

Library of Congress Cataloging-in-Publication Data
Jacques, Brian.
High Rhulain / Brian Jacques ; illustrated by David Elliot.
p. cm.
Summary: Following a dream, the young ottermaid Tiria travels
from Redwall to the Green Isle, where otters have long been enslaved by feral cats but fight back as they await the High Rhulain, a
savior whose coming was foretold.
[1. Animals—Fiction. 2. Fantasy.] I. Elliot, David, ill. II. Title.
PZ7.J15317 Hi 2005
[Fic]—dc22
2005047591
ISBN 0-399-24208-2
1 3 5 7 9 10 8 6 4 2
First Impression

W

N

S

E

GREEN ISLE

OTTERCLAN'S CAVE

SLAVE
COMPOUND

FORTRESS

LAKE

RIVER

STANDING
STONES

HOLT SUMMERDELL

PITRU'S BARRICADE

DEEPLOUGH

GREAT CRATER

WESTERN SEA

When autumn's day grows old,
sad orchard leaves do fall.
Dawn breaks o'er silent gardens,
bereft of sweet birdcall.
Stark winter's dirge then wails,
until the earth appears,
white clad 'neath drifted dunes,
whilst trees bear crystal spears.
My chamber is a refuge here,
against the snowbound night,
a flickering cave of crimson gold,
made warm by firelight,
where images are conjured,
of friends I used to know.
I battled and I marched with them,
one dusty long-ago.
I see them now arise again,
in memory that ne'er will fail.
Their legend is reborn anew,
and thus begins my tale.

BOOK ONE

The Forgotten Tome

1

The wind moaned like a wounded beast in the southwest. Gathering speed, it ripped over the heaving ocean, smashing the dark wavecrests to boiling foam. Evening skies darkened as the bruised heavy underbellies of cloudbanks tumbled into a chaotic stampede of black and leaden grey. Lightning scarred the skies. Thunder boomed out, like the sound of mountains cracking from peak to base. On Green Isle, the still waters of loughs and streams were whipped over their banks, flattening and saturating reed and sedge. Leaves showered widespread as trees shook their heads, goaded by the gale into an insane dance.

None of this concerned the big hawk as it fought for its life. The bird was cornered, even though it had ripped through the catching net with its fearsome talons. It choked and spat at the remnants of the tidbit which had lured it into the snare. But there was something it could not rid itself of: a star-shaped iron barb, which the bait had been wrapped around. It had pierced the roof of the big bird's mouth; one of the tips protruded from under its beak. Blood bubbled onto the hawk's throat feathers as it hissed defiance at two young feral cats. They circled their quarry, yowling and spitting, looking for an opening to catch their fierce prey unawares.

Riggu Felis, Warlord of the Green Isle Cats, stood watching his two sons, scorning their efforts to dispatch the wounded bird. The wildcat chieftain turned impatiently to the pine marten, Atunra, his aide and constant companion.

"Gwurr! Is this a kill or a dance? Look ye, they fight like two frightened frogs!"

Atunra flinched as both young cats leapt back, a hair's-breadth from the wounded hawk's lethal talons. "The big bird is a dangerous fighter, Chief. It is wise they do not rush in at it."

Riggu Felis gave a snort of derision. Casting aside his single-bladed war axe, he threw off his battle helmet and cloak, oblivious to the wind and rain.

"Garrah! I have raised cowards for sons! Step aside, ye weaklings. I can snap that thing's neck like a twig!"

As his two sons gave way, the big wildcat bounded in. Tail waving, ears flattened and fangs bared, he howled his challenge. "Arrrreeeekkaaarrrr!"

The wildcat chieftain made a barbaric sight, but the hawk was a born warrior and not easily daunted. Shaking its wings free of the last net strands, it powered itself straight at the foebeast's face, avoiding the outstretched claws. The savage, hooked talons struck true, deep into the area betwixt eyes and nostrils. Spreading its mighty wings, the big bird flapped a short distance into the air.

Riggu Felis screeched in pain, hanging helpless for a brief moment. Then his weight sent him crashing to the ground as the hawk winged upward and out of the trees. Both the young cats and the pine marten dashed forward to help, but too late. The bird had flown.

High into the raging gale it swooped, where it was flung by the elements into the maelstrom of keening wind and battering rain. Up and away it went, like a dead leaf in an autumnal gale—head over tail, talons over wings, a flurry of dark brown and white plumage, resembling a tattered quilt. Off, off, over glade, swamp, stream, sward and lough,

4

across dune and shoreline. Out over the thunderous might of raging seas.

The warlord Riggu Felis lay senseless on the wet earth. His sons looked on in horrified awe as Atunra inspected the gruesome injury inflicted by the bird. Quickly she held his head facedown, wiping away the gore as she issued hasty instructions to the young feral cats.

"Jeefra, Pitru, run and get help. I'll try to keep him breathing while he's unconscious. Hurry now!"

Jeefra ventured a question. "Is he going to die? Has the big bird killed him?"

The pine marten snapped back, "Nay, he will live, as long as I can stop him choking on his own blood. Go now!"

Pitru leaned over Atunra's shoulder. The pine marten kicked out at him. "Don't tarry there gossiping, go and get help—a healer, carriers, bandages and salves. Half of his face is gone, ripped off, most of the muzzle, all of the nose, and his top lip, right down to the teeth and gums. Go quickly, stop for nought. Hasten, before your father bleeds to death!"

As they dashed off through the trees, Atunra stared down at the ravaged features of Riggu Felis. "Ye still have two eyes, though if ye see that face reflected in water, you'll wonder why I saved ye. Still, half a face is better than none. Now Riggu Felis will be able to slay his enemies with just a look, methinks!"

Lycian still had her best seasons before her. She was rather young to be Mother Abbess of all Redwall. However, nobeast could deny that the pretty, slender mouse possessed wisdom, judgement and the good sense of most creatures twice her age.

On the west parapet of the Abbey's outer walltop, Lycian and her constant companion, the molemum Burbee, basked in the welcome morning sun, sitting on their portable chairs enjoying mugs of hot mint and comfrey tea.

5

Burbee scratched her velvety head with a huge digging claw, exclaiming in curious mole dialect, "Hurr, marm, ee wuddent think this morn wot a terrible stormen et wurr larst noight, burr, nay ee wuddent!"

Lycian, surveying the gentle blue sky, blinked in the warm sunlight. "Thank goodness Mother Nature is in a calmer mood today. Just listen to that lark, what a beautiful song she's singing! Can you hear it?"

The molemum had to listen a while before she could discern the sound. She nodded, smiling. "Hurr aye, marm, 'tis aseedingly noice!"

Lycian began singing a song from her Dibbun days, which harmonised perfectly with the bird's trilling.

"When the new day is dawning
the lark doth ascend.
If I could but speak to her
I'd make her my friend.
She would tell of her journey
to the lands of the sky,
where the soft fields of cloud
like white pillows do lie.
She would sing of the earth
far below that she'd seen,
all patched in a quiltwork
of brown, gold and green.
As she wings on the zephyrs
of smooth morning breeze
to rise from the meadows,
the hills or the trees.
With the evening come down,
little bird, cease thy flight
'til the blue peaceful morning
awakes from the night."

The larksong and Lycian's ditty reached their finale together. Molemum Burbee, a sentimental beast, wiped a tear from her eye. "Thurr now, ee likkle bird bees hoi and far away."

Turning to face the Abbey, Lycian allowed her gaze to wander over the magnificent structure. Lovingly built but firmly fashioned as a mountain, the ancient sandstone walls ranged in hue from dusty pink to soft terra cotta in the alternating sunlight and shadow. From belltower to high slated rooftop, down to the mighty buttresses, twixt tiny attic and mullioned dormitory windows, amongst ornate columns and ledges and the long, stained-glass panels of Great Hall on the ground floor, Redwall Abbey stood, solid and steadfast against countless seasons and the severity of all weathers.

Lycian sipped her tea approvingly, nodding towards the front steps and main oaken door. "No storm could bother our home, eh, Burbee?"

Frowning, the molemum squinted over the rim of her mug at the Abbey grounds. "Hurr, that's as may be, young marm, but lookit ee h'orchard. Trees blowed thisaway an' that, fruits'n'berries be'n knocked offen ee boughs. Gurt pesky stormgale!"

Lycian patted her friend's paw, smiling. "Oh come on, old grumblechops, that's what usually happens in bad weather. Nothing our Redwallers can't put to rights. Drink up now, here comes our refill."

Besides being a Foremole (which is a lofty position among his fellow creatures), Grudd Longtunnel was also the Head Abbey Gardener. A nephew of molemum Burbee, he was good-natured, cheerful and honest as the day is long. Balancing a tray on one powerful paw, he clambered up the steps to the walltop, tugging his snout respectfully to the Abbess and his aunt.

"Gudd mornen to ee, marms, an' a roight purty one et bee's, too. Oi bringed ee 'ot scones an' h'extra tea. Boi okey, you'm surrtingly can sup summ tea in ee course of a day. Moi ole tongue'd float away if'n I drinked that much tea!"

Burbee chuckled. "Gurt h'imperdent young lump, lessen thoi cheek an' pour us'n's summ o' that brew."

Grudd placed the plate of fresh scones, spread with meadowcream and clover honey, between them. Whipping the cosy from a sizeable teapot, he topped up both their mugs. "Shudd see wot ee storm do'd to moi veggibles. Flartenned ee lettuces, snapped off'n celery an' strewed termatoes every whichway. Even rooted up moi young radishers. Burr!"

Lycian blew on her tea to cool it. "Your aunt Burbee was just remarking on the storm damage in the orchard. Is it very bad, Grudd?"

The Foremole's face creased deeply in a reassuring smile. "Doan't ee frett, h'Abbess marm. Oi gotten moi molecrew a-workin' daown thurr, an' all ee Redwallers lendin' a paw. Just bee's two more willin' beasts a-needed."

Lycian shot him a look of mock severity. "We'll be down just as soon as we've finished tea, my good mole, and not a moment sooner. Carry on with your duties!"

Grudd caught the twinkle in her eyes. He bowed low, tugging his snout in a servile manner. "Vurry gudd, marm, as ee says, marm, you'm take yurr own gudd toime, marm. Oi'll look for'ard to ee visit with pleshure. 'Twill be a gurt honner furr uz 'umble molebeasts!"

Burbee shook with mirth at the antics of her nephew. "Ho bee off'n with ee, you'm gurt foozikil!"

Down in the orchard, Banjon Wildlough, the otter Skipper, was organizing the workers. Banjon was not a big creature, as otters go, but he had an undoubted air of command about him. Everybeast obeyed his orders, all working together for the common good—except the Dibbuns, of course. (These were the little ones; Abbeybabes were always referred to as "Dibbuns.") The otter Skipper tried to keep his patience with their rowdy manner, which, after all, was the innocence of playful infants.

"No no, Gropp! Ye can't eat those apples, they ain't ripe yet. You'll get tummyache, I'm warnin' ye. Taggle! Stop chuckin' them hazelnuts around. Grumby! Come down out o' that tree. Irgle, Ralg, where are ye off to with that barrow?"

Banjon turned despairingly to his friend, Brink Greyspoke, the big, fat hedgehog who was Redwall's Cellarhog. "I gives up! Can't you do anythin' with the liddle rogues?"

Brink was a jolly creature and well-liked by the Dibbuns. He tipped Skipper a wink. "I'll soon get 'em organised, leave it t'me, Skip."

Brink began by appealing to what Dibbuns loved most: their stomachs. "Lissen now, ye big workbeasts. I 'eard that Friar Bibble 'as got lots o' candied chestnuts to reward willin' bodies with. So 'ere's the plan. See all this hard sour fruit wot's fallen? Well, that'll go for preservin' an' picklin'. All those green nuts, too—they'll be used in the cheese-makin'. Toss the lot into yon barrow, an' we'll take 'em to the kitchens, that'll please the Friar greatly. Come on now, let's see those big muscles bulgin'!"

Squeaking with delight, the Dibbuns rushed to obey Brink.

Banjon spotted some of the older ones about to leave the orchard. They were led by his daughter, Tiria. He called to the ottermaid, "Ahoy, me gel, where d'ye think yore off to?"

Tiria Wildlough stood a head taller than her father. She was a big, strong otter, with not a smidgeon of spare flesh on her sinewy frame. She shunned the typical dress of a maiden, wearing only a cutdown smock, to allow her free movement. This was belted around her waist by her favourite weapon, a sling, which she had named Wuppit. Despite Tiria's young age, her skill with the sling was readily acknowledged by everybeast within Redwall.

She waved cheerily to her father, whom she always addressed as Skip. "We're going to help the molecrew with their compost heap, Skip. Was there anything else you wanted us for?"

Banjon paused a moment, as if making up his mind.

"Foremole Grudd told me he'd like a load of posts an' staves. He's thinkin' of buildin' fences to act as a windbreak from any more wild weather we might get. It'll cut down on damage to his fruit an' veggibles. D'ye follow me?"

One of Tiria's chums, a young squirrel called Girry, shook his head doubtfully. "No wood like that growing in our Abbey grounds, Skip. . . . "

His friend, a young mole named Tribsy, interrupted. "Nay zurr, h'only in ee Mossflower wuddlands will ee foind such timber—yew, ash an' mebbe summ sturdy willow. They'm all a-growen out thurr."

Banjon nodded. "Aye, Foremole asked me to go for it, but I got me paws full with wot's to be done here. Tiria, me gel, I was thinkin', would you like the job of woodcuttin'?"

The ottermaid's eyes lit up like stars. "What, you mean go out into Mossflower? On our very own, me an' Tribsy, an' Girry, an' Brinty? Of course we can!"

Her father's offer meant that they were grown-up and capable enough to be let out without supervision, alone into the vast thicknesses of the Mossflower Woodlands.

Banjon eyed his daughter with that no-nonsense look he had cultivated. "Right, so be it. Tiria, I'm holdin' you responsible, yore in charge. No larkin' about or strayin' off too far!"

Tiria strove hard to keep from bubbling over with excitement. "Count on me, Skip. Straight out, get the wood and right back here to the Abbey. Right, come on, mates, let's get going!"

Skipper coughed. Turning aside, he stifled a smile. "Not so fast, crew. Take yore time, the wood won't run away. Oh, an' ye'd best take a cart along, an' two of Brink Cellarhog's axes. See Friar Bibble, he'll give ye vittles an' drink for a break at noon. Now remember, Foremole only wants sound wood—good strong branches, straight an' well-trimmed. Right, off ye go!"

Skipper Banjon watched as they strode off together, raucously singing an old work song.

"Oh the seasons turn again again,
as Redwall beasts do work work work,
through sun an' wind an' rain rain rain,
we never never shirk shirk shirk!
To table then each eventide,
as sun is setting down down down,
a-feasting drinking singing,
with ne'er a tear or frown frown frown!
We all! We all! Are happy at Redwall!
Our Abbey! Our Abbey!
We're proud to serve Redwall one and all, one and all!"

Brink Greyspoke stood up from fruit gathering. Rubbing his back, he nodded at the departing group. "First outin' on their own, eh? You sure yore a-doin' the right thing, Skip?"

Banjon nodded. "They'll be right as rain with my Tiria in charge. Ye can't keep young 'uns penned atwixt Abbey walls forever. Do they know where ye keep yore axes in the cellars?"

Brink stroked his chinspikes. "Aye, they know alright, Skip. I just 'ope they bring my new 'un back in one piece. I fitted a beech haft on it only two days back, 'tis a good axe, that 'un. . . . "

He was about to expand on the subject of axes when he spotted the Dibbuns marching off in a determined manner. "Whoa there, liddle mates! Where are ye bound?"

Grumby the hogbabe pointed toward the main gate. "Ho, us is goin' to 'elp Miz Tirrier to choppa wood. Don't not worry, Skip, we keep a h'eye on 'em for youse!"

Brink gathered the little ones up and placed them in the big wheelbarrow amid the windfall fruits. "Yore far too young t'be rovin' about woodlands. I'll take ye up t'the kitchens an' tell Friar Bibble to feed ye all well for yore hard work. Will ye lend a paw 'ere, Skip?"

Banjon took one of the barrow handles. "I certainly will, matey. Friar Bibble might feed me, too. A liddle bird told me that he's bakin' sugarplum pudden today."

The Dibbuns roared with delight. "Sugarplum pudden! Whooooraaaayyy!"

Brink turned his eyes skyward, murmuring to Skipper, "I 'opes to goodness he is, 'cos if'n he ain't, we'll 'ave to run for our lives from those liddle 'uns!"

2

In the woodlands south of Redwall Abbey, other young creatures were abroad that day: a small gang of water rats, eight in all, headed by one Groffgut. Leaving the larger vermin bands, they had wandered up country, seeking any opportunity to plunder, kill or cause terror. This was done in the hope of establishing themselves as a feared vermin band. Thus far they had made patchy progress, but Groffgut's confidence was growing daily.

Warm noontide sun slanted through the trees onto a quiet streambank. Some of the rats lay about by the shallows, fishing the limpid waters, whilst others foraged for nests with eggs in them. Groffgut disdained such menial tasks, letting the others do all the chores. By virtue of his size, strength and quick temper, he was the chief. Stretched flat out, he gazed over the bump of his paunchy gut, idly watching the blue-grey campfire smoke blending amid sun shafts.

One of his minions, Hangpaw, limped up from the shallows, displaying a small perch dangling from a line. "Yeherr, Chief, lookit, I gorra fish!"

Groffgut was not impressed. "Yarr, s'only a likkle 'un. Stick it onna fire, an' go an' catcher some big 'uns."

An excited whoop rang out from farther up the bank. "Yaggoo! Cumm an' see dis, mates, I gorra h'eagle!"

13

Groffgut heaved his bulk up irately. "Wot's dat Frogeye shoutin' about now?"

Plugtail, another of the gang, came scurrying up. "Chief, Chief, Frogeye's catchered a h'eagle!"

Groffgut shoved him to one side. The rest followed him as he went to investigate, grumbling all the way. "Huh, shupid! Rats don't catcher h'eagles, don't dat ijjit know? It's h'eagles wot catchers rats!"

None of the gang had ever seen an eagle before, but there was no doubt that Frogeye had captured a big, fierce bird. It looked a lot like they imagined an eagle should look. Frogeye's lazy eye, the one that normally remained lidded over, was blinking up and down, exposing the milky-hued pupil, as the rat danced around, prodding and tripping his find with a crude, homemade spear. The wounded and exhausted bird stumbled forward, desperately trying to get at the life-sustaining streamwater.

Frogeye slammed his spearbutt into its body, toppling it backward, tail over crest. He laughed callously. "Yeehee-hee! See, I told ya, didden't I? I catched a real live h'eagle all by meself!"

Groffgut drew his sword, which was in reality a broken scythe blade with a rope handle. Approaching the big bird, he stood on one of its half-spread wings, pinning the other with his blade as he inspected it. Had the bird not been injured or fatigued, any rat would have rushed for cover at the sight of it. Groffgut saw clearly that it was unable to resist. The bird's savage golden eyes were clouded and flickering shut, a stream of dried blood apparently having sealed its lethally hooked beak. The magnificent dark brown and white plumage stuck out willy-nilly after being battered for leagues across stormbound seas.

Groffgut gave the gang his verdict. "Aye, it's a h'eagle, shore enuff!"

Nobeast took the trouble to argue, though Hangpaw, a thin rat with a withered limb, ventured to enquire, "Wot's we s'posed ter do wid h'eagles?"

14

Threetooth, who lacked all but three fangs, cackled. "Yer eats 'em, I think."

His companion, Rashback, so named because of an unsightly mange, scratched vigourously at his scraggy tail. "I didden know ye could eat h'eagles!"

Groffgut eyed him contemptuously. "Ye can eat anybeast once it's dead, turnep'ead!"

Frogeye became huffy at not being consulted. "Hoi! Dis is my h'eagle, I catchered it. S'pose I duzzen't wanner eat it, eh?"

Groffgut pointed at Frogeye with his sword. "Tern around willyer, mate."

Frogeye turned obediently, and Groffgut dealt him an enormous kick to the bottom, which knocked him flat. The breath whooshed out of Frogeye as Groffgut stamped a footpaw down on his back, sneering, "I'm the chief round 'ere! Who asked yew, malletnose? Plug, git yore rope round dis h'eagle's claws, lash 'im tight."

Plugtail flung his rope around the big bird's legs and noosed them securely. The bird could only flap its wings feebly in protest.

Groffgut issued his orders to the gang. "We'll eat the h'eagle later. Let's 'ave a bit o' fun wid it first. T'ain't every day yer gits a h'eagle ter play wid. Tow it back ter camp, mates!"

The wood-gathering expedition had been a success. Tiria and her three friends had worked diligently, filling the cart with a selection of long branches and straight, thick limbs. It was mainly good yew staves, some pieces of ash and a selection of lesser but useful bits of willow and birch. The four companions were following the course of a stream, which they knew flowed close to the south path at one point. Once they reached the path, Redwall would be within easy walking distance. Tiria estimated they would reach the Abbey by early evening.

Enjoying the freedom of the outdoors, and being in no

great hurry, they opted to take a break for an afternoon snack on the streambank. Girry unpacked the last of their food, whilst Tiria checked the ropes which bound the cargo of wood to the cart. Brinty and Tribsy skimmed flat pebbles over the slow-flowing stream. The ottermaid felt quietly proud of herself; she had completed her task without any untoward incident. Cooling her footpaws in the shallows, she watched the noon shadows start to lengthen over the tranquil waters. Two green- and black-banded dragonflies patrolled the far reed margin, their wings iridescent in the sunlight. Bees droned drowsily around some water crowfoot blossoms, and birdsong echoed amid the trees.

Tribsy left off skimming and sat down to eat. "Froo' corjul an' hunny sangwiches, moi fayverrit!"

Tiria smiled. "Good old Friar Bibble, he knows how to look after hungry workers, eh Tribsy?"

The young mole smiled from ear to ear. "Hurr, an' us'll be back at ee Red'all in gudd toime furr supper. Oi dearly loikes a noice supper, so oi doo's!"

Brinty took a long swig of the fruit cordial. "Don't you ever think of anything but eating, old famine face?"

Tribsy patted his stomach. "Whut's to think abowt, maister? Oi bee's nought but ee pore choild needin' vittles aplenty to grow."

Brinty watched the young mole demolish a sandwich in two bites. "You're growing sideways instead of upwards."

Girry gestured his friends to be quiet as his ears stood up straight. "Ssshh! Listen, did you hear that?"

They listened for a moment, then Tiria shrugged. "Hear what?"

Girry pointed upstream. "Over that way, sounded like somebeasts enjoying themselves, laughing and shouting."

Tribsy wrinkled his snout. "Oi doan't yurrs nuthin'. You'm squirrels can yurr better'n uz moles, burr aye."

Brinty shook his head. "I don't hear anything, either."

Girry began climbing a nearby elm. "Well, I can hear it,

there's something going on up yonder. You three stay here, I'll go and take a peep."

Tiria cautioned her friend, "Stay in the treetops, Girry. Don't go getting yourself into any trouble. I don't want to face my dad back at the Abbey and have to tell him something happened to you!"

The agile young squirrel threw her a curt salute. "Yes marm, don't fret marm, I'll be fine marm!"

The ottermaid watched him ascend into the upper foliage. "Well, just be careful, and less of the marm, please! I'm only one season older than you, cheekybrush!"

Tribsy commandeered another sandwich. "Oi'll just finish off ee vittles whoile us'ns bee's waitin'. Ho joy, this 'un's gotten cheese on it, moi fayverite!"

Brinty looked at his molefriend in amazement. "Is there any sandwich that isn't your favourite?"

Tribsy shook his head solemnly. "Oi b'aint found one as yet, zurr."

After a while they went back to skimming stones. Tiria was by far the best skimmer, making one flat chip of bankrock jump nine times as it bounced over the water. It was rather pleasant passing an afternoon in this fashion, the ottermaid thought. She began to wonder what the fuss and stern warnings from her father had been all about.

Just then, Girry dropped down out of the elm in a rush of leaves and twig ends. The young squirrel, breathless with indignation and urgency, gabbled out, "They've got a big bird hanging upside down from a tree and they're lighting a fire under it, hitting it with spearpoles. We've got to stop them, Tiria, oh, the poor bird!"

Grabbing her friend, the ottermaid shook him soundly. "Make sense, Girry! What big bird, where, and who's hitting it? Now take a deep breath and start again, properly!"

Girry obeyed, taking several breaths before he recovered. "I went upstream. I was up in a beech when I saw them. There's about eight water rats, nasty-looking scum. Anyhow, these rats, they've got a big bird strung upside down from a bough, and they're torturing it to death, I swear they are. Please, Tiria, we must do something to help the bird!"

Unwinding the sling Wuppit from about her waist, Tiria took charge swiftly. "Take an axe, Girry. Go on ahead of us and get close to the bird without being seen. Then wait for us. Tribsy, Brinty, take two good yew staves from the cart and follow behind me!"

Plugtail and Hangpaw were trying to set light to a heap of twigs, leaves and moss beneath where the big bird was hanging upside down. They had to keep ducking as the other gang rats swung the hawk back and forth by prodding and striking at it with their spears. The bird's wings hung limply outspread. Though it hissed feebly at its tormentors, there was no way it could stop them.

Groffgut was enjoying himself immensely at the expense of his helpless victim. He swung his crude sword at the bird, clipping a few of its throat feathers, while taunting it cruelly. "Once dat fire's ablaze, we'll roast yer nice'n'slow, birdy. May'ap it'll be suppertime afore yore dead an' ready, eh?"

Frogeye took a lunge at the bird with his spear but missed. "Kin I 'ave one of its legs, Chief? It was me wot catchered it."

Groffgut snarled and aimed a kick at him. "I'll 'ave one of yore legs if'n ye slays that h'eagle too quick. Stop stabbin' at it like that, snottynose!"

Parraaaang! A hard river pebble shot out of the trees, striking the swordblade and knocking it from Groffgut's grasp. He went immediately into an agonised dance, sucking at the paw which was stinging from the reverberation of the strike.

"Yeeeeek! Who did that? Heeeyaaagh!"

Tiria sped onto the streambank, whirling another stone in her sling as she shouted, "Get away from that bird, rat!"

Groffgut stopped dancing, tears beading in his squinched

eyes. He saw that it was a lone otter. Waving his numbed paw at the gang, he screeched, "Kill dat riverdog t'bits. Slay 'er!"

Frogeye leaped forward, thrusting with his spear. Tiria sidestepped it. Swinging the stone-loaded sling, she brought it crashing into the rat's jaw as she roared, "Redwaaaaallll!"

Brinty and Tribsy charged out of the bushes, laying about heftily with their long staves. Girry dropped down onto the bough which held the big bird. Leaping from there to the ground, he scattered the smouldering fire with his axe. Tribsy gave Plugtail a crack across both legs with his staff, which sent the rat hurtling into the stream. Brinty brought the butt of his staff straight into Groffgut's belly as he reached with his good paw for the sword. Then he began lambasting the gang chief mercilessly. Tiria was everywhere at once, flailing with her loaded sling, cracking the rats' paws, ribs, tails and heads. Whilst all this was going on, Girry placed his back beneath the bird's head and supported it.

Taken aback by the ambush, most of the rats fled for their lives, leaving only three of their number at the scene. Threetooth and Frogeye were stretched out senseless; Groffgut, unfortunately, was still conscious, wailing and pleading as Brinty whacked on at him in a frenzy, yelling at him with each blow he delivered. "Dirty! Filthy! Torturer!"

Tiria seized the young mouse, lifting him clear of his target. "Enough, he's had enough! Do you want to kill him?"

Brinty was still waving his staff at empty air, roaring, "Aye, I'll kill the scum sure enough. Rotten, murdering torturer. He's not fit to stay alive!"

Tiria squeezed Brinty hard. "Now stop that, this instant!"

The young mouse suddenly calmed down. He dropped his staff at the realisation of the wild way he had been behaving. "Sorry, mate, I must have got carried away!"

Tribsy chuckled. "Hurr, you'm surrpintly did, zurr, boi okey, Miz Tiria. Coom on, let's get ee pore burd daown!"

19

Tiria relieved Girry by holding the weight of the limp hawk. The young squirrel took his axe, clambered up into the tree and cut the rope with a single stroke.

The ottermaid lowered the bird gently to the ground, murmuring softly to it, even though it was unconscious. "There there, easy now. You're among friends. We'll get you back to Redwall Abbey. You'll be taken care of there, I promise."

Girry bounded out of the tree, calling to Tribsy, "Come on, we'll get the cart to carry the big bird on."

Tiria stayed by the hawk's side. "Good idea, mates. Brinty, you keep an eye on that rat, he looks like their leader."

The young mouse strode over to Groffgut, issuing a harsh warning. "One move out of you, lardbelly, and I'll break your skull!"

Then he picked up Groffgut's sword and flung it into the stream as the rat gang chief lay there helplessly, glaring hatred at Brinty through his swollen eyes.

When they returned with the cart, it took three of them to lift the big bird on. It lay limp atop the wood cargo.

Tribsy stroked its head. "Do ee bee's still naow, burd. We'm friends, acumm to 'elp ee."

The bird's golden eyes opened for a brief moment before it passed out again. Tribsy patted it gently. "Thurr naow, ee pore creetur, you'm sleep well. Us'll watch o'er ee 'til you'm gets to ee h'Abbey!"

Tiria settled the bird more comfortably on the cart and went to Brinty. The young mouse was wielding his staff, standing guard over Groffgut. The ottermaid nodded approvingly. "Well done, mate. I think you knocked all the fight out of that one!"

She turned the rat over with her footpaw. "Listen carefully, vermin. We're not murderers like you, that's why you're still alive. But I warn you, stay out of Mossflower, or you won't get off so lightly next time."

Groffgut made as if to snarl, but Brinty jabbed him

sharply. "Listen, scumface. If you ever cross my path again, I'll break your skull. Do I make myself clear?"

The gang leader never answered. He lay there, his whole body one throbbing pulse of pain from the beating Brinty had given him. Then he spat contemptuously, still glaring at the young mouse. Brinty took a step forward, but Tiria pulled him away.

"Come on, leave him. We've got to get the poor bird back to Redwall. I think that vermin's learned his lesson."

Groffgut watched them go. When they were safely out of earshot, he stared balefully at Brinty's back, muttering, "I won't ferget you, mousey, oh no! Next time we meet will be yer dyin' day. But I'll make it nice'n'slow for ye!"

As the friends made their way along the streambank, Tiria noticed that Brinty's paws were shaking and his jaw was trembling. "Are you alright, mate?" she murmured.

The young mouse shook his head. "I've never raised my paw in anger against another creature before, and I've never been in a fight. I don't know what happened to me back there. That rat was much bigger than me. If he could have reached his sword, he'd have slain me easily. You know me, Tiria, I'm usually the most peaceful of mice. But when I thought of the way that rat had treated the bird, well, I just lost control. I'm sorry."

Tiria winked at her friend. "No need to be sorry, Brinty. Some of the quietest creatures can fight like madbeasts when they're roused. You did a brave thing, going at the rat like you did."

Brinty strove to keep his paws from shaking. "Maybe so, but it's not a very pleasant feeling afterward, remembering what you did. I would have killed him if you hadn't pulled me off. I don't think I'd ever like to fight again, it's too upsetting."

The twin bells of Redwall, Methusaleh and Matthias, were tolling out their evening peal as the cart reached the Abbey gates. Tiria banged at the entrance. Hillyah and her husband, Oreal, two harvest mice, served as the Abbey Gate-keepers. The couple lived in the gatehouse with their twin babes, Irgle and Ralg.

Oreal called out from behind the huge timber gates, "Say who ye are. Do ye come in peace to our Abbey?"

Girry answered the challenge. "It's the wood gatherers, open up! We've got an injured beast here that needs help!"

Unbarring the main gates, the Gatekeepers opened one side, allowing the friends to pass through with the cart.

The little harvest mouse twins squeaked aloud at the sight of the big bird draped on the wooden cargo. "Yeeeek! A hinjerbeast!"

Their mother drew them aside. "It's not a hinjerbeast, it's an injured beast, an eagle I think, though I've never seen one before."

Tiria allowed the harvest mouse family to help with pushing the cart up to the Abbey building. "The elders will tell us what type of bird it is, once we get it safely inside."

Abbess Lycian and her friend Burbee awaited them on the Abbey steps, along with Skipper, Foremole Grudd and Brink Greyspoke. Skipper shook his daughter's paw heartily.

"Stripe me rudder, gel! That's a fair ole cargo o' wood, but is that a dead bird you've brought us?"

The little twins piped up together, "It's a hinjerbeast, Skip!"

Abbess Lycian hastened forward to inspect the creature. "It's alive, but only just, poor thing. How did this happen?"

Girry explained eagerly. "A gang of water rats had it tied up, hanging from a tree. They were tormenting it, but we stopped 'em with our staves. Hah, you should've seen Tiria, though, she charged right in and battered the bark off those rats with her sling. They soon cleared off, dirty cowards!"

Brink interrupted. "Tell us later, young Girry. Let's get this pore bird some attention afore 'tis a deadbeast. Tribsy, run an' fetch Brother Perant, he'll know wot t'do. Brinty, go an' get ole Quelt the Recorder. I'll wager he'll know wot kind o' bird this 'un is."

Molemum Burbee hitched up her vast flowery apron. "Hurr, an' oi'l goo an' make ee gurt pot o'tea!"

Abbess Lycian smiled appreciatively at her friend. "Good idea, Burbee. Would you be so kind as to bring it up to the Infirmary? A nice cup of tea never goes amiss."

Brother Perant was Redwall's Infirmary Keeper and Healer. The good mouse's knowledge of herbs, salves, potions and treatments was without peer in all Mossflower. No sooner was the bird borne into his sickbay than Perant began practising his art.

"Hmm, a giant of a bird, not like any hereabouts. Probably some kind of eagle or hawk. There's an object lodged inside its mouth. Nasty thing, looks like a star made of iron. See how it sticks out from beneath the lower beak? Skipper, get that hardwood pestle, force the beak open and hold it still whilst I work. Huh, wouldn't like to lose a paw if it snapped shut as I was operating!"

Most of the gentler woodland creatures had to look away as Perant pried at the object with his instruments. He worked swiftly, muttering to himself, "What sort of villain would do this to a living creature? Ah, here it comes . . . dreadful thing, just look at that!"

Wiping the barb clean, he passed it to Tiria. She felt the sharp edges of the iron star, her face grim as she dropped it into her pebble pouch.

"Someday I may get the chance to pay the scum back with his own weapon!"

3

Beyond the high seas, far away on Green Isle, a monumental bulk loomed over the landscape of swamps, streams and watermeadows. The once-proud timber fortress of the Wildlough otterclan, it had been inhabited for untold seasons by cats. Riggu Felis, and his barbaric ancestors before him, had held sway over Green Isle for as long as anybeast could remember. The isle had become no place for otters to live. Apart from a small band of outlaw otters, the rest were slaves, completely subjugated by the mighty warlord and his cats. It was the cats' home now—a solid fortress, built entirely of pine logs, on the lakeshore. Part of the structure jutted out over the lake, where it was supported upon pillars of stone in the shallows.

On the stairs outside the upper tower chamber, Lady Kaltag, the mate of Riggu Felis, sat in a window alcove with Atunra, the warlord's pine marten aide. Kaltag's lustrous black tail twitched back and forth restlessly beneath her fur-trimmed cloak as she waited to be admitted into the chamber.

On the lower stairs, the two sons of Felis and Kaltag were arguing and fighting. Jeefra was the burlier of the two. His brother, Pitru, was half a head shorter and not as well fleshed, but it was he who was the fiercer.

Pitru lashed out at Jeefra, snarling, "If he dies, I will be

Warlord of Green Isle. Then you will have to watch out, flabbytail!"

Jeefra dodged past him and ran yowling to his mother's side. "Tell him, Mamma! We're both supposed to rule as warlords if Father dies, aren't we?"

She took his paw, calling severely to her other son, "Pitru, come up here right now!"

The young cat did as he was bidden, though he stayed clear of Kaltag's grasp, pouting and stamping his footpaw. "Jeefra's soft, I'd make the best warlord!"

Kaltag reprimanded the pair. "Shame on you both, talking as if your father were going to die!"

Pitru dodged forward, treading on his brother's tail. He smirked maliciously at Atunra. "I saw what the big bird did to him. He will die, won't he?"

The pine marten shook her head, wincing as screeches and growls emanated from the chamber. "Nay, thy father is a true wildcat. The healers will save him."

More screeches came from within, together with the crashing of furniture being hurled about. Suddenly the door slammed open and two old cats were flung out, tumbling down the stairs. The voice of Riggu Felis roared angrily, "Idiots! Impostors! Out, before ye slay me with those foul potions and rusty needles. Begone with ye!"

Then Warlord Riggu Felis stood framed in the doorway. The wildcat's face had been covered when they brought him in, but now it was plain to view in all its hideousness. The black-and-grey-striped fur was normal from ears to eyes, but below that it was red, glistening flesh and bone. The whole muzzle, nose and upper lip had been torn off. Half of the warlord's face was a frightful mask—a spitting, bubbling skeleton, as he continually sucked air to breathe. His blazing eyes raked them.

"Why are ye staring so? Is it not a pretty sight?"

Storming back into the chamber, he slammed the door. They heard him clattering and rattling amid armour, ranting to himself, "Two useless sons who couldn't kill a bird, a single bird! Hah, and the bird flew off, it could not stand and do battle with me. Birds will die! All birds on Green Isle shall be slain! Then everybeast will know that I cannot die, for I am Riggu Felis!"

Outside, Lady Kaltag beckoned to her sons as she descended the stairs. "We will not tarry here whilst your father is in such wrath. Atunra, you will stay and await his orders."

The pine marten bowed briefly. "As ye wish, my Lady!"

The afternoon was waning by the time the wildcat emerged from his chamber. He faced his aide. "So, Atunra, what do ye think?"

The pine marten stared at him, knowing she would die if she did not reply favourably. Riggu Felis had altered one of his war helmets to cover the injuries to his face. He had wrenched the visor from the headpiece and fixed a square of chain mesh to its lower part. It hid the wounds but made him look even more sinister. Now his breath whistled and hissed through the rings of chain mail, and they parted slightly, revealing his naked fangs. Moreover, he kept pushing his tongue through the mask to facilitate his breathing.

Atunra nodded solemnly. "It gives you an air of mystery, Lord."

The wildcat raised his single-bladed war axe. "Gather my catguards. Tell them to take bows and quivers of arrows. My command is that they kill every bird in the skies, large or small. We will feast on their flesh. Destroy the birds, slay them all!"

He strode to the alcove window. Leaning out, he bellowed, "Death to all birds! Death! Death!"

On the lake below, two otter slaves heard the din from the tower window. Looking up, they beheld the wildcat, recognisable even with his face masked.

One of the otters shook his head sadly. "Ah, 'twas a mistake ye made sayin' Felis was dead. That villain will never die! D'ye not hear him?"

26

The other otter began hauling in his nets. "Aye, sure he'll only get wickeder by the day, worse luck for us. Y'know the trouble with us, mate? We're weak. It takes a beast like Leatho Shellhound to defy that Riggu Felis an' his scurvy cats. Aye, Leatho's the buckoe, sure enough!"

Whulky, the elder of the two otters, rounded on his companion. "Keep yore voice down! Ye know wot'll happen if'n yore caught even mentionin' that name. Ye'll end up bein' slung into Deeplough with a stone tied to yore neck, t'be eaten by Slothunog. Now get rowin' for shore. Can't ye see Weilmark Scaut waitin' on our catch?"

As Chab, the younger otter, sculled their coracle toward the pier, Whulky lectured him. "Lissen, Chab, don't ye ever say we're weak. Us otters have to stay an' obey Felis because we've all got families an' young 'uns to worry about. They'd be the ones to suffer if ever we tried anythin'. Shellhound's free as the air. That rogue can afford t'be an outlaw, an' besides, he's a seadog, not a stream otter like us."

Chab rested his paddle. "But wasn't it us that were once the warriors of Green Isle, an' haven't we got the blood of the High Queen Rhulain* Wildlough runnin' in our veins?"

Whulky sighed. "Aye, that's truth to tell, Chab, but 'tis many a hundred seasons since those days. The High Queen is nought but a thing for songs an' poems to tell our little 'uns now."

An irate voice called to them from on shore. "If you two don't move yerselves, I'll skin the hide from yer rudders!" This threat was followed by the crack of a whip.

Weilmark Scaut was a burly, ginger feral cat, hated by all the otters for his arrogance and cruelty. He stood on the pier end, coiling his long whip, watching the little fishing coracle heave to. As a weilmark he was a high-ranking officer of the catguards.

Strutting back and forth, Weilmark Scaut began ha-

*Rhulain (pronounced Roolayn)

27

ranguing the otters. "Stir yer stumps, waterdogs! Git that catch up 'ere, an' stand t'be searched. Move yerselves!"

Whulky and Chab spread their net with its small catch of trout and gudgeon. They both stood to one side, paws spread wide, as a feral cat soldier searched them for concealed weapons (which otters were forbidden to carry) or any type of contraband.

Scaut took five of the eight fish they had caught, leaving them the three smallest. He scowled at the searcher. "Well, are they clear?"

The soldier tossed two sharpened musselshells (which the fisherbeasts were allowed to carry in the course of their trade) down onto the pier. He saluted with his spear. "Aye, they're clear, Weilmark!"

Scaut watched Whulky and Chab carefully. "Go on then, get goin', both of ye."

As they walked away, Scaut's keen gaze was still inspecting them. "Halt right there, don't move!"

The two otter slaves froze in their tracks. Scaut walked over and placed his face close to Chab's, grinning wickedly at him. "You there, guard, lift this 'uns left footpaw."

The soldier hastened to obey. Scaut struck the raised footpaw with his whipstock, and two perfectly symmetrical, purple mussel pearls rolled out onto the pier.

Scaut feigned surprise. "By my claws, what's this?"

Chab murmured awkwardly, "Sir, they're only baubles for me liddle daughter t'play with."

The weilmark swaggered in a circle around Chab. "Baubles fer yer liddle daughter, eh? They're the property of yore warlord, Riggu Felis, the same as everythin' else on Green Isle. Nothin' belongs to waterdogs, nothin!"

He turned to the soldiers, bellowing, "This beast is a thief, take 'im away an' bind 'im under the pier fer the night. No vittles an' a night freezin' 'is rudder off down there'll teach 'im a lesson!"

He scooped up the pearls and admired them. "Lady Kaltag'll like these fer 'er collection!"

Whulky was dismissed to go back to his family. As Chab was being prodded at spearpoint to the pylons beneath the pier, another feral cat soldier came panting along the lakeshore. Throwing a hasty salute with his bow, he called to Scaut.

"Weilmark! There's trouble down on the river. We've got one of 'em pinned down there. They say 'tis the Shell-hound!"

Scaut grabbed a spear, leaping down onto the shore. "The Shell'ound, eh? Quick, take me there!"

He dashed off behind the stumbling soldier. "Cummon, cummon, shift yerself. I need to catch that rogue!"

Bound by his neck to one of the stone pylons beneath the pier, Chab chuckled grimly. "Fat chance o' that, ye pompous bunglin' furball!"

Leatho Shellhound, crouching among the bushes on the riverbank, watched a cat soldier creeping forward stealthily. In a passable cat accent, Leatho shouted out excitedly, "Lookit, there 'e goes, over by those two rocks!"

As the soldier turned his head to see, Leatho let fly with a stone from his sling. It slammed into the back of the foe-cat's skull, laying him out senseless. The brawny sea otter turned to an injured barnacle goose, who was lying alongside him.

"Hah, if'n that feller ever wakes, I'll be surprised. Now then, matey, let's take a peek at that shaft!"

As Leatho inspected the arrow that was sticking from the bird's neck, the wounded goose commented, "It is not a bad hurt I am thinking. Lucky for me it was that the cats are not being as good with the bows than you are with the sling, comrade."

Leatho worked the arrow loose and staunched the wound by binding it with a poultice of mud and wild radish leaves. "Ye'll live, matey. Yore right, t'aint that bad. You keep an eye on those scallywags while I tighten this dressin'. Was you the only one of yore skein they hit?"

29

Flinching slightly as Leatho firmed up his work, the barnacle goose nodded gingerly. "Only I was struck. It was my own fault I am thinking. We of the Skyfurrowers should never be caught napping while we are on the wing. Lagged to the back and lowered my height I had. Silly goose that I am. Two more cats I can see out there, comrade!"

Two feral cat soldiers were creeping toward the limp figure of the fallen one on the shore. Leatho popped up from hiding. Like greased lightning, he slung two more stones. So swift was he that the second stone was in the air before the first had landed. They both fell true. One cat screeched as his tail was cracked near its base; the other rolled over wailing, with a forepaw badly smashed.

The outlaw otter grinned broadly. "That'll keep the mangy rascals' heads down for a while, but we'll have t'be movin' afore they bring reinforcements. Can ye fly, matey?"

Puffing out its chest, the barnacle goose replied, "Ho yarr, fly I can, though I am thinking it will be some while before I am catching up to my skein. But what of you, comrade, will they not seize you?"

The sea otter sorted through his slingstones casually. "Seize the Shellhound? Hah! The cat hasn't ate supper yet that'll ever seize me, old matey. I'll cover for ye while you escape. Get away from Green Isle, across the wide sea, but I suppose ye know whither yore bound. Whenever ye reach land, though, ye must get a healer, or somebeast that knows physickin', to look at that neck. Arrow wounds have a nasty habit of turnin' poison."

Leatho went into a crouch, twirling his loaded sling. "I'm goin' to break cover now, mate. The moment I've got all their attention, you take off. Understand?"

The barnacle goose offered its webbed leg. "It is thankful to you I am. May the good fortune speed you, comrade!"

Leatho shook the proffered web in his sinewy paw. "An' may the good winds be at yore back, fine bird!"

He broke cover and yelled at the six or so cats who came bounding after him, "Heeee aye eeeeh! Who wants to catch a Shellhound? Yore mothers were bandy an' yore fathers were mangy!"

He dropped the fastest of the cats with a well-aimed stone to the jaw, then sped off. Zigging and zagging, ducking and weaving, Leatho shot into the river and vanished underwater.

The cats, terrified of deep water, scrambled along the bank, firing arrows uselessly into the swift current, just as Weilmark Scaut pounded up with six more behind him. Immediately Scaut began yelling, "Wot in the name o' fangs is goin' on 'ere? Where's that bandit Shell'ound?"

The senior of the patrol, the cat whose paw had been smashed, threw a limp salute and explained in a pained whine, "Weilmark, we brought down a goosebird, but the Shell'ound rescued it. Then 'e dropped Rubjer stone dead, broke Viglo's tail an' smashed me paw, every bone of it I think."

Scaut struck the speaker hard in the face with his coiled whip, roaring at him, "I never asked yer wot he did. I'm askin' yer where is he?"

"Yoohoo, Wipwip, I'm over here!"

As Scaut turned to the sound of the voice, Leatho blasted up out of the water like a rocket. He let fly with a ropy length of bedweed, which had a small rock tied to one end. Before Scaut could duck, it caught him, wrapping swiftly round his neck and bringing the rock thudding against the side of his skull. The weilmark fell heavily in a limp heap. Arrows thrummed through the air toward the river surface. But Leatho Shellhound, the outlaw sea otter, had gone.

As the dispirited cats carried their wounded weilmark from the scene, high up, far out of arrowshot, a barnacle goose honked its delight to the skies.

4

That evening at supper, the Great Hall of Redwall was abuzz with the exploits of Tiria and her friends. The ottermaid sat with her father, Abbess Lycian, molemum Burbee, Brink Greyspoke and Foremole Grudd. She had already related her story of the incident, though quite modestly.

The Abbess clasped Tiria's paw warmly. "You were very brave to save the bird's life, my dear, particularly when you were outnumbered two to one by the vermin. You have a courageous daughter, Skipper."

Almost at a loss for words, Banjon swelled with pride as he patted Tiria's back. "I wish yore mamma had lived to see ye now, gel. She always said us Wildloughs were a warrior clan from somewhere. Yore a credit to us, Tiria."

The ottermaid asked a question she had often mulled over. "Do you think I'll become a Skipper someday?"

Her father put aside his tankard of October Ale, explaining almost apologetically to her, "Ye'd make a finer Skipper than any otter I've ever met, myself included. But the Law of Otters says that maids can't become Skippers. I know it's not fair, Tiria, but the law's the law, an' we've always lived by it."

Tiria persisted. "But I've heard tales saying that there were maids who became Skippers in other parts of the land."

32

Banjon took a draught of his October Ale and then slammed the tankard down decisively. "This ain't the time or place t'be talkin' of these matters, me gel. May'ap there are places where it happens, but not in Mossflower territory, an' I ain't responsible for wot sea otters do. We abide by our Otter Law, an' that's that!"

There was a moment's awkward silence, which was broken by the arrival of Friar Bibble. The shrewcook was pushing a trolley, upon which rested a steaming cauldron. He wiped perspiration beads from his snout with a spotted kerchief before he proclaimed proudly, "Look you, Tiria. I've made a pot of special shrimp'n'hotroot soup, just for you, my brave young 'un!"

Freshwater shrimp'n'hotroot soup was a dish dear to the heart of all otters. Tiria sniffed its fragrant aroma, complimenting the kindly friar. "Marvellous! Nobeast can make shrimp'n'hotroot like you do, sir!"

As he began ladling the soup out, Bibble winked at Skipper. "Indeed to goodness, missy, don't be sayin' things like that. You'll be causin' trouble twixt me an' your da!"

Banjon accepted a bowlful eagerly. "Oh no, mate, 'tis a fact. Even I can't make it taste like you do. Ye can make 'otroot better'n an otter, Bibble!"

Tiria chuckled. "Exactly what do you put in it, sir?"

The friar began explaining. "Well, I uses more watercress an' scallions than some does, an' a touch of wild ransom ... " He halted and glared at her with mock censure. "Indeed to goodness, missy, I can't be tellin' everybeast about those secret herbs an' spices I uses in my recipes!"

Foremole Grudd had been watching Brinty, Tribsy and Girry. They were seated at the other end of the table, telling of the day's adventures ... with many embellishments to the facts.

Grudd laughed aloud. "Hurr hurr hurr! Do ee lissen to they'm young 'uns? Oi never hurd such fibbin' in all moi borned days!"

Brinty was positioning various items on the table as he

told of his role. "See these candied chestnuts? Well, they were the water rats. Wicked villains, all twelve of 'em!"

The molebabe Groop interrupted. "Oi hurd Miz Tirree sayen' et wurr h'eight ratters!"

Girry cleared his mouth of plum pudden. "She was too busy whackin' about with her sling to be counting vermin. Actually, there were thirteen rats. I battled with two of 'em, big rascals who'd climbed up onto the branch of the tree while I was cuttin' the big bird's rope."

Tribsy left off demolishing some rhubarb crumble to make his contribution to the fictional action. He took two loaves and stuck a fork in each one, placing them amid the candied chestnuts. "Yon loafers wurr ole Brinty an' moiself. Hurr, wot ee purr o' wurriers we'm was! These yurr forks bee's ee yew staves us wurr a-carryen'. Bain't that roight, Brin?"

Brinty got carried away as he invented further heroics. Using the loaves and forks, he sent chestnuts bouncing and flying widespread as he yelled, "That's right, we fought 'em! Bangbashwallopsplat! We sent all fourteen of those giant rats scurryin'. Wailin' for their mammas they were, the fatty-bottomed cowards!"

After wiping a splash of soup from his cheek, Skipper Banjon peered at the candied chestnut floating in his bowl. "Look, a rat's just landed in my soup. We'd best eat up, daughter, afore they tell the tale again an' increase the number of vermin they defeated!"

After supper, most Redwallers went to sit out on the Abbey steps to enjoy the summer evening's warmth. Tiria and her father joined Abbess Lycian and Brink Greyspoke on a visit to the Infirmary to check on the hawk's progress. Brother Perant and Old Quelt, the Recorder-cum-Librarian, were studying the bird. It had flown up onto a window ledge and was inspecting its new surroundings.

Perant reported his findings avidly. "Well, friends, what can I say? That bird is a most remarkable creature, just look at it! Earlier today you wouldn't have given a split acorn on its chances of survival. However, no sooner had I removed the barb from its mouth and cleaned up its bumps and bruises when it began drinking water. Hah, and not just wetting its beak, it consumed nearly a full basin. Almost a magical recovery you'll agree!"

The learned Brother pointed at his patient. "See how those golden eyes glitter. Notice how it has preened its plumage back into shape, truly remarkable! Admittedly its mouth and beak must be rather stiff and quite sore, but what a grip on life our feathered friend has, eh? A real survivor I'd say, yes indeed!"

The big bird swept its savage golden eyes over the assembly, then went back to grooming its wing feathers. Tiria felt happy for the bird, clearly a brave and solitary creature. "Do you think its thick plumage saved it from severe injury, Brother? Those rats were brutal vermin."

Perant nodded. "I don't think we fully realise just how strong the bird is, Tiria. It's a formidable creature."

Much to everybeast's surprise, Abbess Lycian strode calmly over to the big bird and began gently stroking its head. It stayed quite still, perhaps sensing that she meant it no harm. Lycian spoke softly to it.

"My goodness, you certainly are a big, strong fellow. I wonder what sort of bird you really are?"

Old Quelt had the answer. He was a silver-furred squirrel, an ancient dry stick of a beast, bent by many long seasons. Besides being the Redwall Recorder, Quelt had appointed himself the first Abbey Librarian. He had commandeered the lowest of the attic rooms and made it his own. There he had gathered every piece of written material Redwall possessed. Brink and Foremole Grudd had shelved the room out at his request. Parchments, scrolls, pamphlets, tomes and volumes covered the library from ceiling to floor. The old squirrel held in his paw a slim, bark-bound book. All of the Abbey members who had assembled listened carefully to what he had to say.

35

"This is a record of birds, written by one Abbess Bryony in the far bygone seasons. She had a particular interest in hunting birds. Let me read you what she wrote about this specimen."

Peering through his rock crystal spectacles, Quelt leafed the yellowed parchment pages. "Hmm, here it is. A bird that is rarely seen in the Mossflower territories. They have been reported by geese who have visited Redwall as mainly inhabiting a place called Green Isle, where they hunt the rivers, loughs and streams. They are said to be large, powerful birds; their description runs thus. Dark-brown upper plumage, with white feathers underneath the body. Long wings, with brown-and-white-patterned undersides, angled two-thirds of the way along. The head is white-crowned, with two dark stripes. These are barred across the eyes, giving a masklike aspect. The eyes are broadly gold-ringed, with jet-black centres. These birds have lethally curved beaks. They also possess four black talons of savage aspect on each blue-grey scaled leg."

Closing the book, Quelt favoured Tiria with a rare smile. "So then, do ye not think your bird fits the description?"

The ottermaid agreed readily. "Indeed I do, sir, perfectly!"

The ancient Librarian pointed a bony paw at the bird. "These were known as pandions in olden times. What you have brought to our Abbey is an osprey, the great fish hawk!"

Brink Greyspoke stared admiringly at the osprey. "A fish 'awk, eh? That 'un must need vittles wot he's used to. What d'ye think, Skip? Shall we go an' catch our osprey a fish? There's grayling aplenty in the Abbey pond."

Skipper, who loved to go fishing but seldom got the chance, was all for the idea. "Aye, let's do that, Brink. Can't see that big ole feller starve now, can we? Er, with yore permission, Mother Abbess, me'n Mister Greyspoke would like to go night fishin'."

Lycian could not help smiling at the eager pair. "Just for

the benefit of the osprey, of course? Nothing to do with taking the little boat out on the pond, together with some refreshment for a quiet summer's night."

Brink's eyes went dreamy at the thought. "Just me'n ole Skip, out on the pond in our liddle boat with the moon above, a flagon o' my best pale cider, some cheese'n'mushroom pasties an' a calm, warm night. Aaaah!"

Banjon kicked the Cellarhog's footpaw to silence him. "Er, no, Abbess, nothin' like that, but just like you said, for the benefit o' the osprey. By me rudder, it can be hard work, fishin' all night long for a fish big enough t'feed that feller's beak. That it will, marm!"

Neither could see Lycian's eyes twinkling as she bowed her head gravely. "A charitable and worthy act, my good friends. You have my permission."

Tiria piped up excitedly. "Can I come too, please?"

Her father shook his head. "You've had quite enough for one day, me gel. I reckon a good night's rest is the best thing for ye."

Seeing her crestfallen face, the Abbess suggested an alternative. "Obey your father, Tiria. Who knows? Tomorrow we may have more responsible tasks, now that you're growing up. But first you may go to the kitchens. Tell Friar Bibble I sent you for a treat, after all your good work today. I'm sure he'll have something special for you."

Flashing the Abbess a brief smile of thanks, the ottermaid hurried off downstairs.

Friar Bibble looked up from his ovens. "Indeed to goodness, 'tis the heroine of the woodcutters. What can I do for you, lovely miss?"

Tiria explained that the Abbess had sent her for a treat.

The tubby little shrewcook waved a paw around his domain. "Well now, what would ye like to eat, beauty?"

She shrugged. "I don't really know, sir."

Taking a wooden paddle, Bibble opened one of the long

oven doors. "Indeed to goodness, there's a thing, a young 'un who can't make up her own mind. Come and lend a paw here, missy, maybe I'll treat you to a Friar's Special."

Using the long beechwood paddle, Tiria helped Friar Bibble to pull out loaves, cobs, farls and rolls, all for next morning's breakfast table. "What's a Friar's Special, sir?"

Bibble selected two crispy little golden batch loaves. "It's what I like to treat myself to after a long day's bakin'. You'll like it. Pass me that small pot off the oventop. Wrap a towel around it now, don't want to burn your paws."

Tiria did as he bade, placing the pot in front of him. "Mmm, it smells delicious! What is it?"

Bibble sliced both batch loaves through with his knife. "Damsons an' crushed almonds cooked in honey an' aged cider."

He ladled the mixture onto the cut loaves, then produced a flagon and two beakers. "Elderberry an' burdock cordial, just the thing. Come now, we'll sit on those sacks o' flour whilst we have our snack."

Tiria began praising the wonderful treat. "It tastes really nice, sir."

Bibble held up a flour-dusted paw. "Quiet now, don't go tellin' anybeast about my Special, or I'll have a full kitchen every night, so I will."

The ottermaid promised him that she would keep silent, but only on condition that he would allow her to visit again for more.

The shrewcook shook his head in mock surprise. "Indeed to goodness, Tiria Wildlough, you're a beauty an' a rogue all in one. Be off to your bed, you young scallywag!"

Playfully he pursued her from the kitchens, waving a paddle.

Leaving the kitchens, Tiria wandered through Great Hall, stopping for a while at the beautiful Redwall tapestry. This was an intricately woven work, depicting as its main theme the legendary mouse, Martin the Warrior. He had been one of the Abbey's founders and the famed Champion of Red-

38

wall. Lanterns illuminated his heroic figure, whilst all around him vermin could be seen fleeing for their lives. Tiria often visited the tapestry. She loved to look at the Warrior, he was a valiant fighter, standing courageously against all odds. Formidable, yet with the light of kindness radiating from his eyes. Martin stood holding his great sword, which had been forged from a piece of a fallen star in the mountain fortress of Salamandastron, home of the mighty Badger Lords. Above the tapestry, lying on two wallspikes, the actual sword was displayed. It was nothing elaborate—a real warrior's blade, perfectly balanced, as deadly as chain lightning in a winterstorm, its point as keen as an ice needle. Tiria instinctively touched the only weapon she had ever known, the sling she had named Wuppit, belted about her waist, with its stone pouch attached.

She stared at Martin and his sword, softly reciting a phrase her father had often repeated. " 'Any weapon is the best weapon, as long as ye can use it skilfully and with honour.' "

Tiria blinked, peering at the likeness of Martin. Had he nodded at her, as if in agreement with her father's words? She yawned, unaccountably overcome by tiredness. Perhaps it was just a draught stirring the tapestry. Her yawns echoed around the time-mellowed hall as she stole off to her bed.

The land of dreams is an odd realm, sometimes nightmarish, other times peaceful. Tiria found herself wandering along the still shores of a vast sunlit lake; she felt happy in its silent tranquillity.

From afar, two creatures floated toward her in a nimbus of golden light. As they drew close, Tiria recognised one as Martin the Warrior. Smiling at her, he indicated his companion. Tiria felt her heart jump. The other creature was a tall, stately otter lady, obviously older than she but a mirror image of herself in features, build and height. On her brow rested a slim gold circlet, with a large, round emerald at its centre. The otter lady wore a short, dark-green cloak, richly embroidered about the hem. From neck to waist she was covered by a metal breastplate, silver with a gold star radiating from its centre. What really intrigued Tiria was that the otter lady carried a sling and a stone pouch, belted about her middle, the same way in which Tiria carried hers.

The ottermaid felt an immediate trust of and kinship to the lithe, regal apparition. She stood staring at her in the sunny dream landscape, not knowing what to say but yearning to talk to the otter lady. Turning to Martin, she found herself equally dumbfounded. Though Martin the Warrior had no need of speech, his kind eyes widened expressively. He merely smiled at Tiria, pointing to the otter as an indication that she should listen to what the strange vision had to say. Then, in clear, measured tones, the otter lady spoke:

"Like the sun, High Rhulain will rise anew,
to set the downtrodden free.
A warriormaid with Wildlough blood
must cross the Western Sea.
She who looks ever through windows
at the signs which feathers make,
seek the Green Isle through her knowledge,
for all thy kinbeasts' sake."

Then both Martin and his companion glided on past Tiria. She yearned to follow them but felt rooted to the spot. As the bright noon of her dreams darkened, desolation overcame the ottermaid. She felt them fade into the mists, and she was left alone, standing on the deserted lakeshore amid the sighing breeze, with the otter's words echoing throughout the corridors of her mind. Tiria did not sleep peacefully for the remainder of that night. She tossed and turned fitfully, imbued with a restless energy.

5

Tiria was up with the dawn the next morning with a sense of unfulfilled purpose that she could not name. Dressing hastily, she hurried downstairs. Her normally healthy appetite usually took her to the kitchens; instead, she avoided them and went straight outdoors. It was a fresh summer morn, the grass underpaw heavy with dew. Lawn borders were patches of pastel colours, with daisy, milkwort, rockrose and pasque flower in profusion. She paused at the northwest Abbey gable, catching the sweet chirrup of ascending larksong from the flatlands beyond the west ramparts. The sound blended melodiously with the cooing of woodpigeon from the woodland on the far side of the east wall.

The poignant moment was broken by the interruption of two gruff voices singing raucously. Tiria knew it was her father and Brink, coming up from the Abbey pond after their night fishing. She also realized that a meeting with the jolly pair would result in being questioned. What was she doing outdoors so early, couldn't she sleep, had she eaten a good breakfast yet? Avoiding the tiresome interview, the ottermaid stepped behind a protruding buttress and waited for them to go indoors. However, the happy pair were in no hurry.

Carrying a splendid grayling between them in a net, Brink and Banjon sang away lustily.

"O I knew a worm who turned to his tail,
an' this is wot he said,
I wish that you'd stop followin' me,
as though we both were wed.
Said the tail to the head stop pullin' me,
'cos I've no wish to go,
besides, I think yore really a tail,
an' I'm the head you know!
This caused the worm some great concern,
he said, I'm sure yore wrong,
an' they both began to bicker about,
to whom did the stomach belong?
Both tempers did boil, while disputin' a coil,
they fell into an awful fight,
they wriggled an' squirmed an' waggled an' turned,
for worms as ye know can't bite.
Then a big blackbird, who'd heard every word,
came flutterin' out of a tree,
I'll oblige ye both, the blackbird quoth,
an' he ate them both for tea.
So that was that, he settled their spat,
an' I'll bid ye all good day,
for it's head to tails when reasonin' fails,
a worm should crawl away!"

They finished the song, but Tiria had to wait whilst they performed a little jig on the Abbey steps, shaking paws and patting each other's backs triumphantly. The slam of the Abbey door told the ottermaid that they had gone inside. She came out of hiding and continued her rambling walk.

With no real purpose, Tiria made her way up the wall-steps to the northwest corner of the ramparts, where she stood staring out over the flatlands. Across these plains, she had been told, were hills, mountains and the shores which

42

bordered the Western Sea. Like many Redwallers, she had never traversed that far, but being an otter, Tiria knew that someday she would. Oblivious to the sounds of Abbey-dwellers commencing their day's activities behind her, she remained, caught in a reverie of unknown problems.

At first, she did not notice that the dark shape was coming toward her. Only when it got closer did Tiria see that it was a bird—a large barnacle goose, much bulkier than an osprey. She wondered why it was flying so low, and alone, too. Geese usually flew very high in a V-shaped gaggle known as a skein. It soared straight in over the battlements, landing on Tiria in an ungainly heap.

Fortunately, the ottermaid was no weakling. Holding on to the bird, Tiria was able to stop them both from toppling off the walkway to the lawns below. Once its progress was arrested, the goose scrambled free of her and crouched back into the lee of the wall. It was a striking creature. Greyish black with white underfeathers, it had a quaintly comical face which looked rather friendly.

Tiria straightened up, but all she could think of to say was "Er, good morning!"

The barnacle goose nodded affably. "I am bidding you a good morning also. I am thinking that this is the place of Red Walls. I am of the Skyfurrows. Some of them have been here before, though not for many seasons. Here is where you have healers, I am told?"

Tiria noticed a tattered mass of mud and leaves sticking to the newcomer's neck. "Healers? Oh yes, we have a healer at our Abbey. Has your neck been injured?"

The goose bent his beak toward the remnants of the makeshift dressing. "It is injured by an arrow I am. The Shellhound said that help I must seek. Arrow wounds can go bad, trouble that would mean for Brantalis."

Tiria suddenly forgot her own vague problems. "Brantalis, is that your name? Mine's Tiria, I'm a Redwaller. You stay right there, Brantalis, we'll get you to a healer quickly."

Brantalis clacked his beak. "Wait here I will!"

Hillyah and Oreal, the harvest mice, were emerging from the gatehouse with their twin babes. Tiria called to them from the walltop. "There's an injured goose up here that needs help. You'd best get a stretcher and some bearers, it's quite a large bird. Would you hurry, please?"

Oreal was a creature who could become easily flustered. Hopping from one paw to the other, he called out to his wife, "My dear, it's an injured goose, whatever shall we do?"

His wife, a sensible type, took charge promptly. "Don't get upset, dear. Stay here with Irgle and Ralg, I'll soon get help!"

The harvest mousewife sped off toward the Abbey, with her pinafore hitched high. Irgle and Ralg slipped by their father. The mousebabes scuttled up the wallsteps. Eager to see the visitor, they both squealed excitedly, "A hinjagoose! A hinjagoose!"

Oreal stood undecided for a moment, then chased after them. "Come back, sugarplums, come back! Be careful, it might be dangerous!"

Tiria fended the little twins off, blocking their path as they leaped up and down, shouting, "Us wanna see the hinjagoose!"

Oreal caught them by their tails. "It's not a hinjagoose, it's an injured goose. Come away now, you naughty sugarplums!"

Irgle struggled in his father's grasp. "I norra shuggaplump, I a h'infant Dibbun. Lemme see the hinjagoose!"

Tiria soon diverted their attention with the mention of food. "You can see the injured goose later on. There's raspberry jelly and strawberry fizz for breakfast. If I were you, I'd go and get some before the others eat it all up!"

Within a moment, Oreal was being towed across the lawn by his whooping babes. "Rabbsee jelly anna straw'bee fizz, quick quick, 'urry up Daddy afore it be gone!"

Brantalis gave a honking laugh. "Small ones are always hungry for the good food I am thinking."

Tiria nodded. "Aye, though they'll be disappointed when they find I lied to them. It'll be the same breakfast as usual. Got them out of the way though, didn't it?"

Foremole came trundling up with a crew of six moles, carrying a stretcher between them. He tugged his snout politely to Tiria. "Beggen ee pardun, miz, bee's this yurr ee gurt burd us'n's must carry to ee h'Abbey?"

Brantalis rose hastily and began descending the wallsteps in a series of wobbling hops. "I will not be carried by these strange mice, dropping me they would be. By myself I will walk!"

Tiria restrained herself from laughing at the comical aspect of Brantalis and the indignant look on Foremole Grudd's face. She apologised to the mole leader. "I'm sorry, sir, but it seems Brantalis appears able to get himself across to the Abbey."

Signalling dismissal to his crew, Grudd marched off with his snout in the air. "Boi okey, oi'm not a botherin' abowt ee h'ungrateful gurt bag o' feathers. Gudd day to ee, marm!"

Still stifling her mirth, Tiria bowed deeply to Grudd. "Good day to you, sir, and my thanks for your kind offer of help."

Clack!

Had she not bowed, the ottermaid would have surely been slain by the crude spear which flew in over the battlements. The weapon's chipped-flint head shattered as it struck the parapet.

Whipping off the sling Wuppit and loading it in the same movement, Tiria leaped to the walltop. Below, in the ditch that ran alongside the path stretching from north to south, she glimpsed the water rats. It was Groffgut's gang, racing away north up the dried-out ditchbed. Tiria identified the gangleader's voice as he shouted, "Dat wuz the waterdog! I missed 'er, but 'twas dat mouse wot beated me up dat I wanna kill!"

It was a difficult throw, but Tiria whirled Wuppit wildly and let fly hard. She hit the back of the last runner's head,

45

downing him. Dashing to the main gate, she began swiftly unbarring it.

Skipper Banjon and Brink, together with Tiria's three friends, were walking down the Abbey steps when they spied her flinging the gate open and racing out onto the path. Banjon was off like an arrow. "Wot'n the name o' rudders is that gel up to? C'mon, mates!"

Some distance up the ditchbed, they came across the ottermaid, standing over a sprawled-out water rat. She was shaking her head as her eyes roved north up the dried-out watercourse. "It was those vermin we met yesterday. I was on the walltop when one of them threw a spear at me and missed. I heard him shouting that it was the mouse he wanted to slay, the one who had beaten him. Anyhow, they're well gone now, probably cut off east into the woodlands further up. I managed to hit this one from the walltop."

Girry looked back to the Abbey ramparts. "Good grief, you mean to say you slung a stone that far, from up there, and you hit your target? Is he dead?"

Brink knelt and checked the rat briefly. "Oh aye, this 'un's dead, sure enough!"

Shocked, Tiria dropped her sling as though it were a poison snake. Her voice shook as she explained, "I didn't mean to kill anybeast, honestly. I only wanted to drive them away from Redwall. It was just a wild shot. I wish I'd never slung that stone!"

Skipper pressed the sling Wuppit back into his daughter's paw. "You said there was eight of the vermin. So, one of 'em wants to kill hisself a mouse, eh?"

A tremor of fear ran through Brinty, but he put on a show of bravado. "Huh, I'm not frightened of scummy water rats!"

Banjon eyed Tiria levelly. "An' ye didn't mean to kill the rat. Why?"

She shrugged. "Can't say, really. I've never slain anything before. It's just not a very nice feeling I suppose."

Her father's gaze hardened. Raising his voice sternly, he addressed his daughter. "Not a very nice feelin', ye suppose? You lissen t'me, gel. Those rats are thieves, murderers an' torturers, all of 'em! 'Tis about time ye grew up an' learned about vermin. If'n I'd been with ye when y'found 'em tormentin' that bird yesterday, I would've finished 'em all, instead o' lettin' the villians go free to roam Mossflower. There's seven of the scum out there now, all ready to rob an' kill any decent, innocent creature they come across!"

Banjon nudged the carcass of the fallen one. "Ye can't reason with vermin, Tiria. This rat won't be doin' any more evil, 'cos you stopped him. You did the right thing, protectin' our Abbey an' yore friends. Remember, gel, yore a warriormaid with Wildlough blood!"

The force of her father's final phrase hit Tiria like a thunderbolt. It was the exact line spoken to her by the otter in her dream, which came instantly back to her in vivid detail. She swayed and had to support herself by leaning against the side of the ditch.

The skipper leaped forward and steadied her. "Tiria, are ye alright? What ails ye?"

Brink took his friend to one side, whispering, "Leave 'er be, mate. Pore missy, 'tis prob'ly the shock of it all. I think ye were a mite harsh with 'er, yellin' like that. May'aps she ain't old enough to grasp it all yet."

Banjon turned to his daughter apologetically. "I didn't mean to shout at ye like that, beauty. I'm sorry."

Brink threw a paw around Skipper's shoulder. "Don't fret, mate. She knows ye meant no 'arm. Come on, me'n' you'll see if'n we can't pick up the trail o' those vermin. Brinty, why don't you an' yore mates take Tiria back to the Abbey? Aye, go an' see how yore goose is farin', pretty one. Great seasons, bringin' two big birds back to the Abbey in two days. Wotever next, eh?"

Once they were alone, Tiria could not wait to confide in her friends. She told them everything about her previous night's dream.

47

Girry's eyes were wide with awe at her narrative. "You actually saw Martin the Warrior?"

Now that she could recall it all, Tiria began feeling more positive and cheerful. "Aye, I saw him, true enough, but it was the strange otter lady and what she said to me."

As soon as they reached the Abbey, Tribsy clambered up out of the ditch. "They'm wurr ee gurt load o' wurds she'm sayed to ee. "'Ow can you'm a-member 'em all?"

Tiria heaved Brinty from the ditch. "Because they're burned into my brain. I can repeat exactly what she said. Listen.

"Like the sun, High Rhulain will rise anew,
to set the downtrodden free.
A warriormaid with Wildlough blood
must cross the Western Sea.
She who looks ever through windows
at the signs which feathers make,
seek the Green Isle through her knowledge,
for all thy kinbeasts' sake."

Girry twirled his bushy tail in puzzlement. "It sounds rather mysterious. What d'you make of it, Tiria?"

The ottermaid broke into a trot. "I'll have to think about it, mate, and nobeast thinks well on an empty stomach. I haven't had breakfast yet, I'm famished!"

Speeding into a run, she bounded over the lawns, with the others pursuing her. Tribsy, who was slowest, was shouting, "You'm wait furr oi, gurt ruddery creetur!"

Breakfast was about finished when they arrived at the kitchens, but the kindly Friar could not bear the thought of a hungry creature. "Indeed to goodness, 'tis lucky you are that I have some hot farls and honeymaple preserve put by. Oh, and there's an apple dumplin' for you, Tiria, 'cos I recall these three rascals havin' breakfast earlier, with your da and Brink."

They sat in the almost empty dining room, dipping farls in honeymaple preserve and sipping pear cordial. Girry eyed the ottermaid as she tucked into her dumpling. "Well, have you had any thoughts about your dream riddle yet?"

Tiria poured herself more cordial. "Don't rush me, I'm thinking about it."

Tribsy appeared quite amused by her comment. "Hurr-hurrhurr, you'm thinken abowt thinken abowt ee riggle. Hurrhurr, that bee's a gurt deal o' thinken, miz!"

They were joined at table by another latecomer, little Sister Snowdrop, Old Quelt's Assistant Librarian-cum-Recorder. Snowdrop had a pure white patch of fur on her head, hence her name. She was a dry-humoured old mouse, though nowhere near as ancient as Quelt.

Tiria made room for her. "Sister, you're usually one of the first here every morning. What kept you late today?"

Snowdrop dipped her farl in hot mint tea and sucked at it. "I am rather late, Miss Wildlough, so would you do me a favour? Please don't bring any more large birds to this Abbey at mealtimes. Yesterday it was an osprey, just before supper. Today it was a barnacle goose at breakfast time. Quelt had me dashing around the library, pulling out reference books on geese and their seasonal flying times. It doesn't do a creature's eating habits any good, you know!"

Tiria licked sauce from her paw. "Sorry about that, Sister. So, Quelt has met Brantalis, has he?"

Snowdrop nodded. "He has indeed. It is his opinion that geese are more sociable and forthcoming than ospreys. He likes the Skyfurrows especially, having treated several of their gaggle in bygone seasons."

The ottermaid agreed. "I like Brantalis, too. Did he say how he came by his wound?"

The little Sister poured herself more tea. "Brother Perant said the wound could have been a lot worse. He was cleaning and dressing it as I left the Infirmary. Your friend Brantalis told Quelt that he had been shot by a cat's arrow."

Brinty interrupted. "A cat's arrow? But there aren't any cats in Mossflower Country anymore. I wonder where he was when he received the wound?"

Using her habit sleeve, Snowdrop wiped steam from the tea from her tiny square glasses. "Over the great seas, in someplace called Green Isle, that's what I heard him say."

Girry thumped the table, sending plates clattering. "Green Isle! That's the place you said the otter lady mentioned in your dream, Tiria!"

The ottermaid promptly repeated the line. "Seek the Green Isle through her knowledge."

The Sister looked up from her breakfast. "Through whose knowledge? What are you young 'uns rattling on about?"

Tiria had already left the table and was heading for the stairs. "I'll tell you later, Sister. Right now I've got to go and speak with that goose!"

She hastened up to the Infirmary, followed by her three friends and a curious Sister Snowdrop.

Brother Perant showed them into his sickbay, bowing ironically. "Ah, welcome to the Abbey nesting place. Any more big birds today, Tiria? A swan, or an eagle perhaps, or is it too early for them to come calling?"

Brantalis came waddling behind the Brother. He seemed spry enough and was proudly sporting a clean white-linen dressing around his neck. The barnacle goose pointed his beak at the Infirmary Keeper. "Right you were, Tiria. A great healer this mouse is, I am thinking. See, Brantalis is lively as an eggchick!"

The ottermaid nodded approvingly, then came straight to the point. "What do you know about a place called Green Isle?"

The osprey, perched up on the windowsill picking at the remains of his fish, spoke for the first time. "Kyeeh! Pandion Piketalon knows more of Green Isle than a Skyfurrow. It is my home. His kind only stop to feed there before flying on. Piketalons have always lived on Green Isle!"

50

Brantalis spread his powerful wings and flapped them. "Anywhere would I sooner dwell than the place of cats. A bad and wicked isle it is."

Tiria stepped between both birds, who were now eyeing each other truculently. "Please, let's not start arguing. Pandion Piketalon, do you know where the Green Isle is?"

The osprey looked slightly crestfallen. "Keeharr! I was hurt, and driven high over the great waters in a mighty storm. I could not tell you how I came to Red Walls. Kraaawk, I am far from home and lost!"

Brantalis puffed out his chest. "I am of the Skyfurrows. I am knowing the way, but I am thinking, no earth crawler could follow where I fly!"

Tribsy wrinkled his snout sagely. "Burr, you'm surrpintly currect thurr, zurr!"

Brinty threw up his paws irritably. "Then what's the point of solving dream riddles if you can't get to this confounded Green Isle place, eh?"

Sister Snowdrop looked over the rims of her tiny square spectacles. "Will somebeast please tell me, what is all this business of dreams and riddles?"

The osprey fluttered down from his perch. "Kreeaah! I know nought of dreams or riddles!"

Brantalis edged away from the fierce fish hawk, murmuring, "I am thinking the Piketalon knows nought but catching fish."

Pandion's golden eyes stared unblinkingly at the goose. "Better than dabbling in mud and honking to frighten clouds!"

Brother Perant stamped his paw and raised his voice. "Enough, do ye hear me? I will not have squabbling in my Infirmary. You, Pandion, back up on that sill! Brantalis, under the table and hold your beak!"

Girry winked at the normally mild-mannered healer. "That'll teach 'em, eh Brother?"

Perant pointed to the door in a frosty manner. "Out, the lot of you! Go and solve your problems elsewhere, and leave me in peace. Come on, begone with you, and you, too, Sister Snowdrop!"

They shuffled silently out onto the landing. As the door slammed behind them, the little old Sister pulled a comical face, even though Perant could not see her. "Yah, stuffy old bandage bonce, go and physick yourself!"

Tiria shook her head wearily. "We're not getting very far with this, are we?"

Snowdrop took her by the paw. "Don't be so easily defeated, young 'un. Follow me, I'll help you with your riddles and puzzles. I'm rather good at that sort of thing."

Sister Snowdrop took them upstairs to the lower attics, where she worked as Old Quelt's assistant. "Let's go into the library. I can think better in there."

The friends were reluctant to invade Quelt's inner sanctum, since it was the ancient squirrel's retreat from everyday life. Tiria whispered to the little Sister, "But won't Old Quelt object to us disturbing him?"

For all her long seasons, Snowdrop was quite young at heart. Placing her paw on the library doorlatch, she giggled. "Heehee, not to worry, the old buffer's probably taking his morning nap!"

Without warning, the door opened inward and the Sister fell flat as she went with it. Snowdrop found herself sprawled on the floor, staring up into the face of Redwall Abbey's revered Librarian-cum-Recorder.

Quelt bowed politely. "Come in, friends. As you can see, the old buffer's had his morning nap. Eh, Sister Snowdrop?"

6

It was late night over Green Isle. The river flowed smoothly along toward the sea, reflecting a half-moon and the brief flash of a comet blazing its track across the dark sky vaults. Two figures stole silently through the undergrowth which fringed the bank. They halted as a nightjar called from the darkened shallows. One of the two otters, Whulky, cupped both paws around his mouth and croaked like a frog.

A floating log materialised out of the shadows. Leatho Shellhound, who was poling it, jumped ashore and joined paws with the pair. "Sure I knew ye'd come. Y'weren't followed, I trust?"

Chab, Whulky's companion, reassured him. "The guards are so stuffed with roasted birdflesh that they're snorin' at their posts!"

The outlaw otter's teeth gleamed in the moonlight as he drew in a short, angry breath. "A murderous an' brutal affair, buckoes. All those pore birds killed to suit the whim of Riggu Felis. Ah well, hop on, an' I'll take ye to the gatherin'."

As they poled the log downriver, Whulky whispered, "Is it true Zillo the Bard will be there?"

Keeping his eyes on the watercourse, the sea otter replied, "For sure 'tis. He's been takin' the enchanted slumber agin. 'Twill be interestin' to hear his ballad."

Tall stones protruded up from the scrubland behind the shore dunes. Berthing the log, the three otters headed for them. In the past, sea and stream otters had gathered at this time-honoured venue in the hundreds. However, owing to the regime of Riggu Felis, that night's attendance was no more than twoscore in number.

The site was screened by a ring of scrub bushes, with six sentries posted on watch. Leatho and his two friends waved to them and made their way to the fire at the centre of the tall stones. They were greeted by the others, who sat them down and served out bowls of burgoolla. This was a thick stew of seaweed and shellfish, seasoned with the most fiery of herbs and spices. A mere whiff of the burgoolla aroma, though delicious, could wring tears from a creature's eyes with its sheer heat. Customarily, no words were spoken during the eating of this otter delicacy—except to either compliment or criticise its quality.

Whulky fanned a paw across his mouth after the first taste. "Ah sure, an' isn't this a true drop of the grand stuff?"

Many agreed with him. "Hoho, 'tis grand sure enough!"

But there were always those who liked to disagree.

"Arraway with ye. I've scraped better burgoolla off'n me ould granma's pinny, so I have!"

"Aye, the stuff tastes like a duck in a muddle."

There were many indignant defenders.

"Ah, shut yore gob, sure ye'd complain if a fine, big trout cooked itself an' jumped into yore big mouth, so ye would!"

"Aye, lissen bhoyo, if'n ye could make better burgoolla than this, then put yore paws t'work an' give yore fat lip a rest!"

The good-natured banter was brought to a halt by the flat thump of a rudderdrum.

Leatho stood then, calling out, "Be we well gathered, otters all. Do I see a Wildlough?"

Whulky stood up. "Ye see a Wildlough, once one of the mightiest clans on river or stream!"

Leatho continued with his roster. "Do I see a Galedeep?"

A huge otter raised his paw. "Ye see a Galedeep of the mighty sea otter rovers!"

"Do I see a Wavedog?"

"Ye see a Wavedog of a clan that don't know fear!"

"Do I see a Streambattle?"

"Aye, ye see a Streambattle whose clan know the scars o' war well!"

The list continued, with each clan representative answering proudly. When he had finished, Leatho waited until a voice called out to him, "An' do we see a Shellhound?"

The outlaw sea otter roared back, "Yore seein' a Shellhound that never backed down from a foebeast! I'm the last o' my clan, I have neither kith, kin nor family! But by the thunders I'm still here an' fightin'!"

Firelight gleamed from the outlaw's eyes as he glared around the assembly. "Why, who is it that calls to me?"

Two otters supported an older one to a seat by the fire. He was still a big beast, though he bore many scars. One of his legs had been replaced by a wooden peg, and his left eye wore a black musselshell patch. He held a round, flat rudderdrum, which he struck gently with his tail.

Leatho strode across and embraced him fondly. "Ould Zillo the Bard o' the Watermeadows, haven't ye sunk with the sun beyond the westerin' sea yet?"

Zillo gave him a gap-toothed grin. "Ah no, me buckoe, I wouldn't dream of it whilst there's still one mangy catpaw print on our lovely Green Isle!"

Leatho chuckled admiringly. "Ye ould battledog, what have ye been dreamin' about then?"

Zillo struck the rudderdrum a mighty clout. "The day of deliverance is comin'!"

A roar of joy came from every otter present. Leatho held up a paw for silence. "Whisht now, Zillo has the floor!"

A hush fell over them as the bard sat staring into the fire.

His rudder began beating the drum slowly. Then he began
to sing his story in true bardic fashion.

"On the night that the great storm was ragin' apace,
sweepin' in o'er the high seas to batter this isle,
I heard that a wildcat had lost half his face,
Ah, isn't that grand now, I said with a smile!"

Two otters joined in with flute and banjotta, an odd stringed
instrument that was very popular among the clans. Zillo
let them play a short stanza before continuing.

" 'Twas then by me fire I fell into a dream,
with the wild winds a-keenin' an' wailin' outside,
sure a wisdom came floatin' o'er some magic stream,
that the days of our vengeance were soon to arrive.
'Twas a mouse in bright armour, he spake loud
    an' clear,
an' he carried a sword that was wondrous to see.
'Ould Zillo the Bard,' he said, 'Never you fear,
for 'tis writ in the stars that the clans will run free.
From the seas an' the oceans, from river an' stream,
rise up all ye warriors, arm every paw.
A leader is comin' to fulfill yore dreams,
one who'll stand at your head as ye march off to war.
Ye'll rise like the red dawn, all in a great band,
like a brave surgin' tide such as never was seen,
as ye thunder her title all over this land:
All hail to the Rhulain! The High Otterqueen!' "

The otters leapt up, bellowing and cheering, roaring and
chanting. "Rhulain! Rhulain! Ee aye eeeeeh!"
    Leatho could not stem the noisy jubilation, but the blood
was pounding through his body. He took Zillo the Bard by
the shoulders, shouting in his ear above the din. "Are ye
sure High Rhulain is comin' back to Green Isle, or was yore
dream just a desire to rouse the clans?"

Zillo raised his voice in reply. "My dreams have never lied, Shellhound. 'Tis certain I am!"

Leatho battered for a long time on the rudderdrum before order was finally restored. His voice rang out like steel. "We'll get nothin' done, howlin' an' jiggin' about like a rabble o' wildbeasts!"

Zillo backed him up. "Sure the Shellhound's right. Hold still now like goodbeasts an' lissen to him."

The outlaw sea otter began outlining his campaign. "We need to work together now, buckoes, but our watchword must be secrecy. Don't breathe a word yet of what ye've heard here tonight to anybeast!"

Chab held up his paw. "Not even to our families?"

Leatho shook his head vehemently. "Especially not yore families, mate. Little 'uns will repeat wot they've heard to anybeast, an' old 'uns can't resist gossipin'. If Riggu Felis an' those cats caught wind of ought, they'd soon pry it out of familybeasts. They're good at that, as ye know. When the time's right, I'll let ye know, then ye can tell yore kin."

Zillo added his own warning. "Holdin' yore silence will stop many an otter bein' weighted with rocks an' tossed into Deeplough for Slothunog to feed off."

The very mention of Deeplough's monster brought gasps of fear from many. Leatho let the message sink in before carying on with his plans.

"Right, here's wot we need. Secrecy, or our plans will be ruined. Organisation an' obedience, if we're to see this through together. An' weapons! When the time comes, bare paws'll be useless against Felis's murderers. Last, an' most important, we need our Rhulain, a High Queen that this isle hasn't seen since seasons out o' memory!"

One of the Wavedog clan called out, "How'll we know the Rhulain when we see her?"

Leatho, at a loss to answer, turned to Zillo. "Can you tell us, mate?"

The bard pondered a while. "All I can tell ye is wot I know from the poems an' ballads passed down through my forefathers. One thing is certain, though, she'll be of the Wildlough blood. I've heard old paeans an' lays that tell of a warriormaid, tall an' swift. Fearless in battle, an' more deadly with sling'n'stone than any livin' beast. 'Tis said that she wore a gold coronet set with a greenstone, and also that she wore a surcoat of armour from neck to waist, embossed with a gold star. That's about as much as I can tell ye."

There was a hesitant silence over the meeting. Then Big Kolun, Skipper of the Galedeep sea otters, boomed out in his loud, jolly voice, "Well that'll do for us Galedeeps. Ye couldn't 'ave painted High Rhulain clearer, Zillo. Sounds like the kind o' queen I'd foller to Hellgates an' back. Right, buckoes?"

Yells of approval greeted him. Leatho winked at the big fellow. "Galedeeps were always loyal warriors, matey!"

Kolun spat on a huge paw and held it out. "Here's me paw, an' here's me heart, Shellhound. I'm with ye!"

Dawn of the following day found Riggu Felis, Lady Kaltag and their two sons taking breakfast beneath an awning on the pier which fronted the lake. It was a fine summer morn, with sunbeams dancing on the water from a cloudless sky of cornflower blue. Otterslaves stood by, ready to serve the demands of the warlord and his kin. As usual, Jeefra and Pitru were quarrelling, this time about two gull eggs which they had been served.

Jeefra went whining to his mother, tears beading in his eyes as he wailed, "Mamma, Mamma, Pitru stole my egg. He's finished his own and now he's taken mine!"

Kaltag left off sunning herself in the early warmth. "Will you two stop bickering? Pitru, give that egg back to your brother, this instant!"

Pitru tossed the egg up, then caught it deftly, smirking. "Tell him to come and get it!"

His mother fixed him with an icy glare. "Give Jeefra the egg. Do as I say!"

The chain mail half-mask which covered Riggu Felis's disfigured face chinked as he drew in breath. He was watching his sons with interest. The wildcat rasped, "Let them be, Kaltag. If Pitru wants the egg, let him keep it—though mayhaps Jeefra's warrior enough to take it back by force. Go on, son, let's see what you're made of."

Jeefra feared both his father and Pitru, so he took the soft alternative. Turning to an otterslave, he ordered, "You, bring me another gull's egg!"

"Stay where you are, slave!" The warlord's fangs showed between the quivering chain mail. "Jeefra, go and take the egg back off Pitru. Go on!"

Kaltag complained, "My lord, you should not be urging brothers to fight each other in this way."

The wildcat ruler of Green Isle snarled at her. "Stay out of this! They have to learn to take what they want. Well, go to it, Jeefra. I'm waiting!"

Pitru taunted his weaker brother. "Aye, go to it, Jeefra. I'm waiting, too."

Jeefra had no option. He knew it would go badly for him if he was shamed in front of his father. Gathering his nerve, he made a sudden charge, but his brother easily side-stepped him. Leaping onto Jeefra's back, Pitru forced him to the ground, holding him there as he mocked his feeble attempt.

" 'Mamma, Mamma, Pitru stole my egg!' Here, take it back, you big snot-nosed kitten!" Wilfully, he smashed the raw gull egg over his brother's head. The runny mess splattered down across Jeefra's face. Pitru contemptuously kicked his brother's backside, then freed him. Jeefra fled indoors, sobbing.

Pitru licked yolk from his paw, commanding one of the otterslaves, "Go and bring me another egg, I'm still hungry!"

A gurgling laugh issued from behind the chain mail as Riggu addressed Kaltag. "That one's got the makings of a proper wildcat!"

She sniffed. "We have two sons, both wildcats."

Pulling the face mask to one side, the warlord thrust his hideous features close to her. "Never! I'm the only true wildcat here—I, Riggu Felis! You and all the rest of these cats, you are only feral cats. Your ancestors were tame creatures who served stronger beasts. You could not even fend for yourselves. It took my kin, the real wildcats, to conquer your masters. We brought your kind here from the sunset lands of the far oceans. See my colour, my stripes, these are the marks of the proper wildcat bloodline. I am the only one who is all wildcat, a warlord born. Jeefra is more like you, but Pitru has more wildcat in him!"

Pitru had been eavesdropping on his father's words. "Does that mean I'll be the ruler of Green Isle someday?"

Riggu allowed the chain mail to cover his lower face again. "It takes more than a bully to make a warlord. You have to be fearless, like me. Why could you not have slain that bird on the eve of the storm, eh?"

Both brothers had been reminded of the incident many times by their father. Pitru did not like being criticised. Turning on one paw, he prowled off, leaving his father with a parting shot. "Huh, you tried, and look at the mess it made of you."

Springing up in a fury, the wildcat chieftain seized his single-bladed axe. "You insolent whelp! Why, I'll. . . ."

A cry rang out from the lakeshore, distracting Riggu. "Master, we have taken two prisoners!"

Bound together by ropes, the two otterslaves, Whulky and Chab, were thrust up onto the pier. Surrounding them were catguards, with Weilmark Scaut and Atunra at their head. Still hefting the axe in one paw, Riggu wiped froth from his slobbering lower lip. He composed himself swiftly and sat down.

The prisoners were forced to lie facedown in front of the wildcat as he stared regally at them. "Why do you bring them before me? What have they done?"

The pine marten Atunra bowed. "Master, they were

60

caught outside of the settlement before dawn. Both have been missing all night."

Weilmark Scaut pointed with his whipbutt at the otters. A large bandage covered Scaut's jaw, where the missile from Leatho had broken it. He was in pain and had to speak from between clenched teeth.

"This younger one I caught stealing recently. He's already served a night and a day beneath the pier, Lord. I've had my eye on these two, they're always whisperin' together."

He pawed at the painful swelling on the side of his face before continuing. "Last night I could not sleep, so I did a secret visit to the slave compound. They were both missing."

Scaut winced in agony, while Riggu gestured for Atunra to continue. "After Weilmark Scaut roused me, we took a patrol of catguards and two trackers. We picked up their trail to the riverbank, but there it ended. So we hid and waited, knowing they would return the same way. Sure enough, an hour before dawn, we caught them both skulking back."

Intrigued, Riggu leaned forward. "And where had they been?"

Scaut was not to be outdone if any credit were to be given. He took up the narrative again, despite his aching jaw. "I sent the trackers downriver, Lord. They found lots of pawprints an' the ashes of a fire inside the circle of tall stones. They was attendin' some sort o' otter outlaw meeting, Sire. I'd swear an oath on it!"

The face mask swayed in and out as the wildcat chieftain beckoned the guards to stand the captives up. He peered at their bruised and battered heads. "Hmm, I see, and they've refused to talk, eh?"

Scaut uncoiled his whip. "Leave them to me, Sire. They'll soon talk when their ribs show through their hides!"

Riggu glimpsed the looks of stubborn defiance the otters gave each other. "No they won't. Put away that lash, I have a better idea. Tell me, do they have families?"

Atunra answered smartly, "Master, the younger one has a wife and three offspring. The older one has only a wife."

Riggu looked at the two otters enquiringly. "Why do you not think of your families and talk to me?"

Whulky and Chab remained tight-lipped. The wildcat shrugged. "Bravery in a warrior is an admirable quality, but bravery in a slave with loved ones to care for is just plain stupidity. So, do you wish to speak to me now, or go to your deaths in silence?"

Whulky and Chab were trembling all over, but they stared straight ahead without saying a single word.

The wildcat leaned back in his chair, tapping his claws on the arm. "So be it. Tie them both underneath this pier until tomorrow morning. If they haven't spoken by then, we'll take them to Deeplough and introduce them to Slothunog."

He rose dismissively and wandered casually indoors. Stopping in the fortress doorway, Riggu Felis called back over his shoulder, almost as an afterthought, "Oh, and let their families join them beneath the pier. They can accompany them to Deeplough. That might help to loosen their tongues before tomorrow."

Atunra and the catguards marched the otters off. Whulky and Chab were in deep shock at the horror they and their families would have to face.

7

Old Quelt smiled at the embarrassment on the faces of Sister Snowdrop and her four companions. "Don't stand staring at the floor and shuffling your paws like naughty Dibbuns. Come in, all of you, and welcome. Redwallers have been making jokes about Old Quelt since long before you were born, Sister Snowdrop. Please run along and find these young 'uns something to drink."

Snowdrop brought a flagon of pennycloud-and-rosehip tonic and some beakers from a window ledge, and poured the drinks. Tiria and her friends sat at a long, well-polished beechwood table, gazing about them at Quelt's pride and joy: Redwall Abbey's first library.

All four walls were shelved out from floor to ceiling with good oaken planking. Every possible area was full of books and scrolls. Thin pamphlets stood spine to spine with tall tomes, thick volumes and beribbonned rolls of parchment, all in neat order. To one side of the fireplace was a nook, which held a writing desk with two padded stools. Quill pens and charcoal sticks, together with hardwood rulers, sealing wax and sheafs of parchment, lay stacked, ready for use.

The ancient squirrel peered over the top of his glasses at his gaping guests. "Almost a lifetime's work. I did it, you know. Helped, of course, by the good Sister Snowdrop, our trusty Cellarhog Carpenter and many obliging moles. So, what do ye think?"

Tiria acted as spokesbeast. "It's wonderful, sir, most impressive. I hadn't realised there were so many books and scrolls in our Abbey."

Snowdrop refilled their beakers. "This is now the repository for all the written works of Redwall. Quelt gathered them in this former attic room. It took us long seasons to clear out the gatehouse records, and even longer to empty out the Abbess's chambers, and the kitchens, cellars and dormitories."

The Librarian-cum-Recorder sighed wearily. "Aye, and we're still searching, discovering, dusting, repairing and cataloguing old writings. Huh, and that's beside my work as Redwall Recorder."

Brinty complimented Quelt. "You've worked wonders, sir. I expect you're very proud of your library!"

The oldster wiped a drop of tonic from the tabletop with his sleeve. " 'Proud' is not the word I'd use, 'fulfilled' sums it up better. Yes, I feel fulfilled by my achievement. But you haven't come here to listen to some doddering old fogey rattling on about his library. What exactly are you looking for? Is there any way I can be of assistance?"

Sister Snowdrop glanced at Tiria. "Tell him about your dream riddle."

Quelt began rolling up his wide habit sleeves. "Oh do, miss, I pray you. Riddles, puzzles or conundrums, I've always been pretty fair at that type of thing. Now, you may start at the beginning, and please leave nothing out!"

The ottermaid related her dream in detail—the big lake and its shore, and her encounter with Martin the Warrior and the otter lady. Word for word she recited the poem, then explained about her dream's aftermath.

"It was very odd. After I woke up, I couldn't even recall that I'd had a dream. Then my father unknowingly repeated the line about Wildlough blood, and it all came back as clear as day to me."

Old Quelt picked up quill, parchment and ink. He stroked at his scraggy, silver whiskers reflectively before replying. "Hmm, very interesting. What do you young 'uns make of it all?"

Tribsy wrinkled his velvety snout. "We'm wuz 'opin' you'm or ee Sister cudd make sumthin' of it all, zurr. Arter all, we'm bain't gurt scholarbeasts like you'm bee's."

Girry agreed. "Huh, I wasn't very bright at Abbeyschool."

Brinty shook his head. "Neither was I. What about you, Tiria?"

The ottermaid smiled ruefully. "Afraid not, mate. When I should've been studying, I was always fooling about with slings and stones. Wish I'd paid more attention now."

Sister Snowdrop stared at them through her small square glasses. "Oh, I'm sure you're being too hard on yourselves, you four never struck me as dullards. Most riddles can be solved with some serious concentration. Let's put our heads together and make a joint effort at finding the solution."

Quelt pointed his quill pen at his assistant. "A sensible idea, Snowdrop. Come on, you can be the Recorder for a change. I want you to write down what Tiria has to say. Miss, would ye kindly repeat the poem again for us? Slowly, please."

Tiria spoke the rhyme methodically, allowing the little Sister to keep pace with her words.

"Like the sun, High Rhulain will rise anew,
to set the downtrodden free.
A warriormaid with Wildlough blood
must cross the Western Sea.
She who looks ever through windows
at the signs that feathers make,
seek the Green Isle through her knowledge,
for all thy kinbeasts' sake."

Brinty came up with an immediate idea. "Why don't we go down to the front lawns, stand back and watch all the

Abbey windows? We may catch sight of the one who is always looking through them."

Snowdrop put aside her pen. "Really, young mouse, you've lived at Redwall how long, fifteen or sixteen seasons? Tell me, in all that time did you ever see any creature who had little else to do than stand about gazing through windows night and day, eh?"

Brinty saw how foolish his idea must have sounded. "Sorry, Sister, I see what you mean. I was only trying to help."

Tribsy rapped a huge digging claw upon the table. "Oi says ee bestest way to solve ee riggle bee's to start at ee beginnin' of et, hurr!"

Snowdrop complimented him. "An excellent suggestion! I always said that nobeast could beat sound mole logic. Now, we know that the sun rises anew each day, but we don't know what a Rhulain is. However, this mention of a warriormaid with Wildlough blood fits your description, Tiria."

The ottermaid pointed at herself. "Me? I'm not a warrior!"

A wry look crossed the old Sister's face. "Excuse my asking, but are you not the one who led the charge against a gang of water rats and saved the osprey? And do you not carry around a sling named Wuppit, a weapon with which you slew a vermin with a single throw from an incredible distance? Please correct me if I'm wrong, but doesn't the blood of Wildlough otters run through your veins, hence the very name you go by, Wildlough?"

Tiria attempted to equal her interrogator's irony. "Huh, we know all that! Kindly stop quibbling and get on with your explanation of the poem, my good mouse."

Snowdrop resumed without comment. "It states that you must cross the Western Sea, but let's skip ahead a few lines. The object of your journey is to aid your kinbeasts, doubtless that means other otters. We know that they dwell on this place called Green Isle and are in some kind of difficulty. So that's a start."

Girry interrupted by referring to the lines Snowdrop had skipped over. "Right then, but we're not on Green Isle, neither is Tiria. So our first task is exactly what Brinty meant: We must first find the window watcher who is always looking at the signs feathers make. That seems to be the key to this puzzle. I wonder who it can be."

Tribsy blinked a few times, allowing the information to sink in. "Oi doan't know who et bee's, do ee?"

Brinty looked to the Recorder. "Have you any ideas, sir?"

Snowdrop whispered, "No use asking him, I'm afraid the poor fellow's fallen asleep again."

With both paws folded across his gently heaving chest and both eyes closed, Quelt surprised them by speaking. "On the contrary, Sister, the poor fellow's wide awake and drinking in every word you've spoken. Dearie me, it's you lot whose eyes are really closed. The answer's staring you right in the face!"

Tiria began to feel impatient with Quelt's manner. "If you have the answer, sir, I'd be grateful if you'd give it to us, instead of pretending to be asleep!"

Quelt continued with his eyes still closed. "You were doing quite well for the main part, at least Snowdrop was, though it was young Girry who asked the most pertinent question. Who is the one who looks through windows at the signs made by feathers?"

Opening his eyes, the Librarian pointed directly at Snowdrop. "It's you, my aged assistant!"

The little Sister's voice rose squeakily. "Me? What makes you say that?"

Quelt took an unhurried sip of his tonic drink. "Ask yourself, what do we use to write with? Quills! And what are quills but the feathers of birds? So we dip them in ink and make marks, we write with them. Are you following me?"

Tribsy chortled. "Hurrhurrhurr, loik maggypies follerin' ee frog, zurr. You'm carry roight on!"

The ancient squirrel obliged. "The riddle points to a 'she,' a knowledgeable creature. Observe!" Quelt removed his rock crystal spectacles and held them up.

"Constant seasons of study do not help one's eyesight. Sooner or later, we elders need these windows to see properly through. My spectacles are round, and I am a he, not a she. Now look at Sister Snowdrop."

Instantly the problem was solved for Tiria and her friends. "She wears little square glasses shaped like windows. I've never seen her without them. It is you, Sister!"

The dawn of a happy smile soon faded from Snowdrop's face. She waved her paws in agitation. "No, no, I don't know what a Rhulain is, or how to cross the Western Sea, and I'm woefully ignorant about Green Isle."

Rising stiffly from his chair, Quelt left the table. "Tut tut, my dear friend, what a disappointment you've turned out to be after serving as my assistant for so many long seasons. A trained scholar and Librarian, surrounded by all the knowledge our Abbey has to offer—literature, records and histories. Why, it's like a Dibbun being locked in Brink Greyspoke's cellars complaining that he has nought to drink. Was all the training I gave you for nothing?"

Little Sister Snowdrop smote the tabletop so hard that the beakers rattled and her paw went numb. "Yowch! No sir, it certainly was not! I'll help you, Tiria. In fact I'll start right away, going through the early archives. Thank you, Quelt, my brain's working properly now. Tiria, take Brinty and Tribsy with you. Go and question that goose again. Brantalis knows the way to Green Isle, he said so. And the fish hawk, Pandion, he lives on Green Isle. I'll wager a berry to a chestnut he knows what's going on there with otters and so on. See what information you can glean from him. Right, on your way, friends!"

As Girry watched them hurrying away, his face fell. "But, Sister, what about me?"

Snowdrop pushed him ahead of her as she bustled toward the bookshelves. "You've just been appointed Second Assistant Librarian. A younger pair of eyes, somebeast who can carry stacks of books and reach high shelves, that's what I need. Come on, young squirrel, quick's the word and sharp's the action. Now, shall we start at *A* for anything, *G* for Green Isle, *R* for Rhulain or *D* for dreams?"

Old Quelt looked up from the desk, where he had installed himself to catch up on recording events of Abbeylife. "I'd start with *U*, for upstairs attic. There are still lots of books and scrolls up there, waiting to be identified. Prepare to get your tail dusty, young Girry! Now, where was I? Oh yes! This fine day began eventfully with the visit of an injured barnacle goose, and the slaying of a vermin creature by a warrior ottermaid. . . ."

Sunlight lanced through the foliage of East Mossflower Woodlands, creating a bright kaleidoscope of green, gold and tan. Brimstone, clouded yellow, and small white butterflies fluttered and perched on the marshy banks of a gurgling stream, which flowed out of a watermeadow. Skipper Banjon crouched on the edge, casting about amid the rank black ooze.

Brink Greyspoke tested the soggy mess with a cautious footpaw. "Careful, Skip, ye could go down in that stuff!"

The Skipper retreated, wiping his paws on the grass. "Aye, this is the furthest I'm trackin' any vermin. They've either sunk under that lot or they've made it to the watermeadows. There's more'n ten exits from those meadows. We'd be half a season tryin' to pick up their trail again. Brink, what d'ye think?"

The Cellarhog held his snout to help block out the odours of rotted vegetation and soggy, water-logged wood. "I don't reckon they'll be botherin' Redwall again. Let's go back to the Abbey. That little walk has whetted my appetite for lunch."

The pair strode off, back the way they had come, chatting amicably.

"I didn't know yore appetite had t'be whetted, mate. I've never knowed it t'be blunted!"

"Hoho, lissen who's talkin', ole Banjon barrelbelly!"

"Nonsense! I'm only a slip of a beast compared to you. That apron o' yores would go round me three times!"

As their sounds receded into the woodlands, not a stone's throw from the bank where Banjon and Brink had been standing the sticky morass beneath an overhanging grey willow burst asunder, spewing forth Groffgut and his gang of water rats. Spitting and vomiting the nauseous slime, they staggered up onto firm ground. Every one of the rats was plastered from head to foot with marsh debris and reeked with its stench.

Frogeye dug something from his ear with a piece of twig. "Wot did we hafta jump in der for? I nearly drownded!"

Groffgut clouted him over the head. " 'Cos we woulda got caught. We hadter 'ide, softbrain!"

Rashback spat out a woodlouse, then picked it up and ate it. "Cudden't we 'ave fought 'em off, Chief? Der's eight of us, an' only two of dem."

Plugtail wiped ooze from his eyes as he corrected him. "Seven, ye mean, der's only seven of us now. Pore ole Hangpaw was slayed when we was runnin' away."

Threetooth sat down and started scraping off body mud with his stone spearblade. "Mebbe Hangpaw wasn't kil't. He might be still alive back der."

Groffgut kicked out at Threetooth but missed, slipped and fell flat on his tail. Obbler and Fleddy, the youngest two gang members, burst out into cackling laughs at Groffgut's mishap.

The gang leader jumped upright, fuming. "Wot's so funny, eh, eh? Youse lot makes me sick ter the neck. Ye think we cudda fought dem off—a great big 'edgepig anna giganantic waterdog? Yer think Hangpaw's still alive back in dat ditch, eh, eh?"

Ranting and spitting mud, he vented his temper on them. "Well goo on den, chase after de 'edgepig an' de riverdog.

70

An' when youse've kil't 'em, den go back ter d'ditch an' see if Hangpaw's still alive. Well, who's gunna go?"

None of the gang felt like pursuing the issue further, knowing Groffgut's violent temper. They sat silent, cleaning themselves up and avoiding their leader's angry stares.

Frogeye finally made an attempt to calm the situation. "Yah, who cares about all dose daftbeasts an' their h'abbey? Hangpaw's dead, an' dat's dat! Dis is a big forest, wid plenny o' vikkles about. Let's jus' move on an' find some-wheres else."

It was the wrong thing to say, as Frogeye soon learned when Groffgut bit him on the nose and kicked him in the stomach. The gang leader waved his rusty scythe blade sword at the rest.

"Youse lot ain't goin' nowhere 'less I tells yer so, see! Are we a vermin gang or wot? Dose h'abbeybeasts stoled our h'eagle, ambushed an' battered us, kil't one of our gang an' chased us 'til we 'ad ter jump inter a bog an' 'ide from dem! Nobeast does that ter my gang an' gets away wid it, 'specially not dat mouse who kept wallopin' me wid a big pole. I've got dat 'uns name writ in me brain!"

Threetooth made certain he was out of Groffgut's range before he popped the question, "So, worra we gunner do about it?"

The gang leader actually jumped in the air twice to emphasise his first two words. "Do? Do? . . . I'll tell yer wot we're gunner do! We're gunner get revenge on dem, dat's wot we're gunner do! Cummon, we're goin' back ter that Wallred h'abbey. I'll make 'em sorry dey ever messed wid our gang!"

8

Big Kolun Galedeep had ten small otterbabes, which was almost half of his family, aboard his boat, the *Rustynail*. The sails had been furled on his orders. He sat in the stern, twanging away at his banjotta. Leatho Shellhound sat beside him, holding the tiller steady as the little otters pulled away, two to each oar. Helping them to keep an even stroke, Kolun and Leatho roared out a lusty shanty. The *Rustynail* travelled at a fair clip around the bay, broken occasionally when one of Kolun's small brood pulled too hard, missed the water and tumbled over backwards. They were learning not only to row but also to sing. They were raucous infants, missing some of the lyrics but coming in heartily on every last line.

"Hey now, hark belay there an' listen ole mate,
Hear the high seas a-callin', c'mon let's not wait,
out there on the briny with no land in sight,
just the gold sun above ye an' bright stars at night.
Ho barnacles binnacles bungtops an' blood!

In the kingdom of fishes they sport an' they play,
the herrin' the mackerel the fluke an' the ray,
in bluey green deeps where the long seaweed grows,

there swims an' ould dolphin they call Bottlenose.
Ho barnacles binnacles bungtops an' blood!

Set course by yore rudder an' trim up those sails,
we'll plough on forever through doldrums an' gales,
bound for the red sunset far over the main,
an' leave the landlubbers to roam hill an' plain.
Ho barnacles binnacles bungtops an' blood!"

The little otters thought it was all great fun. They went into
tucks of laughter when their father and Uncle Leatho roared
at them in colourful nautical terms.

"Heave away, ye tiny sea swabs! Bend yore backs an'
straighten yore rudders!"

"Hahaarr, buckoes, we'll put muscles on ye like cockles!
Haul on those oars, or 'tis over the side with ye!"

"Ahoy, can't ye pull better'n that? Ye'd have trouble
pullin' yoreselves out of a pot o' skilly'n'duff!"

Deedero, big Kolun's missus, came bustling along the
bayshore with a young ottermaid in tow. Both were waving
and hallooing to get the Galedeep Skipper's attention.
When one of the otterbabes spotted them, she prodded her
father with her oar.

Big Kolun scowled comically at the tiny creature. "Avast
there, ye bold salty scoundrel, strikin' yore cap'n with a
paddle. Ye'll be keelhauled for that!"

Leatho squinted villainously at his big friend. "Keelhauled? Shiver me tripes, yore gittin' too soft with these
mutineers, matey. Chop 'er up an' chuck 'er t'the sharks,
I say!"

The infant pointed a chubby paw to the pair onshore.
"Daddo, it be Mamam, I fink she want you!"

Kolun waved to his missus, shouting, "Ahoy, me heart's
delight, just ye wait there, me ole treasure chest. We're
headin' in to port full speed!"

As the boat scraped the shallows, Deedero tapped her
rudder impatiently upon the sand. "Move yoreself, Leatho

Shellhound, there's big trouble a-brewin'. This pretty maid's got a message for ye!"

The outlaw sea otter sloshed through the shallows to her side. He smiled kindly at the ottermaid. "Yore all out o' breath, me darlin', an' ye've been weepin', too. Tell me now, wot is it?"

The ottermaid, a slave called Memsy, scrubbed at her eyes as she sobbed out the message. "Oh, Mister Shell'ound, sir. 'Tis Whulky an' Chab. They was caught this mornin' early, taken by the weilmark an' that marten beast. Lord Felis questioned them about where they'd been, but they wouldn't speak nary a word. Oh oh, 'tis a terrible thing, those pore creatures!"

Taking Memsy by the shoulders, Leatho spoke softly. "There now, don't go upsettin' yoreself, beauty. 'Tis nought the Shellhound can't sort out. Do ye know where that wildcat is keepin' Whulky an' Chab?"

Memsy strove to calm herself, but she shook like a leaf. "Tied under the pier in front of the fortress, sir. Both their wives an' Chab's three little 'uns are there, too. Lord Felis says that if they don't talk afore tomorrow morn, they'll be dragged off to Deeplough . . . an' . . . an' . . . throwed in to Slothunog. Oooohhhh!"

She fell to crying in earnest, and Deedero wrapped her comfortingly in her wide shawl, hugging her like a babe.

Leatho's teeth ground audibly. He unwound his sling, muttering to Kolun in a voice tight with anger and urgency, "I'm goin' on ahead to scout out the situation, mate. Get as many armed warriors an' good swimmers as ye can from the clans. When ye come to meet me, do it as quiet as ye can. I'll be lyin' in the rushes, about a quarter way up the south edge o' the lake. If'n I ain't there, then stand by an' keep yore heads low until I show up. Will ye do that?"

Big Kolun Galedeep picked up an oar and hefted it grimly. "Never fear, Leatho. I'll pick a good crew out, an' be on time to meet with ye. You go now, mate, an' fortune go with ye!"

74

Chab and Whulky were moored by their necks and waists to the posts beneath the pier. Their wives and the three little ones were tethered several posts away, though only by a thick rope knotted about the otterwives' shoulders, which still allowed them to hold the babes in their paws. Not knowing what they were guilty of, they stared at Chab and Whulky with wide, frightened eyes. Above them, feral cat-guards paced the boards on both sides of the pier. More could be seen patrolling the lakeshores.

Chab whispered to his companion, "I'd give my whis-kers'n'rudder for an ould shellblade knife t'cut through these ropes. First thing I'd do would be t'free the wives an' little 'uns, so they could swim fer it!"

Whulky strained against the rope about his neck. "No, mate, keep still for the moment, an' stow those wild ideas if'n ye ain't got anythin' to back 'em up with. If'n the wives an' babes had t'make a run fer it, they wouldn't stand a chance with all those catguards around. All we can do is to hope somebeast got word to the clans. If'n the Shellhound gets t'know, he won't leave us t'be slain. I'd take an oath on that!"

A long, thin willow withe was pushed down between the spaces of the pierboards, swung by a cat with a whipping motion. The cane caught Chab a stinging blow to his cheek.

"Sharrap down there, or I'll lay about the lot of ye, little 'uns, too!"

Both Chab and Whulky knew who the voice belonged to: Scorecat Groodl, a minor officer, subordinate to Weil-mark Scaut. Groodl was a brutal and sadistic cat, short in stature and savagely cruel to those beneath him, particu-larly slaves. He twitched the willow withe from side to side, taunting the prisoners.

"Not a peep out of any of ye now. 'Twould be a shame to deliver ye to Slothunog tomorrow, all cut'n'bruised. He likes his meat t'be tender an' unmarked."

He continued flicking them lightly with the long, whippy

75

withe. It was some while before Groodl became bored by his callous sport and wandered off, leaving a guard of ordinary rank to watch the prisoners.

Chab's wife bit her lip to stop a wail of anguish, now that she knew the fate that was in store for them. Angling his neck against the rope, Whulky gave her a confident wink in an effort to keep up her spirits.

"We won't let anythin' bad happen to ye, marm. Don't fret, 'twill only upset the little 'uns."

Big Kolun Galedeep had gathered a crew of paw-picked otters: Streamdivers, Streambattles, Wavedogs and some of his own clan, about fifty in all. They were armed with light javelins, which had fire-hardened tips, and slings, with a few blades in evidence, but these were in short supply. They marched stealthily, with Kolun and his brother Lorgo leading them, to the thick tussocks of reed and rush on the south quarter of the lakeshore. Leatho was nowhere to be seen. They lay low and silent on Kolun's orders.

They had not waited long when a telltale ripple on the lake surface came toward their hiding place. Banya Streamdog, a lithe ottermaid noted for her aquatic skills, pointed. "Lookit, here comes the very buckoe himself!"

Without a single splash, the Shellhound bounded out of the water into the rushes. He nodded a greeting to the crew before addressing Kolun. "Memsy was right, mate. I got up as close to the pier as I could without bein' spotted. Sure enough, that hellcat Felis has got Whulky an' Chab, an' their families, too. They're bound to the supportin' posts. There was no sign o' Felis about, but there's enough catguards standin' sentry an' patrollin' all around the area. Ye picked a fit-lookin' crew there, Kolun. Well done!"

The big otter's craggy face looked grim. He tightened his grip on the oar he had brought along. "Just give the word, mate, an' we'll storm 'em. There'll be fur an' catmeat flyin' everywhere!"

Leatho patted his friend's powerful shoulder. "Take it

easy, buckoe! There's far too many of 'em, we'd be slaughtered. Felis ain't planned anythin' for them otters 'til tomorrow morn. The way I sees it, there's no point in us makin' a move afore dusk. That gives me time aplenty to tell ye the plan I've hatched. Now lissen careful. We'll free our friends, but this is wot ye must do!"

The long, hot morning rolled on into noontide, with the far lake margins shimmering and the surface lying still as a sheet of glass. With his aide Atunra in tow, the warlord emerged from the fortress onto the pier. He sat beneath his awning, enjoying the shade. Of late, he had shunned the dog days of summer; the chain mail mask could get uncomfortably hot in constant direct sunlight. Groodl came out and joined his catguards to watch the prisoners.

Atunra went over and had a brief exchange with the scorecat, returning to inform the warlord, "The otterslaves have still not spoken, Master."

Riggu appeared unconcerned. "Then that is their bad fortune. Tomorrow I will use them as an example to the other slaves. Spectacles like that always keep our otters aware of their position. What's a few slavebeasts to me? The hardest-learned lessons are always the most effective."

The wildcat's reflections were rudely interrupted by the sounds of yowling, screeching and clattering from within the fortress. Riggu sank his claws into the velvet-covered chair arms. He waited a while, but still the din did not subside.

From between clenched teeth, he issued an order to Atunra. "Take those guards with you. Go in there and bring those sons of mine out here to me! Drag them out here if ye have to! Enough is enough, I'll put an end to all this spitting and snarling!"

Flanked by catguards, the two young cats were marched out to stand before their father. As usual, Jeefra was blubbering and Pitru scowling.

Jeefra began complaining tearfully to Riggu. "He said

that when we go to Deeplough, he's going to push me in so the monster can eat me, and he said that he's going to. . . ."

A growling noise that had been welling up in the warlord suddenly exploded, cutting Jeefra short. "Yahaaarg! Shut . . . up!"

Jeefra was totally silenced by the vehemence of his father. Slowly Riggu Felis stood. He prowled about the pair in a circle, his voice dripping contempt.

"My sons, eh? A whining coward and an impertinent bully! You are a disgrace and a shame to the name Felis. I curse the day you were spawned, both of ye!"

He ceased prowling and stood facing them, eye to eye. A cold smile stole across the eyes above the half-mask. "Well, my spoilt little kittens, it all ends right here. Your growing up starts today."

Riggu called to Groodl, who was watching from a short distance, "You there, attend me!"

Groodl marched smartly up, presenting his spear in salute. The warlord appeared to ignore him, speaking instead to Atunra. "Tell me about this one."

The pine marten replied. "Master, he is Groodl, one of Weilmark Scaut's scorecats."

Riggu looked Groodl up and down critically. "A scorecat, eh? And do you instill rigid discipline into your guards with that willow cane you carry beside your spear?"

The mean-featured feral cat rapped out tersely, "I never gives an order twice, Lord. When I gives the word, they jumps to it, sharpish!"

Riggu Felis nodded approvingly. "Good, I like that. Well, scorecat, you have two new recruits in your troop as of now. Take these two useless objects out of my sight. See if you can knock them into shape. Have them fitted out as the lowest of your guards."

He paused, watching the effect upon his sons. Jeefra looked stunned with shock, but Pitru narrowed his eyes lazily and gave a scornful snort. Riggu continued. "Show them no favours and cut them no slack. Use that willow cane on both of them. Let the order be lots of chores, little sleep and plenty of guard duty. Understood?"

Keeping his eyes straight ahead, Groodl swished the willow. "Understood, Lord. Do I bring 'em back to you an' their mother every night?"

The chain mail tinkled as the warlord shook his head. "No no, let them live in the barracks with the other guards. If Lady Kaltag asks to see them, send her to me."

Jeefra fell down weeping as he grovelled at his father's footpaws. "Please, Father, I beg you, don't do this to me! Don't send me to the barracks! I swear I'll change, no more quarrelling or arguing anymore. Mercy, please!"

Riggu Felis turned his face away, nodding to Groodl. "You've had your orders, take them away."

Jeefra had to be carried bodily between four guards, wailing and sobbing brokenly. Pitru did not resist; he merely sneered at his father. "I still have lots of seasons before me, but you're growing older. I can wait, you'll see."

Ignoring Groodl, he sauntered off toward the barracks. The wildcat chieftain was silent a moment, then pointed at Pitru's receding back.

"Atunra, mark him well. That one will grow to be a dangerous beast someday."

The pine marten bowed. "Just as you were at his age, Master."

The chain mail half-mask sucked inward briefly. "Aye, that's what troubles me."

Sunset's crimson curtain faded to dusk, merging into restful darkness. Lights appeared at the fortress turret slits. Two sentry fires burned bright, one to the left of the pier, the other to the right side. Held between the otterwives, Chab's young ones were sleeping.

Banya Streamdog and six sturdy otters emerged from the waters beneath the pier, firelight playing off their sleek backs as they moved like night shades, with scarcely a ripple to betray their presence. Holding a paw to her lips,

Banya made for the otterwives, whispering to them, "Wait and be ready when Lorgo gives the signal!"

Hope surged through Whulky and Chab as the tall, sinewy Lorgo Galedeep surfaced alongside them. "Stay put, mates. Ye can't make a move until the action starts. Chab, don't fret, bhoyo, I've brought some champion riverdogs to git yore babies away safe."

Leatho Shellhound, accompanied by a dozen armed otters, stole from the lake, a short way from the left side of the pier. Directing them by signals, he sent his warriors in a long arc around to the darkness behind the fire. The outlaw set a stone to his sling and waited. Soon he was rewarded by the call of a nightjar from the right side of the pier. Big Kolun and his band had surfaced and were in position. Leatho whirled his sling, aiming at the backside of a catguard who was leaning on his spear close to the fire.

It was a perfect shot: The stone struck its target, not slaying the cat but creating the desired effect. Arching his back and yowling in pain, the catguard stumbled into the flames at the fire's edge. His companions swiftly hauled him back, shouting out in confusion.

"That was a slingstone! What's goin' on?"

"Somebeast's out there, look!"

The outlaw ran forward, whirling his sling as he yelled out a challenge. "Yerra, ye mangy scum, the Shellhound's a-comin'!"

Guards jumped down from the pier to join the others. They advanced on Leatho cautiously, wondering if he had brought clanbeasts with him. The outlaw bolstered their confidence: He slung off a few more stones, carefully calculated to miss them. Roaring with laughter, he danced a jig on the lakeshore, then scampered off into the water.

One of the scorecats urged the rest forward, shouting to them, "It's a single otter. Mad fool, what's he up to? Get him!"

They charged forward but halted at the water's edge.

Aware that the cats were fearful of water, Leatho swam out a short way, then commenced taunting them.

"Come on, ye mangy-tailed cowards! Scared o' gettin' yore paws wet, are ye?"

Spears, lances and arrows were hurled at him. Right at the last moment he submerged, only to pop up again in another place.

"Is that the best ye can do? Send out yore best warrior! Hah, that'd be ole half-face, wouldn't it? I hear he was defeated by a bird—was it a sparrow or a wren?!"

Whilst the diversion was being created, Leatho's crew came out of the firelight and began attacking the catguards' rear. Roused by the commotion, Riggu Felis bounded out onto the pier, single-bladed axe in paw. He was accompanied by Weilmark Scaut, who recognised Leatho's voice. "It's the Shellhound, I've got a score t'settle with that 'un!"

The warlord dropped on all fours, peering through the board spaces to assure himself that the captives were still there, bound to the pier struts. Straightening up, he growled, "Then get down there and take him alive, Scaut. Alive, d'ye hear me? Get some of those otterslave fishing boats and cut him off, encircle him. But remember, I want him alive!"

As the weilmark went off to do his bidding, Riggu Felis turned to Groodl and his guards, who were grouped around the fire on the right lakeshore. "Over here, quick, all of you. Follow Weilmark Scaut!"

Jeefra and Pitru, newly fitted out with helmets, jerkins and spears, were among the group who hurried off to the left.

As soon as the fire on the right was deserted, Big Kolun and his crew emerged from the shadows, thrusting their torches into the flames. Then they began hurling them at the huge timber fortress. Riggu Felis leaped aside as a blazing torch landed on the pier close to him. With his chain mail mask glittering weirdly in the light of the flames, he called urgently to the guards deployed on the left shore.

"Scaut, get your command back over here! They're trying to fire the other side of the fortress!"

The weilmark was loth to leave the outlaw Shellhound uncaptured. He issued swift orders to Groodl. "Scorecat, keep half your cats on shore, send the rest out in the boats. Remember, he must be taken alive. The rest of you, follow me!"

The otters they had been fighting suddenly dispersed into the darkness, leaving Scaut's contingent a free path back. Jeefra and Pitru both wielded paddles in one of the six fishing coracles on the lake. In unexperienced paws, the little craft blundered about as Leatho drew them away in a wild chase.

Once the left shore was clear of guards, the otters came out of the shadows again. Making for the fire, they did exactly as Kolun and his crew had. Igniting more torches from the blaze, they hurled them at the left side of the fortress, causing widespread confusion.

Riggu Felis was screeching hoarsely as he ran hither and thither. "Over here, some of you! Scaut, split your troop, get half of them around to the left side. Hurry!"

Lorgo Galedeep and Banya Streamdog slashed through the captives' bonds. In the chaos which reigned overhead, prisoners were the last thing on any foebeast's mind. Chab's young ones were strapped firmly to the backs of three champion Streambattle swimmers.

Banya and a few of her clanmates surrounded the two otterwives. "Don't forget now, underwater an' straight out. Follow the three carryin' yore little 'uns. They'll take ye over to the right shore. We've spotted a landin' place there that's well away from this lot, quiet an' hidden. Move now, there ain't much time t'waste!"

Lorgo and some of his stalwarts pushed Chab and Whulky after them. "Follow Banya. No need t'look back, we're right behind ye, mateys!"

Out on the lake, Leatho was keeping the coracles chasing after him, making sure they held to the left shore, where he knew they would not come into contact with the escaping slaves.

Groodl was shouting orders to his coracle crews from the shore. "Don't throw those spears, idiots! Hold on to 'em and try to stab 'im. You guards with bows, don't go shootin' at shadows, try t'get a clear target. D'ye hear me?"

What they did not know was that there were now eight otters in the water, not just one. They began popping up in different places, taking turns at mocking the catguards.

"Ahoy there, scruffywhiskers, I'm over here!"

"Ye don't want him, fishbrain, I'm the one yore lookin' for!"

"Belay there, I'm the Shellhound, not that 'un!"

Water sloshed over the sides of the flimsy craft as they wallowed about on the dark lake. Guards wobbled to keep their balance as they hurled spears and fired arrows willy-nilly, completely ignoring their scorecat's orders as they sought to silence their foes.

Groodl was hopping and leaping about in the shallows, ranting hoarsely, "Ye bunglin' mudheads, they're makin' fools of ye!"

Atunra came hurrying from the pier with Riggu's latest order. "Lord Felis says you must break off searching for Shellhound. Call those boats in immediately. We need everybeast on the bucket line!"

Catguards were passing buckets, jugs, bowls and pails, paw to paw, in a line which stretched from the pier end to the fortress. Water hissed and sizzled as they threw it on the flames around the base of the fortress. The guards in the coracles had been lured a fair way out onto the lake. They were only too glad when they heard their scorecat yelling for them to return to shore.

Leatho surfaced and almost bumped heads with Kolun. The big fellow was grinning from ear to ear. "Felis ain't holdin' prisoners no more, buckoe. Our crews got 'em well away an' safe. What now?"

The outlaw nodded toward the retreating coracles. "Let's teach a few o' those landlubbers a lesson!"

Big Kolun shot them a scornful glance. "My babes make a better shape at rowin' than that lot!"

Only three vessels made it to the safety of land. Between them, the two otters overturned the other three. Yowls, splashes and splutters of cats rent the night air as they were tipped into the water. Leatho and Kolun swam smoothly off, satisfied that their plan to free their otterfriends had succeeded.

The last craft that the otters had tipped upside down was the one containing Jeefra and Pitru. Both cats went under immediately, but Pitru was the first to surface. He hauled himself up onto the hull of the coracle and grabbed a paddle from the water. He had made scarcely a stroke shoreward when the vessel heeled, lurching perilously over to one side. Jeefra had a tight hold of it, digging his claws into the birchbark covering as he strove wildly to pull himself aboard. He was in a mad panic, choking and spluttering between mouthfuls of water.

"Help me, help! Don't let me drown, Pitru!"

Pitru glanced around at the other survivors. They were all floundering toward land, oblivious to what was going on behind them. Pitru bared his fangs as he brought the paddle down twice, as hard as he could—the first time, on Jeefra's paws and the second on Jeefra's head.

Throwing the paddle away, Pitru flattened himself on the upturned hull, staring into the dark waters that Jeefra had disappeared under. Then he began paddling landward with his paws, crying out pitifully, "Jeefra, where are you? Has anybeast seen my poor brother?"

Riggu Felis had spoken truly when he had said that one day his son would become a dangerous beast.

9

Brother Perant would not allow Tiria, Tribsy or Brinty back into his Infirmary, even though they pleaded with him. Standing in the doorway, he blocked the entrance, resisting all their efforts.

"No, no, 'tis out of the question, I'm afraid. Those two birds are under my care. I cannot risk you stirring up any more squabbles between them. Please go away!"

But the ottermaid continued trying to reason with him. "I promise you we won't, Brother, really. It's most important that I speak with them. If we can't come in, then perhaps you could allow them to come out. You have my solemn word we'll return them to you as soon as I have the information we require."

The Infirmary Keeper could be rather stubborn when he had a mind to, a quality he viewed more as a virtue than a fault. "Allow them out? Certainly not, miss! The birds are both injured creatures. They need to recover under my care. That's my final word. Now be off with you!"

Perant was about to slam the door when Abbess Lycian arrived upon the scene with the hogbabe Grumby in tow. The Dibbun hid behind her habit, sucking on his paw.

Lycian smiled disarmingly. "Ah, Brother Perant, have you a moment to spare for a wounded kitchen helper?"

The little hogbabe was still sucking lustily on his paw as the Abbess ushered him forward. "Tell Brother Perant what happened to you."

Lycian removed the paw from Grumby's mouth so he could speak. "I'm hurted meself, Bruvva, sticked me pore likkle paw onna 'ot h'oven an' cookered it!"

The good Brother forgot his stubborness, softening instantly. "Oh lack a day and dearie me! Friar Bibble never told me we were having small cooked hogpaws for supper. Come in, young sir, let's see what we can do about your poor paw!"

Grumby hung back reluctantly. "Baby Taggle say you gonna choppa off me paw wivva big knife. Then she say you choppa me tail off, too!"

Crouching down level with Grumby, the healer chuckled. "Don't you take any notice of Dibbun Taggle, she's a dreadful fibber. Wait until I see her . . . why, I'll put nasty ointment on her tongue and bandage it up!"

Grumby giggled at the idea. "Tharra teach 'er to fib!"

Perant led him into the Infirmary. "I'll tell you how I treat cooked paws. First, I bathe them in nice cool water. Then I apply some soothing salve and a dressing. While I'm doing this, you can use your good paw to help yourself to some candied chestnuts from my special jar. How does that sound to you, sir?"

Grumby rattled his spikes with pleasure. "Sounders fine t'me, Bruvva. . . . Yeek, the big birdies gonna h'eat me!"

He scooted out of the Infirmary, straight into Tiria's paws. Recognising an opportunity, she smiled winningly at Perant. "I'm sure they wouldn't, but he's only a Dibbun, probably never seen a hawk or a goose close-up, Brother. Please, won't you reconsider letting us take them off your paws for a while so you can attend to little Grumby?"

Though Lycian did not know exactly what was going on, she spoke up on behalf of Tiria and her friends. "The birds won't come to any harm with these young ones, Brother.

They're almost fully grown-up now. I'll keep an eye on them, too. What do you say, friend?"

Besides being stubborn, Perant was also highly conscious of Abbey protocol and courtesy. He bowed gravely. "If that is your wish, Mother Abbess!"

Afternoon tea was being served on the front lawn, not far from the gatehouse. Redwallers broke off momentarily, some of them showing apprehension at the arrival of an osprey and a barnacle goose. Lycian reassured them calmly.

"We've brought some friends to tea. This is Brantalis, and this is Pandion. They're very well-mannered. Do make them welcome, please."

Tribsy, like all the younger creatures, greatly admired the ease with which Lycian was able to deal with everybeast, even though many of the Abbey's residents were older than their Abbess. "Burr, you'm surrpinkly gotten ee way abowt you'm, marm. H'ole Perant bee'd abowt to shoo us'n's off, but you'm soon fixered 'im. Hurr hur, naow you'm a settlin' h'eveybeast completeful to ease with ee gurt burds!"

Tiria and Lycian took the birds to the buffet table, allowing them to choose what they liked. Brantalis opted for soft cheese and watercress sandwiches, which he immersed in a bowl of pea and cabbage soup and gobbled down with evident relish. Pandion favoured preserved fruits and a leek and mushroom turnover, both of which he seemed to enjoy. The Redwallers dining nearby were amused by the barnacle goose's quaint mode of speech.

"This good food, I am thinking it is very likeful. Soon I am thinking I will try some of that tireful!"

Brinty laughed. "That's called trifle, not tireful. I'm sure you'll like it. Maybe Pandion will, too."

The great fish hawkpecked at his turnover pastry crust. "Kraaah! I will have the soup with watershrimps in it. Pandion likes watershrimp!"

Tiria interrupted politely. "It's also a favourite among

otters. Actually, all Redwall vittles are good. But first I must ask you some questions."

A group of Dibbuns had formed a ring on the lawn. They flexed their tiny limbs, hopping about, as Sister Doral, the Abbey Beekeeper, tuned up her fiddle.

Once prepared, the jolly Sister called out, "Please take your places for the Bee Dance. Abbess Lycian and Hillyah, will you oblige us by singing the verses?" Without further ado, she struck up the lively introduction.

Brantalis began bobbing his head up and down in time with the tune. "Music is good! Tiria, I am thinking I will be answering your questions not now. Later!"

Pandion commenced tapping his talons upon a platter. "Dances, I like dances and song. Kreeeekyaaaaaarr!"

Tiria watched the pair, surprised that they wanted to watch and listen. She settled back with a sigh. "Be my guests, please. I'll wait until it's finished."

Within moments, the ottermaid was tapping her rudder along with the infectious tune.

"Heyla huppla Mister Bee, make some honey just
    for me!
Fly o'er lawn and buzz o'er lea,
fetch that honey for my tea,
visit all your special flowers
blooming through the summer hours.
Heyla huppla Mister Bee, make some honey just for me!
Woodruff clover poppy thyme,
spurrey sorrel columbine,
dogrose heather harebell blue,
violet pansy speedwell too.
Heyla huppla Mister Bee, make some honey just for me!
From the blossom's nectar sweet,
comes a hearty honey treat,
I can't wait 'til you arrive,
at my table from your hive.
Heyla huppla Mister Bee, make some honey just for me!

Golden rich and gooey thick,
sticky likkle paws I lick,
scrumptious munchious gorgeous stuff,
Dibbuns just can't get enough.
Heyla huppla Mister Bee, make some honey just
    for me!"

Abbess Lycian knew the song well, and she sang it prettily.
Watching her Abbeybabes dance always gave her enormous
pleasure. However, she also found it puzzling: The little
ones were normally stumbling, bumbling toddlers, but the
instant they heard music, they were completely transformed. Away they went in perfect rhythm, clapping, jig-
ging, bowing, twirling and performing some artful high
kicks and fancy pawwork. Some of them could actually
somersault and cartwheel.

The applause from the Redwall audience was almost
drowned out by the two big birds as they reared up, beating their outspread wings furiously. Brantalis honked,
whilst Pandion threw back his head and skriked to the
skies. Encouraged by the ovation, the Dibbuns threw themselves into the dance again as an encore. Tiria began wondering if she would ever get the chance to interview the
two birds.

After a while, Sister Doral put the fiddle away and went
to get her tea. Tiria was about to speak with Brantalis when
her father and Brink came and joined them. Banjon sat on
the lawn, enjoying some warm scones, damson preserve
and hot mint tea.

"Ahoy, Tiria, me gel! Me'n Brink been out trollin' the
woodlands for yore water rats. We lost their trail in the
nor'east woodlands, by the marshes borderin' the watermeadows. I don't think ye'll be seein' them again. Ain't that
right, Brink?"

The sturdy Cellarhog seated himself laboriously, trying to
balance a trencher that was piled high with salad, pasties,
soup, bread and cheese. He winked at the ottermaid. "Aye,

beauty, those vermin are either sunk without trace, or they made it o'er the watermeadows an' headed up north out o' Mossflower. Are ye alright now, missy? That was a funny liddle turn ye took, back in the ditch earlier."

Tiria decided to let them in on her dream experience. "I wasn't ill at all. It was that I'd suddenly recalled a dream I had last night. If you've a moment to spare, I'll tell you all about it."

As the shadows began lengthening, Skipper Banjon listened avidly to his daughter's narration of her vision and the subsequent events. When Tiria had finished, he stared oddly at her.

"Rip me rudder, gel, I always knowed you was fated for somethin' other than Abbey life. Ever since we lost yore dear Ma, fates rest her memory. You was nought but a liddle furball then, but I sensed it in ye. Aye, the more ye've growed, the more certain of it I am. Tiria, yore different from the others. A true Wildlough, that's wot ye are!"

Brink peered over the rim of his soup bowl. "Great seasons, if ye've been visited by Martin the Warrior, well that's the proof. Just say the word, darlin', an' yore dad an' me'll help ye any way we can!"

The ottermaid clasped their paws gratefully. "Thank you both, especially you, Skip. I was worried as to how you'd take the news of me having to leave Redwall and seek out the Green Isle. Brantalis the goose knows the way, and our fish hawk was reared there. He should be able to tell us more about the place. I was just about to start questioning them, but now look!"

Both birds had joined the Dibbun circle, and Sister Doral had been persuaded to take up her fiddle again. She played a simple reel, whilst the Abbeybabes gave the osprey and the barnacle goose their first dancing lesson. Squirrelbabe Taggle and molebabe Groop were bossing them about severely.

"No, no, y'kick yore paws uppa like dis, Mista Panjon!"

"Hurr, naow do ee stop a-flappen yurr gurt wingers abowt, zurr, you'm nearly knockered oi snout o'er suppertoime!"

The two birds seemed slightly relieved when Banjon and Brink came to their rescue. "Avast there, mates. Come an' talk to the maid wot saved yore lives. We'll teach ye to dance proper tomorrow. Steer clear o' these liddle rogues."

There was nobeast around the gatehouse wallsteps, so they took their food and adjourned there.

Tiria started immediately with Brantalis. "Listen, my friend. I know I can't fly like you, but I must find the way to Green Isle. Are you willing to help?"

The barnacle goose clacked his beak resolutely. "I am thinking that I will help you, Tiria, after all your kindness to me. Here is the way Skyfurrows always take to Green Isle. Every autumn season we are flying down from the far northlands. Always we fly south, aye, fly south and follow the coast, until we are reaching the old mountain, home of the longears and great stripedog lords. Know you of it?"

Skipper Banjon did. "Aye, that'd be Salamandastron, where the fightin' hares an' Badger Lords dwell. I've heard of it but never been there meself. 'Tis a mighty trek from Redwall to that mountain, I can tell ye!"

Brantalis nodded sagely. "A mighty trek, indeed, for earthcrawlers such as you. But I am thinking, there is a better route. If Brantalis could not fly, he would use the River Moss, north of here. I could speak the way to you, whilst you mark it down. The creatures of the Red Walls are good at marking ways down I am thinking."

Tiria thumped the wallsteps with her rudder. "Of course, a map! It would make things a lot simpler if I had a map to guide me!"

Brink raised his spiky eyebrows. "Oh, lots easier, missy, but ye forgot to mention that ye'll need a boat to make yore journey in. No otter could swim o'er the Great Western Sea alone. 'Tis impossible!"

Banjon merely winked at his Cellarhog friend. "Don't ye fret, matey. If'n my Tiria needs a boat, ye can wager she'll soon git one, won't ye, gel?"

Tiria shrugged, as though the matter were no great concern. "Aye, I'll get a boat, one way or another. Now, after supper we'll ask Sister Snowdrop to draw up the map, exactly the way in which Brantalis describes it to her. Good, that's that settled! So, Pandion my friend, tell me about your home. What's it like on Green Isle?"

The osprey regarded her with his savage golden eyes. "Kaharr! If I knew the way to my home, I would fly there this day. Green Isle is a place of great beauty, with soft morning mists, mountains, loughs and rivers full of fine fish. Kraak! But it is also an island of much evil and danger. Cats rule there—big, cruel, warlike beasts. One called Riggu Felis is their warlord. He it was whom I wounded badly, when he and his two sons tried to kill me for sport. There are also seadogs there, and riverdogs, just like you, Tiria. But, alas, they live under the cat's paw, they are slaves, and runaways, outlaws. There is a big timber fortress at the head of a lake. The cats have ruled there since back into the mists of time. You will not be welcome on Green Isle. It belongs now to Riggu Felis and his warriors!"

Tribsy gave forth a deep mole growl. "Hurrrrr! Us'n's not a-feared o' ee catters. We'm bee's gurt Redwall wurriers!"

Brinty clenched his paws truculently. "Aye, and we're great fighters, too. Those water rats soon found that out when we whacked them with our staves!"

Tiria shook her head. "I'm sorry, mates, but you won't be going. I couldn't risk your lives. Since the dream was mine, I feel I must fulfill it alone."

Skipper placed his paws around the crestfallen pair. "She's right, buckoes. Ye've always been good friends t'my Tiria, young Girry, too, an' I thank ye kindly. But 'twould be too perilous to risk yore lives, far from yore Abbey in a strange land. Besides, there was no mention or sign in Tiria's dream commandin' anybeast to go but her."

Brink suddenly came up with a practical idea. "Why don't ye take the big fish 'awk with ye, miss? Granted, 'e don't know the way, but I wager Pandion would be of service to ye when ye get to the isle, eh?"

Brantalis favoured Brink's scheme. "I am thinking this is a good idea, yes! I cannot go until when the autumn leaves fall, when my skein comes down the coast from the north. I will know when the time is. Then I will be flying to the shores to meet them. Skyfurrows always fly together. So I am thinking, it will be many moons before I join my family. The hookbeak should go with you, Tiria!"

Pandion Piketalon hopped up onto the battlements. Spreading his wings, he stared regally down his lethal beak at Brantalis. "Karralah! I go to Green Isle with my friend Tiria. Let that waddling flatbeak linger here until he ventures forth to meet with his kind. Pandions do not fear flying alone. I need no gaggle around me!"

The barnacle goose flared up, beating his heavy wings aggressively. "Brantalis is thinking he was not named flatbeak. Beware, fish eater! A Skyfurrow's wings can break bones!"

Tiria was forced to come between the big birds. "Don't start again, you two! There's no cause for all this disagreement and wing flapping. Either make your peace or begone from here. It is against our laws to battle within the walls of this Abbey!"

An instant later, the touchy situation was forgotten. Girry came hurtling across the lawn, leaping over flower beds and shouting frantically. "Quick, quick! Come to the attic above the library. Sister Snowdrop's found something which you must see!"

10

Daybreak drifted sluggishly over Green Isle, dull and grey. Thick mist shrouded the lake and shores in a pall of silence, but the peace was rudely shattered by agonised shrieks from the pier.

"Hiiiyeeeee! My son, my Jeefra! Eeeeeeyyyaaaaarrrr!" Lady Kaltag howled and screeched like a wounded beast. Catguards crowded in front of her, barring the way to the sodden form which lay huddled and lifeless on the pier end. She fought tooth and claw to get past them, wailing dementedly.

Scorecat Groodl was in charge of the guards. He tried to slink away as he caught sight of Riggu Felis emerging from the fortress. The warlord was a nightmarish sight, his hideously injured face exposed as he carried his helmet and face mask in one paw. He stopped Groodl in his tracks.

"What is the meaning of this?"

Trembling, the scorecat tried to avoid looking at the wildcat's maimed features. "Lord, we had to search for your son. Atunra told us to drag the lakeshore waters with ropes and hooks."

Swinging his helmet, Riggu Felis caught Groodl a lightning swift blow, which knocked him flat. He snarled sav-

94

agely at his catguards. "Get him away from here, fools, quickly! Bury him out of sight, far along the bank. Go!"

Pitru lounged casually in the fortress doorway, his face betraying nothing. Riggu confronted him. "You know more about this than you are telling!"

Pitru shrugged. "There's not much to tell. Our boat was upturned out on the lake last night. Otters did it, probably that Shellhound one who broke Scaut's jaw. I never saw Jeefra after we both went into the water. I searched for him and shouted for help, but none came. I had to make my own way back to the shore. That's all I know."

Kaltag was following Groodl and the catguards who were bearing Jeefra's body away. Seeing her remaining son, she turned and ran to him. Seizing Pitru's paw, she sobbed brokenly, "What happened to your brother? Tell me, my son, tell me!"

Wrenching his paw free, Pitru pointed accusingly at his father. "Ask him, he was the one who forced us to join the catguards. Jeefra would still be alive if he hadn't!"

Kaltag flung herself at the warlord, scratching and biting. He held her off, shouting in a harsh voice, "Do you not think I grieve for the death of my son? It was you, always shielding and making excuses for them both, indulging their whims. You were responsible for turning them into spoilt cats. I have to rule as Lord of Green Isle, with no time to be a nursemaid, yet I decided to do something for them. I sent them to serve as catguards so they could grow up with some sense of responsibility. The death of Jeefra is a hard thing for me to bear, but he died like a warrior, honourably in battle!"

Riggu signalled to Atunra and two guards standing nearby. They managed to get Kaltag away from him. She was led indoors, yelling at him, "Murderer! Assassin! You killed your own son! What next, Riggu Felis, Great Lord of Green Isle? Will you slay both me and your other son so you can rule alone?"

Pitru shed his guard's attire and gave his father a satisfied smirk before following his mother indoors.

Weilmark Scaut, still with his jaw in bandages, marched up and saluted the wildcat with the stock of his whip. "Lord, there was little damage done by the fire, we contained it before it could get a hold. The fortress walls are old and thick, so they hardly suffered, apart from a bit o' scorched bark."

If he expected any thanks for the information, Scaut was sadly disillusioned. The warlord vented his spleen on the unwitting weilmark. "So, you think that makes everything alright, do you? One of my sons is slain, the otters freed the prisoners, they tried to burn down my fortress and they had all my catguards chasing their own tails. They made fools of us!"

The sight of Riggu Felis with rage stamped on his unmasked face was a frightening thing to behold. Scaut backed off, keeping silent lest his Lord's wrath descend upon him.

Slamming on his helmet, Riggu grabbed his war axe. "You will summon my catguards, every one of them. Have them lined in ranks on the shore by the time this mist breaks. I'll straighten their backbones!"

The weilmark did not know whether to breathe a sigh of relief or apprehension as the warlord strode off to his tower chamber.

Out on the coast, just above the tideline, were cliffs with thick vegetation hanging down over deeply undercut rock shelving. This had once been the habitat of all the Shellhound sea otters, but Leatho was the last survivor of his clan. The long, low-ceilinged cavern was well disguised, and was on a stretch of the coast seldom visited by any creature.

On that misty morning, every free otter gathered there in force to celebrate the victory over their foes. A huge cauldron of kelp and seafood stew bubbled over a sizeable fire of driftwood, charcoal and sea coal. A jubilant air prevailed overall, with little ones playing games of jinkshells and elders gathering round the far side of the fire to gossip and exchange news with friends and relatives. Ould Zillo the Bard sat in a corner, composing a ballad of the night's heroic events. Otterwives doled out freshly baked pawpad turnovers and bowls of stew.

A jolly, wide-girthed old grandfather named Birl Gully was pouring tankards of his home-brewed invention from a barrel to a waiting line of clanbeasts. His vast stomach wobbled with merriment as he passed out the stuff.

"Hohoho! Come on, me bhoyos, drink 'earty now! There ain't nothin' like my Gullyplug Punch t'put the curl back in yore whiskers. 'Twill give ye a rudder like a rock an' backfur like velvet moss!"

Big Kolun Galedeep carried two tankards outside the curtain of vegetation which covered the cave front. Leatho was seated on a rock outside, staring into the thick, rolling mist that lay upon the calm, ebbing tide. Sitting beside the outlaw, Kolun gave him a tankard of Birl Gully's punch.

"Git that down yore throat, matey. 'Twill warm the cockles of yore 'eart!"

Leatho sipped pensively, still silently watching the sea mists. Big Kolun was not renowned as a sipper. Emptying his tankard in two swallows, he wiped the back of a hefty paw across his mouth.

"Well now, Shellhound. The clans seem t'be enjoyin' theirselves in there, while yore mopin' about out 'ere. Wot ails ye, mate? You can tell me."

Leatho swilled the punch around in his tankard. "One single victory don't mean we've won the war, Kolun. That wildcat ain't goin' to hold still after wot we've done. Felis is bound to come back at us hard as he can. I don't know exactly how the villain'll do it. So 'tis up to me to try an' outthink him."

Kolun threw a paw around his friend's shoulders. "Aye, well, you do yore outthinkin' later, buckoe. Yore wanted in there right now. C'mon, stir yore rudder!"

Rousing cheers greeted the outlaw as he joined the throng. Amid copious back slapping and paw shaking, he was escorted to a seat of honour by the fire. Leatho had issues he wanted to address the otters about, but as he made to rise, Big Kolun's missus, Deedero, shoved him firmly back down, proclaiming, "Arrah, sit ye down, Shellhound. The bard's composed a fine lay about ye. Whisht now, the singer's got the floor!"

Ould Zillo's rudderdrum began thrumming the beat, whilst a flute and fiddle joined in. The one-eyed bard launched into his newly written ballad.

"Harroo for the Shellhound, ain't he the bold beast,
he's the hero we've all come to toast at this feast,
for he singed the cat's tail, and put flame to his fort,
the whiskery tyrant, his threats came to nought!
O pity those slaves who were bound 'neath the pier,
an' for the three babies we all shed a tear,
all sentenced to death in the dreaded Deeplough,
'twas enough to put any pore otter in shock!
'Til the Shellhound arrived in the dark o' the night,
an' to the cats' fortress his warriors set light,
with freedom their watchword, they championed the
    cause,
as they battled with catguards along the lakeshores!
With slingstone an' spear they attacked the cruel foe,
an' as for the outcome, well I'm sure that ye know,
they freed the brave captives an' got clear away,
an' were back here safe home by the dawn of the day!
Ye wicked ould wildcat this lesson ye'll learn,
or yore guards will be slain an' yore fortress'll burn,
sure ye'll wail in the ashes an' stamp the bare ground,
an' ye'll rue the sad day that ye met the Shellhound!
Shellhound. . . . Shellhound . . . Shellhooooouuuuund!"

All around the cave, voices and tankards were raised.
"Leatho! Leatho! Speech speech speech!"

Taking the floor, the outlaw held up his paws until order was restored. "Friends, clanbeasts, my thanks to ye! But 'twas not just me who did the deed. There were many brave ones with me who are worthy of yore praise—warriors, who risked life an' limb to free our good friends. Hearken to me now! Riggu Felis will be yearnin' to avenge his defeat. That wildcat is a powerful an' savage foebeast. Aye, an' if I'm yore leader, then I've got this to say. All our otterclans are not yet ready to face the cats. Not until we're all united behind one High Queen, the Rhulain!"

More cheers and chanting broke out. "Eeayeeeeeh! Rhulain! High Rhulaaaaain!"

Ould Zillo the Bard whacked his drum until they stopped. "Sure will ye not hold yore noisy gobs now an' give the goodbeast a chance? Where's yore manners? Leatho has the floor! Best of order now, all round the cave, d'ye hear!"

Nodding his thanks to the old otter, Leatho continued. "We'll get nowhere if'n we don't lay the ground with some hard plannin' now. Do ye not realise that Felis still holds more than a hundred slaves?"

He shook a clenched paw at the chastened otters. "Aye, that many! All that's left o' the Wildlough clan, an' other families, with old 'uns an' babes. They must be freed, afore Felis starts takin' reprisals among 'em!"

Big Kolun Galedeep strode to the outlaw's side. "Wot ye say is true, Leatho, an' everybeast here is with ye. So tell us how ye plan on goin' about it!"

Shellhound warmed to his subject immediately. "First we need to make this place safe an' secure. Every single otter must leave home an' holt to live here from now on. That way we can't be singled out or hunted down family by family. Deedero, Zillo, I leave the runnin' of this place t'ye both. I know ye can be trusted to provision an' protect the cave."

There was a murmur of agreement; clearly, this was a wise choice. Leatho's keen eyes searched the gathering.

"Next, I want two volunteers, otters who aren't readily

99

identifiable. These two must steal back into the fortress and blend in as slaves. 'Tis a risky an' dangerous task. They must learn t'be my eyes an' ears among the enemy. Through them we'll learn what's goin' on in the cats' camp, what Felis's next move will be. Are there two among ye who'll take the chance?"

A mass of paws shot up. Leatho took his time selecting. "You there, an' you, too. Step up here."

Memsy, the former otterslave who had brought news of Whulky and Chab's capture, was one. The other was a slim otter, fully grown but rather nondescript in looks. He walked forward, nodding to Leatho.

"I'm Runka Streamdog, brother of Banya."

The outlaw shook both their paws. "I'm beholden to ye, mates. Stand by for orders."

He addressed the remainder of the clans. "Now I need warriors, beasts who are strong'n'fit. Ye'll have to travel light, live off the land an' be ready to fight t'the death at the wink of my eye. Kolun Galedeep'll come among ye an' pick out those he thinks will do. Remember, if yore chosen, we'll only be back here now an' agin. No more feastin' an' restin' round the fire wid yore friends an' families. If yore with me 'n' Kolun, ye'll travel like the wind, an' strike like thunder'n'lightnin' at the cats. Our aim is t'free all the slaves, an' fetch 'em back here to safety to wait 'til Queen Rhulain comes to Green Isle."

It was fully midmorn before the sun deigned to appear and banish the mists. Dew stood heavy on the helmets, jerkins and spearpoints of over two hundred catguards, marshalled in five ranks on the lakeshore. Feral cats of various hues, shapes and sizes stood rigidly to attention. Among them were archers, axe carriers, spearbearers and pikebearers, their limbs stiff and numb from the long wait. Weilmark Scaut stood on a raised rock in front of the parade, watching as his ten scorecats patrolled the ranks. Each one carried a long willow cane, ready to strike out at slovenly guards.

As he saw the warlord emerge from the fortress in full armour, Scaut called out sharply, "The Lord of Green Isle comes!"

Raising their weaponry, the catguards shouted in strict chant, "Warlord of all! Mighty Wildcat! Conqueror and Destroyer of foebeasts! Lord of the Fortress! Hail Riggu Felis!"

The sound of their chant was still echoing around the lake as Riggu Felis stood on the rock, now vacated by Scaut. The warlord wore a helmet of beaten silver, with horns that resembled twin crescent moons protruding on each side. From these hung a square of heavy black silk, embroidered with silver wire, forming his lower face mask. A long cloak, of black-and-white weave, over a fine chain mail doublet plus the shining, single-bladed war axe hanging from one paw on a thong completed his apparel.

A light lake breeze rippled across his mask as he spoke out scathingly. "I wish I had twice your number. Then would I slay all ye standing before me now, dead where ye stand!"

The wildcat chieftain paused, then watched the ranks jerk with shock as he roared at them, "Fools! Addle-pawed idiots! Brainless buffoons! I, Riggu Felis, Lord of this isle, watched ye being made sport of by a few riverdogs last night! The captives whom I had sentenced to death! Where are they now?"

He raised the axe, pointing at the fortress. "My home was put to the torch, almost burned! Where are the slain bodies of all the otters who did it?"

Leaping down from the rock dais, the wildcat prowled along the first rank of catguards, prodding them on their chests with the axe handle as he repeated, "Tell me! Where? Where? Where?"

Halting abruptly at the end guard on the line, Riggu Felis faced him, dropping his voice to a conversational tone. "Gone, all of them, escaped. What do you think should have happened to them?"

The catguard's voice took on a dithering tremble as he

replied, "Th . . . they sh . . . should have been s . . . s . . . slain, Lord."

The warlord exploded with a sudden angry bellow. "Slain!!"

With a single devastating swing of the axe, he killed the unfortunate guard on the spot. "Slain, just like this one!"

The ranks stood in stunned silence, each catguard keeping his or her eyes straight ahead, scarcely daring to breathe, terrified to look at their fallen comrade lest they draw the attention of the maddened wildcat.

Brandishing the dripping axe, Riggu Felis pounced up onto the rock platform. "Hear me! More of ye will follow that one if my domain is not shortly rid of outlaws and runaways. We will scour this isle from coast to coast, we will root out these accursed otters! The rivers and streams, even the very tidal waters, shall run red with their blood, old or young, all of them! I promise ye, I will make warriors of ye once more!"

Whilst the wildcat had been haranguing his army, Lady Kaltag had come out onto the pier. She stood looking across at Riggu Felis. Atunra and Pitru joined her. The young cat was garbed out like a chieftain himself. He wore a steel helmet with a purple scarf streaming out behind it, a cloak of dark blue and a breastplate set with jet stones. In one paw he carried a small polished shield; in the other, a curved scimitar.

Kaltag pointed at Riggu Felis accusingly, her voice scornful and unafraid. "Look at the mighty wildcat! He is very good at slaying those who serve him. First my son Jeefra and now one of his own guards. Why do you not go and slay some real enemies, the outlaw they call Shellhound and his followers? Or are you afraid that they might fight back?"

Riggu Felis could not keep the sneer out of his voice. "I am planning on seeking out my enemies right away. Why don't you go and attend to your own affairs and keep that overdressed kitten out of my way! Atunra, attend me."

Kaltag stopped the pine marten as she stepped forward. "Atunra stays here, with me and Pitru. Go! We will defend the fortress against attack whilst you are out playing your games!"

Inwardly the warlord cursed himself for neglecting to think of having the fortress defended in his absence.

Leaping down from the rock, he growled to Scaut, "Weilmark, take fourscore guards and attend Lady Kaltag."

Scaut headed the two long ranks of catguards, but on reaching the pier he found Pitru barring his way with drawn scimitar. "I have no need of you here, Weilmark. Get back to your master. I'm in charge of this fortress!"

Scaut was taken by surprise at Pitru's haughty manner. "You? But your father said nought of this to me!"

Kaltag intervened, her tone cold with authority. "I have appointed my son as commander of this fortress. You will address him by that title from now on. Now leave us!"

Though Riggu Felis did not contest Kaltag's words, he sneeringly called out so that all could hear, "So, the fancy-dressed kitten is becoming a dangerous beast at last!"

Before he turned to march off, the warlord exchanged a secret and meaningful glance with Atunra, his faithful life-long aide. The pine marten blinked briefly in acknowledgement. She understood the unspoken order. To her, there could be only one Lord of Green Isle and Commander of the Fortress—her master, Riggu Felis.

11

In the attic above the Abbey Library, the window shutters had been removed. Sister Snowdrop sat on a heap of books, framed in a shaft of early evening sunlight swirling with red-gold dust motes. Books, scrolls, volumes and ancient archives lay thick about the little old mouse. Her reverie was broken when Tiria came pounding in, followed by her three friends along with Brink and Skipper.

"Sister, what is it? What have you found?"

Enveloped by dust, Snowdrop pulled a kerchief from her sleeve as she attempted to reply. "I fou . . . A fou . . . Aaaaaaa-choo!"

Scrambling up, she raced to the open window, sneezing several more times. Breathing in gulps of fresh air, the Sister glared over her tiny square glasses at them. "Really! Do you have to come stampeding in here and raising all that dust? Most inconsiderate!"

Snowdrop paused to clean her spectacles. "You well may ask what I've found, but I'm not showing it to anybeast in here until I've had my afternoon tea on the west walltop. We'll talk about it there."

Brink scratched his headspikes. "But why would ye be takin' tea up there, Sister?"

Skipper interrupted his friend. "Wait, Sister, I'll tell this ole buffer. That'd be 'cos Friar Bibble ain't servin' on the lawn. Afternoon tea's ended. But if'n ye was to go to the walltop, ye'd find our Abbess there with molemum Burbee. Without lookin' I can tell ye. They'll be sittin' on those liddle foldin' chairs, sharin' a pot o' tea an' a tray o' goodies. Same as they do every mornin', noon, late noon an' evenin', every day. Right, Sister?"

Snowdrop beamed at him. "Right, Skipper Banjon, very observant of you, I must say. You go on now, I'll get my beaker from the library and meet you all up there with my discovery."

Having installed herself on top of the gatehouse steps at the west walltop, Sister Snowdrop took full advantage of the generosity of the Abbess and Burbee. Dunking arrow-root and almond biscuits into a steaming beaker of mint and comfrey tea, she indicated a large, thick, green volume she had brought with her.

"Feast your eyes on this, my friends. What do you think of it?"

Abbess Lycian topped up Snowdrop's beaker from her seemingly ever-full teapot. "Pray, what are we supposed to think of it? The thing looks very much like a dusty old green book to me."

Snowdrop spluttered on a soggy biscuit, as though she could hardly believe what the Abbess had just said. "Can't you see? It's the rare, original Geminya Tome, that's what it is. Dusty old green book, indeed!"

Abbess Lycian was completely unruffled by the revelation. "How nice, but what exactly is a rare original Geminya Tome, if I may make so bold as to ask?"

The little Sister was wide-eyed with disbelief. "Surely you're joking, Mother Abbess! You mean to tell me you've never heard of it?"

Breaking off, Snowdrop stared around at the others. "Have none of you ever heard of the Geminya Tome?"

Molemum Burbee came out with one of her gems of mole

105

logic. "No, we'm bain't, moi dearie, an' oi aspeck we'm never will, unlest you'm tell us'n's. Boi 'okey, scholarybeasts can bee's gurtly aggurvatin', hurr aye!"

Tiria supported the good molemum firmly. "Please, Sister Snowdrop, can you just get on and tell us about your precious Geminya Tome?"

Stroking the volume's faded green cover, the old Assistant Librarian explained. "This is something that has been lost to the sight of Redwallers since Old Quelt was young. He has often told me of it. Sister Geminya was a mouse who lived at our Abbey in the long distant past. She was a highly knowledgeable scholar, specialising in the solving, and setting, of all types of riddles and puzzles. Many considered Geminya to be the cleverest creature in all Mossflower. However, genius has its drawbacks: She was also renowned as an odd, reclusive and quirky beast, very secretive and annoyingly condescending to all. Just examine her name, it was a title she gave to herself. Look at the name of her book, the Geminya Tome! Artful I grant you, but extremely vain!"

Skipper tapped his rudder impatiently. "Ye'll forgive us who ain't scholars, Sister, but wot makes a book called the Geminya Tome so extremely vain?"

Taking a piece of charcoal from her waist pouch, Snowdrop began scribbling on the walltop paving. "Look, I'll show you. Take the letters of her name, Geminya. Switch them about and it becomes Enigma Y."

Brinty looked at the writing. "What's an enigma?"

Abbess Lycian kindly explained to the young mouse, "It's merely an educated name for a riddle or a puzzle."

Snowdrop continued writing. "Exactly. Now take the letter Y. It has the same sound as the word we use when asking a question, 'why.' Then there's the word 'tome,' which means a great weighty volume. But split it in half, and it becomes two smaller words. Do you see?"

Girry piped up. "Of course! 'tome'—'to me.' Haha, clever, eh?"

The Sister had finished writing on the wall paving. "There you have it. Read it out please, Tiria."

The ottermaid read out the curious translation. " 'Enigma to me. Why?' "

Snowdrop drained her beaker and held it out to be refilled. "Exactly! Now we can see the vanity of Sister Geminya. She's telling us that she could solve anything. An enigma to me, huh, why?"

Abbess Lycian smiled. "She was very clever, though."

Sister Snowdrop put aside her beaker. "Old Quelt is taking a nap right now. Just wait until he wakes up and I show him this!"

Tiria was still mystified. "I don't quite understand, Sister. You've found this book and translated its meaning, but how does that help me? Is there anything about Rhulain or the Green Isle in it?"

Snowdrop began leafing through the yellowed pages of the ancient work, muttering to herself, "Actually, I believe there is something. Now, which page was it on? Hmm, I should have inserted a marker."

She stopped at each page she came to, painstakingly inspecting it. "Ah, this is interesting, but that's not it. Hmm, neither is this. I'm sorry, friends, I'll get to it sooner or later. One just can't go riffling slapdash through a work so rare and valuable as this, you know."

The onlookers began snorting and tapping their paws impatiently at the dilatory old Sister. Feeling rather sorry for her, Abbess Lycian ventured a helpful suggestion.

"We realise you're doing your best, Snowdrop, but it's starting to get dusky out here. Perhaps if we go inside, conditions may be more favourable for you to study."

Sister Snowdrop bobbed a small curtsy to the Abbess. With a speed which was surprising for one of her long seasons, she hopped nimbly off down the wallstairs, calling back as she hurried toward the Abbey, "What a splendid idea! They'll be serving supper soon. Would one of you kindly bring the book along?"

107

Skipper picked up the volume, watching the sprightly Snowdrop skipping up the Abbey steps. "Stan' on me rudder, there goes a bossy liddle marm, an' no mistake. I wonder would she like a servant?"

Girry chuckled ruefully. "She's already hired one. Me! But we wouldn't have got this far without her."

Lycian began helping Burbee to clear away the tea things. "That's a kind observation, Girry. We'd all do well to remember it. Come on, young Tribsy, you can carry this teapot."

Supper was held in Great Hall for the main body of Redwallers. After saying grace, Abbess Lycian requested that a separate meal be served in Cavern Hole for the riddle solvers. Though smaller, Cavern Hole was more cosy, with armchairs and cushioned wall ledges. It was also well lit by lanterns, and a fire burned in the hearth. Friar Bibble and his assistants set up a buffet for Tiria and her friends. The meal included a long chestnut and apple plait with a crispy golden crust, bean and scallion soup and summer salad. The dessert was a batch of redcurrant tarts with meadowcream. There was cherry cordial to drink, plus the obligatory pot of tea for Lycian and Burbee.

Old Quelt put in an appearance, happily roused by the discovery of the Geminya Tome. He and Snowdrop took it off to a moss-padded niche. Ignoring the company, they set to work on an eager study of the book.

Not wanting to disturb the avid scholars, Tiria and her father, joined by Brinty, Tribsy, Girry, Lycian, Burbee and Brink, sat in an opposite corner, discussing the ottermaid's forthcoming journey to the as-yet-mysterious Green Isle. Brink was most concerned about a boat for the voyage.

Once again, the helpful Abbess had an idea to propose. "Skipper, you and Brink were close to the watermeadow in Mossflower Wood yesterday. I'm fairly certain that the Guosim shrews meet there for their midsummer festival around this time. Do you think they might be there now?"

Banjon perked up considerably. "Wot would we do without ye, Mother Abbess! Me'n'Brink'll set out for the watermeadow first thing tomorrer. If'n my ole mate Log a Log Urfa is there, he'll soon sort a boat out for that gel o' mine!"

Tribsy took his snout out of a soup bowl long enough to enquire, "Wot bee's a Guosim an' a Log a Log Urfa, zurr?"

The Abbess explained patiently to the young mole. "Guosim are our shrew friends. Each letter of their name stands for what they are: Guerilla Union Of Shrews In Mossflower. Guosim! Their chieftain is called the Log a Log. Skipper, I never knew that Log a Log Urfa was a friend of yours."

Banjon cut himself a slice of the wholesome-looking plait. "Oh aye, marm, that 'e was, though it was afore you was Abbess. We was young buckoes t'gether. I sailed many a stream with Urfa before they chose 'im as a Log a Log."

Tiria helped herself to a tart. "And you think he'll help me to get a boat, Skip?"

Her father winked broadly at her. "Urfa don't forget 'is ole mates. You'll see, gel!"

Burbee poured more tea for herself and Lycian. "Hurr, that bee's if'n Miz Tiria doan't get too h'old to sail ee boat, boi ee gurt toime they'm scholarybeasts taken to solve ee riggle!"

Girry called over to Quelt and Snowdrop, "Well, have you two found anything in that old book yet?"

Without looking up, the old Recorder answered, "Yes, it seems we have, young 'un."

Girry's tail rose stiffly, a sure sign of indignation in squirrelfolk. "Well, thanks a lot for not telling us!"

The Abbess reproved him instantly. "Girry, don't be so rude to your elders! We must make allowances for old scholars. They don't see things as we do."

She turned politely to Old Quelt and his assistant. "Pardon me, but would it be possible to see what you've discovered, please?"

Between them the pair carried the open book over. Sister

Snowdrop tapped the page. "Right here you will see two references concerning the information you seek. However, we have yet to solve them. Girry, perhaps you'd like to read the first clue out."

The young squirrel read aloud from the Geminya Tome.

"Linger sure for the lee,
I set my trick carefully,
my home lies o'er the sea,
you'll find the title names me . . . Is."

The ancient Recorder Librarian peered over his glasses. "Personally, I think Sister Geminya was only doodling, but you'll find that out, if you've wit enough. Well, can any of you bright creatures throw some light on it?"

They stared at the four lines a while, then Brinty spoke. "I think it's telling us to discover a name. Right, sir?"

Old Quelt shrugged. "Don't ask me, my brain is old and slow. Try having confidence in your own judgement."

Girry chimed in. "I think Brinty's right. We're looking for the name of somebeast, agreed?"

Sister Snowdrop adjusted her glasses. "That much is fairly obvious, but where among the lines of the poem do we begin to look?"

Skipper, who was studying the rhyme intently, spoke without taking his eyes from the page. "I think I know, Sister. I've read this thing through six times now. Most of it makes sense, all except one line."

Tiria interrupted her father. "You mean the first line, Skip? 'Linger sure for the lee.' I noticed that, too. Hmm, wonder what it's supposed to mean?"

Brink tried to help with a suggestion. "I know the lee is the sheltered side of anythin'. Is that a clue? Are we lookin' for a shelter?"

Quelt shook his head. "No no, Mr. Greyspoke, you're just confusing the issue. Try using the whole line as a guide."

Tribsy wrinkled his snout comically. "Hurr, you'm means all ee wurds'n'letters of ee line?"

Sister Snowdrop began giving out charcoal sticks and scraps of parchment for everybeast to use. "Precisely! We must treat the entire line as an anagram. You know what that is—a lot of letters which you can jumble up to arrange into a new phrase."

Molemum Burbee sucked her tea noisily. "Hurr, oi never see'd that dun afore, marm. Oi bain't used to riggles'n'puzzlers. They'm makes moi 'ead ache."

Abbess Lycian topped her friend's mug up with fresh tea. "There now, don't you fret about it, Burbee. Girry, maybe you and I could work at it together."

They paired off into twos. Only Quelt sat alone, watching them like a master observing his pupils.

Tiria and Brinty were first to come up with something. The ottermaid cried eagerly, "Listen to this: 'Eels rue fling her tore'!"

Brink scratched his headspikes. "Wot does that mean?"

Tiria shrugged. "I don't know. Sounds silly, doesn't it? Have you two got anything yet?"

Skipper Banjon, who was Brink's partner, read out their effort. " 'Forges the line ruler,' or 'Rules the line forger.' Huh, I think we left a letter *E* out. It's hard alright!"

Old Quelt polished his glasses nonchalantly. "Dearie me, you aren't even close. Would you like me to tell you the answer?"

Girry called out abruptly, "No, we wouldn't!"

Quelt answered with a touch of irony in his tone. "Please yourself, young 'un. I suppose you've solved it, eh?"

Abbess Lycian's eyes twinkled. "Yes we have, actually. It says 'The Ruler of Green Isle.' Then there's the last word of the rhyme, it says 'is.' I'd forgotten about that, but now it makes sense."

Girry was elated. "Abbess Lycian and I solved it, by arranging all the letters of the line in a circle and staring hard at them. It suddenly just popped out at us. The Ruler of Green Isle . . . Is!"

Brinty looked expectantly at his young squirrel friend. "Is who?"

Sister Snowdrop pointed to the Tome. "We don't know yet, apart from the fact that it's somebeast who lives over the sea. Now listen carefully while I read you the second part of the puzzle."

The little Sister recited the odd words slowly.

"Three aitches, two ee's, two *I*'s, two *N*'s,
Wherever there's *Q*, there's a *U*, or two.
One *G*, one *L*, one *A*, one *R*,
So I leave the answer to you."

Molemum Burbee covered her ears with both paws. "Ho gurt seasons! 'Tis enuff to droive a pore beast to discratchun!"

Lycian and Girry were already forming up the letters into a circle. The Abbess whispered to Girry, "She means distraction. Right, let's see what we've got!"

Girry rubbed his paws together, chuckling happily. "Really enjoy doing these puzzles, Mother Abbess!"

Brink Greyspoke wiped charcoal dust from his paws in disgust. "Well, I'm glad ye do, Girry mate, 'tis all a duck's dinner to me. I'm only good at bein' a Cellar'og!"

Girry addressed Quelt in a bantering manner. "You're the scholar here, sir. I don't suppose you've got the solution yet?"

The Recorder Librarian eyed him severely. "No, I haven't, and I don't suppose you've got it in so short a time, young fellow!"

Girry stood up and began pacing the room. Clasping his paws behind him, he did a little hopskip, twirling his bushy tail.

Tiria stared at him incredulously. "Girry, you haven't solved it, have you?"

Girry nodded, smirking like a Dibbun who had evaded a bath. "Got it as soon as I set eyes on it. Straight off!"

Molemum Burbee shook a huge digging claw at him. "Then take ee smugg lukk off'n ee face an' tell uz!"

The young squirrel was enjoying his moment. Performing another hopskip, he stuck his nose in the air. "Shan't!"

Sister Snowdrop pleaded, "Oh please, tell us. I'll have Friar Bibble cook something special just for you!"

Girry grinned sweetly at her. "No, shan't!"

Skipper rose menacingly from his seat. "Tell us right now, ye young rip, or I'll kick yore fluffy tail down the stairs!"

Abbess Lycian cried out severely, "No you will not, sir!" She cast an icy glance at Girry before continuing. "I will, and I'll box his ears into the bargain. Come here, you annoying rascal!"

She made an undignified charge at Girry, who fled shouting, "Yaaaah! 'High Queen Rhulain,' that's the answer!"

Lycian strolled back to her seat, smiling calmly. "So then, there we have it, straight from the mouth of my obedient assistant."

She held out her paw to Girry, who had regained his composure sufficiently to announce, "The Ruler of Green Isle is High Queen Rhulain!"

He bowed elegantly but could not resist one last hopskip as he bounded to the Recorder Librarian's side. "Hoho, this is the stuff! Come on, Quelt sir, and you, too, Sister. Where's the next puzzle, eh? Just show it to us and we'll crack it like Friar Bibble cracking a hazelnut with a bung mallet. Won't we, mates?"

There was ready agreement from the rest until Sister Snowdrop put a damper on their enthusiasm. "I'm afraid we haven't found anything else yet. You'll just have to wait."

Girry's tail stood up like a flagpole. "You don't mean to tell us that's all, do you?"

Old Quelt closed the book, patting its cover. "Not at all, young sir. There's probably lots more about Miss Tiria's dream and the journey she'll be making."

Tiria could not conceal her disappointment. "Well, why can't you find it for us now?"

Removing his glasses and dabbing at his eyes with a kerchief, the ancient squirrel explained. "I'm certain there has to be more, because Sister Geminya has given us a keystone clue, the High Queen Rhulain. I can follow her reasoning, though she could be an exceedingly aggravating creature. But when she has a tale to relate, or a mystery to set out, this is the roundabout way she has of writing it down. Sister Snowdrop and I must study the Tome carefully. Just one oversight, and we lose it all. It is not the work of a moment, you must understand. Our research will be long and arduous, but we'll get there. Now, my friends, I am very old and very tired. It will have to wait until tomorrow morning. I bid you good night!"

Sister Snowdrop arose, rubbing her back as she joined him. "Please don't judge us harshly, friends. Sleep can be a bother and a waste of time to the young, but as the seasons pile heavily upon one it becomes a blessing and a comfort. I, too, will see you all in the morning. Good night!"

The pair shuffled off, carrying the big book between them.

After the door of Cavern Hole had closed behind them, Abbess Lycian threw up her paws in frustration. "Oh bother! Just when we were getting somewhere. I'm not a bit tired yet. Oh well, what must be must be. Is there any tea left in the pot, Burbee?"

"Burr, nary ee drop!" Burbee said, as she held the teapot spout down to demonstrate. "Oi bain't one fur fancy likkle teapotters, oi'll go an' make summ in our own gurt big 'un."

Lycian picked up their large earthenware mugs. "Good idea. I'll get our folding chairs and meet you up on the wall-top. There's a full moon out, and it's a pleasant summer night. I like it up there, don't you?"

The molemum was feeling tired herself, but she agreed. "Yuss, marm, oi'll see ee up thurr!"

12

It was a beautiful night outside, still warm from the long, hot summer day. Like a ball of newly churned butter surrounded by stars, the moon reigned over a dark, cloudless sky. Groffgut and his gang lay in the ditch opposite the Abbey's west wall. They had been passing the time there since midnoon, napping and eating food they had gathered along the way. The water rats had been content during daylight hours, but they were distinctly uneasy now that night had spread its canopy over all. They were awed at the sight of Redwall and none too anxious to pay it a visit or meet its inhabitants. However, it was fairly obvious that their leader was planning something by the way he sat apart from them in the dry ditchbed, focussing his attention on the monumental building which loomed over them.

Pointing his rusty makeshift sword at the west walltop, Groffgut tried to whip up the gang's enthusiasm. "Willyer lookit dat place, mates? Just sittin' there, all fulla good stuff fer us!"

Threetooth provided the only response, which was not overly encouraging. "Dey got a h'eagle in dere, an' anudder big burd, too. I saw dem!"

Groffgut contradicted him, lying blatantly. "O no, yer

never! Didden't I show youse de h'eagle flyin' away, jus' afore it went dark?"

Threetooth knew what he had seen, and he said so. "Dat burd was too 'igh up inna sky. 'Twasn't no h'eagle, neither, it was a seagill."

Groffgut threw himself on Threetooth and gnawed on his ear. "Are yew callin' me a liar, eh? I said it was a h'eagle!"

Threetooth was sorry he had spoken. "Owowow! Awright awright, it was a h'eagle. Wowoow! Stop eatin' me lug'ole, Chief, it was a h'eagle!"

Groffgut kicked him to one side. He curled his lip in scorn at the other vermin. "Yer know the trouble wid youse? Ye've all gone soft on me! Yer frykinned of yer own shadders. Right, y'see dis sword?"

He brandished the rusty scythe blade under their noses. "Well, I'll be usin' it ter slay anyrat wot's not wid me. 'Cos if'n yer not wid me, yer agin me, see! Now, up wid yer paws all dose who's wid the chief o' dis gang!"

Knowing Groffgut's dangerous temper, the gang had no option but to raise their paws. Groffgut made a point of counting and naming them to reassure himself.

"Dat's Frogeye, Plugtail, Rashback, Obbler an' Fleddy. Oi, Threetooth, is yore paw up or down?"

Threetooth, who had been nursing his chewed ear with both paws, sullenly raised one. "S'up, Chief."

The gangleader nodded. "Dat's good, 'cos I'm gunna need yew.'"

Frogeye knew that he was waiting for somebeast to ask, so he obliged. "Are yer gunna tell us de plan, Chief?"

Groffgut dropped his tone dramatically. "Der's seven of us, right? Lissen, we sneaks up to dat wall, an' four of us, me'n Frogeye'n'Rashback, an' Plugtail, lets Obbler an' Fleddy climb up an' stand on our shoulders. Next, the climber gets up onto Obbler'n'Fleddy's 'eads. It's easy den. All the climber does is slings my sword up onna rope an' catch der top o' that wall, pull hisself over an' open dat big door to lerrus all in. Good plan, eh mates?"

Threetooth began protesting as he backed off down the ditch. "Y'mean I've gorra be de climber? I'm no good at climberin', I swear I ain't, Chief!"

Groffgut shoved Rashback and Frogeye forward. "Grab 'im!" They seized the unfortunate Threetooth firmly.

Groffgut spat on his rusty blade, eyeing his victim. "I told yer, if'n ye ain't for me, yer agin me. So, where d'ye want it, eh? In the gut, across yer throat or in yer lousy 'eart, 'old 'im tight, mates!"

Threetooth babbled like a brook in flood. "I don't wanna get kil't, I'll climb, don't slay me, Chief! I'll climb der wall for ye!"

Groffgut thrust his face close to Threetooth. "Ho yer'll climb right enuff, or I'll skin yer alive afore I kills yer. Plug, where's dat rope we tied de h'eagle up wid? Knot it round me sword 'andle, will ye."

All the gang members were young rats, Obbler and Fleddy the two youngest. The latter was becoming quite taken with the idea of burgling Redwall Abbey, but he had a question to ask of his leader first.

"Ye said der was all sortsa good stuff in dat place, Chief. Wot sorta good stuff?"

Groffgut saw this as an opportunity to fire his gang to great efforts. Unfortunately, he was not good at speech making. "Er, lotsa good stuff! Everythink's in der, mates."

Young Fleddy pressed him further. "Y'mean good stuff like nice vikkles, Chief?"

The gang leader nodded sagely. "Aye, more'n yew could eat, loads more!"

Obbler picked his teeth with a grimy claw. "Huh, I 'ope der's more'n Fleddy kin eat, 'cos I wanna fill me belly, too. I likes h'apple pie, 'cos I 'ad a bit once, an' it tasted nice!"

Groffgut clapped him heartily on the back. "Don't fret yer 'ead, mate. They got enuff h'apple pies fer all of us!"

A moment later, Groffgut was sorry that he had spoken.

It seemed that the rest of the gang were fond of pies, though each had his own individual favourite.

"An' strawb'rry pies, too, Chief?"

"My ole granny used ter bake tater pies, wid onions in 'em. D'yer think dey'll 'ave tater pies like me ole granny's?"

"Blackberry pies is bestest, big fat juicy ones!"

"Worrabout plum pies, bet they're juicier, eh, Chief?"

"Roobab pies is good, wid lotsa 'oney on, though. D'yer think dey puts 'oney on their roobab pies in der, Chief?"

Groffgut kicked the last speaker soundly, having heard enough about their favourite pies. "Will youse all shurrup? Yis yis, dey've got loadsa diff'rent pies in der. Now let's gerron wid it, eh!"

Creeping out of the ditch, the gang made it across the path, into the shadow of the wall. Groffgut and the three he had nominated flattened themselves against the wall.

Their leader whispered urgently to Fleddy and Obbler, "Cummon youse two, up yer get. Stand tight, mates!"

It was not as easy as it had sounded. There were muttered complaints as soon as the two younger rats began clambering over the four who formed the bottom line.

"Nyyurk! Don't stand on me nose like dat, clumsypaws!"

"Oooh, yew stuck yore footpaw in me eye, gerroff!"

"Stop ticklin' an' git yer tail outta me ear, willyer!"

Groffgut gasped as his stomach was kicked hard. "I'll tickle yer ears wid me sword if'n yer don't shut yer big noisy gobs. Threetooth, it's yore turn. Gerron top of their 'eads afore yer sling der rope!"

Unknown to the gang, they had been observed as soon as they left the ditch. Abbess Lycian had spotted them as she stood up to pour tea for herself and Burbee. She quickly informed Oreal Gatekeeper, who shot off to the Abbey and brought Skipper, Brink, Foremole Grudd and his entire crew up to the west wall.

They took a secret peep at the rat gang and held a whispered conference. Skipper's initial idea was to exit the

Abbey by the south wickergate, surround the rats and finish them off. The Abbess was horrified by the plan.

"But Skipper Banjon, they're the same age as your own daughter. How could you kill such young creatures?"

"Vermin, Mother Abbess, they're vermin!" Brink reminded her. "If you don't kill vermin they'll kill you, or some other innocent creatures who can't defend themselves. Skipper's right, marm, they're young alright, young an' evil!"

Abbess Lycian stole a hasty glance at the rats on the path below. She turned away quickly, biting on her habit sleeve to stifle the laughter which was threatening to burst forth. "You should take a look down there. They've all collapsed in a heap. One of them is kicking the others' tails. Good gracious, what language! Can you hear it?"

Foremole Grudd shook his velvety head in disgust as he peered down at the rat gang. "They'm a-tryin' t'stand h'on each uther's thick 'eads agin, so's they'm can cloimb up yurr. Boi okey, oi never see'd such bunglybeasts in all moi borned seasons!"

Skipper set his jaw grimly. "Vermin are vermin, no matter which way ye look at 'em!"

However, the Abbess was not one to back down on her principles. "Be that as it may, Skipper Banjon, I will not have them slain. They're nought but a few scruffy young water rats. I don't consider them to be a threat to our Abbey, or a danger to us, in their present position. As Mother Abbess of Redwall, I forbid the slaughter of those vermin!"

The Abbess blenched with fright as Skipper grabbed her roughly and pulled her to one side. It was a swift and timely act. The curved scythe blade, with its attached rope, came looping over the walltop. It would have struck Lycian had it not been for Banjon's intervention. The rope was jerked tight from below, leaving the blade lodged firmly around the angle of a battlement.

Skipper kept his voice calm and level. "Well, marm, what do we do now?"

Loud, hoarse whispers could be heard from the rat gang as they urged their comrade on.

"Gudd t'row mate, up yer go!"

"Aye, get dat big gate h'opened, let's see wot dey got in der!"

"Yeeheehee! An if'n der cook don't cook gudd pies, we'll roast 'im in 'is own h'oven!"

It was the first time any Redwaller had ever seen their Abbess bare her teeth and growl fiercely. "Kindly leave this to me, please!"

As Threetooth's villainous head appeared over the walltop, Lycian was waiting for him. She dealt him a mighty blow with the teapot, which was still half full of hot tea. It made a peculiar sound. *Punngggg!* The water rat fell backward with a shocked gurgle, plummeting down onto the rats below.

Flinging the teapot at them, Lycian yelled out in a most un-Abbesslike manner, "Give 'em blood'n'vinegar! Redwaaaaaallllll!"

Skipper chortled, but the smile was quickly wiped from his face as Lycian turned to confront him. "Roast the cook in his own oven, eh? Skipper Banjon, my order against killing still stands. But you have my permission to take a party down there, armed with heavy sticks. Give those vermin the beating of their lives and send them packing!"

By this time, everybeast was leaning over the walltop to view the effect of their Abbess upon the would-be raiders.

Molemum Burbee shook her head gravely. "Ee woan't catcher yon vurmints naow, Skip, they'm taken h'off loik arrers. Burr, an' moi gurt teapot with 'em!"

Banjon watched the rat gang scurrying off up the ditchbed until they were swallowed up in the darkness. "Good grief, marm, you certainly fixed 'em up right'n'proper. Those vermin are drenched with 'ot tea an' spittin' tea leaves. Hah, I fear that's the last ye've seen o' that best teapot. I could swear it was stuck on one rat's 'ead!"

Now that the excitement was over, Lycian collapsed into

her little folding chair and gulped down what tea was left in her mug. She seemed totally overcome. "Oh dear, I can't believe I did that! Look, Burbee, my paws are all a-tremble, I'm shaking like a leaf!"

The molemum had almost a full mug of tea, which she kindly donated to her friend. "Ho, you'm a gurt terror, marm, an' no mistake. But oi wish't you'm hadden't given ee best teapot to yon villyuns. Hurr, 'twas far too noice furr ee loikes o' they'm!"

Grudd Foremole tugged his snout politely. "Off to ee beds naow, marms. Brink'n'Skipper, too, off ee go, zurrs. Me'n moi crew'll stan' guard up yurr 'til ee mornen loight. Us'll give 'em owd 'arry if'n ee ratters cooms back yurr agin furr more!"

Panicked, dispirited and chastened, the rat gang did not stop running until they were well into Mossflower Woodlands. Slumped on a streambank, they panted for breath, nursing hot water scalds and spitting tea leaves.

Rashback moaned as he slopped cooling mud on his afflicted back. "Aaaaargh, wot was dat dey t'rowed over us?"

Fleddy had missed most of it. He licked a paw where a bit of the liquid had splattered. "Dunno worrit was, but it don't tastes bad t'me."

Obbler sniffed at his companion's paws. "Smells nice, too, not like dat swamp we felled in. Hawhawhaw! Lookit ole Plug, 'e's wearin' a new 'elmet!"

Plugtail, who had been lagging behind, tottered in to join the gang. The teapot was jammed on his head at a rakish angle, the spout covering one ear and the handle sticking out above the other. The rim covered his right eye, so he could only see with the left. Showing not a vestige of sympathy for his plight, the gang laughed at his woeful pleadings as he staggered about.

"Will youse stop laughin' an' get dis t'ing off me 'ead?"

Bonggg! Plugtail walked sideways into a tree trunk and tripped over Groffgut's paws. The gang leader, who was sitting with his back to the trunk, dealt him a hefty kick, snarling, "Gerritoff yerself, thick'ead! Can't yer see I'm wounded?"

Frogeye, probing at a loose tooth he had suffered in the melee, stared over at Groffgut. "Where are yer wounded, Chief?"

Groffgut returned his stare sourly. "None of yer bizness, squinty lamp!"

Still seated with his back to the tree, the gang leader muttered savagely, "By the 'ellgates an' bluddtubs, I'll make dose Wallred crowd sorry dey ever messed wid me, jus' yew wait'n'see!"

Threetooth, who had now lost every tooth he possessed, winced as he felt the enormous lump between his ears. "It wuz a mistake tryna take a place dat size. I ain't goin' back der no more!"

Groffgut sprang up, waving the rusty scythe blade. He chased Threetooth along the streambank. "Yew'll go where I tell yer to, or I'll flay yer mangy 'ide. Get back 'ere right now!"

Hoots and guffaws greeted the rearview of Groffgut as he ran after Threetooth.

"Hawhawhaw! Lookit, 'e ain't got no tail!"

"Haharrharr! Wot 'appened t'yer ole wagger, Chief? Did yer leave it be'ind?"

"Thunderin' tripes! I bet dat 'urted, 'e's got even lesser'n ole Plugtail now!"

Groffgut left off chasing Threetooth. Standing with his back to some bushes, he glared hot anger at the scoffers. "One more snigger, go on, jus' one more laugh from any of yer. Anybeast who t'inks it's funny, say so, right now, go on!"

The gang fell silent and went back to tending their own hurts. When the teapot landed on Plugtail's head, he had dashed about madly, trying to get it off. The rope and scythe blade that followed it got tangled about one of his footpaws. Unfortunately, Groffgut got in the way, and the swinging blade slammed into his backside, severing his tail right at the root. The humiliation of a gang leader losing his tail far outdid any pain he felt from the wound. Groffgut knew he had to restore his position with the others. He put on his darkest, most vengeful scowl, grinding out every word savagely.

"I lost me tail in battle, der ain't no shame in dat, see! But I swear a blood oath afore ye right now, afore dis season's out, I'll be wearin' a cloak made outta the tails o' them as did this t'me. Aye, an' a necklace of their eyeballs!"

None of the gang dared to say a word. They knew he was in deadly earnest.

Unaware of the drama that had taken place on the walls, Tiria slept soundly, transported to the realm of dreams. She was in a room, a huge rock chamber. Cool breezes soothed her brow, yet she could feel radiating warmth upon her back. She felt no curiosity as to her surroundings, nor any compulsion to turn and look at the room. It was the view of the nighttime sea that fascinated her. She was standing at a broad, unshuttered window, staring fixedly at a spot on the moonlit waters, somewhere twixt tideline and horizon. Tiria knew that she was in a high place, far above shore level. Without looking, she knew that Martin the Warrior was standing beside her. His strong voice echoed through her mind.

"Maid of the Wildlough, hearken to what the High Queen Rhulain will say to you. Remember her words, for your very life will depend on it."

He pointed with his sword to the place in the sea where Tiria was still watching. A shape began to emerge from the moon-burnished waves. Tiria instinctively knew it was the otter lady of her previous dream. The apparition was cloaked and hooded, the face within the hood appearing as a dark void, but the voice was unmistakable—melodious yet commanding.

"Bide ye not on Mossflower shore, hasten to Green Isle.
Thy presence there is needed sore, in coming time
　　of trial.
Leave thy Redwall friends to read that tale of
　　ancient life,
when Corriam the castaway took Mossguard maid
　　as wife.
Their secrets follow in thy wake, lost symbols will
　　be found
to aid both Queen and Clanbeast regain their
　　rightful ground.
Trust in the fool of the sea, to the Lord of the rock
　　pay heed,
but remember a hawkstar must fly,
on the day thy domain is freed."

The vision faded like smoke, being drawn down into the sea. Far out between shore and horizon, Tiria saw what looked like the tip of the hood the otterlady had worn, sticking up out of the waters. The young ottermaid was overcome by a sense of loss; then the entire scene vanished into the bottomless well of slumber.

Dawn's first rosy rays aroused the birds to song all over Mossflower Woodlands as Tiria wakened. She remembered every detail of the dream distinctly—Martin, the rock fortress, the Rhulain and her message. The ottermaid dressed swiftly. Now she knew exactly what she had to do.

BOOK TWO

The Fool of the Sea

13

Riggu Felis, an able general and a cunning tactician, deserved the title of warlord. He sent six scouts out, ahead of his main body of catguards, to comb the woodlands and hills for traces of his enemy. It was midnoon when they picked up the trail, pursuing it to the bank of a wide stream. Being cats, and not overly fond of water, they waited by the shallows for the wildcat and his command to catch up with them.

In the bushes on the opposite bank, the otters lay hidden, watching the catguards. Big Kolun Galedeep and Banya Streamdog crouched alongside the outlaw Leatho Shellhound. After grasping the oar, which was now his favourite weapon, Kolun nudged his friend.

"You were right, mate. They've arrived, though there ain't many of 'em. Wot d'ye think their next move'll be?"

Leatho never took his eyes off the scouts. "Let's wait an' see, Kolun. I wager Felis'll be along with the rest soon enough. I want to count how many he has with him."

Banya volunteered her services. "I'll do that, Shellhound, but wot d'ye want 'em counted for?"

The outlaw explained his strategy. He was the wildcat's equal when it came to planning ahead. "I know that Felis has two hundred or more catguards in his army. If they're

129

all with him, then we'll make this place our battlefield. We could chop 'em to ribbons afore they cross the water. Now durin' the fight, I've got a job for you, Kolun. When I gives the word, take yore clan an' all the Streambattle clan out of here in secret. I'll hold the cats off with what I've got left. You circle round the back, get clear away, then march for the fortress. The slaves'll be unguarded if Felis has all his guards with him. You can hit the place hard an' free all our friends."

Big Kolun grinned. "Good idea, matey, but wot if'n Felis don't have a full force along with him?"

Leatho nodded. "I've thought o' that. If Banya counts less than the full number, then we'll decoy 'em. We'll pull out an' make a lot o' noise, so they can follow us easily. I know a good hill, it's inland, an' any beast on the high slope can give a good account of themselves there. . . . Stow it, mates, here comes Felis an' the rest!"

The catguards gathered in four ranks on the opposite bank; their warlord stood to one side, sheltered by a large willow tree. Weilmark Scaut took the tracker's report before joining his master.

"Lord, the tracks ended at this stream. The otters 'ave a far greater force than ours."

A satisfied hiss came from behind the chain mail mask. "Good, just as I had hoped, Scaut. Send six of your guards to cross the stream. Take a score of archers back into the brush. I know they're waiting for us on the other side of this water, I can feel it. Listen now, they'll send lances and slingstones at the six in the stream. Check what direction the weapons come from and send your arrows over that way. Then we'll see what happens."

The six guards were not too happy to enter the stream, but they had their orders. Immediately as they entered the shallows, a fusillade of slingstones and light javelins dropped four of them.

Big Kolun brandished his oar. "Well, 'ow many of the scum did ye count, Banya?"

130

The tough Galedeep maid flung off a slingstone. "About fivescore, give or take a few. . . . Look out!"

A volley of arrows hummed viciously down among the otters. Leatho saw two clanbeasts fall, and another injured. "Kolun, give the order to fall back, but keep slingin'. Don't retreat too far, then cut off into the trees to yore left. Make sure they know we're runnin' away."

A scorecat named Fleng hurried to Riggu Felis and Scaut beneath the willow. "Lord, the otters are beaten, they're abandonin' their position!"

Abandoning the cover of the willow, the warlord watched intently as the undergrowth and bushes swayed. He heard the shouts of the fleeing otters. "They're travelling inland. What do you make of that, Scaut?"

The weilmark's voice was heavy with scorn. "We've got 'em beaten, Lord. Otters can't stand up to yer catguards. Look, they're well on the run!"

Chain mail chinked as the wildcat shook his head. "It's just as well that I'm in command and not you!"

Ignoring Scaut, he turned to Scorecat Fleng and issued his commands. "Take your squad and pursue them from this side until you can find somewhere easy to cross the stream. Keep after them, and make as much noise as you can to let the otters know they're being pursued. Go now, we'll follow up before dark."

Fleng saluted smartly with his spear. A moment later, he and his twenty guards were dashing along the bankside, shouting aloud.

Riggu Felis shouldered his war axe. "Get the rest of our force and follow me, Scaut." He strode off in the opposite direction, to the right.

Issuing orders to his scorecats, the weilmark got everybeast under way. He trotted forward to the warlord's side, obviously bewildered. "Lord, twenty guards aren't enough to defeat all those otters. Aren't we going to follow an' defeat 'em, like you said you would?"

Riggu Felis moved his axe haft sharply, catching Scaut's bandaged jaw. He gave the puzzled feral cat a contemptuous glance. "Listen, and see if this sinks into your thick head. I will defeat the otters in my own way. I know twenty guards won't defeat them—they'll probably all be slain. But I will have won a great victory over the otters. Do you know why, Scaut?"

Keeping his distance from the axe haft, the weilmark stroked his injured jaw ruefully. "No. Why, Lord?"

The wildcat gave a hissing laugh. "Why, indeed! Pay attention, my idiot friend, and I'll tell you. Those otters have families, the same as any otherbeast. They want to keep their loved ones safe, so they try to fool me by drawing us off inland. I don't know of any otters who live at the centre of Green Isle. They make their homes and dens in rivers and along the coast."

Scaut temporarily forgot his aching jaw. A slow smile spread over his brutal features. "So we're goin' to the coast to attack their families, Lord?"

Riggu Felis let his tongue slither out to lick at the gold metal chain mail that masked his lower face. "Aye, Scaut. Imagine how the one called Shellhound and his followers will feel. Picture them coming back, crowing about how they slew a score of my guards, then finding their own families—who I'm sure number a great deal more than twenty creatures—lying dead amid the scorched ruins of their homes. Who will have won the victory then, eh?"

The feral cat officer gazed at his leader in awe. "Truly you are the Warlord of Green Isle, Sire!"

The cruel eyes of Riggu Felis narrowed to slits. "Anybeast who does not agree with that is a deadbeast, Scaut. That is why I left my faithful Atunra back at the fortress today. She will make certain that no upstart brother-killer will ever usurp his father."

Pitru was still young, but he was a quick learner. Revelling in his position as the fortress commander, he went about his devious plans gleefully. His first task was to seek out minions who would serve him well and obey orders without question. These came in the form of three feral cats: Yund, an old and experienced scorecat; and two of his guards, Balur and his sister Hinso, who were not much older than Pitru. Lady Kaltag largely kept to her tower chambers, allowing her remaining son the run of the fortress, which he took full advantage of. Atunra was not taken into the new commander's confidence. Pitru and the pine marten had disliked each other for a long time. Pitru knew that Atunra lived only to serve his father.

In the late afternoon, Pitru sat out on the pier with Yund and the other two cats. They basked in the sunlight, nibbling at cooked lake trout and sipping wine. Yund, an intelligent scorecat, knew how to please his young new master. Pitru was delighted with the latest plan they had hatched up together. It concerned the defence of the fortress. They had emptied the catguard barracks and had housed the guards inside the fortress. Half of them were on day duty, some standing by the windows and some up on the sentry posts, armed with bows and arrows. The half who were off duty idled their time away, eating, drinking and sleeping indoors. Each night the rota was changed, and they took the place of their comrades on guard duty. But the master stroke against otter attacks, which Pitru and Yund had devised, was the slaves themselves. They were also taken out of the compound, into the fortress, but only the parents. The young ones and elders were forced to camp in the shade of the fortress, all the way around the building. They would be first to receive the brunt of any assault on the place.

Yund glanced over the shoulder of the slave who was serving the wine. He alerted Pitru. "Look, Lord! Atunra is coming out of the main gate."

Pitru winked at the scorecat and settled back with his eyes closed. He waited until the pine marten was close before addressing her. "Still skulking about, eh? What do you want now?"

133

Atunra knew it was wise to keep a civil tongue in her head. "Your father would not approve . . ."

Before she could finish, Pitru sprang up, whipping out the large, broad-bladed scimitar which he now carried at all times. "Silence! You will begin again by addressing me as Commander. That is my title until I become Warlord."

After a moment's silence, Atunra bowed stiffly. "Commander, your father would never permit all the guards to be inside the fortress, and all those slaves, too. Lord Felis would never allow it. Guards have always lived in the barracks, and otterslaves in their compound. It is your father's law."

The young cat placed his swordtip against the pine marten's shoulder, pressing forward and then pushing her backward as he sneered in her face. "What some old, half-faced cat chooses to do is none of my concern. I make the rules now as commander of this fortress. Now get out of my sight, you spying lickpaw!"

Atunra did not stop to argue. She turned on her paw and strode silently back indoors. Pitru put up his blade and swaggered back to his seat.

Yund raised his goblet in salute. "That's the way to deal with your father's spy, Sire, though I'd watch my back while that 'un's around if I were you."

Pitru spread his paws appealingly. "Perhaps if I had three good friends, then they would watch my back for me. And who knows, mayhaps those three friends would know how to deal with a spy in our midst?"

The scorecat replied, with a look of enquiring innocence, "Indeed, Commander, and mayhaps such friends would be well rewarded when your time comes to rule as warlord?"

Pitru closed his eyes and stretched out luxuriously. "A new warlord of Green Isle would need a fortress commander and two trusty weilmarks to serve him. He would remember his loyal friends."

Yund looked at Balur and Hinso. Both nodded wordlessly. Laying his spear at Pitru's footpaws, Yund bowed deeply. "We live only to obey your commands, Sire!"

Fleng and his squad had kept up their noisy pursuit of the otters from the far streambank. As darkness fell, they found a narrow rocky outcrop and forded the stream. The otters' trail was not difficult to pick up. Leatho had halted the clans on a stony hilltop he had chosen to await the arrival of the cats.

Fleng arrived shortly at the base of the hill. He hid his guards in the bushes, ordering them to fire a volley of arrows. The heavy barrage of rocks, javelins and slingstones that came back at them left Fleng's squad pinned down so hard that they could not raise a paw to retaliate. The scorecat kept glancing back over his shoulder, waiting for his warlord to arrive with reinforcements. Leatho's forces continued to batter the bushes relentlessly. It took Fleng only a short time to realise that half his squad lay slain around him. If he stayed, he would be killed along with the remainder of his guards. For some reason unknown to the scorecat, both he and his squad had been left abandoned. Signalling a retreat to his catguards, Fleng crawled backward from the bushes and fled.

Big Kolun Galedeep, standing out in full view, lifted a boulder above his head and hurled it downhill at the enemy position. He complained to the outlaw, "Ain't much goin' on down there, Leatho. Those cats don't seem to be puttin' up a decent fight at all. Wot d'ye suppose is goin' on?"

Leatho slung a stone and peered downhill. "I'm not sure, mate. Either we lost 'em along the way or some are still tryin' to cross the stream. Maybe we should take the fight to them an' see wot happens."

That was all Big Kolun needed. Seizing his oar, he thundered off downhill, roaring, "Galedeeps to me! Yayla-hooooo! Chaaaaaaarge!"

Leatho could not halt Kolun and his clan, but he called

out to the rest, "Watch yoreselves, it might be a trap. Follow me!"

Leatho and Banya arrived on the scene together, only to find it devoid of foebeasts apart from ten slain guards. Kolun and his clan looked thoroughly disgruntled.

The big otter hailed the outlaw. "Huh, just as well ye didn't charge with me, Shellhound. There wasn't any fightin' t'do, they've gone!"

Leatho rolled up his sling. "There's somethin' wrong, Kolun. It was all too easy. Wot do you think, Banya?"

The tough ottermaid was a short distance away, supporting the head of a badly injured catguard until it drooped limply back and she let it go.

"I got to that 'un just afore his lights went out. He managed to say that there wasn't more'n a score of catguards. Said they was ordered to follow us an' t'make the most noise they could, so that we'd think it was a full troop."

Leatho interrupted her. "But where'd Felis an' the rest of 'em get to?"

Banya touched the dead guard with her footpaw. "He said they stayed back at the streambank where we first met up with the cats. I was goin' to question him a bit more, but he just drifted off."

Kolun gritted his teeth. "Huh, lyin' cowards, they won't admit we beat 'em fair'n'square. That's cats for ye!"

Banya did not agree with him. "No, he spoke the truth. Look around, there was never over a hundred catguards here. Wot d'you think, Shellhound?"

But Leatho was already on the move as the chilling realisation dawned on him. His voice was tight and urgent. "Kolun, get the clans on the move. Quick, at the double!"

The big otter saw the alarm in his friend's eyes. "Why, mate, wot's goin' on?"

Leatho was running as he shouted out his explanation. "Felis outsmarted us. He's gone the other way, t'the coast where the families are hidin'!"

The outlaw was out ahead of everybeast, speeding like an

arrow. Kolun and his brother Lorgo, together with Banya, headed the main band as they sped through the night. The big otter's chest was heaving.

"That scummy cat, goin' after our families like that!"

Banya steadied him as he stumbled against a tree. "Aye, 'tis just the sort of thing Felis'd do. Save yore breath, an' let's hope we can stop 'im, mate!"

Word had passed through the clans of what might happen. The packed mass of otters increased their speed. Regardless of rock, bush or shrub, they stampeded madly toward the coast.

14

It was shortly after sunrise at the Abbey. Sister Snowdrop watched Friar Bibble filling a tray with breakfast foods for herself and Old Quelt. "A touch more honey on the Recorder's oatmeal, if you please, Friar. He likes a lot of honey—oh, and some of those whortleberries, too, thank you."

Bibble obliged her. "There y'are, Sister. Oh, did ye hear? Tiria's gone. An' that Pandion bird, thanks be to goodness!"

The aged Sister looked over her glasses. "Gone, Friar? Where to, what do you mean?"

Bibble filled two beakers with coltsfoot and dandelion cordial. "Indeed to goodness, I thought you knew. She's off on that journey of hers. I filled haversacks for them—her da, Brink and Tiria. They left before sunup."

Snowdrop appeared bemused by the news. "But she can't do that! We haven't gathered all the information she needs yet."

Friar Bibble wiped his paws and took a parchment from his apron pocket. "Well, I don't know about that, Sister, but gone she has. Said I was to give this to you."

The little Sister tucked the parchment into her habit sleeve. "Thank you, Friar. Oh, when you see Brinty, Tribsy and Girry, will you please send them straight up to the library?"

Bibble watched her skittering off with the laden tray. "Indeed to goodness, I'm more of a messenger than a cook this morning. Now then, baby Groop, what can I do for you?"

The molebabe held her dish out solemnly. "No messinjers furr oi, jus' vikkles, zurr. Lots of 'em!"

Sister Snowdrop and Old Quelt shared the Recorder's desk as they pored over Tiria's letter. They looked up as the library door slammed open. Girry and Brinty dashed in, followed at a more sedate pace by Tribsy.

The young mole was balancing a tray loaded high with food. "Hurr, Miz Tirry bein' goned bain't a-stoppen this choild gettin' ee vikkles. G'mawnin', zurr'n'marm!"

Brantalis appeared in the doorway and honked. "I am thinking Tiria is gone from here!"

Quelt peered at him over the rim of his oatmeal bowl. "Yes, she has. Why are you looking so pleased?"

The barnacle goose did a waddling turn and started off downstairs, calling back to the Recorder, "I will look as pleased as I please, old one. No more hook-beaked fish eater to bother me. He went, too. I am thinking I will ask the Bibbler for two breakfasts now."

Snowdrop went back to studying the parchment, murmuring, "I'm sure that will please the Friar no end."

Brinty helped himself to a baked apple from Tribsy's tray. "Huh, scooting off like that without so much as a thank-you or farewell. The Friar said Tiria left a letter. Is that it? Can I have a look, please?"

Old Quelt straightened the creases from the parchment. "No, you can't! Your paws are all full of cooked apple."

Girry stood on tip-paw, trying to see the letter. "My paws are clean."

The ancient squirrel's eyes twinkled behind his glasses. "Good, well, let's see if you can't keep them that way, young sir. I'll read the letter out to you. Listen."

He held the missive at paw's length, commenting before

he read it, "Dearie me, spelling is not that ottermaid's strong point, though she does write with a neat paw. Er, right.

"Dear friends,
Sorry I couldn't stop to say good-bye. I had a dream last nite, and the High Rhulain said I must go to Green Isle rite away. I hope you find lots of things in the Geminya Tome book. Here are some words from my dreem which may help you: 'Bide ye not on Mossflower shore, hasten to Green Isle. Thy presence there is needed sore, in coming time of trial. Leave thy Redwall friends to read that tale of ancient life, when Corriam the castaway took Mossguard maid as wife. Their secrets follow in thy wake, lost symbols will be found.'
"There's lots more, but my father and Brink are wateing, so I've got to go now. Pandion's with me, too. I'm sure he'll be a great help to me. I'll miss you all very much, and Redwall, too. Thank you for your kind aid and frendship. I hope we'll meet again someday.
"Tiria"

Tribsy dropped his tray and broke out sobbing. "Boo-hurrrrrr! Us'll never see Tirry no more, she'm goned. Boohurhurhurrr! Oi wurr gurtly fond of 'er, she'm wurr allus koind an' noice, an' she'm wurr moi friend. Boohurrr!"

Girry and Brinty were affected by their molefriend's tears. They, too, turned aside and wept quietly. Old Quelt reached out a bony paw to lift up Sister Snowdrop's chin. She was sniffling also, a tear rolling from beneath her small, square glasses.

"Such a pleasant young ottermaid. Oh dear, I hadn't re-alised how fond of Tiria I'd become!"

Old Quelt shook his head in gentle reproof. "My my, just look at you all, blubbering away like Dibbuns at bathtime. Well, what's it to be, eh? Are you going to waste time cry-ing the day away, or are you going to do something to help your friend by solving the clues which she left for us?"

There followed much wiping of paws and habit sleeves across eyes. Tribsy sat down by his fallen tray and sighed deeply. "Oi'll be with ee direckly, zurr, soon as oi've 'ad moi brekkist!"

A moment later, they were all hard at work.

Tiria bounded along through Mossflower's summer woodlands as though there were springs on her paws. Her regrets at leaving her home and friends soon vanished with the excitement of embarking on the quest. Pandion circled overhead, whilst Skipper and Brink trudged along behind, burdened by two large haversacks of supplies.

Though she had pleaded with them to let her help with the packs, her father and the good Cellarhog would not hear of it.

"Nay, missy, we'll 'elp ye for as longs as needs be!"

"Aye, me gel, ye might have to carry both of 'em alone afore yore journey's done. Don't get too far ahead of us now. Take a right turn at the bend o' the next stream and stay away from the water's edge. 'Tis deep an' swampy there."

As she forged ahead, Banjon called after her, "Oh, an' tell yore fish 'awk to walk from here. We don't want no great bird frightenin' the Guosim shrews."

Tiria guessed that they were not far from the watermeadow from the sounds of revelry which began echoing through the normally silent woodlands. It was a blend of singing, shouting and merriment.

Pandion did not seem to like it. Spreading his wings, he addressed Tiria. "Kraaaaah! They will frighten off the fish with that din. I will hunt among the streams. When I have eaten, I will come and find you."

He winged off, and the ottermaid waited for her father and Brink to catch up. As they pressed forward through the trees, Brink chuckled at the growing sounds of raucous singing.

"Those Guosim certainly know how to enjoy theirselves, Skip."

Banjon agreed. "Aye, that they do, mate, especially at their summer watermeadow festival."

There was a swift rustle of undergrowth, and a gruff voice called out, "Halt right there!"

Tiria was surprised by her first meeting with the Guosim. The travelers were suddenly surrounded by twelve or more shrews, tough-looking little beasts with spiky fur. Each one wore a coloured headband, a short kilt with a broad-buckled belt and a ferocious scowl. They were all armed with short rapiers.

A youngish shrew flourished his blade aggressively at them. "Stand still, or ye'll be deadbeasts!"

Skipper murmured to Brink and his daughter, "Don't say anythin', leave this t'me."

Banjon looked the young shrew up and down fearlessly. "Well, Dobra Westbrook, ye've sprouted up a touch since I last clapped eyes on ye. Where's yore dad? Still swiggin' grog an' wrestlin' with the best of 'em, is he?"

Dobra stared hard at Skipper for a moment. Then he put up his blade and hugged him fondly. "Nuncle Banjon, ye ole gullywhumper! Where've ye been all these seasons? What brings ye t'the watermeadow?"

Skipper pulled himself loose and held Dobra at paw's length. "I've come t'see yore dad. I thought you was him at first. By the rudder, ye look just like him!"

Tiria cast a sidelong glance at her father. "Nuncle?"

Skipper explained, "Dobra's always called me that, since I made him his first liddle sling. That was about four seasons afore you were born."

The watermeadow was practically a carpet of gypsywort, sundew, water plantain, bulrush, reed and wide-padded water lilies. The three visitors were escorted to a logboat which transported them out to a big island at the centre of the meadow. Dobra leaped ashore as the prow nosed into land. The place seemed to be packed with Guosim shrews—families picnicking, maids dancing, elders arguing, groups singing and various contests of skill taking place. They followed Dobra through the carnival atmosphere to the middle of the island, where it seemed the main event was being held. A number of veteran Guosim warriors were seated in the treeshade, eating and drinking as they watched a slinging competition.

Dobra called out to a sturdy, tough-faced shrew, "Ahoy, Dad! Lookit wot the frogs just dragged in!"

Log a Log Urfa, Chieftain of the Western Guosim tribe, stood up. He swaggered over, growling savagely, "Haharr, 'tis a mad ole plank-tailed waterwalloper who thinks he kin wrestle. Let's see wot ye can do, cully!"

They leapt upon each other, crashing to the ground and setting the dust flying as they grappled and grunted like madbeasts. Tiria became alarmed. Just as she was reaching for her sling, they both sprang up and began hugging and laughing.

"Urfa Westbrook, ye great grog tub, how are ye, buckoe?"

"Banjon Wildlough, me ole matey, if'n I feel half as good as yore lookin', then I'm fine!"

Introductions were made all around. The guests were seated and given tankards of Guosim Grog, accompanied by huge thick wedges of pie, which turned out to be leek and turnip with savoury herbs.

Skipper started right in telling Urfa about Tiria and her need for a boat, but the Guosim chieftain touched a paw to his lips. He pointed to the slinging competition.

"Hush now, matey, I'll talk to ye in a moment. The Dipper's about to throw. I don't want to miss this!"

Brink whispered, "Which one's the Dipper?"

Urfa pointed out a tall, sinewy shrew who was stepping up to the mark and selecting stones from his pouch. "That 'un there, Brink. Ole Dipper's got an eye like a huntin' eagle. Ain't nobeast in all the land kin sling a stone like the Dipper can! You just watch an' see."

Banjon sized the shrew up keenly. "Yore Dipper must be a good 'un if ye say so, mate. Wot's the target he's slingin' for?"

Urfa nodded to a figure suspended from a beech limb some distance off. It was a crude likeness of a weasel, with torso and limbs made from stuffed sacking. The head was carved from a turnip, with two hazelnuts for eyes.

Dobra explained the rules as Dipper began twirling his sling experimentally. "If ye hit the body, that's two points. The paws are five points apiece, an' the head scores a full ten. Each slinger gets three throws. There's a rare barrel o' best grog as a prize for the winner. But afore ye sling, y'must nominate wot ye plan on hittin'."

Tiria made a polite enquiry. "What do the eyes score?"

Urfa shook his head, chuckling. "Nobeast ever nominated an eye an' hit it, missy. Quiet now—the Dipper's goin' to sling."

The tall, lean shrew twirled his loaded sling, calling out, "One head an' two footpaws!"

A gasp of admiration arose from the spectators. Evidently it was something of a feat which the slinger had chosen. Dipper hurled off his first stone. It grazed the turnip on the left side of the face. There was a deathly silence as he loaded his sling again and tested the breeze with a licked paw. Dipper slung his second stone. It hit the right footpaw fair and square, causing the leg to flop about. The hush was intense now, as other Guosim crowded in to watch. Dipper loaded his final stone, crouching low as he whirled the sling. It thrummed in the hot noontide air, snapping back as he whipped off the missile. It barely skimmed the underside of the left paw, hardly causing the leg to stir.

A small fat shrew, acting as scorer, scurried out to inspect the target. After studying it a while, he called out officiously, "Theree 'its, thee Dippah scoharrs terwenty points!"

The Guosim cheered Dipper to the echo, clapping his back and shaking his paws as they roared, "Dipper's scored a score!"

Urfa turned proudly to his guests. "Wot did I tell ye? The Dipper's a champeen slinger alright!"

Banjon nodded. "Oh, he ain't a bad 'un, mate. Did I tell ye my gel Tiria slings stones? D'ye think she could have a go?"

Urfa had a slightly condescending note to his tone. "A maid wot thinks she can sling, eh? Wot next! Aye, go on then, Tiria, give it a try."

The scorer took Tiria's name, announcing her as she stepped up to the mark. "Siiiilenza perleeeeze! H'a Misser, Tehiria, Werhildlock h'of Rehedwall H'abbey issa serlingin' nehext. Thank yew!"

There was a light smatter of applause, plus a few sniggers from the onlookers. Evidently they did not rate slingmaids very highly.

Tiria waited for quiet, then called out her targets. Her sling, Wuppit, was already thrumming as she shouted, "Two eyes and a head!"

Splakk! The left hazelnut eye was driven deep into the turnip head. Reloading the sling swiftly, she whipped off her second shot. *Crack!* Pieces of shattered nutshell flew in the air as the stone drove through into the other turnip eye socket. The head was swinging from side to side with the impact as Tiria hopped three paces back from the mark. The sling was a blur, making a deep musical hum, owing to the extra large stone she had picked for her final shot. *Whooosh! Whack!* The force with which the stone struck the head sent it flying from the body into the bushes beyond.

The whole of the Guosim tribe went wild, cheering, yelling and rushing to congratulate the ottermaid. Tiria was completely overwhelmed by the crush of shrews and had to be rescued by Skipper, Brink, Urfa and Dobra, who escorted her out of the melee, off to a quiet spot on the tree-shaded bank. Log a Log Urfa detailed a group of his Guosim warriors to disperse the excited crowd of shrews.

Skipper winked at Urfa. "So then, matey, wot d'ye reckon to my Tiria, eh?"

The shrew chieftain wiggled his snout energetically (always a sign of admiration and wonderment among Guosim). "I tell ye, Banjon, if'n I didn't see it with me own eyes, I never would've credited it. Yore Tiria made it look so easy, mate. I'd give me tail'n'ears to have a slinger like that in my tribe!"

Skipper threw a protective paw about his daughter. "Hah, there's no chance of ye gettin' my gel. She's got a long journey t'make. That's why we came to see ye, mate. She needs a boat."

Log a Log Urfa refilled their tankards. "A boat, ye say? Wot sort o' boat, Tiria? An' where d'ye plan on goin' in it?"

The ottermaid replied politely, "Any sort of boat, sir. The Guosim ones look fine to me. But you know a lot more about boats than I do, so I'll leave the choice to you, if I may. I've got to sail to a place called Green Isle, somewhere across the Western Sea."

Urfa did a choking splutter, spraying grog widespread. "Wot? You three are plannin' on crossin' the Western Sea? That ain't no sea, it's a wallopin' great ocean!"

Tiria patted Urfa's back until he finished spluttering. "My father and Brink won't be going, sir, just myself and Pandion."

Urfa wiped his mouth on a spotted kerchief. "An' who, pray, is this Pandion, an' where's he at?"

Tiria caught sight of the osprey circling the watermeadow. She pointed. "That's him up there, he's an osprey."

Placing both paws in her mouth, she gave a piercing whistle. Pandion zoomed down like a slingstone.

Guosim shrews scattered everywhere, shouting in alarm. Urfa flung himself into a nearby bush. "Git that thing out o' here afore it slays us all!"

Pandion Piketalon landed, kicking up clouds of dust as he flapped his powerful wings. He stared about with fierce golden eyes. "Where did the little spikies go?"

Tiria wagged a reproving paw at him. "You frightened them all away, you great show-off! I think you'd best go off

146

fishing again. I'll whistle when we need you, but be careful how you make your entrance next time."

Pandion launched himself into flight once more. "Pandion likes fishing. Lots of big fat ones around here!"

Only when he had gone did Urfa scramble out of the bush. "Me'n' my crew'll take ye down the river Moss t'the sea, miss, but that great bird ain't sailin' on my boat. He can fly!"

Dusting himself down, the Guosim chieftain tried to look bold and unconcerned as he called to his tribe. "Come on out. The bird won't harm ye, I had a word with it."

He murmured to Skipper out of the side of his mouth, "Got to show 'em who's the Log a Log round here, don't I?"

Urfa resumed his seat. "Now then, Miss Tiria, there's a matter of a barrel o' grog ye won for yore slingin'. D'ye want to take it with ye?"

The ottermaid tapped her rudder thoughtfully. "Is it good grog?"

Urfa seemed taken aback that anybeast should ask. "Good grog? It's the finest ten-season mature brew. I'd give me tail'n'whiskers for a flagon of that nectar!"

Tiria smiled. "I'm not really a grog drinker. Perhaps you'd like to accept it as a gift from me, sir."

Urfa shook her paw gratefully. "Thank ye kindly. I'd be a fool to refuse it. But let me put ye straight about sailin' craft, miss. All we have are logboats, carved from the trunks o' trees. 'Twould be madness to try an' cross that Western Sea in one. Ye'd be drowned!"

Urfa saw the look of disappointment on her face. "Now don't ye go frettin', beauty. I've got an idea. For a long sea voyage ye'll need a proper ship, an' I know the very creature who has one. At dawn tomorrer I'll take ye down the ole River Moss to the Western Sea an' introduce ye to him. All he'll need by way o' payment is vittles aplenty. I'll supply them meself."

Skipper patted Urfa's back heartily. "I knew ye wouldn't let us down. Yore a real mate!"

147

The Guosim chieftain waved his paw airily. "I'd be a mizzruble beast if'n I couldn't do a favour for me ole friend Banjon."

Brink helped himself to another wedge of pie. "Wot's yore friend's name?"

Log a Log replied straight-faced, "Cuthbert Frunk W. Bloodpaw, Terror of the High Seas!"

15

Dawn brought pale-washed skies, drizzle and a layer of mist over windless land and sea. The cavern beneath the ledges was thick with acrid smoke. Leatho Shellhound skidded in, striving with rudder and paw to hold his balance on the glistening floor.

Big Kolun Galedeep held tight to the rocky walls, the smoke stinging his eyes as he coughed and yelled out to Banya Streamdog, "Git some torches lit an' fetch 'em in here, will ye!"

Both he and the outlaw sea otter hung on, gagging and spluttering until a half-dozen torches were brought.

Kolun rubbed his streaming eyes, staring about him in the flickering light and deep shadow. "Wot'n the name o' fur'n'rudders has been goin' on here?"

Banya held her torch high as she held on to a ledge. "The place is empty. There ain't nobeast anywhere!"

Leatho slid across to the hanging curtain of vegetation which screened the cave from the sea. From there he pondered the scene before him. "Seaweed an' damp wood have been piled on the big cookin' fire to make all this smoke. I can't say wot this slippery mess all over the floor is."

Lorgo Galedeep dipped a paw in the slime, sniffing at it several times before hazarding a guess. "Smells like Gullyplug Punch an' seafood stew, an' leftovers mixed with veg-gible oil. But where's our families? D'ye think Felis an' the cats took 'em all prisoner?"

Big Kolun dispelled the idea with a snort. "No, never! My missus an' the others wouldn't have been taken without a fight. Look around, mate. D'ye see any slain or wounded beasts from either side layin' about? There's not even a trace o' blood, the place is empty. Ahoy there, Shellhound, where are ye off to?"

Leatho had parted the trailing curtain and plunged into the mist-shrouded sea. He surfaced a short distance from the cave. "Yore right, mate. They weren't ambushed, even though I noticed lots o' cat signs outside by the land en-trance. There's a good chance yore families escaped. We'd best start a search for them. You Streamdivers an' Wave-dogs, come with me. Kolun, take the rest an' follow along the coast. See if'n ye can pick up any trails."

The clans of the Streamdivers and Wavedogs formed a spread-out phalanx behind the outlaw. They swam smoothly along the quiet coastal waters, watching for any signs of life. There was no letup in the dull early morn. Mist and drizzle persisted, limiting both sound and vision in the calm, waveless sea. Worries, doubts and fears for their fam-ilies plagued the clanbeasts' minds. Was Leatho right in his supposition, had their loved ones avoided the murderous wildcat? Leatho pressed on into the enveloping mist, lis-tening keenly for the slightest hopeful sound.

The tall, ragged rocks of a headland loomed up out of the gloom. The clanbeasts swam in Leatho's wake as he changed course seaward. There was a space of open water between the cape and a massive dark rock that stood apart from it.

Raising his voice, the outlaw yelled an otterclan cry: "Yaylaaahoooooooo!"

An echo bounced back from the rock. A moment's silence followed, broken only by the lap of water against stone.

Then a booming call rang out. "Hawoooooooom!"

Leaving his comrades behind, Leatho cut the water speedily. He headed for the rock and a hulking figure perched upon it. Once he could make out the nature of the creature, he returned its greeting. "Yaylaaahooo! Gawra Hom! Hawooooom!"

The grey bull seal, Gawra Hom, threw back his head and reared up. "Hawoooom! Glokglokglok!"

Just then, Kolun's boat emerged from around the side of the rock. It was packed with little ones, all showing off what they had learned as they pulled the oars lustily.

Deedero, Kolun's missus, was at the tiller. She waved to the grey seal. "Many thanks to ye, Gawra Hom!"

She turned to the outlaw, paws akimbo. "Well, Mister Shellhound, you took yore time gettin' here! There's pore weary families sittin' in the rain on the other side o' this rock. D'ye reckon y'might rescue 'em some time this season, or is that too much to ask, eh?"

Relief flooded through Leatho as he threw the sturdy ottermum a mock salute with his rudder. "Right ye are, marm. We'll get 'em off there, marm!"

He gave another salute to Gawra Hom. "If'n I can ever help ye, mate, just give me a call. Yore a goodbeast, Gawra Hom."

The big grey bull waved a flipper. "Hoooom wharraa-woooooh!"

As the mist began thinning, Deedero spied Big Kolun and the clanbeast swimming out from the shore to the rock. She glared at him, calling to him dryly, "Ahoy there, ye great sloprudder! Are you goin' to play about there all day, an' leave yore family marooned? Or are ye thinkin' about res-cuin' 'em?"

Cheerfully, the big Galedeep otter waved a meaty paw. "Ho, but it does me 'eart good t'see yore charmin' face, me liddle thistleblossom. Rest yore dainty paws, we'll soon have ye home'n'dry!"

It took some considerable time to get the families safe ashore. The elders and the very young were exhausted from their nighttime flight through the dark sea and the time they had spent clinging to the rock.

When the task was accomplished, Banya Streamdog asked the question that was uppermost in everybeast's mind. "We can't go back t'the caves or the tall stones anymore. So where do we hide all these families?"

Leatho was at a loss, but Ould Zillo the Bard had an answer. "Sure, an' why not take 'em all to Holt Summerdell?"

Everybeast knew the name, Holt Summerdell, through an old song that was sung around the fires at night.

Deedero looked askance at the bard. "There ain't no such place. Holt Summerdell's only a nice song. It ain't real, is it?"

Zillo tapped his nose knowingly. "Ah, but that's where yore wrong, marm. I knows it's a real place. My grandpa showed it t'me when I was only a liddle snip. But I remember exactly where it is. Y'see, Holt Summerdell was a holiday home of the clans afore the cats came to Green Isle. Aye, an' a grand ould time they used to have there all summer long. But 'tis long forgotten now—except in the song. There's only meself knows where 'tis, an' I'm the bucko that can take ye there. It lies inland, beyond Deeplough in the highlands, a fair stretch o' the paws. Though if'n we set out now, I could have ye there soon after dusk. Well, Shellhound, what d'ye think?"

Leatho picked up one of Kolun's brood, a tiny ottermaid. He set her on his shoulders. "Don't seem we've got much choice. Lead on, matey!"

They struck off inland, with the rain still drizzling, though the mist was breaking up into patches over the valleys and woodlands. Zillo kept their spirits up by tapping

152

out the pace on his rudderdrum and singing the song about Holt Summerdell.

"All the long-ago seasons we loved high up there,
in those warm afternoons an' the sweet evenin' air,
alas though they're past I remember it well,
that dear little spot we called Holt Summerdell.
When ye'd rise in the mornin' the air was like wine,
through the curtain came stealin' the golden sunshine,
with the twayblade the clubrush the burr an' the sedge,
round the clear crystal waters that flow o'er the edge.
Ye could ride on the slide there or sport in the pool,
where trout roamed the deep reeds so green an' so cool,
on some flat mossy rock ye could lie there an' bask, as
the ould ones would say, now wot more could ye ask?
But the times are all fled like a mayfly's short day,
though sometimes within me a small voice will say
go follow yore dream to the place ye loved well,
that dear little spot we call Holt Summerdell."'

The otterbabe riding on Leatho's shoulders whispered in his ear, "Uz gunner go ta H'old Suddermell? Soun's ferry nice!"

The outlaw tickled the little one's footpaw. "Aye, darlin', I'm sure Mister Zillo will take us there."

The old bard chuckled. "Sure I'll take ye there, right enough. Wait'll ye see it! Then ye'll wonder how anybeast doubted me."

The outlaw nodded. "I don't doubt ye, Zillo. Tell me, though, how did ye manage to escape from the cave without Felis harmin' or capturin' anybeast?"

Ould Zillo shrugged. " 'Twas all Deedero's doin'. Ye recall how ye left me'n'her in charge afore ye went off? Huh, I didn't have much say in the runnin' o' things at all. That big ottermum just took over. Aye, an' 'tis just as well she did, mate. Let nobeast ever tell me that Deedero Galedeep ain't got a head on her shoulders!"

Kolun tapped Zillo on the shoulder from behind. "Go on, tell us how my missus did it."

The bard had to smile as he recalled the deeds of Deedero. "Sure, 'twas worth writin' a ballad about. First thing she did was to get yore boat pulled up alongside the cave. Then she fed all the little 'uns an' bedded 'em down in it so they were out o' harm's way. Then she split us into two groups. I was in charge of the gang who went out collectin' seaweed an' water-logged driftwood. We had to stack it all by the main cookin' fire. Next thing she had us doin' was pourin' all o' Birl Gully's punch into the seafood stew, that an' a jar o' veggible oil an' any other leftovers we could find. I tell ye, Kolun, that missus o' yores should've been a warlord!"

Leatho pressed the bard. "Go on, wot did she do then?"

Zillo took up the tale again. "Lissen t'this. Deedero takes her gang out by the land entrance o' the cave. They strip all the branches from two blackthorns, the ones with the big sharp spikes. So she lays 'em out, where any foebeast would tread on 'em in the dark. Then she posts some o' the wives close t'the cave an' tells 'em to report to her any sudden yowls or miaows."

Leatho interrupted. "But supposin' it would've been us comin' back to the cave ahead of Felis. What then?"

Birl Gully roared out laughing. "Harrharrharr! That would've been yore bad luck, mate. But as it 'appens, things turned out right. 'Twas the wildcat an' his guards who came chargin' along that way. Harrharrharr!"

Zillo continued. "Must've been close to midnight when our sentries 'eard the yowls an' catcalls. They hurried back, an' Deedero sent everybeast off into the sea, pushin' the boat away up the coast. The little 'uns thought it was no end o' fun. Now there was only me'n'Deedero left there. She orders me to heap the seaweed an' dampwood on the fire. Right away there's smoke billowin' everywhere. I saw Deedero take a long pole an' push the big cauldron over, topplin' it all over the floor. It smelled pretty strong, I can

154

tell ye. Well, that was it. Me'n'Deedero got out o' there an' went swimmin' after the others . . . leavin' Riggu Felis an' his catguards t'clean up after us, o' course!"

Leatho thumped his rudder down in admiration. "Blood'n'thunder, I think we'll have to call yore missus General Deedero from now on, Kolun!"

The big otter tucked his oar under one arm, puffing out his chest proudly. "Aye, an' to think she chose me as her husband. Yowch!"

Deedero had caught up with them and stepped on Kolun's rudder. "Quick march there, dumblepaws, step out lively. An' you two, Zillo an' Shellhound, stop skylarkin' about an' move yourselves. If'n we don't get these little 'uns someplace safe by dark, with good hot vittles in 'em an' a pillow to lay down their heads on, it ain't no wildcat ye'll have to worry about. It'll be me. Understood?"

They stepped out smartly, saluting all the way.

"Aye, marm, very good marm!"

"We're kickin' up a bit o' dust now, marm!"

"Now don't ye fret, me liddle apple dumplin', everythin's goin' right to plan. Ouch! Will ye stop stampin' on me rudder like that, er, my sweet honeybee."

Riggu Felis would have stamped his paw with rage had it not been for the broken blackthorn spike embedded in it. He roared up at the first guard he saw passing a window inside the fortress.

"Open the main gate! Get Atunra and Pitru down here! What in the name of slaughter'n'fangs is going on here? Why are all these otterslaves camped outside in the open? Get that gate open on the double, or I'll rip ye in half with my own two paws!"

Weilmark Scaut assisted the limping warlord up onto the pier. There was a wild scurry of paws from inside. Then the main gates creaked open.

The wildcat howled at the clutter of catguards milling about within, "You, you, you and you! Get those otterslaves locked back in their compound right now. You, scorecat, attend me!"

The feral cat in question marched up and came to rigid attention. "Lord!"

Hot, angry eyes glared through the chain mail at her. "What do they call you?"

She gulped. "Scorecat Rinat, Sire."

Her face was sprayed with spittle as Felis thrust aside his face mask and yelled at her, "Get these guards back inside their barracks immediately! Where is my counsellor, Atunra? Where's that useless son of mine? Why isn't he here to meet me, eh?"

Rinat's voice trembled nervously as she replied, "The Fortress Commander is with Lady Kaltag in her chamber, Sire."

The wildcat shoved her roughly aside. Limping toward the stairs, he struck out at catguards with his axe handle. "Out! Out all of ye, back to your barracks!"

Balur and his sister Hinso were on guard outside of the chamber. Acting on Pitru's orders, they challenged Riggu Felis. "Halt there, we must announce you!"

Grabbing both guards, the enraged warlord hurled them headfirst down the stairs. With his axe, he dealt the door a blow that left it toppled on one hinge. Scorecat Yund was inside the chamber with Kaltag and Pitru, who signalled him with a sideways glance. He turned, holding his spear horizontally at chest height, barring the wildcat's path. Without breaking his limping stride, the warlord wrenched the weapon from Yund's grasp and smashed it in two halves on his head. Lifting the scorecat bodily, Riggu flung him down the stairs also. Now, with no guards left to block him, Riggu confronted his son. His breath from behind the chain mail mask hissed viciously.

Pitru had never seen his father so wrathful. He moved swiftly behind his mother's chair, crying out, "Stop him, he means to kill me, just like he slew Jeefra!"

The Lady Kaltag faced Riggu fearlessly, her voice calm

156

and slightly ironical. "I stood at my window and watched your arrival. There was no sign of captive otters, bound tightly, being dragged back here for punishment. What happened to your footpaw? Were you wounded doing battle with the foe?"

Riggu Felis stumped over to a table and perched upon its edge. He took a knife from a plate of half-eaten fish and began probing at his footpaw with it. "This is nothing, a broken thorn. Where is Atunra? I need to consult with her."

Kaltag ignored the question, wrinkling her nose in distaste as she sniffed the air. "What is that horrible smell you bring into my chamber?"

The warlord continued digging at his footpaw, sweeping aside his cloak, which was getting in the way. "Where, what foolishness is this, what smell?"

Pitru pointed at his father. "It's all over the back of his cloak. Some kind of slop, that's causing the smell!"

Kaltag's smile was humourless and icy. "Did those who wounded you also do that—plaster you with filth?"

Riggu Felis grunted as he pulled out the broken blackthorn spike. "A thorn, that's all it was, a thorn I stepped on!" Skirting the question of his cloak, he pursued his former enquiry. "Where is Atunra? Send her to me now."

Kaltag shrugged carelessly. "She is of no consequence to me. I have not seen her since you marched away from here to destroy your enemies."

The wildcat's blazing eyes sought out his son. "What have you done with Atunra, you little worm?"

Pitru could not meet his father's gaze, but he was regaining his confidence. He stared at his mother, addressing her in wide-eyed innocence. "Tell him I know nought of his pine marten lackey. As Fortress Commander, I was far too busy organising the defences against the enemies he was supposed to have defeated. I am not Atunra's nursemaid. Why should I watch over her?"

There was a clatter of dishes as Riggu drove the knifepoint deep into the tabletop. "You stupid young brat! Is that

157

what you call organising defences—allowing half the otter-slaves to wander about outside the walls and letting a load of guards idle their time away indoors, eating and sleeping? Hah, Commander! All you'll ever be is a silk-clad kitten, cringing behind your mother's skirts!"

Kaltag's voice dripped scorn as she came to Pitru's defence. "Well, I hope he never becomes a warlord like you, skulking back here with a wounded paw and a stinking cloak! Where are all the prisoners you vowed to bring back? Scorecat Yund noticed you returned twenty-one guards short. What happened to them, O Mighty One, eh? At least we weren't attacked, thanks to Pitru's defence plans!"

Her words stung the wildcat worse than blackthorn spikes. He knew he had lost the argument and was not prepared to bandy further. However, he was determined to have the final word as he swept out of the chamber.

"I've ordered the guards back to their barracks and the slaves back to their compound. It is my command that they stay there. I will seek out Atunra now. If any harm has befallen her by either of your doings, then you will see just how merciless a warlord can be!"

Riggu Felis found Weilmark Scaut awaiting him alone on the pier. He barraged him with orders. "Search my fortress from top to bottom, and all the surrounding area. Use all your guards to do it. Find Atunra and bring her to me, dead or alive. I'll be in my chambers. As of tomorrow, we will no longer seek out the otters."

Scaut looked puzzled. "Lord?"

The wildcat ripped off his muddied cloak and threw it into the lake, watching the water carry it under. "Why chase about after a bunch of outlaws? I'll make them come here to me. Don't look so blank, Scaut. I have what they want—this fortress and a whole lot of otterslaves. Mark my words, they'll come. Fortunately for me, otters are noble creatures. They won't leave their own kind in slavery. They'll make an attempt to liberate them."

16

Happy sounds of Dibbuns laughing and playing drifted up through the open library window at Redwall Abbey. Old Quelt, Snowdrop and the three young puzzle solvers sat around the long, polished table. The Sister had one paw on Tiria's farewell letter and the other on the Geminya Tome.

"I think the answers lie somewhere twixt these two. First we need to study the clues Tiria left for us. Then we can look up any references to them in the Tome."

Girry stifled a yawn. "Is it nearly lunchtime yet?"

Old Quelt looked over his glasses at the young squirrel. "Bored with study already, are we, young sir?"

Girry flicked a paper pellet he had made through the window. "Huh, there's no sense in saying that I'm not, sir."

The Librarian Recorder turned his attention to Tribsy and Brinty. "Has your interest become dulled also, friends?"

The young mole yawned. "Hoo urrh! Oi'm a-doin' moi bestest, zurr, but 'tis 'ard wurk, a-studyen' gurt ole books."

From where he was slumped in his chair, Brinty nodded to the open window. "There's a lovely sunny day going to waste while we're stuck in this gloomy library. 'Tisn't fair!"

Sister Snowdrop sniffed meaningly. "That's because you lack a true scholar's dedication."

Girry slouched over to the window, scowling rebelliously.

159

"That's alright for you to say, Sister. You've been studying since long before we were born, but we're still young. We want to be outdoors in the summer days, like all the others. Hah, I'll bet Tiria's having a great time right now, travelling on a long journey and having all sorts of adventures probably. Somebeasts have all the good fortune!"

Brinty pouted. "Aye, and here's us, swotting away and getting old'n'dusty. What did her letter say—'Leave thy Redwall friends to read that tale of ancient life'? Ancient life! Huh, that's what we'll become sitting round here!"

Snowdrop looked to the letter. "That's exactly what it says: 'Leave thy Redwall friends to read that tale of ancient life, when Corriam the castaway took Mossguard maid as wife.' "

Tribsy sighed. "You'm read that twoice afore, marm. But et bain't gotten us'n's much furtherer."

Snowdrop tapped the letter decisively. "But these lines mean something important, I'm sure!"

Old Quelt made a suggestion. "Snowdrop, why don't you and I ponder on this awhile? Meanwhile, our young friends can pop down to the kitchens and ask Friar Bibble to pack a picnic lunch for five. Then we can all meet up at the Abbey pond to do our work. Perhaps the open air will do us good."

Cheered up by the idea, the three young ones were already making for the door. Brinty called out happily, "That's the stuff, Mister Quelt. We'll ponder by the pond!"

The ancient Recorder thought for a moment, then chuckled. "How very droll, ponder by the pond. I like that!"

Many other Redwallers had the same plan. Taking lunch by the pond was quite popular on warm summer days. They spread out around the bank, ever watchful of the Dibbuns, who were drawn like magnets to water. The little ones frolicked gleefully in the shallows.

Hillyah Gatekeeper and her husband, Oreal, were constantly calling out warnings to their twin babes.

"Irgle, come back here. Don't go too far out, d'you hear me?"

"Stop splashing that water about, Ralg, you'll soak us all!"

Quelt opened the hamper that the three young ones had brought. "Oh, I say, Bibble's done us proud! Damson pie, hazelnut crumble, sage and turnip pasties, celery cheese and dandelion cordial. Hmm, I would have enjoyed a cup of tea, though. Cordial always makes me dozy at lunchtime."

Molemum Burbee came promptly to Quelt's rescue. "Yurr ole zurr, 'ave summ tea out of our new h'urn!"

The Abbess and Burbee had replaced their lost teapot with an ingenious new invention. It was a small copper boiler, which Brother Perant had donated to their cause. Lycian and Burbee had cleaned it up and mounted it on a little trolley. The urn had a small charcoal heater in its base, enabling them to have a constant supply of hot tea wherever they went, always on tap.

The five puzzlers had plenty of help from the pondside diners. Interest was aroused as they gathered around to hear Girry read again the two relevant lines from Tiria's letter.

" 'Leave thy Redwall friends to read that tale of ancient life, when Corriam the castaway took Mossguard maid as wife.' "

Brinty opened up the discussion to their audience. "Well, does anybeast understand that?"

Sister Doral put forward a timid enquiry. "Er, excuse me, but who is Corriam the castaway?"

Tribsy replied through a mouthful of pastie. "Us'n's doan't be knowen, marm. That's whoi we'm arskin'."

Snowdrop leafed slowly through the Geminya Tome. "Let's see if there's any reference to it in here, shall we?"

As they waited on Snowdrop's study, Hillyah Gatekeeper began rocking back and forth, eyes shut and paws clenched.

Oreal, her husband, looked quite concerned for her. "What is it, dear, are you feeling ill?"

Hillyah opened her eyes. "No, it's just something that flashed through my mind a moment ago. Ralg, I'll not tell you again, stop splashing that water about! Oh dear, I've gone and lost it again, just when it was right on the tip of my tongue. Most annoying!"

Abbess Lycian poured tea for the harvest mouse mother. "What was it, Hillyah? Were you trying to recall something?"

Hillyah wiped little Irgle's snout distractedly with her apron hem. "Oh, pay no attention to me, Abbess. It probably wasn't important anyhow."

Brinty shouted excitedly as he watched Snowdrop turning the pages of the Tome. "There it is, there it is! No, not there, turn back a few pages, Sister. Stop there! Middle of the page. Do you see? There's that name, Corriam!"

Finding the line, the little Sister read aloud. " 'Corriam's lance, a gift from Skipper Falloon of the Mossguard. See T.O.A.L. Chap two, F.W.' "

Old Quelt polished his glasses hastily. "Let me see that, please. What else does it say, Sister?"

Snowdrop showed him the page. "Nothing else. This was only a note jotted in the margin. All the rest is about the great sword of Martin the Warrior, stuff that we already know, not relevant to our puzzle."

Girry munched on a slice of hazelnut crumble. "What's a Chap two supposed to mean, I wonder?"

Quelt answered promptly. "It's merely short for chapter two. Most scholars know that. T.O.A.L. and F.W.—they're the letters that are baffling me."

Hillyah startled them all with a whoop. "I've got it! T.O.A.L., Tales of Ancient Life! That's what I was trying to remember. I've seen it somewhere before, I know I have. It's a book!"

Oreal smiled helpfully. "Where did you see it, dear?"

Hillyah tugged at her apron strings in frustration. "That's the trouble. I can't remember!"

162

Oreal hauled little Ralg from the pond shallows. "Well, don't get upset about it, my love. You'll recall everything sooner or later, you usually do. Listen, I'll see to our babes. Why don't you go and have a lie-down on the bed in the gatehouse? That always helps."

Hillyah's eyes widened in realisation. "Of course, the bed! Come on, you scholars, I've got something to show you!"

She bustled off with a crowd in tow, relating to the Abbess, who was keeping pace with her, "When Oreal and I first moved into the gatehouse, long before the twins were born, you understand. . . . Well, my goodness, that place was in a dreadful mess, after lying empty half a season after Old Gruggle passed on. He was never the tidiest of mole Gatekeepers, but you couldn't imagine the dust and disorder! So I rolled my sleeves up and went straight to work on it. The first thing I tackled was that big bed in the corner. I think it was put there when the gatehouse was first built, a great, solid old thing. There must've been a hundred seasons of dust and fluff underneath it. Anyhow, there I was, flat out underneath the bed with my broom, sweeping and cleaning. Sneezing, too. That was when I saw it."

Girry leaped over a flower bed as they hurried across the lawns. "What was it, marm?"

Hillyah explained eagerly. "The bed fitted square to the walls in one corner. I noticed that the leg that fitted into that angle was broken off short. It was propped up by two thick books. One was called *Gatewatcher's Poems*, written by somebeast named Porgil Longspike, and the other was *Tales of Ancient Life*, by Minegay. They're still in the same place, I never got round to asking Brink Cellarhog if he'd make a new bedleg for me."

Little Sister Snowdrop, walking slightly behind Hillyah, cried out. "Huh, Minegay, I'll wager that's one of the names Sister Geminya made up for herself. Same letters!"

Old Quelt was last to arrive inside the gatehouse. He saw three pairs of footpaws sticking out from beneath the big, old four-poster bed. "What have you found, is there anything there?"

Girry's voice sounded rather hollow and stifled. "Oh, the book's here alright, sir, but it's jammed tight, and this bed's far too heavy to lift!"

Grudd Foremole moved Quelt gently to one side. "You'm cummen out'n thurr, youngbeasts. This yurr bee's a tarsk furr moi crew. Rorbul, fetch oi summ proppen an' foive gudd liften beasts!"

Foremole's sturdy assistant, Rorbul, ambled out of the gatehouse. He returned in a short while with five able-looking moles and two blocks of beechwood from the kindling pile by the north wall. Headed by Grudd Foremole, the crew scrambled under the bed. The watchers saw the big bed slowly begin to rise under Grudd's directions.

"Yurr naow molers, put ee backs oop agin et an' lift. Wun, two, h'up she cumms. Hurr, roight crew, 'old et thurr!"

Following some knocking and bumping, Grudd called out, "Hurr, take et daown noice'n'easy, moi 'earties."

Effortlessly, the bed fell down into its former position. The molecrew emerged, dusting their digging claws off, satisfied with a chore well done.

Grudd passed the books over to Quelt. "Yurr, zurr, they'm cummed to no gurt 'arm." He tugged his snout politely to Hillyah. "Thoi bed bee's as furm an' cumfy as ever 'twas, marm."

The onlookers crowded out onto the sun-warmed wall-steps alongside the gatehouse. Old Quelt sat in their midst. He opened the book in question and sought the appropriate page, from which he read aloud, " 'Chapter two. Fabled Weapons. Concerning the lance of Corriam Wildlough, brother of the High Queen Rhulain.' "

Two logboats sailed downstream. Tiria sat in the stern of the leading craft, listening as both Guosim crews plied their vessels skillfully, singing a shrew waterchant in their gruff bass tones.

"Pass to me my good ole paddle, steady as ye go,
bend y'backs ye sons o' Guosim, row mates row!
First a spring comes from the mountains,
fed by rainfall from the sky,
'til it joins up with another,
bubblin' from the rocks on high,
spring to rill an' rill to brook,
growin' stronger constantly,
blendin' flowin' always goin',
on its journey to the sea.
Pass to me good ole paddle, steady as ye go,
bend y'backs ye sons o' Guosim, row mates row!
As the day runs into night,
brooks do meet t'form a stream,
travellin' through dark an' light,
where the silver fishes gleam,
here's a river deep an' han'some,
windin' o'er the grassy plain,
speedin' with the current onward,
soon we'll taste the salty main.
Pass to me my good ole paddle, steady as ye go,
bend y'backs ye sons o' Guosim, row mates row!"

Morning sun twinkled through the tree foliage which formed a leafy canopy over the water. The current was fairly fast, running through a high-banked slope, chuckling as though it were enjoying a secret joke of its own. Dobra was in the prow of the second logboat, which had a crew of four Guosim paddlers and was carrying a cargo of food. Log a Log Urfa commanded the leading craft. Tiria could see his back, for'ard of their four shrew crew. Skipper sat amidships with Brink alongside him. The Cellarhog's face looked drawn and wan. Not the best of sailors, he clung to the slim logboat's side miserably.

Feeling sorry for the poor hedgehog, Tiria called out to Urfa, "How long will we be on this River Moss, sir?"

There was a hint of laughter in the Guosim chieftain's

voice as he shouted back to her. "This ain't the Moss, beauty. 'Tis only a sidestream that leads to it. See the bend up yonder? Well, the river lies beyond it. Hold tight now, miss, it gets a bit bumpy soon. We'll be headin' downhill, y'see, over a few rapids, but nothin' t'worry about. Ye'll know yore on the River Moss when we jump the ripflow that joins it with this stream. If'n ye likes sailin', then ye'll enjoy that part."

Though Tiria sympathised with Brink's discomfort, she had to admit to herself that she was enjoying the experience immensely. As the crew slewed the logboat deftly around the bend, spray cascaded high, and the stream really began to race along downhill. The ottermaid felt like yelling aloud with joy at the wildness of it all.

Log a Log Urfa stood balanced expertly in the prow, bellowing out orders as they weaved and tacked down the wild, watery slope. "Keep 'er down at the stern an' up by the head, buckoes! Back water to port, take 'er round those rocks! Don't reef the banks now, keep ridin' 'er to midstream!"

Bankside trees shot by in a green blur as water sprayed everywhere, with Urfa still roaring over the melee. "Luff yore starb'd oars now, luff I say! Steady to port! Steady . . . steady! Now give 'er full oars, me buckoes! Get yore backs into it! Heave! Pull! Heave! Pull! Up oars an' ship 'em, Guosim!"

Tiria felt the logboat leave the water, leaping like a fighting fish. Then it slammed down hard, catching the boiling rift of breakwater. Both boats skimmed out like arrows onto the broad swirling surface of the River Moss.

They were out of the trees, with the sun beaming on them from an open summer sky. Everybeast cheered loudly as they slid sleekly along. The crews slowed their oars back to a normal stroke. The river was wide, with shallows and sandbanks either side.

Banjon pointed upward. "See, Tiria, there's yore matey!"

The ottermaid waved to Pandion Piketalon as he wheeled

166

overhead. The osprey hung briefly on a thermal, then went into a sidelong skim and called, "Kraaahakaaaah!"

As they drifted through the bright morning, Tiria watched the countryside gradually change. Green-mantled flatlands merged into hummocks, lilac and yellow with heather and gorse. Now the ottermaid understood why the Guosim loved to travel in their logboats.

She was about to mention this to her father and Urfa but found them busy attending to Brink. The Redwall Cellarhog was still suffering from his water-motion sickness. Skipper bathed Brink's face with a cold, damp cloth, whilst Urfa dosed him with herbs and encouraging advice.

"You chomp on these special 'erbs, matey. They'll put the roses back into yore spiky ole cheeks!"

The faithful hedgehog mumbled pitifully as he chewed on the odd-tasting herbs. "Don't ye fuss now, friends. I'll be right as rain afore ye know it. Phwaaaw! I wish I was sittin' in my cellars, back at the Abbey right now. Nice'n'peaceful an' still, an' not rockin' back'n'forth an' to'n'fro like this."

As Dobra's logboat drew level, he hailed them. "Nobeast stoppin' for lunch today? I'm famished!"

Brink replied mournfully, "I wish ye wouldn't mention food, young 'un. The thought o' vittles makes me want t'die!"

Urfa pointed to a line of dunes in the distance. Between them glimpses of sun-sparkled sea could be viewed. "We'll hang on 'til we reach those sandhills afore we put in to land. Then ye can eat yore fill."

Tiria's appetite was well whetted when they reached the dunes at midnoon. However, nobeast was more thankful than Brink Greyspoke as the logboats nosed into the sandy shallows. He leaped ashore and threw himself flat, hugging the ground fervently.

"Never again, Skip, not if'n I lives more'n a thousand seasons. I'm done with sailin', mate!"

The shrews were kindling a cooking fire. As Skipper

watched them laying out huge quantities of food, he did a swift head count.

"There's four paddlers apiece to each logboat, Tiria and meself, Urfa, Brink, an' Dobra, an' Pandion somewheres up there. So why are ye layin' out enough vittles for an army? Does yore friend have a crew with him?"

Log a Log Urfa was scattering some stale shrewbread on the dunetop. It was already attracting seagulls. "No, Skip. My friend Cuthbert sails alone. He's a real odd 'un. I'd be hard put to explain him to ye. So ye can judge for yoreself when he gets here."

Coming down from the dunetop, the Guosim chieftain forestalled Tiria even before she asked the question. "Seabirds'll come from afar for vittles. My friend Cuthbert usually sails these waters. Once he sights gulls flyin' over this way, he'll follow 'em. Cuthbert ain't a beast to give up a chance o' vittles lightly, miss. Ahoy, Dobra, git up on that other dune an' give a shout when ye sight a sail out at sea."

Pandion landed amid the gulls and frightened them off, so Tiria went and had a word with him. "You can't stop here! You're scaring the gulls off and making the Guosim shrews nervous."

The big fish hawk glared hungrily about. "Yarraka! Then I'll fish out on the sea. When shall I return?"

Tiria stroked the osprey's lethal talons. "When you see me aboard a sailing ship, come down and land on it. Go now, my friend."

Pandion soared swiftly off. Soon he was nought but a dark speck out above the waves, hunting for food.

Sunset had settled over the western horizon in a glorious riot of scarlet, purple and gold when Dobra shouted from his vantage point, "Ship ahoy, layin' offshore!"

Everybeast climbed the dune to look. A vessel with one large, square sail, rigged amidships, was standing off from the shallows. Urfa identified it.

"The *Purloined Petunia*, that's Cuthbert's ship, shore

enough. He's waitin' for floodtide—that'll carry 'er up the rivermouth an' across the shore close to these dunes. Come on, mates, let's eat. Ole Cuthbert should join us soon."

Guosim shrews could not be faulted as cooks: They laid on a feast fit for many warriors. There was a cauldron of beetroot, potato and radish soup; massive portions of summer salad, cheeses, breads and pastries; and a sizeable bowl of fresh fruit salad. Hot blackberry cordial and a keg of special Olde Guosim Nettlebeer completed the spread. Even Brink perked up, declaring himself fit enough to sit with the dining party. Tiria was curious to learn more about the creature who would be joining them, but Urfa was not very forthcoming on the subject, telling her to wait and see for herself.

At one point the ottermaid went up to the dunetop to view what progress the ship was making. It was halfway across the beach, with the floodtide behind it. She could not see the captain, but Pandion perched on the masthead, seemingly unbothered by anything. Tiria made her way back to the fire and sat by Urfa.

"Your friend's not far off these dunes. He'll be here shortly. What do we say to him, sir?"

The Guosim chieftain sliced a cheese with his rapier. "Don't ye say a word, miss. Leave the talkin' to me!"

As a half-moon rose in solitary splendour over the coast, their guest made his appearance. He turned out to be a big, capable-looking hare. But Tiria was surprised to see him dressed as a Guosim shrew, complete with coloured headband, kilt, broad belt and a rapier far too large for any shrew to wield. His body was crisscrossed with old scars, and he lacked half of his left ear. He loped silently up and sat by the fire. Then he began eating as though he had lived through several famines. Not a word passed his lips as he ravenously tackled soup, salad, cheese, bread and pastries.

Urfa rose quietly, beckoning everybeast except the hare to follow him. He led them to the shoreside of the dune and

169

signalled them to sit. Tiria fidgeted impatiently, but Urfa waited a while before speaking in a low voice.

"Hush now, an' lissen t'me, mates. No jokin', though, I'm deadly serious. Tonight Cuthbert thinks he's a shrew, so his name'll be Log a Log Boodul. Have ye got that?"

Brink scratched his headspikes. "But I thought you said his name was Cuthbert somethin' or other Bloodpaw. Why's he changed his name all of a sudden?"

Urfa cautioned the Cellarhog, "Keep yore voice down, Brink. Ye call him Cuthbert when he's a sea otter pirate, but whilst he's a shrew his name is Log a Log Boodul. Understand?"

Tiria sighed with frustration. "No, I don't understand. What sort of a game is he playing, anyway?"

Urfa stared out at the moonlit sea. " 'Tis a long story that I don't have time t'tell, but trust me. This hare is the bravest of the brave. At the mountain of Salamandastron, where he comes from, he's wot they call a perilous beast. If'n he takes a shine to ye, then he's loyal to death—there ain't a more honourable or faithful friend than that hare. I don't know the full story, but I heard he ain't right in his mind anymore. That 'appened from all the wounds an' knocks'n'blows he's taken in battle. So play along with me, an' I'll see he takes ye to Green Isle, Tiria. Just leave it t'me, fair enough?"

The ottermaid shook Urfa's outstretched paw. "Of course, sir, I trust you completely!"

They trooped back to the fire and sat down with the strange hare, who was still eating. Without warning he dropped his food, staring at them as if seeing them for the first time. He laughed happily.

"Well, sink me in the bay, if'n it ain't Urfa Westbrook. Wot brings ye to these waters, ye bottle-nosed rascal?"

Urfa smiled and poured nettlebeer for them both. "Log a Log Boodul, good to see ye, me ole shipmate! These 'ere are me otterpals, Banjon Wildlough an' his daughter Tiria. That other cove's a Redwall Cellarhog, he's called Brink. They're good, trusty messmates."

The hare did not even acknowledge them. He split open a pastie and packed it with salad, then wolfed it down in two gulps. "Oh, I knows about 'em. My eagle Pandion told me. Have ye met my ole eagle matey Pandion? Funny, that, ain't it? Us shrews don't usually take to eagles, but me'n' him gets on 'andsomely t'gether. So then, wot can I do for ye, me ole logboat swamper?"

Urfa brought Tiria forward. " 'Tis this 'ere ottermaid. She needs t'get to Green Isle, ye see. But nobeast has the guts to take 'er, 'cos of the big battle goin' on over there."

A wild light gleamed in the hare's eyes. "Haharr, a battle, ye say? Can I take part in it, me darlin'?"

Tiria responded eagerly. "We were hoping you would, sir, knowing your reputation as a perilous warrior."

Without another word, the hare bounded up and streaked off in the direction of his ship.

Tiria looked at Urfa in dismay. "Did I say anything wrong? Is he offended?"

The Guosim chieftain shook his head. "Nay, ye did just fine, gel. Wait'll I see who he is when he comes back, an' then take yore lead from me."

They sat by the fire a while, picking at the wonderful food and puzzling over the strange hare. Long before they saw the hare, they could hear him. He was bawling out a sea shanty in a raucous voice.

"O shiver me timbers an' swab me decks,
ye bullies to me hark,
Or I'll gut yore tripes an' dock yore necks,
an' feed ye to the shark!
'Twas in the winter we set sail,
ye bullies to me hark,
in the eye of a storm an' the teeth of a gale,
I fed 'em to the shark!
Their cap'n was a greasy oaf,
ye bullies to me hark,
I tied him to an ole stale loaf,

an' fed him to the shark!
I stewed his crew in seaweed punch,
ye bullies to me hark,
an' seein' as 'twas time for lunch,
I fed 'em to the shark!
So if ye think yore big'n'tough,
ye bullies to me hark,
I'll stuff ye all with skilly'n'duff,
an' feed ye to the shark. Haharrhaaaaaarrr!"

Scowling and growling ferociously, the hare swaggered into view. This time he was wearing a tricorn hat with a big fluffy feather, which he kept blowing upward to stop it flopping into his right eye. His left eye was hidden beneath a musselshell patch. A brass ring, large as a barrel stave, dangled from his good ear. He wore a tattered pink silk frock coat, tied with a broad yellow sash, into which were thrust two cutlasses, a knife, fork and spoon. His outfit was completed by an enormous pair of folded-down seaboots, which beggared description.

The hare winked dramatically at them with his uncovered eye. "Stap me stays'ls! Vittles, an' prime ones, too! Come an' fill yore beak, matey!"

Pandion, who had been trundling along in his wake, settled down by the fire. The hare launched into the food as if he had not eaten in days, tossing choice morsels to the osprey. Salad and crumbs sprayed the company as he addressed them.

"Vittles, where'd we be without 'em, eh, I ask ye? So then, young Tillie, me otter, are ye the one I'll be battlin' alongside when we gets to this Green Isle place? Speak up, me liddle periwinkle!"

Tiria tried hard to keep a straight face as she replied, "Aye, Cap'n, providing we make it to Green Isle."

The hare sprang up. Grabbing for but missing his cutlass, he brandished a spoon instead while roaring out, "Make it? Haharr, o' course we'll make it, Tillie me darlin', or my name ain't Cap'n Cuthbert Frunk W. Bloodpaw, Terror o' the 'Igh Seas. We'll set sail at first light tomorrer, 'ere's me paw an' 'ere's me 'eart on it. A sea otter pirate can't say fairer'n that now, can he?"

Tiria realised that Cuthbert was now in the role of a sea otter pirate captain. Life was certainly going to be complicated, sailing with a hare whom she had met as a shrew but was now transformed into an otter! How many other identities did he possess, she wondered. The one cheering fact was that she was now guaranteed a passage to her destination.

That night, Tiria went to sleep with the Rhulain's words echoing through her mind: "Trust in the fool of the sea."

17

Holt Summerdell was still some distance off as the otter-clans and their families made it into the start of the high country. It was early evening, not quite dusk, as they skirted the rim of a vast crater. The otterbabe riding on Leatho's shoulders gazed, sleepy-eyed, down the steep shalestrewn sides at a big lake. Flat and dark, it covered the bottom of the crater, its water dull and lustreless, its slate-hued surface without a ripple.

"H'is dat Suddermell down dere?"

The outlaw smiled up at the little one. "No, me beauty, that's the place they call Deeplough. Summerdell's much nicer, just the right place for otterbabes."

Deedero looked away, shuddering. "I should hope it is. Zillo, how much farther to Summerdell?"

The bard pointed inland. "See the rim beyond this 'un? Well, there's a valley covered in woodland with a waterfall runnin' through it. Holt Summerdell's right there, marm, hidden amongst the trees. A grand secret place 'tis."

Big Kolun picked up a chunk of rock from the crater rim. "Loose stones round the edges, mates, so don't walk too close t'the edge now. One slip an ye'd go straight down that slope into the lough, with nought to save ye. Zillo, how deep would ye reckon that water is?"

174

Ould Zillo stared at the still waters, far below. "Well now, they say 'tis bottomless. Nobeast has ever plumbed the depths o' Deeplough. Sure, an' who'd be fool enough to try such a thing? Will ye look at it, 'tis smooth as dark glass! Ah, 'tis an evil lough, the home of Slothunog the monster!"

Deedero glared at the bard. "Will ye stop that sort o' talk in front o' the little 'uns? 'Twill frighten the life out of 'em!"

Big Kolun hefted the rock he had picked up. "Take no notice of that ould ballad warbler, me 'eart's delight. Nobeast I ever knowed has seen Slothunog. He's prob'ly just a tale somebeast made up ages ago."

He flung the rock upward and outward. It plummeted down, missing the sides of the slope, and hit the lough with a booming splash that echoed around the rim. Before the ripples had spread halfway over Deeplough, a monstrous black shape broke the surface, blew up a shower of spray, then plunged beneath the murky waters in pursuit of the rock, probably thinking it was something to eat.

"Blood'n'thunder, did ye see that?" Banya Streamdog leaned over the rim, wide-eyed with shock.

Roughly, Deedero hauled her back. "Come away, missy, an' let's be shut of this awful place!"

She gave Kolun a hard stare. "An' you, ye great lump, wot did ye do that for, eh? Huh, just a tale somebeast made up . . . some tale!"

Even the normally jovial Kolun looked subdued. "Yore right, me ole buttercup, let's git out of here!"

Darkness had fallen over the high country by the time the weary travellers made it into the woodlands. Ould Zillo guided them toward the sound of rushing water, warning everybeast to tread carefully. The watersounds increased in volume as the bard and his followers pressed on through the trees. Emerging onto a broad rockledge, Zillo waited until they had all joined him. Then he called out above the roar of the waterfall, "There she is, friends, Holt Summerdell!"

Even in the darkness they could see the magnificent valley. The woodlands were split by the falls, which flowed from the mountains above. Cascading down, the water fell into a pond, spilling over into a broad stream that meandered off down a gentler slope until it was lost amid the woodland trees.

Zillo had to shout to be heard. "Keep in a single file an' follow me along this ledge. Stick close to the side an' hold tight to yore little 'uns. We'll be goin' through the falls, but don't worry, 'tis safe enough."

He led them a short way along the ledge until it looked as though he could go no further because of the rushing waters of the falls. Turning, the bard grabbed the first two otters in the line. He pushed them straight into the waterfall, shouting, "Get through there. Go on now, keep goin', nobeast ever died of a wet head! Come on, mates, who's next? There's a cave through there—it's good an' dry!"

The families pressed forward, shouting and yelling as they pushed through the noisy curtain of rushing water.

Leatho and the clan chieftains waited until everybeast was safe inside before entering the cave. It was dark but still and dry inside.

Zillo called through the gloom, "Sit down an' wait where ye are. Banya, Birl Gully, Lorgo, bring flints an' tinder. Come forward an' see if'n ye can make it to the back wall!"

After a few moments, the chink of flint against steel set sparks flying in the darkness. Then a faint glow grew into a pale single flame, illuminating Zillo's face.

"There's kindlin' over here—wood, dried grass an' charcoal."

His words created a burst of activity. Soon fires were flaring in all corners, and a large blaze was blossoming in the centre of what appeared to be a spacious and high-ceilinged cave. Deedero gave a cry of alarm as something dark brushed by her face. Zillo calmed her.

"Ah sure, 'tis only some friendly bats, marm. They won't harm ye."

The ottermum regained her composure speedily.

"Friendly, eh? Well, if these little 'uns don't get some hot vittles an' soft beds soon, it won't be friendly bats ye'll have to watch out for. It'll be me, an' a lot of unfriendly mothers, so let's see some action around this cave!"

A quick meal was cobbled together by willing paws. Soon there were flatcakes baking on hot stones, and a cauldron of thick soup, made from peas, lentils and carrots, bubbling over the main fire. An herbal tea was brewed, and warm cordial was prepared for the young ones. Though there was plenty for everybeast, most of the babes were too tired to eat much. Whulky, Chab and Big Kolun found moss and dead leaves piled by one wall. They spread them in an alcove, covering the lot with cloaks and some blankets. The young ones of the families snuggled up on this communal bed. It was dry, warm and, above all, safe.

Leatho sat by the main fire with Kolun, Banya and the clan chieftains, sipping tea and listening to an ottermum singing to the babes. The everflowing curtain of water outside cast a veined pattern of red-gold moving light, reflected from the fires, around the roughhewn rock walls of the cave.

Chab whispered proudly to nobeast in particular, "That's my missus singin'. She's castin' a sleepin' spell over the babes with that soft voice of hers."

Big Kolun blinked and rubbed his eyes. "Aye, mate, she's got a pretty way with a tune. I think yore missus's spell is workin' on me."

Soon they were all dozing off to the ottermum's lullaby.

"Oh you sun now run away, run away,
little stars come out to play, out to play,
baby mine come close your eyes,
sleep until the new dawnrise,
I will sing thee lullabies, through this peaceful night.

All the earth is standing still, standing still,
darkness blankets field and hill, field and hill,

birds do slumber in the nest,
busy bees have gone to rest,
all good mothers know what's best, for the babes
    they love.

When tomorrow comes anew, comes anew,
there'll be lots of things to do, things to do,
'neath a summer sky of blue,
roses blooming just for you,
birds will sing so sweetly, too, for my own dear one."

Warmed by the fireglow, Leatho Shellhound allowed his leaden eyelids to fall for the first time in two days. He dreamed of a mouse warrior who carried a wondrous sword. The visitor from the kingdom of dreams had little to say, but the outlaw sea otter dwelt on his every word:

"Masters who lack slaves cannot serve themselves well, and an empty compound is a trap without bait."

Dawn was casting its rosy tendrils over the hidden valley when Deedero stirred Big Kolun and Leatho from the edge of the whitened embers.

"Rise'n'shine, you two, make way for a workin' otter. Come on, shift yoreselves from under me paws, I've got to liven this fire up t'cook brekkist. Outside with ye both!"

It was not wise to argue with Big Kolun's missus, so they roused themselves fully by breaking through the curtaining waterfall, out onto the ledge. Shaking and stretching, Leatho took stock of their new surroundings. Birdsong in harmony with the sound of the falls echoed around the valley.

Kolun sat on the rim of the ledge, dangling his footpaws over the drop to the pool below. He nodded admiringly. "Ould Zillo picked a prime spot here, mate. Just lookit those veggibles growin' over yonder, an' fruit, too!"

Leatho sat down beside him. "Aye, the stuff's growin' wild now, but I can see it was once laid out in terraces by the clans of long ago. I'll wager some of our mates could knock it back into shape, like it used t'be. There must be fish an' freshwater shrimp in that pool an' the stream below it."

Kolun stood up. "No wonder otters loved Holt Summerdell. Wot d'ye say me'n'you go an' gather some vittles for brekkist? That'll put a smile on my Deedero's face."

The outlaw had to smile at his big friend's enthusiasm. "Aye, let's do that, matey, but I can't hang around here all day, no matter how nice it is."

The big otter shrugged. "Fair enough. Where are we off to?"

Leatho winked. "Just followin' a dream."

Between them, Leatho and Kolun carried a heap of produce they had gathered. Deedero sorted through it. "Apples, pears, leeks, mushrooms an' damsons, too. You mean we've got a damson tree out there?"

Kolun threw his paws wide. "There's more growin' on those terraces than ye could shake a stick at, me ole petal. The damsons ain't quite ripe yet, but there's plums an' all manner o' berries out there. I even seen some ramson an' hotroot bloomin' among the herbs."

Whulky and Chab entered the cave, carrying a woven reed net they had made.

"We did a spot o' fishin' down in that pond, an' look at wot we got!"

"Freshwater shrimp, the water's swarmin' with 'em, ain't it, Chab?"

"Aye, nobeast's fished 'em for a long time. Did I hear ye mention hotroot, Kolun?"

Lorgo rubbed his paws together gleefully. "I'll go an' get some right now. Er, Deedero, d'ye think there might be some shrimp'n'hotroot soup for brekkist?"

The ottermum wagged a ladle at him. "I might think about it after I've made vittles for the little 'uns, but ye'll have to wait."

Birl Gully shoved Lorgo toward the water curtain. "Come on, mate, I'll help ye gather the hotroot. Kolun, Leatho, are ye comin' with us?"

The outlaw declined Birl's offer. "No, we've got other business today. But while yore out there gatherin' hotroot, see if there's any ingredients that'll help ye to brew up some o' yore Gullyplug Punch."

The jolly old otter slapped his rudder down heartily. "Stan' on me whiskers, Shellhound. That's a great idea! I'll brew a big barrel o' Gullyplug to celebrate our new home. C'mon Whulky, Chab, lend a paw. You, too, Zillo, an' you, young Banya."

They splashed through the water curtain, laughing and shouting, all except Banya. Kolun waved his oar at her.

"Ain't you goin' with 'em, young 'un?"

The tough ottermaid winked knowingly at him. "No, I'm goin' with you an' Leatho. You two are up to somethin', so I'm comin' along with ye."

Leatho whispered in her ear, "Then ye'd best tread wary, an' come armed, Banya Streamdog, 'cos we ain't goin' pickin' hotroots."

Smiling grimly, Banya patted her sling and stone pouch. "Somehow I didn't think ye were!"

The day was fine and the going was easy. By midmorning they were skirting the rim of Deeplough, with the dark, still waters far beneath them. Striding along either side of Leatho, his two friends listened as he outlined their mission.

"We're bound for the slave compound behind the fortress. We've got to find a way to free the slaves. Once we've got 'em away from Felis, we'll be able to take the offensive against him without worryin' what that villain would do by takin' reprisals an' punishin' our friends."

They marched onward, discussing their plans, unaware that they were being closely watched.

It was Scorecat Fleng and eight surviving catguards of his command. After being vanquished by the otterclans, they had dashed off willy-nilly into the night, expecting to be pursued and slain. Fleng had pushed his guards hard, not stopping until after dawn. They hid amid some rocks, exhausted, defeated and totally lost. Even when his guards were fit to travel again, Fleng feared returning to the fortress to face Riggu Felis. Despite the fact that the wildcat had deserted him and his patrol, Fleng knew that the warlord would punish him for his failure to stay and do battle with the enemy. So they wandered hither and thither, scavenging for food, uncertain what to do next. They were camped by a stream which ran through a small copse when Fleng suddenly realised where he was. Glancing upward, he recognised the high slopes of the hillside which led up to Deeplough. He was about to remark to his guards about this when he spied the three otters leaving the rim and descending the slope toward them.

Immediately he hissed out an urgent command. "Quickly, hide! Get down an' lay low, all of ye!"

Fleng's thoughts were racing furiously as he whispered further orders. "Don't let the otters see ye, let them pass by us!"

Following their leader's command, the catguards secreted themselves amid the bankside bushes, scarcely daring to draw breath, as Leatho and his friends forded the stream and pressed on through the copse.

When it was safe to speak, Fleng heaved a sigh of relief. He turned to the eight guards, smiling craftily. "Well, mates, there goes our ticket back home. I'll wager those three are headed for the fortress, so here's what we do. Keep silently on their trail until they're close to the fortress. Then when I give the word, we cut loose an' raise the alarm. Mark my words, we can come out o' this as heroes. It's our lucky day, did ye see who one of those otters was? The outlaw Shellhound! Hah, Lord Felis an' Weilmark Scaut'll be pleased to get their claws on that 'un. An' I'll tell 'em we was the ones who chased the otters into the trap. Right, up on your paws an' follow me!"

181

18

Noontide sun warmed the worn wallsteps of Redwall Abbey. Old Quelt's audience sat entranced, listening to him reading from the book which had lain hidden under the gatehouse bed for countless seasons: *Tales of Ancient Life,* by Minegay (yet another alias of the devious Sister Geminya). The Recorder read aloud to his attentive friends. The archive took the form of a story related to Geminya by a very old otter granmum:

"I am Runa Wildlough, daughter of Alem Mossguard, Skipper and Chieftain of the Norwest otters, and wife of Corriam Wildlough. This is my tale. The weight of age upon my grey head tells me that I will not see many more seasons, but that is the way of all living things. My time at Redwall has been long and happy. I have sons and daughters whose offspring now care for families of their own. In short, I am surrounded by kinbeasts who wish to care for me. However, since last winter, when I lost my husband, Corriam, the light has faded from my life. My only wish now is to join him by the still waters which flow through the quiet places of eternal summer.

"I was nought but a young ottermaid when I first met Corriam Wildlough, many long seasons ago. My friends and I were gathering shells and driftwood on the shores south of the River Moss when we came across him. He was lying amid the debris of the tideline, covered in sand and long kelp. We all took him to be dead. The others ran off, fearful to go near him, but I was not afraid. I went to him and began cleaning him off. He was a tall, handsome otter, older than me by some six seasons. Clutched tightly in his paws was a magnificent lance, which was snapped at its centre, and a coronet. This was a narrow band of beaten gold set with a wonderful green stone, an object of rare beauty. I tried to release his grip on the lance and coronet. Imagine my feelings when he grasped them tighter and then let out a groan—he was still alive! My friends had all fled, so I took it on myself to care for him and to get him back to my father's holt, though this was no easy journey. As best as I could, I half carried, half dragged his sorely wounded body back to where our tribe dwelt, where the River Moss joined the woodlands.

"Alem, my father, was not too pleased. He said that the daughter of a Mossguard chieftain had better things to do in life than nurse some half-dead beast washed up by the tide. This made me only more determined to care for my mysterious otter (I was rather headstrong, as most young ones are at that certain age). Looking back, I think my disobedience drove a wedge between me and my father, but I continued to care for my patient. I fed and cleaned him for many days, during which he never uttered a single word. Then one evening he suddenly began to talk. He told me that his name was Corriam Wildlough, younger brother to the High Queen Rhulain, ruler of a place far across the Great Sea called Green Isle.

"I asked him how he came to be lying on the shore, wounded and close to death. He had been sailing the seas in a great ship, he told me, together with his sister, the Rhulain, and a crew of Wildlough clan warriors. They were pursuing a vessel full of wildcat raiders who had been attacking the coasts of Green Isle. The wildcats

183

were believed to have come from beyond the great seas to the south. They were ruthless beasts who hungered for the conquest of other lands. But the High Queen Rhulain was a great warrior in her own right and the equal of any wildcat conquerors.

" 'Our ship chased after the wildcat vessel,' he said, 'ranging far across the Great Sea. Unfortunately, she gave us the slip one foggy night. Next day we saw land, a great mountain called Salamandastron, where a Badger Lord named Urthwyte—a huge, silver-furred beast—made us welcome and provisioned our ship with food and fresh water. We stopped at the mountain for three days. On the fourth dawn, we sighted the wildcat ship out to the west. Despite a fierce storm arising we set sail after the enemy. Heedless of the weather, we rushed headlong into the rising storm, which soon had us fighting for our very lives. The waves came at us like mountains, battering our ship about like a cork in the offshore waters. Out on the high seas, the wildcat vessel stood off, riding the gale and watching like a bird of prey. Our captain did not see the reef until we were right on it. A great jagged rock rose from between the waves before we had chance to steer clear of it. The side of our ship was stoved in, and we felt the keel crack beneath us. Waves as tall as big trees swamped our craft, trapping it fast on the reef like a wounded beast. Many a warrior was lost in the relentless avalanche of water.

" 'Then the wildcats came. They hung off the reef, put down boats and swarmed aboard our crippled vessel. There, in the midst of jagged reef and howling gale, they fell on us mercilessly and slaughtered the flower of the Wildlough clan. I remember standing alongside my brave sister until we both went down, battling furiously. I think the wildcats supposed I was dead and tossed me into the sea. It remains a total mystery to me how I came to be washed up on the shore, many leagues away from that reef, still holding on to my lance and my sister's coronet. Whether she gave it to me before they slew her, or whether I seized it from her brow, I will never know.'

"That was his harrowing tale. I felt so sorry for Corriam—his terrible wounds, the haunted look in his eyes and the loss he must have felt. All his clan comrades lost, and his beautiful sister cruelly slain. Here he was in a strange land, with only me to care if he lived or died, far from his home, which he would never see again. I devoted my every living moment to his welfare and the task of getting him better.

"My father showed open dislike of Corriam. This brought us close together, setting my father and me further apart. So it was that I fell deeply in love with my injured warrior. When Corriam was fit enough to travel, we left the holt of my father and sought a new life together elsewhere.

"We found peace and a happy existence at Redwall, this beautiful Abbey, whose doors are always open to good creatures everywhere. There it was that I took Corriam's name: I became Runa Wildlough, his wife. So we lived together, rearing a family throughout many joyous seasons, without fear or regret. Corriam took long, painstaking days repairing his lance. When he finished, it was a weapon of perfect balance, the envy of all who beheld it. I tested it myself—it was light and a joy to handle. The lance was also slightly longer, owing to Corriam joining it at the centre by fashioning a sleeve of solid silver into which he fitted both ends. It was perfectly symmetrical and truly straight from tip to tip.

"When the time comes for me to follow my beloved Corriam, I leave both the lance and coronet to the care of my dearest friend and companion, Sister Geminya. She assures me that the two treasures will stay together for some future generation of the Wildlough clan, who will be noble enough to need them for the good and well-being of her kinbeasts.

"Runa Wildlough."

As Old Quelt finished reading, a sigh of dismay came from Sister Snowdrop. The ancient Recorder peered over his glasses at her.

"What seems to be the trouble, Sister?"

Snowdrop shook her head ruefully. "I thought Runa's tale was going to tell us where the lance and the coronet could be found."

Girry stuck out his lip sulkily. "Huh, that would've been too simple. That old otter granmum had to go and give them to the confounded Sister Geminya. Aye, and you know what that means?"

Brinty buried his face in both paws. "More blinking riddles and puzzles to solve!"

Tribsy put on a pitiful face. "Boohurr, wot's ee pore choild t'do? Moi brains'll be furr wored out boi all ee rigglin'n'puzzerlen!"

Abbess Lycian looked over Quelt's shoulder at the page he had been reading. She peered closely at it before exclaiming brightly, "Oh, cheer up friends. There's some tiny scribbles at the bottom of this page. They may be our first clues from Sister Geminya."

Old Quelt took off his glasses and rubbed his eyes. "I can't see anything, Mother Abbess, my old eyes aren't much good now. See if you can decipher them."

He passed the book to Lycian, who read it easily. " 'C. the G.T. Chap. Seasons by seasons times seasons.' That seems to be all it says."

Molemum Burbee wrinkled her snout. "Boi okey, wot'n ee names o' gudness bee's that aposed t'mean?"

Quelt replied, "It's obviously a clue, marm."

Foremole Grudd gave his opinion. "Bain't nothen obvious 'bout et, zurr. If'n ee'll excuse oi sayen, lukks gurtly 'ard to oi!"

Girry was staring at the page intently, as if he were beginning to understand. He traced a paw along the scribbled letters. "Maybe not, sir. I'm thinking of what we've learned so far from studying Sister Geminya's puzzles. Now, the first letter is a C. That's a letter like Y, and I and U, it says a sound. So C becomes the word 'see.' "

Sister Snowdrop nodded eagerly. "Well done, Girry! See, then it says 'G.T.' Remember we were searching not long ago for 'T.O.A.L.' This book, *Tales of Ancient Life*. 'G.T.' could be the name of a book!"

"Ho aye, loike ee Geminya Tome."

Quelt stared at Tribsy. "How did you know that?"

The young mole wriggled his snout. "Oi aspeck oi guessed it, zurr!"

Brinty was already dashing down the wallsteps. "The Geminya Tome, we left it by the pond!"

Abbess Lycian, by far the best runner, reached the pond ahead of Brinty. Groop the molebabe and her accomplice, Grumby the hogbabe, were about to launch the tome into the water. Lycian snatched it from the two indignant Dibbuns.

"Give me that book this very instant!"

The infant molemaid protested. "We'm only a goin' for ee sail onna pond h'Abbess."

Lycian stamped her footpaw down forcefully. "Not today or any other day, missy. The very idea of it, sailing a precious tome on the water. Really!"

Hogbabe Grumby was the picture of dejection. "It bee'd a gudd h'idea, us was makin' a boat."

The tome was carried to the orchard, where it would be much safer. Old Quelt took charge of the proceedings once more.

"Right, what have we got so far? 'See the Geminya Tome.' What comes next, Sister?"

Snowdrop uttered a single word. "Chap."

Girry scoffed. "Huh, 'Chap.' is for 'chapter,' even I know that!"

The Abbess patted his paw fondly. "Which shows that you're making progress as a scholar. Bet you can't solve the last bit, though. It says 'Seasons by seasons times seasons.' "

Girry scuffed the grass with his footpaws. "No, Mother Abbess, I haven't a clue what it means."

The kindly Abbess smiled at his embarrassment. "Not to worry, young 'un, neither have I. Does anybeast know?" She scanned the circle of blank faces.

Molemum Burbee raised a paw. "May'aps usn's be thinken better arter dinner."

Lycian hugged her old friend. "Where would we be without mole logic? What a good idea, Burbee! Brinty, Girry, bring those two books along. We don't want them ending up as boats for the Dibbuns."

Skipper Banjon and Brink Greyspoke arrived back from their journey to the coast neatly in time for dinner. They were inundated with questions about their trip and Tiria's departure. Brink was thankful when Brother Perant called silence for the Abbess's grace. Lycian's gentle tones echoed clearly through Great Hall. Skipper gazed around at the faces of his friends, tinged by soft pastel lights flooding down through the tall stained-glass windows. It was good to be home again. He hoped someday his daughter would return to the beloved Abbey, where she could sit with him and listen to the evening grace which the Mother Abbess intoned calmly.

"Mother Nature bountiful, we thank thee one and all,
for good food the summer yields, to creatures at Redwall.
May our Abbey prosper, through seasons yet to be,
helped by those who tended the earth, in harmony
  with thee."

The Redwallers fell to with a will. Bowls and plates clattered as the various delicacies were shared among young and old—summer salads, new-baked breads, cordials, teas and October Ale.

The Skipper smiled gratefully as Friar Bibble lifted the lid from a steaming tureen. "Aharr, good ole freshwater shrimp'n'hotroot soup. How did ye guess I'd arrive in time for it, mate?"

Bibble chuckled. "Indeed to goodness, I only had to open one o' my kitchen windows wide an' let the aroma waft out. There, I said to myself, anybeast within a league of that ain't worthy of the name otter if'n he don't come runnin', an' here ye are, Banjon Wildlough!"

Skipper winked cheerfully at Lycian. "Our Bibble's a wonder, ain't he, Mother Abbess?"

Lycian commented wryly, as she sliced into a sweet chestnut flan. "Oh, he has his uses, even though he doesn't know what seasons by seasons times seasons is. Eh, Bibble?"

The good Friar pulled a long face. "Look you, marm, neither does any other creature, yourself included. Seasons times silly seasons, huh!"

Brink looked up from a deeper'n'ever turnip'n'tater'n'beetroot pie that he was sharing with Foremole Grudd. "Dearie me, an' I thought you was all cleverbeasts. Hah, ye don't know wot seasons by seasons times seasons is?"

Lycian paused with her slice of flan halfway to her mouth. "Oh, and I suppose that you do, Mr. Brink Greyspoke?"

The stout Cellarhog could not resist grinning smugly. "Oh, indeed I do, Miz Mother Abbess Lycian. I've knowed that 'un since I was only a liddle pincushion of a Dibbun!"

Silence fell over the diners at this revelation.

Old Quelt treated Brink to a jaundiced glare. "So you know? Well, are you going to sit there, grinning like a duck with two tails, or are you going to tell us?"

Brink dug into his plate of deeper'n'ever pie decisively. "No, sir, I ain't goin' to tell ye, not when you asks in that manner I ain't!"

Sister Snowdrop tried a more friendly approach. "Pray tell us, O Wise Keeper of our fine Abbey Cellars, how would you like us to ask you?"

Brink munched away as he considered the question. "Hmm, in a polite an' helpful manner, Sister. I can be coaxed, y'know."

189

Skipper poured a foaming tankard of ale for his friend. "May'ap a nice drop o' prime October brew'd move ye, sir?"

He winked at the others, who soon caught on. They began bribing Brink with all manner of tidbits.

"Give that good hog a bowlful o' woodland trifle."

"Aye, an' pour lots o' meadowcream on it!"

"Here, Mr. Greyspoke, take my mushroom an' gravy pastie."

"Maybe ye'd like a warm scone with some comb honey?"

The Cellarhog was graciously accepting all blandishments, when squirrelbabe Taggle rapped his paw with a spoon. "Gurr! You tellum, or I choppa tail off wiv a big knife!"

Brink threw up his paws in mock terror. "Sixty-four, the answer's sixty-four!"

Tribsy scratched his tail. "How did you work that out, sir?"

Brink shrugged. "Well, there's four seasons, ain't there? So, four seasons by four seasons is sixteen. Times that by another four, an' it adds up to sixty-four. I was always good at figurin' when I was a liddle 'un, still am."

As soon as dinner was finished, the Geminya Tome was sent for. Amid great excitement, Old Quelt opened it to chapter sixty-four and started reading.

"Twixt supper and breakfast find me,
In a place I was weary to be,
Up in that top tactic (one see)
Lies what was the limb of a tree.
It holds up what blocks out the night,
And can open to let in the light.
For a third of a lifetime one says,
Looking up I could see it sideways.
Tell me what we call coward (in at)
Then when you have worked out that,

190

You'll find your heart's desire,
By adding a backward liar.
Ever together the two have been set,
Since Corriam's lance ate the coronet."

An awed silence followed the reading of the riddle. Then Skipper asked airily, "Is that all there is to it?"

The glasses dropped off Quelt's nose as he spluttered, "Is that all! Don't you think that's quite enough, sir?"

Banjon held up a placatory paw. "Now don't go gettin' yoreself in a tizzy, old 'un, I was only jestin'. Though I'll tell ye this, on me affydavit. I never, in all me seasons, heard a puzzle or a riddle that even comes close to bein' as hard as that 'un!"

Little Sister Snowdrop's voice rose into a tirade. "That Sister Geminya! Oooohh, the bottle-nosed, twidgetty-tailed, prinky-pawed, mumbledy-toothed old busybody! What right did she have, thinking up brain-bending puzzles like that? It's a confounded . . . oooh, it's a . . ."

"Why, it's an enigma, just like her name, and it will do no good getting upset like that, Sister." Abbess Lycian patted Snowdrop's paw soothingly. "I for one am not going to be defeated by Geminya's riddle. You were right, Snowdrop, she's all you said she was, and more. The barrel-bottomed, flinky-eyed, twoggly-eared old nuisance! There, that feels a lot better. What d'you say, friends, are we going to solve the riddle of Corriam's lance and Rhulain's coronet? Who's with me?"

Skipper grasped Lycian's paw. "I am, marm, if the solvin' will help that lovely gel o' mine. Wot d'ye say, mates?"

The roar of approval that followed bounced off the hallowed walls of Great Hall several times. Molemum Burbee removed both paws from her ears when the din had passed.

"Oi'll make ee tea furst, then us'll get a-started."

Mother Abbess Lycian shook her head in admiration. "Who could say better than that?"

191

19

Tiria's first dawn aboard the *Purloined Petunia* was heralded by a rude awakening. The ottermaid was sound asleep in the little galley by the bows when the stentorian bellowing of Cuthbert Frunk W. Bloodpaw cut through her slumbers like a bucket of cold water being thrown into her face.

"Hahaarr! Belay yore bows'ls an' begin burnin' brekkist! Fire up yore galleystove an' get some vittles underway!"

Pandion stayed at his perch on the masthead, regally ignoring the hare's nautical tirade, which was directed at Tiria. Cuthbert watched as she staggered out of the galley onto the swaying deck. Then he continued.

"Top o' the mornin', shipmate Tillie! The sun's in the sky, the waves 'neath our keel, an' a fair wind at our stern. So let me read ye the articles o' this vessel. Bein' as I'm cap'n, the navigatin' an' steerin' are my task, an' there ain't a bully afloat does it better'n me! Ole Pandion up yon is the lookout an' fish catcher. Now, cock yore lugs an' lissen, me briny beauty. Yore the first mate, head cook, bottlewasher, deckscrubber an' scoffburner!"'

Tiria felt it appropriate to throw a salute. "Aye aye, Cap'n, what's your orders?"

Cuthbert scowled. "Orders! Are ye still asleep, Tillie? Yore cap'n craves vittles, so let's see wot sort o' grub ye can dish up. Jump to it, me 'earty!"

The ottermaid decided to play along with the eccentric hare and adopted her best seagoing manner. "Aye aye, Cap'n, I'll whomp you up a prime scoff, sir! But you'll excuse my asking, Cap'n, I thought we were bound westward, but we're sailing south. I can still see the coast. Why is that, Cap'n?"

Cuthbert kept the vessel on its southward tack, replying, "Haharr, that's 'cos we're hard on course for the mount o' Salamandastron, Tillie gel. Got t'call in an' pay me respects to ole Lord Mandoral afore we turn west into the main. Now get those vittles scorchin' afore I throws ye to the jellyfish!"

The small galley was equipped with a water barrel and a slate oven. Tiria was not familiar with cooking, having been served superbly prepared meals by Abbeycooks all her life. So she set about experimenting, using the heap of stores that the Guosim had loaded aboard. Tiria soon had a fire going with seacoal, wood and charcoal, which she added to the stove embers. First she took carrots, barley, white turnips, lentils, cabbage leaves and dandelion roots and chopped them finely. Then she added sea salt and crushed peppercorns. Finally she tossed the lot into a pan of boiling water and allowed it to simmer. After a while the concoction began to thicken, as Tiria continued stirring away, trying to ignore her ravenous captain's shouts.

"Tillie, ye plank-ruddered swab, ain't me vittles ready yet?"

Tiria shouted back, exchanging insults with Cuthbert. "No, they aren't, you lollop-lugged old tyrant, and they won't be ready until I say they are, so there!"

She expected the hare to come back at her with some salty threat about being thrown to the sharks, but instead he merely chortled and broke out into a comical ditty.

"Don't steal your grandpa's wooden leg an' run away
    to sea,

193

an' leave yore family sheddin' salty tears.
That cap'n only needs ye 'cos his ship ain't got a sail,
an' you was born with two big floppy ears.
Yore innocent an' stupid, so stay home with me, o child,
'cos if ye takes a voyage with sailors rough,
ye'd soon be usin' language that'd rot yore
    grandma's frock,
an' roarin' out for skilly an' plum duff!
For a life at sea is hard an' rather lonely,
especially if you've got no hankychief.
With no mother hov'rin' near to scrub out yore
    scruffy ear,
you'll catch the lurgy an' you'll come to grief!
Stay home, stay home, don't buzz off o'er the foam,
stay home, don't break yore aged mother's heart.
You can use yore grandpa's wooden leg to stir the
    porridge with,
an' Grandma's teeth to crimp the apple tart!"

Tiria could hardly stop giggling long enough to call out that the meal was ready. Cuthbert lashed the tiller on a straight course and dashed down to the galley.

Pandion took a brief leave from his lookout post to flap down and give the food a scornful glance. "Kwaaaark! No fish stew!" He soared out over the waves to catch his own meal.

Tiria filled a bowl for herself, leaving the gluttonous hare with the ladle and the pan. She watched him apprehensively as he guzzled down a great mouthful, then smacked his lips approvingly.

"Haharr, prime scoff, Tillie me darlin', wot d'ye call this burrgoo?"

Tiria sampled her own bowl. Surprisingly, it was very tasty. "Oh, er, it's called Nofish stew, sir. And my name is Tiria, so would you kindly stop calling me Tillie?"

Lifting the musselshell patch from his eye, Cuthbert

peered closely at her. "Tiria, eh? I don't know no Tiria. My ole mate Urfa said I was takin' a gel called Tillie to the Green Isle. I reckon we'd best turn round and head back t'the dunes, so we can look for Tillie. Wot d'ye think?"

The ottermaid sighed resignedly. "I was only joking, Cap'n. My name's not Tiria, it's Tillie."

The hare treated her to a glare of disapproval. "One name should be good enough for anybeast, Tillie. T'aint a matter to joke about, you mark my words."

Tiria almost choked on her stew at this observation. The hare had already changed his name twice since they had met and would doubtless adopt other titles before long. She swallowed hard and saluted.

"Aye aye, Cap'n. Tillie's my name, no more jokes."

Cuthbert licked the ladle clean. "Well said, Tillie. Right, I'm off back to me steerin'. If'n I was you, I'd get down t'makin' some skilly'n'duff for supper. Us seadogs is very partial to skilly'n'duff."

Tiria shook her head as she watched him swagger off astern. "Skilly'n'duff, what in the name of goodness is that? They never served skilly'n'duff at Redwall. I wonder how much skill it takes to make duff. Oh well, here goes!"

Over the next few days, Tiria became accustomed to the odd habits of Cuthbert Frunk W. Bloodpaw. They got on well together. Pandion, too, though for the most part the osprey kept to his perch or sailed aloft scouring the sea for fish. Tiria gradually realised that she had a natural talent for cooking. Virtually any dish she attempted turned out well, even skilly'n'duff. Cuthbert became exceedingly fond of her cheese and leek bake, followed by a dessert of dried apple and preserved plum tart. The pair also began composing songs together and often could be heard singing out lustily.

On the evening of the fourth day out, Tiria was in her galley, baking a large-sized potato, carrot and mushroom pastie. She was singing alternate verses of a duet they had made up the previous day. Cuthbert warbled out his parts from his position as steersbeast. He had a somewhat wobbly baritone. Pandion did an awkward hob jig on his lookout perch, contributing an odd squawk. It was a raucous pirate song, boasting about what infamous creatures the cook and the captain were, with both joining in on the chorus.

"Ho wreck me rudder, stove me planks,
an' rust me anchor chain,
salute me twice as you walk by,
or ye'll never walk again, hahaarr!

I'm Tillie the wild'n'terrible, the fiercest cook afloat,
I was born in a storm one icy morn on a leaky
    pirate boat,
I can lick me weight in vermin, so don't dare mess
    with me,
I'm a high-falutin' plunderin' lootin' terror o' the sea!

Ho rip me riggin, batter me bows,
an' splinter my mainmast,
when I says move out of me way,
ye'd better move right fast, hahaarr!

I'm Cap'n Cuthbert Bloodpaw, an' me father was
    a whale,
so stay clear of me vittles, or I'll bite off yore tail,
I cut me teeth on a cutlass, oh I was a savage child,
I'm a hairy scarey go anywherey buckoe bold'n'wild!

So tear me tiller, scrape me stern,
an' gut me galley twice,
I'll send ye to the ole seabed,
with y'tail tied in a splice, hahaarr!"

As Tiria and the big hare finished their duet, Pandion was squawking uproariously.

Cuthbert scowled up at the osprey. "That bloomin' bird ain't got no sense o' harmony!"

Tiria watched the fish hawk hopping about on his perch. "Aye, he's just ruined our last chorus there!"

Pandion swooped down to the deck and flapped his wings. "See, it is the big rock, the big rock!"

Tiria peered ahead down the coast at the dark monolith standing out against the crimson sunset in solitary majesty. She gasped. "So that's Salamandastron!"

20

Through the overhead foliage, midday sunlight dappled a lacy pattern upon the three otters resting in a woodland glade. Big Kolun Galedeep rubbed his midriff ruefully.

"I never realised the journey'd be this long. We should've brought some vittles along with us, mate."

Leatho flicked a curious insect away from his eyelid. "D'ye think ye'll last the day out, or will ye perish of starvation afore sunset?"

Kolun sighed gustily. "That's alright for you t'say, Shellhound, but I've got to eat to keep up with me size. A midget like you only has to eat once every season!"

Banya Streamdog patted the big fellow's paw in mock sympathy. "Pore Kolun, it must be awful bein' a giant. You stay here an' save yore strength, mate. I'll go an' see if'n I can find somethin' to tempt yore appetite."

She rose giggling and slid off through the undergrowth, while Leatho continued teasing his big friend.

"Aye, Kolun, rest yore famished rudder a while. Try not to think of that lovely freshwater shrimp'n'hotroot soup Deedero will be cookin' up back at Summerdell. I'll wager she's bakin' flatcakes an' a damson pudden, too."

Kolun's huge paw shot out, covering the outlaw's mouth.

"Now don't ye start goin' on about vittles, y'rascal. It ain't funny. It's torture, that's wot it is!"

Leatho wriggled away from the gagging paw. "Fair enough. I'll give up if'n ye promise not to smother me with that great mauler of yores."

They had lain there a while when Banya returned. She dropped some button mushrooms, a pear and a few bilberries into Kolun's lap.

"There! That should keep the life in ye a liddle longer."

She slouched down between her two friends. Leaning close to Leatho's ear, the tough ottermaid dropped her voice to a whisper. "Don't make any sudden moves, Shellhound. I've just found out we're bein' followed!"

The outlaw did not stir, his lips scarcely moving as he enquired further. "Who is it, an' where are they?"

Banya closed her eyes as if she were napping. "Cats, nine of 'em altogether. Don't know where they came from. They're not far behind us, but out of sight. I only spotted 'em by accident. I've got no idea how long they been trailin' us. What'll we do, mate?"

Kolun had been listening in. He twitched an eyebrow. "Nine, eh? That's only three apiece. Give the word, Leatho, an' we'll rush the villains. Shouldn't take long."

The outlaw retained his relaxed position. "No, stay where ye are an' let me think awhile. Take a nap."

One of the cats came tip-pawing back to where Scorecat Fleng and the remainder of his crew crouched behind some rocks. The scout made his report.

"The ottermaid never saw us. She gathered some vittles an' gave 'em to the big 'un. They're takin' a rest in the woodlands up ahead."

Fleng peered over the rocks, but the otters were too far off for him to see. "Takin' a rest, eh? They surely ain't guessed that we're on their tails. Good! Now I want ye to get forward to where ye can see 'em. Come back an' tell me the moment they make a move. The rest of ye lay still back here 'til I gives the word. This should work out nicely."

Banya began to think that Leatho had taken sufficient time to think. She whispered hoarsely, "Ahoy, Shellhound, are we goin' to lie here all day?"

The outlaw stirred. He rose with a yawn, then murmured, "Time to go, mateys. I've got an idea we can use those cats to our advantage. Banya, keep yore eyes peeled on the trail behind. Let me know when you think we're out of their sight."

The three otters strolled off unhurriedly. Banya's sharp eyes spotted the cat scout. She waited until he had run back to make his report, then winked at Leatho.

"Their spy has just shifted. We're on our own, but it won't be for long. They'll soon be back on the track."

Leatho went into a swift crouch. "Right, stay low an' keep goin', as fast as ye can. I want to get well ahead of 'em. Move yoreself, Kolun!"

The trio sped forward noiselessly.

Day was sinking into dusk as Weilmark Scaut leaned over the pier end. He watched a dozen coracles heading back in. Each one had an otterslave paddling and two guards as passengers. The cats carried a variety of nets, hooks, ropes and grapnels.

Riggu Felis joined his weilmark, the swinging mesh of chain mail on his helmet catching the last sunrays as he addressed Scaut. "Still no trace of her?"

Scaut coiled his long whip slowly. "Nay, Lord. They've dragged the lake from end to end without a single sign of Atunra."

The warlord stamped his footpaw against the pier boards. "Under here, did you make certain they searched beneath this pier? Lots of things get caught twixt the stanchions."

Scaut saluted with his whip as he replied dutifully, "That was the first place we searched, Sire!"

The chain mail veil rattled as the wildcat hissed angrily. He turned and saw his wife and son emerge from the fortress, with a retinue of catguards.

Pitru was clad in an armoured breastplate and greaves, overlaid with flowing red silk. Using his scimitar tip, he clipped blithely at the timber decking as he swaggered up to greet his father.

"A pleasant evening. Did you have any luck with your fishing? Those guards have been at it all day. They should have a fine haul between them!"

Riggu Felis looked the young cat up and down witheringly. "Still strutting around in borrowed finery I see, my wayward whelp, and not short of clever remarks, too. Take my word on it, sooner or later I'll find my pine marten, and you'll pay dearly for Atunra's death!"

Pitru gave his mother a look of wide-eyed innocence. "I can't imagine what he's talking about. Poor Atunra, do you know what happened to her, lady?"

Kaltag stared in disgust at the warlord. "The pine marten was not of our blood, yet you search all day for her. Would your time not be better served trying to find and punish the murderer of my son Jeefra?"

Just as the wildcat was about to snarl a reply, a slingstone whirred out of the dusk. The missile clanged as it dented the warlord's helmet. Temporarily stunned, Riggu Felis fell on all fours.

After a shocked silence, Scaut pointed at the shadowy figures of two otters retreating back into the shrubbery on the left shorebank.

The weilmark began shouting, "Call out the guards! Sound the alar . . . unhh!"

He crumpled over from the savage kick Pitru aimed at his stomach. The young cat grabbed him roughly, hauling him upright. "Silence, fool, we'll do this my way! Take what guards we have here, and make no noise. They're in those bushes—it's otters again. Get over there at the double, now! Go quietly, ambush them, wipe the scum out!"

As the weilmark bent to assist Riggu Felis, Pitru laid his scimitar edge across Scaut's neck. "Leave him. I'm in command here. Obey me or die. Now go!"

Gathering the guards from the pier and those from the boats, Scaut led them swiftly toward the bushes. Still with reverberations echoing round his head, Riggu Felis staggered upright, regaining his bearings.

Pitru made no move to assist him, remarking with casual insolence, "It seems we're under attack from the otters again, but don't let it concern you. I've taken care of everything, see!"

He pointed to the catguards plunging into the bushes. Strangely, Riggu Felis nodded calmly. "So you have, and you've proved yourself a bigger fool than I thought you were. You don't know what's going on, do you?"

He shot Pitru a scathing glance as he marched off toward the rear of the fortress, where the barracks and slave pens were situated.

"You carry on playing your stupid games. I know exactly what those otters are up to—and what to do about it!"

Pitru sneered at his father's retreating figure. "Doddering old idiot! Leave this to a real warrior."

The slave pens were only sparsely guarded. Leatho dropped the only catguard in sight with a swinging blow from his loaded sling. Taking the guard's spear, the outlaw used it as a vaulting pole to reach the top of the high timber fence which surrounded the pens. He bounced a few slingstones off the roof of one crude dwelling. An old otterslave emerged, rubbing sleep from his eyes. Leatho gained his attention with a low whistle.

"Ahoy, friend! 'Tis me, Shellhound. Go quietly now and bring Runka or Memsy to me."

The oldster nodded, then hurried off. Leatho did not have

long to wait until Runka and Memsy, the two young otters he had placed there as spies, arrived alongside the fence. Runka acted as spokesbeast for them both.

"Shellhound, we were wondering when we'd see you again. There ain't much to report here. Things are no different, apart from the fact that there seems t'be some conflict twixt Felis an' his son Pitru. For us it's much the same as usual under the cat's paw—short rations an' hard labour. Have ye come to free us?"

Leatho shook his head. "Not tonight, mates, but soon. Let's say about four nights from now. Can ye have the rest ready t'move at quick notice then?"

Runka nodded. "We've got to think o' the old 'uns an' the babes. Four nights, ye say? Hmm . . . me'n'Memsy'll see that they're ready an' waitin'. Anythin' else, Leatho?"

The outlaw replied, "Aye, it'll be yore job to keep every-beast from gettin' too excited. Tell 'em to stay calm and not do anythin' that'd alert the cats. Right, I've got to go now. Remember, both of ye, four nights from now, at about this hour."

Leatho dropped from the walltop, straight into the waiting paws of a dozen catguards who had stolen silently up. He was seized tight with a spearhaft forced across his throat.

Removing his helmet, Riggu Felis thrust his loathsome face close to the captive. "Hah, so you're the outlaw they call Shellhound, eh?"

Leatho bared his teeth at the wildcat, replying defiantly, "Aye, an' yore the cat with half a face. I heard a liddle sparrow did that to ye!"

The warlord brought the butt of his axe crashing down on the otter's head. Then he strode off, calling to the guards who were holding up the unconscious figure, "Bring him round to the pier, but don't harm him. I want this one alive!"

As the guards laid Leatho's limp body upon the pier, the warlord snarled at his son, "I captured their leader, the

Shellhound, while you were chasing shadows around the bushes."

Still glaring at Pitru, the wildcat addressed Scaut ironically. "Make your report, weilmark. Did you obey Commander Pitru's orders? What exactly took place?"

Keeping his eyes to the front, Scaut recounted the ambush. "Lord, we only sighted two otters, but they escaped. It was dark in those bushes. We wasn't t'know it was Scorecat Fleng an' eight guards, so we fired on 'em!"

Felis cut him short. "And?"

The weilmark swallowed hard. "An' we slew Fleng an' six others, Sire. But we was only carryin' out orders. Commander Pitru said to ambush anythin' that moved in the bushes."

The warlord moved with astonishing speed. Striking the scimitar from Pitru's grasp, he knocked the young cat flat. Stamping a footpaw down on his chest, Riggu Felis held his single-bladed axe to his son's throat and spat in his face contemptuously.

"Fortress Commander? Huh, I wouldn't leave ye in charge of a greasy cooking pot! You mincing young oaf, couldn't ye see it was another decoy? I knew the otters would try to set their friends free. That's why I went straight to where you should have been, the slave pens. Now I've lost six guards and a scorecat. You deserve to lose your head for such stupidity!"

"Put up that axe and leave my son alone!" Lady Kaltag had picked up the fallen scimitar and was holding it between the wildcat's shoulder blades. Her voice was frightening in its harsh intensity. "I said, get away from my son, or I swear I'll slay you!"

The warlord was forced to obey. He put up his axe and stood to one side, smiling scornfully as he freed Pitru. "What a bold warrior the great commander has turned out to be! Does your mother fight all your battles, milkpuss?"

Pitru scrambled upright, gritting through clenched teeth, "One day I will kill you!"

Riggu Felis twirled his battle axe skillfully. "One day, you say—why not now? Come on, ask your mother to give you that fancy sword back, then stand and face me. You won't get a better chance unless I'm fast asleep, unarmed and have my back turned to you. Give him his sword!"

Without relinquishing the blade, Kaltag berated him. "You would do better facing the real enemy, those otters, instead of trying to take the life of my only living son!"

Riggu Felis kicked the unconscious Leatho before replying. "You are as foolish as your son. I no longer have to do battle with outlaws. How does the saying go? Chop off the snake's head, and you have killed the body. The rebels have no head now. I have their leader in my claws. Believe me, I have my own special plans for the outlaw Shellhound!"

21

Brantalis the barnacle goose was enjoying the quiet summer morn. He paddled around the Abbey pond in leisurely fashion, pursuing a dragonfly playfully. The goose liked to spend time in the quiet waters. It was peaceful there amid cool willow shade and bulrushes, surrounded by the tranquil green depths. He often considered spending the rest of his seasons at Redwall, which had so much to offer: good friends, places to take one's ease and wonderful food. But then the inherent nature of a migratory bird would steal over him, and he would long to be with his kin, his skein, soaring high over uncharted acres of open sky.

His reverie was broken by Abbess Lycian and molemum Burbee, who wheeled their breakfast, atop the tea urn trolley, to the pond bank. They settled down, slicing scones, pouring tea and gossiping. Both were in a somewhat indignant frame of mind.

Lycian pursed her lips. "Ooh, that Old Quelt! Sometimes he can act so superior to those who are younger than him. Huh, he thinks he knows just about everything about everything!"

Burbee poured hot tea into her saucer and blew upon it, supping noisily as she remarked to her friend, "Hurr, they'm alla same at brekkist, a-goin' on an' on bowt things they bain't got ee clue abowt. But ee ole Quelter, he'm the wurstest!"

Sailing sedately up to the bank, Brantalis nodded at them. "I am wondering what has upset you on such a pleasant day?"

Burbee topped up her saucer, answering truculently, "Ee riggul, that bee's wot h'upsetten' everybeast!"

The big bird stared down his beak at her. "What is this riggul thing, please?"

The Abbess sighed unhappily. "A riddle is a puzzle, something that's hard to explain and difficult to solve."

Brantalis waddled out onto the bank, shaking his tail. "If it is hard and difficult, why do you bother with it? I am thinking it would be better just enjoying your life on such a good day as today."

Lycian spotted Sister Snowdrop coming to join them. She whispered hastily to the molemum, "Burbee, don't mention how we feel about Quelt to Snowdrop. She's been friends with that old squirrel a long time. I wouldn't want to offend her feelings."

The little Sister plumped herself down upon the bank and flung a pebble into the pond with some force. "Honestly, that Old Quelt, sometimes he makes me so angry with his uppity attitude. You'd think he was the only creature in Redwall who could solve riddles!"

Lycian and Burbee could not help breaking out into giggles. Snowdrop looked bewildered. "Sorry, did I say something funny just then?"

Brother Perant stormed up unexpectedly. Flinging himself down, he began spreading a parchment on the ground. It was a copy he had made of the rhyming puzzle.

Perant muttered, "Right, let's take a look at this riddle in peace. I'm tired of sitting at the breakfast table, listening to that Recorder drivelling on about it. Who does he think he is, anyway?"

Perant looked oddly at Lycian, Burbee and Snowdrop, who were hooting with merriment. "Er, excuse me, ladies, but is this a private joke, or am I allowed to join in the mirth?"

Once the Abbess had her laughter under control, she dabbed at her eyes with a kerchief. "Oh, it's just a bit of silliness. Pay no attention to us, Brother."

Brantalis was a little more forthcoming with his explanation. "Friend, I am thinking it is about the Old Quelt squirrel, who is annoying everybeast with his tiresome wisdom."

The Infirmary Keeper's normally sober face lit up in a grin. "Well said, my feathered friend, and so he is!"

Any kind of praise was apt to flatter the barnacle goose. Flapping both wings, he swelled his chest and honked. "Read me out your riggul. I am thinking this bird might be good at solving rigguls!"

The good Brother commented wryly, "Yes, and it seems you're becoming good at molespeech, too. The word is pronounced 'riddle,' or if you can't manage that, try the word 'puzzle.' Oh well, I don't suppose it can do any harm. Listen carefully now:

" 'Twixt supper and breakfast find me,
In a place I was weary to be,
Up in that top tactic (one see)
Lies what was the limb of a tree.
It holds up what blocks out the night,
And can open to let in the light.
For a third of a lifetime one says,
Looking up I could see it sideways.
Tell me what we call coward (in at)
Then when you have worked out that,
You'll find your heart's desire,
By adding a backward liar.
Ever together the two have been set,
Since Corriam's lance ate the coronet."

Brantalis waddled about, gathering his thoughts before he spoke. "What is twixt supper and breakfast? I am not understanding."

Molemum Burbee simplified the phrase with her logic. "Ee darkness bee's atwixt suppertoime'n'brekkist. Noight!"

Perant regarded her with newfound respect. "Good grief, you're right, marm!"

Burbee poured him a beaker of tea, adding, "Hurr, uz molers allus are, zurr. We'm no foozles!"

Sister Snowdrop interjected eagerly. "So, you could read the first two lines thus: 'At nighttime find me in a place I was weary to be!' "

The barnacle goose clacked his beak to gain attention. "I am thinking that would be in those strange nests you creatures call beds. Is that correct?"

The young Abbess smote a paw to her brow. "Very clever! All it really comes down to is this: 'At night I am tired so I go to bed.' Gracious me, who needs Old Quelt when we can solve the riddle ourselves! Read on, Brother. What's the next bit?"

Perant recited the next two lines of the poem:

"Up in that top tactic (one see)
Lies what was the limb of a tree."

Nestling his beak down into his arched neck, Brantalis did his best to appear knowledgeable. "I am thinking that is . . . er, that is . . ."

The big bird ruffled his feathers huffily. "I am not knowing what to think. This riggul is stupid!"

Reluctantly, Abbess Lycian agreed with him. "Dearie me, it looks like we're confounded by another of Sister Geminya's strange quirks. What in the name of goodness is a top tactic one see? Really, I don't know who's the more irritating—Geminya or Quelt!"

"Oh, I'd say Geminya every time, Mother Abbess."

They whirled around to the sound of a familiar voice. There stood Old Quelt, accompanied by Brinty, Girry and Tribsy. The ancient Recorder had crept up quietly, smiling disarmingly over his glasses at them.

"I do beg your pardon, stealing up on you like that. Is

there any room for a few young friends to join you? And, of course, an irritating old busybody?"

The company was totally embarrassed except for Brantalis. "I am thinking there is room for anybeast who can solve rigguls, old one. Sit down and drink tea with us."

Quelt gratefully accepted a beaker of tea. He sat down and began scanning Perant's copy of the riddle. "No doubt you've all solved the first two lines, my friends, and I have, too. Alas, it was this odd twist in the third line—'Up in that top tactic (one see).' I confess it had me quite perplexed. Like yourselves, I was baffled—until young Girry provided the answer."

Lycian seized the young squirrel and hugged him soundly. "You solved it? Oh, you combination of brains and beauty, tell us the answer this very instant!"

Girry spread his bushy tail down over his face, wriggling out of the Abbess's embrace. "It was all by accident, I think. Instead of starting at the beginning of the line, I began at the end. One see, that's a typical Geminya trick. The word 'see' really means the letter C. 'Tactic' was the only word that contained two letter C's, so I removed one from it. When I spelled it out without the C, it read 'tacti.' That didn't sound right, so I replaced it and removed the other C. 'tatic.' It sounded a bit better, so I kept repeating it, and thinking hard. Tatic, tatic, tatic! I suddenly twigged on that this was one of those mixed-up word puzzles. What was the name you called it, sir?"

Quelt explained. "It's called an anagram, a jumble of letters which can be sorted out into a proper word. Tell them, Girry."

"Five letters: an *A*, two *T's*, an *I* and one *C*. 'Attic'! "

Quelt shook the young squirrel's paw warmly. "Solved like a true scholar! So, what do we have now? Somewhere at night that Sister Geminya would retire to when she felt tired. A bed. And where will we find that bed?"

Brinty could not stop himself from blurting out, "In that top attic!"

The Recorder beamed. "Exactly! The very place that my young friends and I were just on our way to find. However, I thought it best to let you know, Mother Abbess, so you good creatures wouldn't feel left out. How would you feel about accompanying three young rips and one old fogey on a little quest?"

Though Quelt did not say it, the Abbess guessed that this was his way of apologising for his behaviour at breakfast. She replied with a twinkle in her eye, "Thank you for your gracious offer, sir. We accept. Er, by the way, which are you—the fogey or one of the rips?"

Tribsy took Lycian's paw cheerily. "He'm an ole rip, h'Abbess, 'n oi bee's a young fogey!"

Brantalis ruffled his feathers and honked. "I am thinking we should stop talking all this gobbledygoose and go to find the top attic!"

Lycian chuckled as she whispered to Tribsy. "Gobbledy-goose? That's a new one on me!"

Brink Greyspoke and Skipper Banjon were sitting on a barrel in the cellars. Between them they were sharing a flask of rosehip and redcurrant wine, accompanied by a wedge of strong yellow cheese with roasted chestnut flakes in it. The two friends were trying to recall forgotten lines of an old Cellarbeast's song, taking alternate verses and singing the chorus together.

"I keeps my ole cellars cool an' still,
stacked up with great oaken casks.
I'll serve ye up with right goodwill,
with any fine drink ye asks!

October Ale or cider pale,
or dannelion wine,
ole nettlebeer, I got som 'ere,
by 'okey it tastes fine.
Cordial brewed from plum'n'pear,
or raspb'rry crimson ripe,

211

try my whortleberry sherry,
'tis wot the ladies like.

I keeps my cellars fresh'n'clean,
each barrel keg or firkin,
an' day an' night I tends 'em right,
I'm a Cellarbeast hard workin'!

Strawberry fizz, that's nice that is,
the young 'uns like its flavour,
dark damson wine matured by time,
that's wot the old 'uns savour."

Skipper paused, scratching his rudder. "Wot comes next, mate? Was it 'beetroot port, poured long or short'?"

Brink cut himself a sliver of the strong cheese. "Nay, as I recalls, that's the last verse. Hmm . . . let me see. Er, I think it went like this: 'sweet burdock cup, just fill it up, de dah dee dum de deedee.' "

"Excuse me, Mr. Greyspoke, but Mother Abbess wants to know if you've got any spare lanterns please?"

Brink turned to Brinty, who was standing in the doorway. "We got lanterns aplenty, young 'un. Wot d'ye need 'em for?"

The young mouse gestured upward. "To search for the top attic. We've discovered some clues in the riddle, y'see, sir."

Skipper Banjon threw a paw about Brinty's shoulders. "We're comin' with ye, matey. Brink, where d'ye keep spare lanterns for searchin' top attics with?"

The big Cellarhog trundled over to an empty ale barrel. "In here. How many d'ye want, sunbeam?"

Brinty tugged his ear politely. "As many as ye can spare, Mr. Brink. There's a lot of us going on the search."

A huge party was gathered at the bottom of the dormitory stairs. It seemed that everybeast in Redwall wanted to participate in the adventure. Friar Bibble waved a floury paw at the heavily laden trio who had staggered up from the cellars.

"Indeed to goodness, they must be on light duties, look you!"

Skipper distributed the lanterns, issuing a warning. "All stay together up there. We don't want to lose anybeast. Top attics is a dark ole place."

Old Quelt made his way through a gang of Dibbuns, who were milling about noisily. "Do we have to take these little ones along? I don't want Dibbuns getting under my foot-paws, do you?"

Howls of dismay and outrage went up from the Abbey-babes as Quelt tried to shoo them away.

The kindly Abbess intervened on their behalf. "Oh, I'm sure they'll be alright. None of our little ones have ever been beyond their own dormitory stairs. It will be a bit of fun for them. I think they should come."

Squirrelbabe Taggle agreed wholeheartedly. "On'y a birra fun, we be good, me promises. Us' don't gerrunder a foot-paws if'n we gets carried!"

The Dibbuns raised a cheer when Skipper lifted an ot-terbabe called Smudger upon his shoulders. "Aye, it'll be no trouble to give these rogues a ride."

Smudger perched smugly on the otter's shoulders, wrin-kling his nose impudently at Quelt. "See, now we go wiv ya, teeheehee!"

There was no need for lanterns on the first floor, where most of the dormitories were situated, nor was there on the sec-ond floor, where Old Quelt kept his library. The third floor, however, was a different matter. It was all in darkness, apart from the chamber above the library where the uncatalogued books and scrolls were stored. Everywhere else it was black and gloomy, coated thick in the dust of untold ages. One or two of the more fainthearted searchers suddenly found they had other chores downstairs to tend. Mumbling excuses, they dropped out of the quest. The remainder, headed by Skipper, Brink and the Abbess, pressed on.

The third floor was a maze, a veritable warren of passages, steps, chambers and side rooms. As the group made its way down a winding corridor, Sister Snowdrop shuddered uneasily.

"Little wonder that Sister Geminya was an oddbeast, living up here all alone. It's very creepy, isn't it?"

Brushing away curtains of gossamer cobwebs with his bushy tail, Girry took the Sister's paw, speaking with a boldness he did not feel. "Come on, Sister. If the place is empty, what's to fear?"

The procession bumped one into the other, as they were forced to halt. A big, old, locked door barred the way. It was shut tight, its hinges and locks rusted together.

Sister Doral's voice quavered as she called to Skipper, "Oh dear, we'll never get that open. Let's go back, it's nearly lunchtime, you know."

Brink took the bung hammer, which he had been using earlier, from his belt. He rooted in his broad Cellarhog's apron pocket and came up with a broad, stubby chisel.

"Don't fret now, marm. Me'n Banjon'll take care o' this!"

Between them, the two sturdy beasts broke the lock and pushed the door open. It gave a long, eerie-sounding creak, which echoed through the lantern-shadowed gloom.

Burbee was trembling from snout to tail with fear. Little Ralg, the Gatekeeper's babe, leaned down from his father's shoulders and stroked the molemum's head sympathetically.

"Hushee now, marm, I mind you, 'cos I ferry ferry brave!"

Burbee patted Ralg's tiny paw. "Thankee, choild. Boi 'okey, wot oi wudden't give furr ee 'ot cup o' tea roight naow!"

They entered a chamber as vast as Great Hall, though much lower ceilinged. Foremole Grudd got his powerful digging claws into a wooden shutter and tore open a window. Much to the relief of all, bright midday sun flooded in. Sparkling dust motes hung thick on the air.

Abbess Lycian espied a small door in one corner. "Look, I wonder where that leads to?"

There was no lock on the door. Skipper pulled it open. "We'll soon find out, marm!"

He held his lantern high and peered in. It was a narrow space with circular walls of rough sandstone. An ancient flight of rickety wooden stairs were fixed to the wall. The whole thing wound upward into stygian darkness and oppressive silence.

After lifting little Smudger down from his shoulders and passing him to Burbee, Skipper ventured onto the first stair. The wood gave a protesting groan, causing Skipper to step back carefully.

"We can't all go up there, those stairs'd collapse. They won't even take my weight. So, what's t'be done?"

Otterbabe Smudger wriggled free of the molemum. Without a backward glance, he trundled to the stairs. "Alla stay down 'ere. Me go h'up!"

The Abbess caught the little fellow before he could venture further. "Come here, you bold creature!"

Sister Snowdrop made a suggestion. "Actually, that Dibbun's right, in a way. Nobeast of any size or weight could make it up the stairs. But if a few smallish, light ones—like myself, say, and two others—went carefully, one behind the other, I think we could make it to the top."

The Abbess took the initiative. "I think Sister Snowdrop and I should go. Girry, would you like to join us?"

The young squirrel's tail stood up straight. "Yes, please!"

Taking a lantern between them, the trio began the ascent, with Girry in the lead.

Skipper cautioned them, "If'n there's ought up there that ye don't like, then come straight back down here. Or if'n ye get in trouble, just give us a shout."

Brink gripped his bung mallet tightly. "Aye, you just shout, mates, an' no rickety stairs'll stop us. We'll come runnin'!"

The wooden spiral staircase was extremely narrow and unsteady. Every step had to be taken carefully.

Girry laughed nervously. "Ha ha, it's like being inside a well with stairs."

Sister Snowdrop shielded her eyes from the dust that he was unintentionally kicking down. "That's probably why it's called a stairwell. Can you see anything up there?"

The young squirrel held the lantern high as he managed a few more steps. "Yes, there's a sort of landing above us, and I think I see a door!"

They speeded up their pace, but the stairs began swaying, and there was the sound of a piece of timber falling below them. The Abbess froze.

"Stand still, both of you. Wait until these stairs stop moving. I think one of the struts has fallen away. Be perfectly still now!"

They stood motionless, scarcely daring to breathe, until the structure stopped swaying. Climbing upward gingerly, step by step, Girry arrived at the landing. He was glad to feel that it was fairly solid underpaw. Lying flat, the young squirrel assisted his two companions up.

Snowdrop went straight to the door, brushing away the cobwebs and dust which lay thick upon it. "I can't find a handle or a latch, but there's some letters carved on the lintel."

Lycian held the lantern close. "What do they say?"

The little Sister read out the graven script. "As far as I can make out, it says 'I say regiments!' "

The Abbess sounded bemused. "Are you sure, Sister? 'I say regiments'? I can't recall hearing of any regiments in the attics of our Abbey!"

Snowdrop replied, almost apologetically, "Well, that's what it says, Mother Abbess. 'I say regiments.' "

Girry narrowed his eyes as he scanned the words. "Put the lantern down, Abbess. Over there, where the dust is still undisturbed, please."

Unquestioningly, Lycian placed the lantern on the floor. Using a pawnail, Girry traced the words "I say regiments" into the dust in a circle, like the figures on a clockface. After studying the ring of letters for a moment, he nodded to Sister Snowdrop.

"Well, do you see it, marm?"

She stared a while and nodded knowingly. "Yes, indeed. I see it now."

Lycian looked from one to the other. "See what? Will you please tell me?"

Girry swept his paw around the dusty circle. "It's another anagram. I'm getting pretty good at them. This is the place we're looking for, Mother Abbess. Huh, 'I say regiments'! It's only a mixed-up name, and guess whose name it is?"

Lycian recognised it suddenly. "Sister Geminya!"

Girry dusted off his paws. "Correct. So let's get that door open, shall we?"

In the big chamber on the lower floor, Quelt shuffled to the foot of the stairs. He peered up into the darkness, twitching his grey whiskers impatiently. "What in the name of confounded seasons are they doing up there all this time, eh?"

Grudd Foremole replied, with typical mole logic, "Oi aspeck they'll tell ee, arter they'm cooms down, zurr."

Sister Doral, who was trying to stop otterbabe Smudger from climbing out of the window, confided to Burbee, "They have been up there for rather a while now. I'm beginning to feel concern for them."

The molemum dusted little Smudger off absentmindedly. "Hurr, an' so'm oi, marm. But no matter 'ow us'ns bee's afeelin', t'won't affeck they'm beasts up ee stairs."

A loud bang suddenly came from the room above. This was followed rapidly by the most unearthly shriek and clattering noises. The Redwallers rushed to the door at the foot of the stairs, with Skipper in the lead, roaring, "Stand by, mates. I'm comin' up!"

He bounded onto the stairs, which shattered in a rending crash of ancient timbering. There was another earsplitting screech. Then thick clouds of dust billowed out into the chamber, enveloping everybeast.

22

Under cover of darkness, the *Purloined Petunia* sailed in toward the mystic mountain fortress of Salamandastron. Somewhat puzzled but obedient to her captain's orders, Tiria manoeuvred the tiller, steering the vessel into the broad, curving bay. Twin beacons on the shoreline burned holes into the night, guiding her in. The ottermaid could make out figures running to and fro onshore. She surmised that these must be the legendary fighting hares of the Long Patrol, the Badger Lord's perilous warriors. Cuthbert had gone for'ard, concealing himself in the tiny lean-to between galley and prow. Tiria guessed he had his own purpose in doing this; she had long given up questioning her odd companion. Vast and primitive, the mighty mountain loomed above her as she hove in, blocking out the eastern sky.

A hare waded into the sea. Standing waist deep, he waved a torch as he hailed the *Petunia*. "Ahoy the ship, identify yourself!"

Cupping paws to her mouth, Tiria shouted the answer, as Cuthbert had instructed her to. "The *Purloined Petunia,* bound for the destruction of all vermin and the protection of goodbeasts!"

She heard the hare chuckle as he replied, "Heave us a jolly old headrope, an' we'll bring you in."

A line was already fixed to the bowsprit. Tiria ran for'ard. Separating the coils, she slung it in the hare's direction. He was joined by a score or so of his comrades, who set their weight on the rope and pulled the ship to shore. More hares came to assist, throwing down logrollers and hauling the vessel over the tideline until it was fully beached, high and dry. Looking over the side, the ottermaid saw that she was surrounded by Long Patrol hares, all uniformed and fully armed. They parted, leaving an aisle through which came striding the biggest badger Tiria had ever imagined. Torchlight shimmered off his armoured breastplate as his dark eyes gazed up at her.

The huge beast's voice was a thunderous rumble. "Permission to come aboard?"

Tiria was in a quandary. Her captain had not warned her of this. She was taken aback as a clipped military voice rapped out a reply to the badger.

"Permission granted, by all means, sah, but one'd much rather toodle ashore to bandy words with you, wot wot!"

Cuthbert emerged from hiding, completely transformed into a full-blown regimental major. Gone was the mussel-shell eyepatch and tawdry captain's rig. The odd hare had waxed his moustache into two fine points, and he was wearing a monocle. Around his waist was a broad black silk sash with a straight sabre thrust through it. A short pink mess jacket was draped elegantly about his shoulders, tasselled, gold-embroidered and bearing two rows of medals pinned to it. Cuthbert was carrying a silver-tipped swagger stick, which he waved in salute.

The big badger nodded, smiling. "Step ashore, Major Cuthbert Frunk W. Bloodpaw, and be so good as to bring your friends with you."

As two young subaltern hares assisted her ashore with needless gallantry, Tiria introduced herself and the osprey. "I'm Tiria Wildlough from Redwall Abbey. This bird is Pandion Piketalon of Green Isle."

The badger bowed solemnly. "Welcome, friends. I am

219

Lord Mandoral Highpeak of Salamandastron. Come along, Tiria. Subs Quartle and Portan will attend to you, though I imagine that fine osprey can take ample care of himself."

They strolled toward the mountain, with Mandoral and Cuthbert chatting animatedly in the lead. Tiria walked behind with the two young subalterns, who were obviously fascinated with the pretty young ottermaid. Both talked incessantly.

"I say, Miz Tiria, are you actually a jolly good chum of Old Blood'n'guts Blanedale?"

Tiria nodded. "I am indeed, Portan. Why do you ask?"

Portan grinned self-consciously. "No need for full titles, marm. Y'can call me Porters, an' that flippin' great droop-ears is Quarters, wot!"

His companion made a swift leg, tripped and almost fell. "Hawhaw, a pal of Old Blood'n'guts, eh? How many vermin have you slain between you? A jolly good few, I'll wager!"

The ottermaid shook her head. "None, really. I only met him a short while ago. But what's all this about slaying lots of vermin? I'd like to know more about my friend Major Cuthbert Frunk W. Bloodpaw."

The company entered the mountain through an impressively large oaken double door. From there they went straight to the main mess hall. There was a host of other hares already there. The place was filled with noise. Long Patrol members laughed, joked, sang barrack room songs and banged on the tables, demanding dinner.

"I say, wheel in the bally tucker before I jolly well perish!"

"Good show, old chap. You carry on an' perish. I'll scoff yours an' look sad for you later. Hawhawhaw!"

"Where's that blinkin' grubswiper got to with our scoff, eh?"

"Let's casserole the confounded cook. There's enough on that flippin' old lard tub for two helpin's apiece, wot!"

"Oh, go an' boil your fat head, Wopps minor!"

"Shan't! You go an' toast y'tail, Chubbscott!"

Tiria found herself seated at a corner guest table with her two subalterns. She ducked as a stale crust flew overhead. "Are they always like this?"

Quartle denied the accusation strenuously. "Good grief no, miz! They're pretty quiet tonight. I expect it's 'cos we have guests, manners y'know."

Regimental Major Cuthbert Cuthbert Frunk W. Bloodpaw was seated at the top table with Lord Mandoral and some high-ranking officers. Pandion was nowhere to be seen; Tiria assumed the osprey had gone fishing in the bay for dinner.

She pressed on, questioning her two friends about Cuthbert. "Tell me about Major Blanedale. I don't know much about him."

Portan seemed quite taken aback. "Great seasons, the chap's a blinkin' legend among Long Patrol types. I've heard that Lord Mandoral sometimes refers to him as the Deathseeker. Says he's been lookin' to get himself jolly well slain ever since he lost his daughter."

Quartle nodded in Cuthbert's direction. "That chap's been sewn t'gether more times than a bloomin' patchwork quilt. Just look at those scars, y'can see them from here. Huh, talk about perilous!"

Tiria was growing impatient with her garrulous escorts. "I know that. He's obviously been in lots of battles. But could you please tell me why? Was it because of his daughter?"

Portan tossed a clean serviette to Tiria. "Whoops! Gangway there, chaps, here comes the old nosh, an' not before flippin' time, eh Quarters?"

An outsize platter of salad, a big bowl of soup, a full loaf of wheatbread and a tankard overflowing with burdock and nettle squash clattered down in front of Tiria. She regarded it with awe.

"There's enough here for the three of us!"

Quartle chaffed her. "Oh, come on now, old thing, it's only a light summer repast. Personally, I'm always jolly well hungry by suppertime. Ain't that right, Porters?"

His tablemate gestured airily. "Anythin' y'can't cope

with, sling it over to me an' old Quarters. We'll deal with it, wot!"

Tiria glared from one to the other. "Will you please stop avoiding my questions?"

"Pay no heed t'these two gormless scoffin' machines, young 'un. I can tell you all you want t'know. Move over there, ye famine-faced wastebins!"

The hare who seated himself at the guest table was a rough-looking customer. He was tall and sinewy, sable-furred, with a scar running through his face from eartip to jaw. Both subalterns went politely quiet.

The new guest unsheathed a very long, basket-hilted rapier and laid it on the table. "Captain Raphael Granden at y'service, young 'un. I take it you're enquirin' about Major Blanedale?"

Tiria answered respectfully. "I am, sir. If you'll pardon me saying, the major is a rather odd creature."

The captain indicated the crowded mess hall with a sweep of his eyes. "We're all odd creatures in one way or another. No doubt y've heard the sayin' 'madder than a March hare.' There's more'n a few of 'em here, miss, but I know what y'mean.

"I served under Major Cuthbert when I was a sergeant. In those seasons he was a perilous fighter, the bravest warrior on this mountain. Anyhow, to cut a long story short, I'll tell ye what made him wilder than a Badger Lord with the Bloodwrath. He had a daughter named Petunia, a real beauty, quiet an' gentle. She was the flower of the Long Patrol. Many a young ranker lost his heart to her, I can tell ye. Well, one autumn day she was out on the shore, a league from here, gatherin' shells an' coloured stones, as many haremaids are apt t'do."

Captain Granden paused, staring at his long swordblade. Both young subalterns urged him on.

"What happened then, Cap'n Rafe?"

"Was it the vermin, sah?"

He nodded sombrely. "Aye, sea raiders, a whole crewload of the scum. They'd anchored around the north point an' come ashore. Petunia saw them, o' course. When she tried to run back here an' raise the alarm, they brought her down with arrows—slew her, an' left her layin' in the shallows. A poor innocent haremaid, who'd never harmed anybeast."

Tiria felt the hair on her nape prickling. "Major Cuthbert found out, of course, Cap'n Rafe?"

The captain blinked several times, and his voice shook. "I was out walkin' with him. It was me who found her. Rollin' in the surf, dead, with four shafts in her back."

Tiria shuddered. "It must have been a terrible thing for him, seeing his daughter like that."

The stone-faced captain never took his eyes from the long rapier blade as he continued. "He picked her up and held her close, then his eyes sort of filmed over. He gave her to me and said, 'Take my daughter back to the mountain.' Then he screamed."

Captain Granden drew in a deep breath. "It was a long time ago, miss, but I can still hear that scream, like some wounded madbeast. It just ripped out of the major's throat. Then I was left holding his daughter's body as he thundered off along the shore after the vermin. I raced back here and raised the alarm. An instant later, I was racing after him at the head of a hundred warriors. But nobeast would ever catch him. He must have run with the speed of madness driving him onward. We lost him completely, even though we searched 'til long after dark."

Quartle and Portan sat forward with tight-clenched paws.

"The filthy villains, I wish I'd jolly well been there!"

"Aye, but Old Blood'n'guts got 'em! Didn't he, Cap'n Rafe?"

They fell silent as the tough hare nodded slowly. "Three days later, the sea raiders' ship drifted into the bay outside of here an' ran aground. I was one of the party, led by Lord

223

Mandoral, who boarded the vessel. Her crew was a mixed bag—rats, stoats, weasels, ferrets, even a pair of foxes. A score an' a half of the villains. Every last one of 'em was dead as a doornail. Slain!"

The ottermaid interrupted. "And the Major?"

Captain Granden smiled grimly. "We found him, though at first we took him for dead, too. He was covered from scut to ears in rips an' gapin' wounds. I was tryin' to pry the broken sword from what I thought was his death grasp when he opened his eyes an' said to me, 'This is my daughter's ship. I took it for her and called it the *Purloined Petunia*. Good name, don't y'think, wot?' "

The captain picked up his rapier and sheathed it. "We carried him back here. Took him four seasons to recover, but he did. Well, his body healed, but I fear his mind was affected forever. So there y'have it, miss. Now, if you're finished eating, Lord Mandoral would like a word with ye."

Regimental Major Cuthbert Cuthbert Frunk W. Bloodpaw was in his element. He had retired to an alcove with a group of fellow officers to drink spiked punch and regale them with a bloodthirsty ditty.

"Oh I dearly do love vermin,
I've oft times heard it said,
that the finest type of vermin,
are those vermin who are dead!

Show me a rat that's been laid flat,
or a ferret that's food for fishes,
or a wily fox laid out in a box,
an' you've got my fond good wishes.
'Cos a vermin that's slain gives nobeast pain,
he'll never harm honest creatures,
nor steal no scoff, with his bonce chopped off
an' a scowl on his wicked features.

224

Oh I dearly do love vermin,
I think I always will,
while I can afford to draw me sword,
there's always time to kill!

'Tis true that a stoat will never float,
with a javelin through his liver,
an' a rat'll never get thirsty,
after sinkin' in the river.
Ole Blood'n'guts they call me,
'cos I sends 'em to Hellgates,
a fox, a weasel or anybeast evil,
along with their foul messmates!"

Tiria bowed to the ruler of Salamandastron. "You wished to see me, Lord?"

Mandoral held a massive paw out to the ottermaid. "Yes, I think you'd best come with me. We'll go somewhere quieter. It can get rather rowdy in here at mealtimes."

As they passed the alcove, Cuthbert could be seen standing on a table, waving his sabre whilst treating his audience to an even more bloodthirsty ballad.

The badger shook his huge, striped head disapprovingly. "Normally I wouldn't allow that sort of thing in the mess. It's a bad example to the younger hares. But Frunk is a law unto himself—he says what he pleases and comes and goes whenever the mood takes him. I take it Captain Granden told you his story?"

Tiria replied. "Yes, sir, a sad and terrible tale it was. I don't think he can really be blamed for the way he is, in view of what happened."

Mandoral agreed. "That's the way I feel also. The major has become a berserker, one who courts death. I allow him more leeway than any of my Long Patrol. It would come as no great surprise if he left here one day and never returned. I'd know then that he got his wish."

Tiria followed the Badger Lord down a passage, then up several flights of rock-hewn stairs. They passed dormitories and barrack rooms, all quite spartan but very neat. Salamandastron looked to be an even more solid proposition than her Abbey home of Redwall, but after all, she reasoned, it was a military fortress. They ascended more stairs. Tiria had begun to wonder how much further up they would go, when Mandoral halted in front of a wide beechwood door. He opened it, showing her in.

"This is my personal chambers and forge room."

Tiria found herself in a wide, spacious blacksmith's shop. Three of the walls were hung with armour, shields and weapons. On the seaward wall a long, unshuttered window faced a view of the restless main beneath a moonlit canopy of star-strewn darkness. At the centre of the room was a great glowing forge with two iron anvils and barrels of oil and water close by. The ottermaid went to the window where she stood admiring the panorama.

Lord Mandoral joined her there. "Salamandastron has always protected the western shores of Mossflower Country against foebeasts and wrongdoers. Of late we have been fortunate to live through long peaceful seasons, but it has not always been thus. Many times we have taken up arms against invaders from both land and sea. I myself prefer the peaceful life. Besides being a warrior lord, I have learned to study. I have educated myself in the legends, lore and history of this mountain, its various rulers and our proud traditions."

Tiria could feel the soft night breeze caressing her face and the heat from the glowing forge upon her back. She chanced a sideways glance at the Badger Lord, well believing that he was a fearsome warrior, with his formidable size, firm, thrusting jaw and quick, hooded eyes. However, there was no doubt, by his words, that he was a creature who possessed both knowledge and wisdom.

Mandoral pointed out at the sea, directing her gaze.

"Look there, Tiria, slightly north and straight ahead, between the bay and the horizon. What can you see?"

She peered into the night sea intently. "What am I supposed to be looking for, sir?"

The badger was moving away from her as he replied, "The tide has started to ebb. Keep looking if you want to know more of the High Queen Rhulain."

Tiria was totally taken aback. "Lord, how do you know of the Rhulain?"

Tiria turned to ask the badger more, but she was facing an empty room. He had vanished!

23

Returning swiftly to her former position at the window, Tiria continued to scan the sea, though her mind was in a state of turmoil. How did Mandoral know about the Rhulain? Why had he told her to watch that area of the sea, and where had he disappeared to? She tried to fathom it all out. In the midst of her deliberations, Tiria suddenly saw something which set her senses tingling.

The ebbing tide had receded sufficiently to expose a rock, in the very spot she was watching. In a flash, Tiria recalled the dream she'd had on the night before she left Redwall Abbey: the Rhulain appearing out of the sea to deliver the message which had sent Tiria in search of Green Isle. When the High Queen had sunk back beneath the waters, she had left what appeared to be the tip of her hooded figure, showing above the waves. There it was now, far out on the deep—a rock shaped like the top of the Rhulain's hood!

A deep voice sounded close by. "The rock is only visible when the tide is at its lowest ebb. It shows quite clearly in moonlight, don't you agree?" Mandoral had returned. He was carrying a sheaf of scrolls, which he placed on a barrelhead.

The ottermaid stood wide-eyed. "I've seen that rock in my dreams! What is it? I mean, what does it stand for, sir?"

228

The dark eyes of the Badger Lord widened in surprise. "You mean you don't know?"

Pointing to the rock, he explained solemnly. "That is where the Queen of Green Isle was lost forever—she, her brother and an entire crew of Wildlough otters. Their ship was wrecked on that rock, and they were slain by murderous wildcats!"

Tiria felt very young and ignorant in Lord Mandoral's presence. "But how do you know all of this, sir? It must have taken place in the far distant past, long before your time."

The Badger Lord indicated the pile of scrolls. "Recorded history, Tiria. Did I not tell you that I have become a student of all the events at Salamandastron?"

The ottermaid gazed longingly at the scrolls. "Let me study the history, too, Lord. I must find out more about the High Queen."

Mandoral allowed one of his rare smiles to the young otter. "No need for that, I can tell you all about the Rhulain. I have researched the subject thoroughly."

The big badger swept Tiria up, as if she weighed no more than a leaf, and deposited her on the windowsill. "First, you must understand that the queen was no stranger to Salamandastron. She had visited here before. This was in the reigning seasons of Lord Urthwyte, the great white badger. Through my studies I learned that they were friends. Throughout the ages, Badger Lords have possessed formidable skills in the making of weapons and armoury. Take, for instance, Boar the Fighter. It was he who made the fabulous sword for your Martin the Warrior. Lord Urthwyte was gifted with a particular talent, the manufacture of armour. Nobeast before or since ever produced shields or armour of such strength and beauty."

"And did he make armour for the Rhulain, sir?"

Mandoral's massive paw touched Tiria's mouth gently, silencing her. "I am always saying to the young hares here, the only way you will ever learn is by listening, not by speaking."

229

Tiria watched in silence as Mandoral went to the pile of scrolls. He selected one, which he spread on the windowsill alongside the ottermaid.

"This is a sketch drawn by Lord Urthwyte. It was to be a new armoured breastplate he had designed for the High Queen. Now you know why I mentioned her to you. Look!"

It was the regal otter lady, just as Tiria had seen her in that first dream. About her brow was the slim gold circlet, containing the large round emerald. Beneath her richly embroidered cloak of dark green, the breastplate could be seen. It was burnished silver metal, with a gold star radiating from its centre. She wore a short kilt, around which her sling was belted, with a stone pouch attached. Tiria took in all of this at a glance, but she stared hard and long at the face.

Tiria was aware of Mandoral voicing his thoughts aloud.

"The moment I saw you down on the shore, I felt that Queen Rhulain was reborn. Now I am certain of it."

The ottermaid was still gazing at the sketch. "Aye, sir, she could be my older sister for sure!"

The Badger Lord lifted her effortlessly down from the sill. "Come with me, I have something to show you."

When Tiria saw him draw back a hanging wall curtain, she knew where Mandoral had vanished to previously. He unlocked the door which stood behind it.

"This is my own personal bedchamber-cum-study-cum-refuge from mess halls packed with noisy Long Patrol hares."

She inspected the badger's retreat. It had one smaller window, shelves full of volumes and parchments, a table, a comfortable chair and various pieces of armour and weaponry hanging from two walls. The Badger Lord took a bundle from a cupboard and placed it upon the table.

"That last ill-fated voyage made by the Rhulain has been documented by Lord Urthwyte. She came from Green Isle to Salamandastron to be measured for a new armoured breastplate. Urthwyte was planning on making one for her. Apparently he thought the old one was getting rather thin and battered. Like that of Badger Lords, Otter Queens' apparel can get some fairly rough treatment. From Urthwyte's records, I gather the new armour would take a full season to manufacture. Alas, she was never destined to see it. But even after the High Queen's death, Urthwyte continued with the breastplate until it was completed. He was a beast with a love for his art, you see. I had the regimental tailors re-create the cloak and kilt from the drawing you saw. As for my own contribution, I made the sling and stonepouch. Unfortunately, there is one piece of the regalia missing, the coronet. We possessed gold enough, but nothing remotely resembling the great round emerald which would have completed it. I want you to take these things, Tiria Wildlough. They are yours by right, I think. I'm sure they will fit you well."

Tiria opened the bundle slowly. The cloak and kilt were tailored skillfully from a thick, dark-green velvet, the hue of mossy streamstones which lay in shaded shallows. The ottermaid could not suppress a gasp of awe as she beheld the breastplate. It was a true example of the armourer's art, a waist-length, sleeveless tunic. The back was a mesh of fine silver links, forming a chain mail. The front was also pure silver, beaten, smoothed, and burnished to a mirrorlike finish. This was surmounted at its centre by a radiating star of bright gold. The inside was padded with a soft, azure blue silk.

Tiria exclaimed as she picked it up, "Goodness, it's light as a feather!"

Mandoral nodded. "Indeed it is. I wish I knew what sort of secret metals Urthwyte infused into it. Don't let its lack of weight fool you, Tiria. It would stand against any blade, even a spearpoint. Do you like the sling I made?"

It was slightly longer than Tiria's sling Wuppit and a little broader, a grey-black in colour and rough to the touch. Tiria tested its balance and pliability. Taking a stone from her own pouch, she loaded the weapon, twirling it experimentally, then smiled her approval.

231

"This is a marvellous sling, sir, far better than my old one. The material is tough and very coarse, good to grip. It would never slip, I can tell. What's it made of?"

The Badger Lord pointed out the window. "The hide of a great fish, a shark that was washed up dead on our shore. There's more than a few lances and arrows among my hares, tipped with the teeth and bone shards of that beast. I knew the skin would come in useful for something, so I had it treated and cured. I see by the way you twirl that sling, you can use it. Can you throw far?"

Speeding up the sling's revolutions, Tiria suddenly whipped off the stone, sending it whirling through the open window. As it sped off into the night, Mandoral watched the sea until he saw a faint phosphorescent splash, far out over the calm waters.

"I have some good slingers in the Long Patrol, but none as good as that. You can use a sling!"

Tiria joined him at the window, her eyes seeking out the rock where the Queen's ship had sunk so long ago. "All I need now, so that the otters of Green Isle will know me, is the coronet. If the Rhulain went down with her ship, it must still be there. Gold does not rot, nor will it rust away, even in seawater. I will go there once it is light. If the crown is there, I will find it!"

Mandoral glimpsed the light of determination in her eyes. "I believe you will. I can see that nobeast would attempt to stop you. I will come with you, Tiria."

She bowed courteously. "I will be glad to have you with me, sir."

Even before dawn had properly broken, a gang of hares had hauled the *Purloined Petunia* down to the floodtide and set her in the flow. Cuthbert, as the commander of the vessel, cut a bizarre figure. In his dual role as ship's captain and regimental major, he wore the musselshell patch over one eye and his monocle in the other. Over his Long Patrol tunic, he had donned his tawdry nautical frock coat. Pointing with his swagger stick, he bellowed out orders.

"Haharr, buckoes'n'chaps, take 'er out a point to port, wot!"

Quartle and Portan, who were jointly in charge of the tiller, began to complain.

"I say, sah, it's high flippin' tide! How are we supposed to see the bloomin' rock, wot?"

"Porters is right, Cap'n sah. You can only see the jolly old rock when the blinkin' tide's out!"

Seated together on the prow, Tiria and the badger smiled as they listened to Cuthbert roaring at the subalterns.

"Who asked yore opinions, ye blather-bottomed buffoons? You just steer as I tells ye, or I'll have yore jolly old scuts for sammidges! Tides don't matter, the water's clear enough t'spot that rock. Why d'ye think I've got a lookout?"

He bawled up to the osprey who was napping on the masthead, "Pandion, matey, go an' sort out that rock an' waggle yore wings over it 'til we gets there, will ye?"

As the osprey took off over the rolling waters, Cuthbert continued to berate his hapless steersbeasts. "Ye slab-sided scoffswipers, wot d'ye know about navigatin', eh? If'n I wasn't commandin', ye'd get lost in a bucket o' water. Now steer a course after that bird yonder, or, so 'elp me, I'll kick yore bottoms into next season!"

It was not long before the fish hawk's keen eyes picked up the top of the rock below the surface. Pandion Piketalon hovered over the location, fluttering his impressive wingspan like some exotic black-and-white-barred fan.

Mandoral pointed. "Your good bird has found the rock, Captain."

Quartle muttered to Portan, "Amazin', he must have eyes like a blinkin' hawk, wot!"

Portan guffawed. "That's 'cos he is a blinkin' hawk, old lad."

233

Dawn breezes wafted the ship gently to the location. Pandion resumed his perch on the masthead, whilst Cuthbert ordered the subalterns to furl the sail and drop anchor. The Badger Lord took a long coil of rope with a chunk of rock attached to one end. Securing it to the prow, he dropped the weighted end into the sea. By this time, the sun was spreading its light over the waters.

Tiria watched the stone falling through the semitranslucent sea. It fell rapidly, bouncing off the sides of the underwater rock peak. When it had vanished into the depths, Mandoral instructed the ottermaid. "You must hold on to the rope at all times. Don't let go of it, Tiria. When you want to come up, just give one normal tug and I'll haul you up. Is that understood?"

Tiria winked at him confidently. "Don't worry about me, sir, I'll be fine. Otters know their way about underwater."

She winced as the big badger gripped her paw, his voice becoming stern. "I know you're an otter, but you listen to me, young 'un. It's not the same as Abbey pools or forest streams, being down under the deep seas. Nobeast really knows what dangers may lurk down there, so you hold on to that rope tight. If you get into any real danger, then give it two sharp jerks, and I'll have you out of there."

Tiria took a firm grip on the lifeline. "I understand, sir, and thank you for all your help."

She slid over the prow into the cold sea, with the crew's best wishes.

"Haharr, Tilly me gel, you keep yore eyes peeled down there!"

"Aye, miz, best of jolly good luck an' all that, wot!"

"Toodle pip, old thing, hope it ain't too flippin' cold down there. Rather you than me, I say."

Then she submerged completely into cold, eerie silence.

BOOK THREE

Across the Western Sea

24

Leatho Shellhound regained consciousness painfully, discovering that he could only see through one eye. The captive outlaw found he could not move his paws; they were bound, outspread, to the bars of a wooden cage. He tried to wriggle free, but the whole structure wobbled and shook. Leatho gave up struggling and waited until his senses were fully restored before taking stock of his situation. The cage was suspended by a thick rope, high on the fortress tower. It hung beneath the windowsill of Riggu Felis's personal chamber.

The top of Leatho's head ached abominably from the blow of the wildcat's axehaft. He tasted dried blood on his lips and guessed that his eyelid was sealed shut by some of that same blood, which had flowed from his headwound. Wrenching his face to one side, he rubbed the affected eye against his shoulder, blinking until it was cleared and he could see properly once more.

Below him, the pier was crowded with otterslaves, hemmed in by armed catguards. Gazing down on the sea of upturned faces, the outlaw's defiant spirit rose as he roared at the catguards, "Heeee aye eeee! I am the Shellhound! Loose me, cowards, an' I'll fight ye all with my bare paws!"

A bucket of water drenched Leatho, causing him to gasp with shock. Riggu Felis leaned over the windowsill, still holding the bucket, his chain mail mask tinkling as it hung down from his ruined face.

"Shout all you like, Shellhound, your fighting days are gone forever. I have plans for you, outlaw. Would you like to hear them?"

Leatho raised his dripping face, teeth bared in a snarl. "Let me out of here and I'll fight you to the death, half-face. Even with my paws bound behind my back, I'll slay ye!"

The warlord laughed. "Brave words, that's all you have left, outlaw. Listen now whilst I speak some words of my own."

Throwing the bucket away, the wildcat leaned out over the sill, his voice ringing out to those below. "Hear me, I am Riggu Felis, a true wildcat, and Warlord of Green Isle! No longer will my domain be troubled by runaways and rebels. See, I have captured their chief, the bold Leatho Shellhound. He will remain up here until his friends surrender. Either they can give themselves up or they may sneak back here in future days to look up at this cage. They will see the bones of Shellhound bleaching in the sun and rotting in the weather. Gulls and carrion birds will pick at his remains. That will be on their heads. If the rebels do not give themselves up, he starves to death! Nobeast defies Riggu Felis. This is a lesson every creature on Green Isle must learn!"

Below on the pier, Weilmark Scaut unfurled his whip and cracked it viciously over the slaves. "Back to work, idle-beasts! Gather the crops, forage for kindling wood, fish the lake. Tonight there will be a great feast in honour of Lord Felis's triumph!"

The captives went back to their enforced chores, despair stamped on their faces, some openly shedding tears. The wildcat foe had finally won. Their leader, Leatho Shellhound, was a prisoner, strung up in a high cage to die. Now their last sweet dreams of freedom had truly deserted them.

That afternoon, the wildcat sat out with Scaut beneath a pier awning, watching the coracles fishing out on the lake.

Just as the weilmark was beginning to doze off in the warm sun, a prod from the warlord's axehaft stirred him back to wakefulness.

"Who's that coming along the shore?"

Scaut blinked. "It looks like your son Pitru with some of his guards. Shall I go an' see wot he wants, Lord?"

Riggu Felis leaned back, closing his eyes. "No, let him come to me. We'll know soon enough."

The young cat swaggered up and stood in front of his father, who was feigning sleep. Pitru rattled his scimitar on the pier boards to gain attention, addressing his father insolently.

"Hah, the mighty Lord of Green Isle, eh? Taking a nap while his slaves are escaping!"

Felis opened one eye disdainfully. "Oh, it's you. What's all this nonsense about escaping slaves?"

Pitru signalled to his catguards, who tossed a slain otter down on the pier. It was the body of Runka Streamdog, brother of Banya. Pitru indicated it with a wave of his blade. "This is one of them. He was supposed to be fishing. I spotted the empty coracle floating round by the reeds. There were two slaves—one managed to get away but we killed this one. And all the time our bold warlord was snoring the afternoon away. But I shouldn't be complaining. The very old are like babes, they need their daytime nap."

Instead of replying to his son's insult, the wildcat turned upon Scaut, growling menacingly, "Didn't you give that young idiot my instructions?"

The weilmark came to his own defence hastily. "Sire, I was half the mornin' tellin' everybeast yore orders, but Pitru an' his guards weren't to be found, Lord. I swear, I searched for 'em everywhere!"

The warlord began advancing on his hapless minion, backing him toward the lake as he prodded him with a punishing claw. "My orders were that some slaves should escape! Otherwise, how would the rebels know about their leader's capture and the fate I had decreed for him, eh?

Who would deliver my message to them, you thick-eared dolt!"

He gave Scaut a final, savage shove that sent him splashing into the lake, which was fairly deep by the end pylons. Scaut went right under. He bobbed up once, banged his head on the pier's underside and went down again.

Riggu Felis shook his head in disgust as he beckoned to the guards. "Get that buffoon out of there before he drowns."

Pushing their spearpoles under the pier, the catguards probed about. Scaut surfaced, a moment later, hanging onto the spears and spewing out muddy water as he yowled like a madbeast. "Haaaaarggggg! Yooooaagh! Gemme out!"

They hauled him out, tangled up with the ropes that bound him to the rotting carcass of Atunra, the missing pine marten. Two guards slashed away with their spearblades, hacking through the ropes and freeing the weilmark from his horrific burden. Scaut frantically scrambled out of the decomposing Atunra's embrace, clambered onto the pier and fainted in a pool of lakewater.

Pitru peered distastefully at the body floating in the lake. "Ugh, what is it?"

From behind his chain mail half-mask, the warlord hissed, "Don't take me for a fool. You know it's Atunra, my faithful counsellor!"

Pitru smiled innocently. "So that's where she went? Well, nobeast told me. Like your order that the slaves should escape. Nobeast told me that, either."

The warlord spoke accusingly. "Yet you slew one of my slaves?"

The young cat looked guilelessly at his father. "Who, me? I never slew your slave. That was Scorecat Yund, my trusty servant. My catguards are very loyal to me, I believe they'd kill anybeast I told them to."

It was a war of words. Riggu Felis nodded knowingly. "Aye, my guards would also slay anybeast for me, and I have far more guards at my command than you do."

*

Evening shades fell over Holt Summerdell after a long, hot day. The music of gently cascading water cooled the air, lending an aura of tranquility to the scene. Otter clanbeasts sat around on the ledges amid fragrant flower scents, listening to the birds trilling their evensong. Young ones played on the waterslide or swam about in the lower rock pools.

Only Big Kolun Galedeep could not relax. Pacing up and down, back and forth, he watched the sun sink lower in the west. Kolun constantly repeated what he had been saying since midnoon. "Where can that Shellhound have got to? Where?"

Deedero looked up from a baby tunic she was embroidering. "If'n I knew where he was I'd be the first to tell ye, Kolun. Now sit down an' relax! Yore makin' me dizzy."

The big otter continued his pacing. "Huh, me'n'Banya were back here just afore lunchtime. I don't like it, Leatho should've been back long since."

Deedero's patience began wearing thin. "So ye keep sayin', ye great worrywart. Why not go an' do somethin' about it? Banya has. She's gone back along the trail lookin' for Leatho. Go an' lend her a paw!"

Kolun waved his paws about irately. "Wot's the point if'n Banya's already gone? We'd both be out there lookin' for Leatho, an' he might've arrived back here by another route!"

From where he was sitting on a higher ledge, Kolun's brother Lorgo pointed. "Ahoy, here comes young Banya now. There's another with her, but it don't look like the Shellhound."

Banya came staggering in, supporting the ottermaid Memsy, who was obviously half dead with fatigue. Both appeared to be numb with shock. Kolun ran to them. Sweeping Memsy up in his powerful paws, he carried her to where Deedero and some other ottermums were sitting. Setting Memsy down in their midst, he immediately began questioning her.

241

"What's happened to Leatho? Have ye seen him, miss?"

The ottermaid was in no state to answer. Burying her face in Deedero's apron, she wept uncontrollably.

Kolun's missus snapped at him, "Leave her alone, ye great lump! Can't ye see she's upset?"

The big otter was bewildered. "But where's Leatho?"

Banya answered. "Memsy told me that Shellhound's been captured by that Riggu Felis an' his cats."

Deedero's voice went shrill with disbelief. "Our Shellhound . . . captured?"

Banya ignored the twin rivulets of tears coursing down her face as she explained. "Aye, captured. The wildcat had an ambush laid for Leatho. He was trapped just outside the slave compound. Now they've got him strung up in a cage, high on the fortress tower. Nobeast can reach him up there. The Felis cat said if'n the clans don't surrender, he'll leave Leatho up there an' starve him to death. He said we could come an' see the carrion birds pickin' over his bones. Two otters escaped to bring us the news, but Memsy was the only one of 'em that made it. The other one was slain by a beast named Scorecat Yund. He was my brother, Runka Streamdog. I'll catch up with his murderer. He'll pay dearly, I swear it!"

News that Leatho was in the clutches of the enemy went out like wildfire. A Council of Clans was called immediately. Gathering in the cave behind the waterfall, everybeast listened in stunned silence as Banya retold the story. The moment she finished speaking, there was an angry uproar.

Ould Zillo had to pound his rudderdrum to restore order. "Ahoy now, hold yore gobs! Shoutin' never got a body anywhere. Kolun Galedeep, let's hear from ye!"

Wielding his long paddle, the big otter addressed the clans in the only way he knew—blunt and direct. "I ain't here to palaver or argue. We've got to free our mate Leatho, an' the sooner the better!"

Kolun gripped the paddle tight, his voice ringing out like steel. "Aye, an' I'll tell ye somethin' else, too. I ain't surrenderin' my missus an' young 'uns up t'be slaves for a mangy cat! If they want war, we'll give it to 'em!"

Zillo banged his drum furiously to be heard over the thunder of approval from the clan warriors. "Sure that's all well'n'good, but wot'll be happenin' to the wives an' babes if'n we lose the battle?"

Deedero raised her voice firmly. "Hah! We'll survive like we always have. Every one of ye owes too much to Shellhound. No foebeast's goin' to starve him to death whilst there's one of us left alive! Leatho never left any of us in the lurch, he was always more'n ready to fight our cause. Lose the battle, is it? Lissen, Kolun me dear, you go an' win that battle, an' don't come marchin' back t'me without Leatho Shellhound!"

Brandishing a lance, Banya Streamdog leapt up. "Streamdogs! Wildloughs! Wavedogs! Streamdivers! Riverdogs! Streambattles! Gather yore weapons! Rouse the clans! Eeeeeee aye eeeeeeeeh!"

As an avalanche of sound shook the cavern, Deedero nodded to her husband. "There's yore answer, wot are ye waitin' for?"

Big Kolun hugged his missus. "A nice bowl of hotroot soup an' a big kiss from you, my 'eart's delight!"

Narrowly avoiding a whack from her rudder, Kolun was swept up in the stampede for the entrance. Any reply that his missus called out was drowned by echoing clan warcries. Lances, slings, bows, spears, blades and all manner of arms bristled from the warrior horde as they bounded uphill out of Holt Summerdell.

It had been a long, hot day. Leatho watched from his high prison as the westering sun set in a blaze of crimson glory. His paws ached abominably from where the ropes cut cruelly into them. The last moisture he had tasted was when the warlord emptied the bucket of water over his head. He licked thirstily at his dried lips and closed his eyes, trying to ignore the pain from his wounded head, which denied sleep to his weary body. As the evening dragged daylight to an unhurried close, the outlaw fought mentally to avoid thoughts of food or drink.

When dusk fell, Leatho's head drooped forward, his eyes no longer able to stay open, his entire body feeling dizzy and light as air. Then a torpor overcame him: All pain receded into a dull throb. His body slumped against the ropes, and he passed out.

A mouse warrior, armed with a fearsomely beautiful sword, was at his side, holding his paw. Then, like a pair of leaves in an autumn breeze, they were travelling through the air. Below him, the outlaw could see Green Isle unfolding, its loughs, hills, streams and woodlands. The mouse warrior directed his gaze to where the Great Sea lapped the pale-sanded shores, his voice gave counsel to the dreaming prisoner.

"To die is easy for you, Shellhound, but you were ever a fighter. Do not let life slip away whilst there is hope. Behold the High Queen bringing a new dawn to Green Isle. Keep repeating her name. Rhulain! Rhulain!"

Leatho saw her then, the tall ottermaid clad in her green cloak and shining breastplate, marching purposefully. Queen of Green Isle! The High Rhulain!

The vision was shattered suddenly as the cage struck the wall and banged about crazily. Leatho woke only to look up and see the Lady Kaltag battering at the bars with a spear from above. Her face was twisted into a vengeful sneer as she shrieked at him.

"Murderer! Now you will pay for slaying my son Jeefra!"

Raising the spear high, she thrust downward at him.

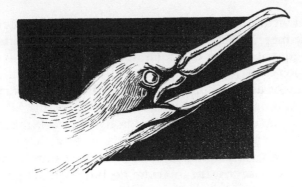

25

Choked and blinded by thick clouds of billowing dust inside the stairwell, Skipper Banjon took a flying leap upward. The tough otter grabbed onto a pawhold in the rough sides of the stone funnel. Buffeted by falling slats of rotted wood, he caught the sounds of wild screams and cries coming from the room above. He drove himself frantically onward, scrabbling and clawing at rocky outcrops and splintered stair ends until he managed to haul himself onto the lopsided landing. Without a second thought for his own safety, Skipper hurled himself at the door, bursting into the room. Grubbing dust from his eyes, he found himself confronted by a fearsome sight.

In one corner, Girry had bravely placed himself in front of Abbess Lycian and Sister Snowdrop, shielding them both. The centre of the room was dominated by a huge male gannet, which was shrieking aggressively. As the bird turned to face him, Skipper noted that one of its legs was lame and that the wing on the same side flopped awkwardly. The gannet's bright-blue ringed eyes focussed on the newcomer. Throwing back its big, cream-capped head, the bird opened its long, sharp beak and gave voice to an ear-splitting scream. "Yaaarrreeekeeekeeek!"

Skipper showed no fear but stood quite still, staring intently at the fierce bird. Calmly, he spoke to his friends. "Stay there, mates, don't make a move or a sound 'til I tell ye. I ain't got a clue wot a gannet's doin' up here so far from the sea."

"Keekaaaheeee!" Pointing its beak at the otter chieftain, the gannet hobbled toward him swiftly.

Skipper was forced to dodge backward but continued speaking. "I think that bird's been injured an' driven in here by a storm, maybe the same one that brought the osprey to us. Now I don't want to alarm ye, but it's a big gannet, an' it must be starvin'. I reckon it'll have to kill to eat soon. So, anybeast got an idea wot t'do next?"

Girry kept his voice to a low murmur. "I was trying to steer it out of the window until it turned and cornered us. It got in that way, so it must be able to make its way out by the same route."

Skipper chanced a quick glance at the open window with its broken frame and flapping rags of curtaining. "Good idea, young 'un, but we need somethin' to help with the job, maybe to use as a shield."

The Abbess came up with a swift solution. "Skip, just behind you, to the left, there's an old bed against the wall, all broken and battered. I think the bird must have used it to rest on. If we could get behind the bed, it could be useful as a barrier. We may be able to force the bird out of the window with it."

The gannet made a stab at Skipper with its sharp beak, but he dodged to the right, narrowly escaping it. "Aye, that's wot we'll do, marm. I'll decoy this villain to one side. Soon as it moves, you three make a dash for the bed. Right, here goes, mates. Redwaaaaaalllll!"

Skipper launched himself at the bird, feinted to the right and thwacked its good leg with a powerful swipe of his rudder. It gave a surprised squawk as it fell in a flurry of feathers. Seizing their chance, Girry, the Abbess and Snowdrop raced to the bed. Skipper backed off hastily and joined them. Heaving the cracked old frame of timber and burst mattress upright, they got behind it.

246

Sister Snowdrop yelled exultantly, "Charge, mates. Charge!"

Holding the bed in front of them, they bulled straight into the gannet, catching it square on. With its damaged wing flapping loosely and its lamed leg not able to gain any purchase, the bird was driven back and bundled through the window in a mad flurry of black-tipped white feathers. It tried clinging to the sill, screaming and hissing, but the Abbess and Girry kicked at it until it had to let go.

Leaning out of the window, the four Redwallers watched as the gannet made a bumbling attempt at flight but lost height immediately. The huge bird fell onto an outward sloping roof below, then rolled off and plunged earthward, still flapping about like a huge, rumpled quilt. A thickly blossoming rhododendron, growing beside the Abbey wall, finally broke the bird's fall. From there, it tumbled to the lawn, where it flapped about, apparently unhurt.

Dusting off her paws, little Sister Snowdrop called down to the fallen gannet, "There! Let that be a lesson, you great plumed bully!"

Abbess Lycian put a paw to her brow and sat down with her back against the wall, exclaiming, "Whooh! Dearie me, I'm all atremble!"

Gallantly, Skipper helped her up. "You did fine, marm, just fine. An' you, too, Girry!"

Sister Snowdrop nudged him indignantly. "Excuse me, but did I take no part in all this?"

Skipper laughed as he threw an affectionate paw around the old mouse's shoulders. "Oh, you did better'n all of us, Sister. Yore a rough ole customer, an' I wouldn't like t'cross yore path up a dry stream on a dark night, no marm!"

Snowdrop smiled sweetly. "You're a dreadful flatterer, sir!"

A shout echoed up through the ruined stairwell. It was Brink. "Ahoy, Skip, is everybeast alright up there?"

The otter chieftain called back down to his friend, "Right

as rain, matey! We'll be down as soon as ye throw a rope up to us."

He turned to the Abbess. "Well, did ye find wot ye were lookin' for up here, marm?"

Lycian cast a reflective eye over the deserted bedchamber. "Not just yet, Skip, but I have a feeling that we soon will. Sister Snowdrop, do you have a copy of the rhyme?"

The old mouse tapped the side of her head. "No need, Mother Abbess, I can remember every word. It goes like this.

"Twixt supper and breakfast find me,
In a place I was weary to be,
Up in that top tactic (one see)
Lies what was the limb of a tree.
It holds up what blocks out the night,
And can open to let in the light.
For a third of a lifetime one says,
Looking up I could see it sideways.
Tell me what we call coward (in at)
Then when you have worked out that,
You'll find your heart's desire,
By adding a backward liar.
Ever together the two have been set,
Since Corriam's lance ate the coronet."

Skipper nodded admiringly. "Well done, marm! Wish I had a memory like that. So, ye've found this place, the top attic. Next thing to look for is the limb of what once was a tree. What d'ye think that'll look like?"

Girry gave a prompt reply. "Oh, I've already guessed that—it's Corriam's lance. It's probably made of wood, so it must have once been the limb of a tree. Right?"

Skipper agreed. "Right, young 'un, but have ye sorted out the rest o' the riddle?"

Girry pursed his lips, endeavouring to look wise. "Er, not right now, sir, but I soon will, never fear."

Sister Snowdrop smiled fondly at her young friend. "No need to, I've already done it, Girry. I've been repeating that rhyme to myself for so long that some of it's starting to actually make sense. When I saw the bed, it began to click into place."

The little Sister smiled smugly until Abbess Lycian spoke to her rather sharply. "Well? Don't stand there grinning like a ferret at a feast, Sister. Tell us!"

For answer, Snowdrop went to where the bed had stood against the wall. She lay down on the floor, facing the window.

The Abbess sighed impatiently. "What are you doing now, trying to get your habit dustier?"

Snowdrop ignored the comment and began her explanation. "I was wondering what 'a third of a lifetime' had to do with our search. Then I remembered. We have three parts to each day—one third is used for work, the second for eating and enjoyment, the third part is set aside for sleep. So, for a third of her lifetime, Sister Geminya would be lying in her bed, which was about here, right? I'm lying on my side, just as she might have. So, what could she see from her sideways position?"

Girry spoke up. "The window and the curtains, I suppose. Though the curtains are nothing but tattered rags now."

Snowdrop continued, "Yes, but a long time ago they could either block out the night or let in the daylight. Now tell me, what holds the curtains up?"

Skipper shrugged. "Prob'ly a curtain rail."

Without warning, Girry gave a great leap. He went bounding up the windowframe and tore the curtain rail from the staples which held it. "Geminya used it as a curtain rail. This is the lance of Corriam!"

Skipper scratched his whiskers in bewilderment. "Sink me rudder, it's been layin' up there in full view all the time. How did ye guess that was it, young 'un?"

Girry brandished the ancient weapon triumphantly. "I never guessed anything, Skip, I worked it out a moment ago. You know how good I am at anagrams. Well, listen to this: 'Tell me what we call coward (in at).' Well, what would you call a coward?"

Skipper pondered a moment before replying. "A lily-livered spineless toad! Beggin' yore pardons for the language, marms."

Girry shook his head. "They're not the names I'm after. How about calling a coward a cur?"

Skipper repeated the name. "Cur, aye, that's a good 'un."

Girry continued. "Now look at the last two words of that line: 'in at.' Move them about, and they become 'tain.' Add the 'cur,' and what do you have?"

The otter smiled brightly. "Cur . . . tain . . . curtain!"

Sister Snowdrop looked over her small square glasses. "And 'you'll find your heart's desire, by adding a backward liar.' 'Liar' spelled backward is 'rail.' You see?"

Abbess Lycian clapped her paws. "How clever, curtain rail! What splendid creatures my Redwallers are. The lance of Corriam has been up there for ages, pretending to be a curtain rail!"

Skipper took hold of the lance, examining it carefully. " 'Tis a fine ole weapon, sure enough. Made o' good hard wood. I've never seen timber like this afore. Good balance, too, a real warrior's lance. Look at the middle, made o' silver!"

Spitting on the metal, he rubbed dust upon it, then polished it against his tunic until it glittered. "Aye, silver! Didn't the story say that the lance was smashed, an' ole Corriam mended it by wedgin' a silver sleeve over the broken bits? A clever piece o' work."

Touching one of the lancetips, the Abbess shuddered. "Beautiful but dangerous, like most weapons. Built for only one purpose—to kill. Things like this frighten me!"

"Ahoy upstairs, here's yore rope comin' up!"

Brink had returned again. He threw the rope, but not high enough. It snagged on a ledge lower down. Skipper reached out and looped it over the lancetip. He hauled the rope up and tied it round himself.

"I'll lower ye down one at a time. You first, Sister."

Once they were safely back with the main party, mole-mum Burbee hugged her friend the Abbess. "Oi'm surrpintly glad to see ee back in one piece, moi dearie. May'aps us'n's should be takin' tea an' cakes down in ee kitchings."

Lycian kissed Burbee's velvety old cheek. "A splendid idea, lots of tea and plenty of cakes for everybeast. I certainly think we all deserve it!"

Happy that their mission had proven successful, the Redwallers made their way downstairs, laughing and chattering. They had hardly entered the kitchens when Brother Perant came hurrying up in a state of great agitation.

"Skipper, Brink, come quickly, before that crazy bird kills somebeast. It's out on the lawn!"

Gripping the lance, the otter chieftain raced out across Great Hall. "Keep those Dibbuns inside. Brink and you others, come with me!"

As they reached the Abbey door, a cacophony of sound could be plainly heard from outside. The harvest mouse Gatekeepers, Oreal and his wife, Hillyah, were frantically trying to distract the gannet away from Irgle and Ralg, their twin babes. The hungry predator loomed over the little ones, determined to eat them. Oreal and Hillyah kept running at the big bird, shouting and waving their paws, which were bleeding from where the maddened bird had pecked them. The babes were wailing piteously, hugging each other tight, trying to hide in a clump of lupins. Having tasted blood, the gannet was shrieking and squawking defiantly, bent on taking its prey. Adding to the din and confusion, Brantalis waddled speedily into the fray. Honking and hissing, the barnacle goose attacked the gannet, beating wildly at it with outspread wings.

Sizing up the situation at a glance, Skipper roared out above the melee, "Everybeast, stay back! Brink, take Girry, Tribsy an' Brinty with ye! Circle round an' get the main gate open! We've got to herd that bird outside an' lock it out!"

251

Wielding the lance of Corriam, Skipper charged the gannet. Brantalis was fighting gamely but was getting the worst of the exchange. He was no match for the ferocious bird's webbed talons and lightning-swift beak.

Skipper came quickly to his rescue. The courageous otter plunged into the brawl of feathers, flapping wings, beaks and claws. He dealt the gannet a punishing blow to the neck, using the lance like a quarterstaff. *Rap! Thud!* Two more hard smacks across the gannet's back sent it reeling. Immediately it came back at Skipper, who jabbed at it as he circled. The Gatekeepers took advantage of the moment to nip in and rescue their babes.

Skipper was calling to Brantalis, "Don't let that bird get back to the Abbey. Keep it movin' toward the main gate!"

The Cellarhog and his three helpers had the gates open wide, all shouting words of encouragement as Skipper and the barnacle goose drove the enraged gannet toward it.

"Keep the villain comin', Skip!"

"Burr, watch ee owt furr he'm beak, zurr!"

"Don't let the rascal get behind ye, mate!"

"Oh well done, sir! Give him another whack on the tail, he didn't like that at all!"

The gannet was still looking for a chance to do some damage, though now it was in retreat and almost out of the main gate. In their anxiety to get the bird out, Brantalis and Skipper collided. They went down in a heap.

Girry saw the gannet turning to renew its attack. Throwing caution to the winds, he ran out from where he and his companions were sheltering behind the gate. Flinging himself bodily on the gannet, he kicked, pummelled and punched the startled bird, yelling, "Gerrout, you big bully, out of our Abbey!"

The gannet stumbled, regained its balance and dealt Girry a vicious peck, which pierced his ear. Brinty came dashing to the aid of his friend. His assault on the foebird was so sudden that he forced it out of the gates, onto the path. Shaking with fright but amazed at his own audacity, the young mouse turned, waving and grinning at the Red-wallers, who were pouring across the lawns.

"Redwaaaaalll! Haha, we did it!"

Nobeast was prepared for what happened next. Behind Brinty's back, a young rat leaped out of the ditch on the opposite side of the path. He was brandishing a crude sword fashioned from a scythe blade. The rat struck Brinty down with one cruel slash.

"Told yer I'd pay ye back someday, didden't I?!"

It was Groffgut, leader of the young water rat gang. He turned to run but was stopped by the lance of Corriam. Skipper had thrown it true and hard. Groffgut stared stupidly at the lance sprouting from his chest. Then he fell dead without a sound.

The gannet had stumbled into the ditch. The screams emanating from there indicated that he had at last found food, the remainder of the water rat gang. Brink Greyspoke, the first Redwaller to reach Brinty, carried him hastily into the gatehouse. Girry and Tribsy followed him anxiously. Skipper went to retrieve the lance and found it broken for the second time. Groffgut had fallen clumsily, his weight having knocked the lance sideways, causing it to snap. Picking up the broken halves, Skipper pushed Groffgut's carcass into the ditch. It fell in a heap on two other bodies: Plugtail's and Frogeye's. The gannet glared up at the otter, who had disturbed its grisly feast. The otter chieftain met its gaze with narrowed eyes.

"Here's another one for ye. I suppose the rest have run off—well, no matter, mate. You carry on with yore vittles, then go an' track 'em down, easy meat, eh? But I warn ye bird, show yore beak in Redwall again, an' I'll slay ye!"

The gannet got the message. It watched Skipper stride back into the Abbey grounds and lock the gate. The big bird gave a satisfied squawk and returned to its gruesome fare.

Skipper could not bear to go into the gatehouse. He skirted the doorway, which was packed with shocked Redwallers who could not get inside.

Brink was sitting on the west wallsteps, weeping unashamedly. "Pore young Brinty! He didn't stand a chance, Skip."

The otter sat down beside his friend, at a loss to say something about the untimely death of Brinty. He dropped the broken halves of the lance into Brink's lap.

"At least I got the scum who murdered him. This lance is wrecked, mate. Cellarhogs are good at carpentry. D'ye think it could be repaired?"

Sniffing loudly and scrubbing a paw across his eyes, Brink strove to get back to normality. He inspected the broken ends closely. "May'aps I could, Skip. 'Tis only the wood at the middle come adrift from this silver sleeve wot's been holdin' it t'gether. Here, what's this? There's somethin' jammed inside the sleeve."

Brink tapped the tube of beaten silver against the wallstep until a piece of yellow metal protruded from its end. He took a grip of the metal in his strong, blunt claws. "You hold onto the sleeve, Skip. I'll get this out."

Skipper grasped the sleeve tightly, whilst Brink jiggled the thing free. It was a slender circlet of pure gold, which had been squashed flat to fit inside the sleeve. Set into the gold was a big green stone of uncanny brilliance.

"Ever together the two have been set,
    since Corriam's lance ate the coronet!"

They looked up, discovering Old Quelt as the speaker. "What you have there, my friends, is the crown of the High Queen Rhulain!"

After a while, Abbess Lycian had to clear the gatehouse of mourners. Molemum Burbee, with Grudd Foremole and his crew, would take on the sad task of dressing Brinty in a clean habit and preparing the young mouse for his final rest. Even amid all the sorrow, word had got out of Skipper and Brink's discovery. To take their mind off things, the kindly Brink invited all the Redwallers to his cellars, where they could watch him restoring the coronet.

Lycian sat with her paws around Girry and Tribsy, trying to cheer them up. "Come on now, imagine what Brinty would say if he could see you both, wailing like a pair of Dibbuns on bath night! We've found Tiria's crown for her. Now watch what Mister Greyspoke is doing."

Brink had covered the head of a wooden mallet with a soft cloth. He had looped the squashed coronet around the spur of his anvil. Moving the coronet around slowly, he beat at it gently, explaining the process as he worked.

"Pure gold is a soft metal, easy to shape. If'n ye go gently, it shouldn't crack or break. Softly does it now, never beat too hard, an' be careful not to hit the pretty green stone. There now, that should do it!"

He held the restored coronet up for all to see. "A crown fit for the head of a queen, eh?"

The onlookers stared admiringly at the beauty and simplicity of the object.

When drinks had been served all around, Abbess Lycian made a small speech. "Redwallers, it is always sad when we lose one of our friends. More so, when it is a young creature who was not fated to live out his full seasons. We will never forget Brinty. Let us drink to all the happy memories we have of him. To Brinty!"

Everybeast repeated the name and drank. In the silence that followed, Skipper had a word to say. "He was a good an' cheerful young mouse, an' a true friend to all, includin' my daughter Tiria."

Girry felt he had to say something. "He saved me from the gannet. Brinty was very brave!" Then the young squirrel touched the bandage around his ear and fell silent.

Tribsy made a visible effort to finish the tribute. As he spoke, tears coursed down the young mole's homely face. "Hurr, our pore Brinty, he'm wurr ee bestest friend us'n's ever haved! We'm be a missin' 'im furrever."

26

Tiria had never been beneath the sea before. It was strangely silent, with only the muted sound of an air bubble or two. Translucent green light from above gave the subterranean world an oddly sinister aspect. As Tiria descended, keeping one paw on the rock face and the other gripping her lifeline, the water grew colder and colder. The outlook became decidedly gloomy as the ottermaid progressed downward. Soon she could see no further than her extended paw. The young ottermaid began to wonder just how far down the Rhulain's wrecked ship lay.

Then she felt her rudder scrape the seabed—a mass of gritty sand, kelp, rock and little else. Feeling slightly cheated that she had not landed on the deck of the submerged vessel, Tiria groped about with her free paw. Nothing! She began to wonder if maybe the wreck had been moved by undersea currents or perhaps, after all the long ages, it had disintegrated and sunk beneath the sand. Who was to say? Then her footpaw struck something. She bent to discover what it was and felt a heavy ship's timber protruding from the seabed amid a jumble of rocky debris. Sifting her paw into the sand, Tiria encountered another object and pulled it free, holding it close to her face. It was smooth, with some holes in it, a sickly pale white thing. A large bubble burst from her mouth as she gasped in horror. It was the skull of an otter! She was standing on top of a mass grave. All the bones of the crew were trapped within the sunken hulk, lying beneath an impenetrable weight of sand and rock. Searching for a slim gold coronet in these cold lonely depths was a fool's errand, an impossibility. Tiria pushed off from the scene, bitterly regretting the failure of her mission.

She did not see the long dark shape streaking out from amid the kelp-festooned rocks. It struck her hard in the back, knocking the air from her lungs in a bubbling gush. Then the thing had her in a vicelike grip. Panic caused the ottermaid to struggle wildly, but the heavy coils enveloped her in their cruel embrace. Still holding on to the rope, Tiria wrenched both paws free. Amid the morass of debris-filled water, she saw a brutishly evil head striking at her face. Grabbing the bulky neck she fought to hold it off, thrusting frantically against the onslaught of a gaping mouthful of serrated teeth. The monster's black, gold-rimmed eyes stared pitilessly at her as it pushed savagely toward her face. Then it squirmed, spinning her around to increase its purchase. In that moment, bereft of any breath of air but with a surge of energy brought on by naked terror, Tiria twirled the rope around the creature's huge head. The lifeline looped twice, just below its jaw. The ottermaid jerked the lifeline sharply. One! Two!

Half conscious and still battling the thick, sinuous body, Tiria felt herself shooting toward the surface. She was hauled roughly into bright sunlight, with Mandoral's battle-cry ringing in her ears. "Eulaliiiiaaaaa!"

Spewing seawater and flailing feebly in the grip of the thing from the depths, both Tiria and the monster were dragged aboard the *Petunia*. Instantly, Cuthbert and the two subalterns flung themselves on the thing. Kicking, punching, battering and biting, they freed Tiria from its crushing stranglehold. Mandoral seized the rope, slashing through it with his fearsome teeth. Quartle and Portan were knocked flat by the thick, writhing body, but Cuthbert and the Badger Lord grabbed it between them. They bundled it over the side, coil by coil, into the sea, where it slithered off, with surprising alacrity, down into the dark depths.

Still conscious, Tiria staggered across the deck on all fours, gasping, "Wh . . . wh . . . what was it?"

Lord Mandoral shook his great striped head. "It looked like some kind of large water serpent!"

Cuthbert helped Tiria to stand upright. "Hahar, 'tweren't no sarpint, that was an ole conger, the giant eel o' the seas! Yore lucky t'be still alive, Tilly, mate. I never knew nobeast t'stand up to a conger, 'specially a giant one like that rascal!"

Quartle and Portan thought otherwise.

"Except Lord Mandoral an Ole Blood'n'guts, wot!"

"Absolutely! Three cheers for Lord Mandoral an' Ole Blood'n . . . beg pardon, Major Blanedale Frunk. Hip hip!"

From the mast top, Pandion joined in raucously.

On her return to the mountain, Tiria sought out her room in the guest quarters. She slumped on the bed, overcome by a sense of depression. She had failed to retrieve the coronet and, to compound her misery, had had to be rescued from an eel. Having had little sleep the previous night and wearied by her ordeal in the sea, the ottermaid closed her eyes and fell asleep.

Judging by the angle of the light slanting through the window, Tiria guessed it was early evening when she was awakened by somebeast knocking on her door. She sat up, yawning and stretching.

"Come in, please."

Captain Rafe Granden marched smartly in and deposited the regalia which Mandoral had given Tiria on the bedside table. The tough-looking hare saluted her.

"Lord Mandoral's compliments, miz. He requests that y'join him at top table for dinner this evenin'. He sent these togs so's you can attend in full fig, wot."

Tiria took one look at the regalia and shook her head. "I'd rather not, Cap'n Rafe. Give his Lordship my apologies. I'll be staying here on my own."

The stern-faced captain looked straight ahead, continuing to speak as if he had not heard the ottermaid. "Dinner'll be served shortly, miz. I'll send Subalterns Quartle an' Portan to escort ye t'the mess. Ye'll be dressed an' ready to attend!"

Tiria protested. "But I've just told you—"

Captain Granden interrupted her abruptly. "I must inform ye, miz, any refusal would be taken as an insult t'the ruler o' Salamandastron. Nobeast refuses a Badger Lord, not done, young 'un, rank bad form, y'know. So, I'll leave ye t'make yourself presentable. Y'servant, miz!"

The captain's tone left Tiria in no doubt that she was to be Mandoral's dinner guest, willing or not. He saluted stiffly and marched speedily off.

Tiria had hardly donned the new attire when her two subalterns arrived. Both were taken aback at her appearance. Quartle bowed several times, and Portan tripped over his own footpaws whilst trying to make an elegant leg.

He grinned foolishly. "I say I say I say, blow me down an' all that, wot wot!"

His companion was equally voluble. "By the cringe an' by the flippin' left, Miss Tiria, if you ain't a perfect picture, I'll eat me aunt's pinny!"

Tiria had to admit to herself that the regalia fitted her exquisitely. She felt every inch the warrior queen, even though she lacked a coronet. Taking both the young hares' proffered paws, she smiled regally.

"Let us proceed to the mess, chaps, wot!"

As they strolled down the corridor to the main mess hall, Tiria could hear massed voices raised in a regimental song.

"Here is our mountain an' this is its Lord,
now sit we down at festive board,
come put aside weapons, both lance an' sword,
let's honour the regiment.

259

One two! I'll drink to you!
an' all my comrades good an' true!
We'll raise the tankard, fill the bowl,
to Salamandastron's Long Patrol!

For warriors fallen from the ranks,
defending western shores,
let's toast 'em all, each gallant hare,
who died for freedom's cause!

Let blood'n'vinegar be our cry,
forward the buffs an' do or die,
we don't know fear or failure,
Eulalia! Eulaliiiiiaaaaaaaa!"

Amid the rousing cheers, shouts and paws pounding tables,
Tiria was escorted to her place. She was seated between
Lord Mandoral and Cuthbert, flanked by Captain Granden
and some very senior-looking officers. When the noise had
reached deafening proportions, the brazen boom of a big
gong echoed through the mess. With the exception of those
at top table, every hare shot bolt upright in rigid silence.

An old colonel, rake thin and sporting long, drooping
mustachios, waited until he received the Badger Lord's nod.
Then, in a wobbly voice, he announced, "Gentlebeasts, ye
may be seated!"

There followed a resounding clatter of benches and
chairs. Then the customary din broke out afresh. Good-
humoured ribaldry went back and forth as the orderlies
wheeled out laden serving trolleys.

"I say, chaps, who's that beautiful gel sittin' next to his
Lordship, wot?"

"Well, it ain't you, Mobbs! You could blinkin' well turn
apples sour by just lookin' at 'em!"

"Oh, go an' boil your fat head, Gribbsy, you've got no
eye for beauty at all. Hah, your motto is, if ye can't eat it,
then it ain't nice!"

"Give your bloomin' jaw a rest, Mobbs old lad. What's for dinner, cookie old thing?"

The supply master sergeant, a huge hare with a broken nose, glared at the offender. "A dry crust an' a short whistle if'n you call me cookie again, me laddo!"

A stout lance corporal chuckled. "Hawhaw, that's the stuff to give him, cookie, you tell the blighter. Hawhawhaw!"

He withered under the sergeant's icy stare. "Ye've never tasted my lance corporal pie, have ye? One more remark from you, young Flibber, an' I'll send a slice home to yore mother!"

The food was excellent and the portions enormous. Tiria was relieved to be sitting by Cuthbert, who devoured everything she nudged to within his paw range. Not a crumb that came near the gluttonous hare was spared.

"Good show, wot! The old mountain pie, ain't tasted that in a blinkin' badger's age, wot!"

He dealt rapidly with summer salad, baked mushroom and turnip flan, cheese and carrot turnover, barley and leek soup and a plate of potato and chestnut pasties. Licking crumbs from his whiskers, Cuthbert began chivvying the servers for dessert.

Lord Mandoral eyed Tiria with obvious approval. "I was right, you are truly a High Queen, Tiria Wildlough."

With a downcast gaze, the ottermaid mumbled, "I'm a queen without a crown. I failed miserably at that wreck today, sir. It was a disaster!"

Her paw was enveloped by the big badger's own. "Nonsense, you were very brave! Huh, just the thought of you down there in the dark depths, battling with a monster, made my blood run cold. I don't mind telling you, it's not a thing I would have fancied attempting. But you went to it without a second thought. Mark my words, miss, that was the true sign of a leader, a real warrior!"

When dinner was over, the usual din of rowdy ballads and loud jokes broke out. This was halted by a big, barrel-chested hare. Colour Sergeant O'Cragg had a thunderous voice.

"H'atten . . . shun! Silence h'in the ranks, ye gobboons! Milord Mandoral 'as the floor. Sah!"

Staying seated, the badger made his announcement. "At noon tomorrow, Major Blanedale Frunk will be sailing for Green Isle. His purpose, to establish Lady Tiria Wildlough in her rightful position as queen there!"

Tiria looked about to say something, but a forbidding glance from Captain Granden bade her to hold any questions.

Mandoral paused, his eyes roving the mess. "There will be some opposition to this move from vermin foebeasts, wildcats, I am led to believe. Therefore, I would be remiss in my duty, sending the Lady with only Major Frunk and a hawk for protection. Major, how many of our Long Patrol could your vessel accommodate?"

Cuthbert's ears twitched pensively. "Hmm, let me see, sah. The *Petunia* could take a limit of twoscore. But if ye count weapons, vittles an' all that tackle, I'd say a score'n a half safely, Milord."

Mandoral had no reason to doubt the old hare's estimate. "A score and a half it is, then. Captain Granden, you'll command when they reach Green Isle. Please select thirty hares for the task. Mind, I only want seasoned warriors, the best our Long Patrol can offer."

Every hare in the mess sat stiffly to attention, each longing to be chosen for the mission. Captain Granden drew his long rapier and began striding slowly between the tables. He tapped the chosen ones on the shoulder with his blade, naming them.

"Colour Sergeant O'Cragg, Master Sergeant Bann, Corporal Drubblewick, Lieutenant Sagetip. . . ."

He continued until he had the required number. Tiria saw her two subalterns sitting with moist eyes, the very pictures of dejection. Standing up, she called out, "Excuse me, Cap'n

Rafe. I'd like to take Quartle and Portan along with me to Green Isle."

Granden shook his head vigourously. "Not possible I'm afraid, m'Lady. They're both too young!"

Tiria objected. "How can you say that? They're about the same age as I am!"

Mandoral interrupted. "You heard the captain, Lady. He's in charge of the expedition. If he says they're too young, then you must take his decision as final."

The ottermaid looked from the Badger Lord to the captain. Aware that everybeast in the mess was watching her keenly, she drew herself up regally and spoke out firmly. "If I am to become Queen of Green Isle, I have to learn to make my own decisions. I say the subalterns will go!"

Granden's face hardened. Thrusting out his jaw, he responded firmly, "I have made my choice, miz, and it stands. They stay!"

Tiria sat down slowly. Her reply was somewhat cool and distant. "Then I stay, too. That is my decision, Captain."

In the awed silence which followed, Granden looked in bewilderment to Mandoral, whose booming laugh broke the suspense. "Hohoho! You don't disobey a queen, Captain. I think you should defer to Her Majesty."

Granden locked eyes with Tiria, staring hard at her. Not to be intimidated, she stared back just as hard. Suddenly the glimmer of a smile twitched the stern captain's lips. He bowed elegantly and sheathed his rapier.

"As you wish, Milady. The subalterns sail with us!"

Thunderous cheers and loud applause rang out for Tiria. Quartle and Portan hastened to her side, grinning madly.

"I say, stifle me flamin' scut, miz. Top hole, well done!"

"Rather! That's the first time I've ever seen old granite-gob Granden backin' down to any blinkin' beast, wot!"

Still chuckling, Mandoral beckoned to her. "Make sure you treat Captain Granden right. He was only carrying out my orders."

263

Tiria kept a straight face as she replied graciously. "Milord, we queens treat everybeast fairly, both our subjects and our allies!"

Both Tiria and Mandoral suddenly broke out laughing.

The following afternoon, a light breeze ruffled the suntipped waves in the bay as the *Purloined Petunia* rode, fully laden, at anchor. Regimental Major-cum-Captain Cuthbert Bloodpaw Frunk stood high on the stern. With a ladle in each paw, he hovered over the upturned barrel which would serve as his stroke drum. The vessel's oar ports had been opened, twelve each to port and starboard. Twenty-four hares sat waiting, each gripping a long oar. Quartle and Portan sat either side of the tiller, ready to steer outward bound. Pandion Piketalon perched at the masthead; below him, two hares straddled the crosspiece. Up for'ard, the two burly sergeants stood by the anchor cable. Tiria was alone, out on the prow, facing west to the open sea.

Cuthbert was in his element as he began roaring orders to all and sundry in his roughest maritime tones. "Ahoy, let's go to sea, me buckoes! Haul anchor, ye slab-sided scallawags! Make sail aloft, ye blunderin' bluebottles! We're bound for death or glory, whichever comes first!"

Boom! Boom! Boom! Boom! As he belaboured his drum, he bellowed out orders to the rowing crew. "Bend yore backs, ye skinny sideswabs! Avast there, ye paddle-pawed poltroons! Pull! Pull! Pullllll!"

The big hare felt happier than he had for many long seasons. "Steersbeasts! Hold her westward, ye dither-pawed dodderers! Sweep oars! Pull, ye gripe-gutted galoots! Heave ho, me blunderin' buckoes! I'll make seabeasts of ye, or I'll wallop yore whiskers, keelhaul yore scuts an' nail yore noses t'the mainmast! Pull! Puuuuullllll!"

The ship, caught by the breeze and swept on by two dozen long sweep oars, shot forward like a flying fish.

Pandion raised his beak to the sun-kissed skies. "Karraheeee! Take me to my home! Karreeehaarr!"

264

The two subalterns gripped the tiller tight between them, amazed at the speed the ship was gaining by the moment.

"I say, Quarters, in a bit of a blinkin' hurry aren't we, wot!"

"Rather, Porters. D'you think Ole Blood'n'guts is tryin' to gain a march, so's we can stop for tea?"

Cuthbert leaned over them both, squinting villainously. "Either of yew chubby-cheeked charmers lets go of that tiller an' I'll make subaltern skilly'n'duff out o' ye both. How'd ye like that for tea, eh?"

Lord Mandoral stood at the window of his high chamber. He saw reflecting sunlight flashing from Tiria's armour as she stood on the bowsprit, waving good-bye to him. The Badger Lord merely nodded his big striped head in acknowledgement. He watched the vessel receding over the water, its long sweep oars making it look like a damselfly skimming over a vast millpond.

Mandoral's lips barely moved as he softly chanted an old warrior's farewell to the tall young ottermaid he had come to respect and admire.

"May fair winds attend thee always,
may thy days be bright and long,
may good weapons ever serve thee,
may thy limbs wax fleet and strong.
I will dream of thee by moonlight,
I will watch for thee by day,
until on thy returning,
I will come to thee and say,
'Drink ye the wine of victory,
now lay aside thy sword,
for home and hearth and friendship
are the warrior's reward!'"

27

Leatho Shellhound struggled wildly to avoid the spear as Kaltag stabbed viciously down at him. Bound as he was by both paws to the cage bars, he did not have much room for manoeuvre. The outlaw ducked his head forward, wrenching his body to one side as the wooden cage rocked madly against the high tower wall. He felt a stinging pain close to his left paw as the spearhead glanced off it.

Kaltag's eyes glittered in the darkness as she drew back the weapon and thrust it down, screeching out vengeance for her dead son. "Eeeyaaaah! Go to Hellgates, murderer! Die! Die!"

Twice more the spear grazed Leatho as he wriggled about within the confines of his narrow prison. Defiant to the end, he roared insults at his tormentor. "Is that the best ye can do, Mangetail? Ye need a few lessons with the spear. Cut me loose, Scruffcoat, an' I'll show ye how it's done!"

Kaltag yowled with rage. Gripping the spearpole with both paws, she centred on the back of the otter's neck, readying herself for the killing strike.

Leatho knew his fate was sealed. Bound and helpless, he could not last much longer. He tensed himself, listening to the cat's rasping breath above him. Suddenly a hubbub broke out from the upper chamber. The spear slithered down through the bars and stuck, quivering, point first, in the pier far below.

Kaltag began wailing insanely. "Let me go, take your stupid paws off me! Shellhound must pay for my son's death!"

Weilmark Scaut and two catguards held her tight, dragging her back from the windowsill. Kaltag bit, scratched and kicked at them, but to no avail, as the three cats hauled her roughly from the chamber.

Riggu Felis stood outside. Quickly he slammed the door shut, snarling, "Get her downstairs. Nobeast comes into this room but me!"

Kaltag was borne away, yelling accusations at the wildcat. "Coward! Traitor! Will you see Jeefra's killer left alive?"

The warlord yelled down the stairwell after her, "Keep that madbeast away from here. She'll ruin all my plans. I need Shellhound alive!"

Felis went into the chamber and stole across to the window. Leaning out, he rattled the cage with his axehaft, taunting the captive. "Well, I'm glad to see you still alive, my friend."

As Leatho looked up, he could see the disfigured face beneath the chain mail half-mask. He growled scornfully at the wildcat. "That's more'n I can say for you, ripface!"

Felis continued baiting his prisoner. "Would you like a drink of water? I'll spare you some if you beg for it. Lovely cold, fresh, clear water, just beg nicely and I'll tell the guards to fetch some."

For answer, Leatho bared his teeth and rattled the cage. "All I'll beg for is a chance to get out of here an' stand facin' yore ugly mug. Then it'll be yore turn to beg!"

The wildcat backed off slowly, calling to his captive, "Oh, I'll let you loose soon enough, the moment your friends surrender to me. Then they can watch you licking my footpaws every day, with Scaut whipping you whenever you stop. That should make a pretty sight, eh?"

The outlaw heard the chamber door slam shut. He sagged forward in his bonds, head drooping. To his surprise, the rope holding his left paw creaked, stretching slightly. Hope surged anew through Leatho. He jerked and tugged on the rope, feeling the fibres starting to part. The spear, of course, it had to be! In the darkness, Kaltag's frenzied stabs must have hit the rope, partially slicing through and weakening it.

Leatho could not twist his head far enough to inspect the rope, but he knew he could eventually snap it. Even though his limbs were swollen and numbed with cramp, the tenacious otter pulled, twisted and jerked against his bond. Each fresh assault tore more of the fibres, snapping away the closely woven strands. He grunted with pain as one final wrench parted the rope, allowing the deadened paw to hang limply at his side. Dizzy with the effort, Leatho rested for a moment. Then, with no firm plan in mind, he set about freeing his other paw. Hauling himself up on the bars, the outlaw got his teeth into the other rope. He gnawed away, strand by strand, until he had chewed right through it. With a deep sigh, he allowed himself the luxury of sitting down on the cage floor. Leatho slowly rubbed the life back into his aching limbs and shoulders, thinking hard. Now, what next?

Early birds began their twittering chorus in the first rays of dawn as the otterclans arrived at the far shores of the lake. Crouching in the rushes, surrounded by his warriors, Big Kolun Galedeep cooled his paws in the cold water. He peered through the mist, which hung like a milky veil over the stillwater.

"Wot d'ye think, should we go in now?"

His brother, the tall, sombre Lorgo, spat on his paws, rubbing them together in anticipation. "Aye, dawn's a good time to attack. The cats won't be up an' about just yet!"

Banya Streamdog interrupted them. "Hold on, mates. We can't go chargin' in without a plan. If'n the Felis cat's got Leatho a prisoner, he's bound to have the fortress well guarded. Stands t'reason he'll be expectin' us to try somethin'."

Kolun dug his big oar into the water moodily. "I s'pose yore right, so wot d'ye suggest we do? We can't just lie here all day twiddlin' our rudders!"

Besides being a tough warriormaid, Banya was seldom short of practical ideas. "A sensible plan would be t'send out scouts first. Whulky, Chab, you take the left bank. Lugg, Ganno, you take the right. See if they're patrollin' the pier an' the slave compound. Make a count of the cats y'can see an' wot sort of weapons they're totin'. That way we'll know just wot we're up against. Oh, an' most important, keep yore eyes skinned for the Shellhound."

In the main gate lodge which led onto the pier, Riggu Felis took a leisurely breakfast. The wildcat felt that, with his plans reaching fruition, his position was becoming more secure. Picking at a freshly caught trout and sipping pale wine, he reflected on other matters which required his attention. It was one of the warlord's strengths: He never left loose ends untied.

Weilmark Scaut stood attendance upon his master, a task which invariably made him nervous, owing to the wildcat's unpredictable nature. After accidentally slopping wine onto the table while refilling the warlord's beaker, Scaut murmured apologetically, "Yore pardon, Lord."

Without helmet or mask, the face of Riggu Felis was set in a tight, fearsome grimace, owing to the severe injuries inflicted on him by the osprey. Scaut wiped up the spillage as the wildcat questioned him.

"Is my prisoner well guarded?"

The weilmark nodded vigorously. "Aye, Lord. I posted two guards on the chamber door, an' two more at the bottom o' the stairs."

The warlord's tongue licked pensively at his flayed upper gums. "Good. The Lady Kaltag, where is she?"

Scaut wondered where this conversation was leading. "In her room, Sire. I posted three guards on her door."

Felis sipped more wine. "See that she is closely watched. Well, we should be expecting those outlaw otters to pay us a visit sometime today, Scaut. Listen now, make sure the slave compound is well guarded, but keep the rest of my force out of sight. Don't send any guards out scouting or patrolling. Now, about the slaves, keep them penned tight in their quarters. I don't want them out working or fishing the lake. Is that understood?"

The weilmark bowed clumsily. "I hear you, Lord!"

The wildcat's next question caught the feral cat officer totally off guard. "Tell me, who do you think murdered my faithful counsellor?"

Scaut stared dumbly at the floor. "Sire, I don't know who slew Atunra."

Riggu Felis chided him mildly. "Come on, you must have some idea. Was it Pitru?"

The weilmark murmured unhappily, "Lord, it is not my place to accuse yore son."

The warlord put aside his beaker. "You recall that when we returned here after hunting the Shellhound and his crew, we learned that Atunra had gone missing. That was when Pitru appointed himself Fortress Commander, was it not?"

Scaut's head bobbed dutifully. "Aye, Lord, yore right."

The wildcat continued, staring fixedly at Scaut. "Pitru had some very close friends about him, three as I remember. One of them was an officer."

Scaut replied. "I don't recall the other two, but the officer was Scorecat Yund, Sire."

The warlord's torn features creased in a hideous grin. "That's the one, Scorecat Yund! Find him, bring him here to me. I'll find out who slew my pine marten."

It was now over an hour since daybreak. Bright summer sunlight had banished the mists from the lake surface.

Banya Streamdog called out to Kolun, "Will ye quit paddlin' round out there an' get back behind these reeds? Any beast with half an eye could spot an otter of yore size out in the open!"

Big Kolun Galedeep waded grumpily back into the reeds. "Where've yore scouts got to, missy? Huh, I could've done their job in half the time!"

Lorgo came up on tip-paw, then bent down again. "I can see Lugg an' Ganno headin' back along the bank."

Banya was watching twin ripples approaching along the lake. "That'll be Whulky'n'Chab if'n I ain't mistaken."

Both the aforesaid otters surfaced. They waded in through the reeds, arriving at the same time as Lugg and Ganno.

Kolun cautioned them needlessly, "Stay low, mates. Ye might be spotted by the cats!"

Whulky stood up and stretched his paws. "Wot cats? All we saw out there was birds an' a few fishes."

Banya sounded clearly baffled. "Ye saw no cats?"

Chab shook his head decisively. "Nary a frog, let alone a cat. An' there was no sign of Leatho, either. Everythin' was quiet at the fortress."

Kolun scratched his rudder. "Nobeast around, sounds funny t'me. Wot about you two?"

Lugg spoke for himself and Ganno. "We saw catguards posted all around the slave compound. I think they're keepin' the slaves locked up—there wasn't any about, workin', or fishin'. Didn't see the Shellhound, though. Don't know where they're keepin' him."

Lorgo spat away the reed stem he had been chewing on. "I think it's a trap! Those cats are sly villains."

Chab pawed water from his ear and shook himself. "Well, if it is a trap, mate, it's the easiest one I ever walked into, an' away from!"

Banya stared around at the puzzled and unhappy faces of the clanbeasts. She reached a sudden decision. "Well, we can't sit here forever. Make ready to march, mates. But pay heed—don't go chargin' an' dashin' into anythin'. We'll go slow'n'steady, split into three groups. Roggan Streamdiver, take yore clan an' the Wavedogs along the left shore. Kolun, you an' Lorgo take yore Galedeeps an' the Wildloughs to the right. I'll take my clan an' the Streambattles up the middle o' the lake. Remember, slow'n'steady. Watch out for traps an' ambushes, an' don't take no foolish chances!"

Big Kolun hefted his oar. "Aye, an' if ye do get into any trouble, just give a yell, an' we'll be there at the double. Good luck to everybeast. Let's hope we all make it back safe to our families at Summerdell. Let's go an' rescue Leatho Shellhound now!" The otterclans moved off silently.

Pitru was on his way to the barracks when he saw Weilmark Scaut and a six-guard escort approaching. He ducked into the cover of the guardhouse. Watching them closely, he observed firsthand their capture of Scorecat Yund as he emerged from the barracks.

Disregarding Yund's protests, they had grabbed him roughly and were now frogmarching him toward the main gate lodge. Pitru, immediately realising what this was all about, cursed himself for a fool. He should have guessed that his father would not leave Atunra's murder unavenged.

The young cat hurried into the barracks, where he was met by his other two close allies, Balur and Hinso. Both catguards appeared badly shaken.

"Commander, they've just dragged Scorecat Yund off!"

"It was Weilmark Scaut and a band of guards. Your father'll make Yund talk, he'll find out the truth about Atunra!"

Pitru grabbed them both by their whiskers, hissing at them, "Shut up, fools! Don't you think I already know that? Stop panicking and listen to me. Balur, get to the lodge window. See if you can hear what's going on in there, then report straight back to me! Hinso, gather all the guards that are loyal to me behind the barracks. Wait for me there. Quick now, both of you, our very lives depend on getting things right. Go!"

Yund was pushed inside the lodge, where Scaut and the rest dragged him to an iron ring set high in the wall. In a trice he was bound to it, with both paws stretched painfully over his head. Riggu Felis stalked over to him like a huge beast of prey, shoving his naked, skinned face close to Yund's horrified eyes. The scorecat could feel the warlord's rasping breath in his quivering nostrils. He quailed visibly, his limbs trembling uncontrollably as the wildcat began the interrogation with a harsh, blunt question.

"Tell me, who killed my counsellor Atunra?"

It took Yund several moments to find his voice. "Lord, I don't know. I swear it, Sire!"

Riggu Felis nodded, as though he had accepted the explanation. He continued in a more reasonable tone. "Yund, my friend, do you know that I can skin a beast with this axe of mine? It's a very sharp weapon."

The scorecat caught his breath as he felt the single-bladed war axe pressing against his throat.

The warlord continued in a casual, almost chatty tone. "Oh yes, and I'll wager you didn't know that I can keep that beast alive for nearly half a day after I've skinned him. He'll scream quite a lot, but that's only to be expected. Now, the one thing I can't abide is a liar. So this is your last chance, scorecat: Do you wish to tell me the truth? Who murdered my friend Atunra?"

Yund gave a prolonged whimpering sob, then spoke. "Lord, I was only carrying out orders."

The warlord removed the axe from Yund's throat. "I understand. You did what any obedient servant would. So, tell me more, who gave you the order? Speak, friend, don't be afraid. I wouldn't slay any true warrior of mine."

The scorecat uttered a deep sigh of relief. "Lord, it was your son, Commander Pitru, who ordered me to slay Atunra. I had to obey!"

Riggu Felis turned to Scaut, smiling. "You see, I knew it all the time, I only needed proof."

The weilmark came to attention. "Sire, shall I take the guards and arrest him?"

The warlord replaced his helmet and chain mail half-mask. "Not just yet, there are other matters to be dealt with. First, we must resolve the otter problem. After that, I will settle accounts with Pitru, once and for all."

Scaut saluted. "What about Scorecat Yund, Sire?"

Riggu Felis shrugged. "He is no true warrior of mine, only a traitor who would betray his commander. You may execute him, but not too swiftly. Make him realise the reward of treachery."

Scaut possessed a naturally cruel nature, so this was the sort of thing he enjoyed. A despairing shriek burst from Yund's lips as he saw Scaut draw a long, slim dagger from his belt. Suddenly, an urgent rap on the door distracted the warlord's attention.

"Yes, what is it?"

Scorecat Rinat entered, making a swift salute with her spear. "Lord, the outlaw otters have been sighted in large numbers. They are approaching from the far end of the lake!"

Riggu Felis gave a purr of delight. "Perfect! I'll put on my finest cloak and armour to welcome them!" Leaving the pier lodge, he went off to his chamber.

Balur crept away from the window and ran off to report to Pitru, with the screams of Scorecat Yund adding speed to his footpaws.

28

With the exception of Cuthbert, most of the Long Patrol hares were ill-suited to seafaring life. The *Purloined Petunia* had been outward bound little more than a day and a half from Salamandastron, yet she was making remarkable progress. The odd hare, in his role as the sea otter captain, Frunk W. Bloodpaw, had driven them hard both night and day. Initially, nearly all the crew were seasick, but Cuthbert, playing the bully skipper to the hilt, had worked them so severely that all thoughts of illness had been knocked out of them. He further compounded the treatment by singing them a shanty entitled "The Landlubber's Lament," accompanying himself on the ship's drum with his two ladles.

"There ain't nothin' like a life at sea,
when yore on pleasure bent,
so hearken crew, I'll sing to you,
The Landlubber's Lament
  bold lads, the Landlubber's Lament!

I dearly loves a storm each morn,
when the ship heaves up an' down,
an' up an' down an' up an' down,
an' oftimes round an' round
  bold lads, an' oftimes round an' round!

Wild gales rip through the riggin',
all the decks aflood with sea,
wid waves as high as mountains,
Ho, that's the life fer me
        bold lads, ho, that's the life fer me!

So I boils up some ole skilly,
an' I stirs the duff in too,
in me greasy liddle galley,
'tis the stuff t'feed the crew
        bold lads, the stuff t'feed the crew!

Pots o' cold'n'watery cabbage,
lots o' slimy turnip ends,
an' some fish heads with the eyes in,
to see that we're all friends
        bold lads, to see that we're all friends!

Then I'll feed ye second helpin's,
just t'keep ye well content,
an' at night I'll serenade ye,
with the Landlubber's Lament
        bold lads, the Landlubber's Lament!"

Tiria had put off her regalia whilst onboard, redressing in her old tunic and kilt. The ottermaid did not stand on the ceremony of her exalted rank; instead, she chose to take a turn at the oars with the hares. Sitting on the bench alongside Colour Sergeant O'Cragg, she rowed out the late-night watch, with both of them pulling lustily on a long sweep oar. The sergeant, a big sturdy hare, was usually taciturn by nature, seldom questioning things. But as they toiled together, he murmured to Tiria, "Beggin' yore pardon, miss, but h'are ye sure we're a-goin' the right way?"

He paused a while before voicing his thoughts. "Wot h'I means is this. When yore surrounded by water, h'everythin' looks the bloomin' same, miss. 'Ow d'ye suppose Cap'n Major Frunk knows where this 'ere Green h'Isle is?"

Tiria did not really know, but she thought up an answer.

"I expect he knows by the position of the moon and stars. Though in the daytime, the cap'n steers by the sun, which always rises in the east and sets in the west. Also, we have our osprey. If the ship strays off course, Pandion can fly out and find the right way to go."

Sergeant O'Cragg was satisfied with her explanation. "Thankee, miss, 'tis good t'know. Though h'if 'twas me steerin' by those stars, we'd soon be lost. 'Ave ye ever seen 'ow many stars there is h'in the sky at night?"

Tiria turned her gaze upward. What the sergeant said was true. On first glance, there seemed to be the usual amount of stars, but as she continued to look, more stars than she had ever dreamed of became visible. All the vast tracts of the nightdark sky were aglitter with innumerable pinpoints of light—some large, some small, others so minute that they resembled dust, covering infinite areas of the uncharted dark vaults. It was a staggering sight.

Tiria lowered her eyes, blinking as she agreed with her companion. "Good grief, Sergeant, there seems to be more stars than sky up there. I've never looked long enough to notice it before, it's almost beyond belief!"

As they bent their backs to the oar stroke, Sergeant O'Cragg came up with another question. "Wot d'ye suppose they really h'are, miss?"

This time Tiria was stuck for an answer. "I don't know, I've never really thought about it. Have you any ideas, Sergeant?"

He surprised her with his reply. "They're the spirits h'of warriors, miss, h'every brave beast that ever fell h'in battle. Leastways that's wot ole Colonel Gorsebloom used t'tell me when h'I was nought but a liddle leveret. The colonel brought me h'up, y'see. H'I don't recall 'avin' no parents, miss."

Tiria glanced sideways at her hulking oarmate. He looked embarrassed by his own words. She gave him a friendly smile. "Really, I wonder what made him say that?"

277

O'Cragg shrugged. " 'Cos h'I asked 'im. The colonel taught me this 'ere poem h'about stars. Would ye like to 'ear it, miss?"

Tiria replied readily. "I'd love to, if you can still remember it."

The colour sergeant winked at her. " 'Course h'I can, just lissen t'this."

Proudly, he recited the poem taught to him by his old mentor.

"There are many places a spirit may rest
when life's long march has ended.
Every creature returns to its home,
exactly as nature intended.
The cowards and traitors, the liars and cheats,
each in their turn is awarded,
someplace that they deserved to go,
as their actions in life accorded.
Those who proved untrue to their friends
lie thick in the dust of the earth,
trodden on forever by all
to show what treachery's worth.
In the mud of swamps, in rotting weeds,
they lie imprisoned by evil misdeeds.
But the warriors true, the brave of heart,
who valiantly upheld the right,
they are raised on high, to the velvet sky,
bringing light to the darkness of night.
They'll stand there as long as the sky will,
their honour in brightness will glow,
a lesson to see, for eternity,
of where the real warriors go!
So ere my eyelids close in sleep,
these are the words I will say,
may I have the courage and faithfulness,
that my spirit should join them one day."

The ship sped on through the night as they rowed in silence. Tiria was lost for words. Who would have thought that the big colour sergeant, hard as granite and tough as oakwood, had a heart so innocent and simple? In the midst of these thoughts, she was startled by the arrival of their relief, Quartle and Portan.

"I say, shove over, you chaps. The blinkin' buffs have arrived, wot!"

"Rather, we'll be rowing the jolly old tub until dawn!"

Tiria and the sergeant rose from the bench as the two subalterns scrambled into their places at the sweeps.

Quartle twiddled his ears in a jocular manner. "Expect your old royal royalness is about ready for some flippin' shuteye, eh, miz?"

Portan winked impudently at the sergeant. "Nighty night, Sarge, off y'go, wot! I'll bet you dream about bullyin' green-nosed recruits round the old barrack square. Leff right, leff right, pick those paws up, laddy buck!"

Colour Sergeant O'Cragg riveted them to their seats with his famous parade-ground glare. "One more word out of ye, an' h'I'll pick yore paws h'up an' sling ye h'into the sea, you 'orrible liddle beasties!"

Tiria was still chuckling as she wrapped herself in an old cloak and lay down behind the small galley. Slumber was not long in claiming her after half a night of rowing. Cuthbert never slept; when on board, he was constantly on duty. The odd hare sat at the tiller in a sort of half-doze, steering his vessel by instinct. Apart from the gentle lap of waves, it was quiet. The *Purloined Petunia* ploughed smoothly over the deeps, on into the starstrewn night. Thirty-one hares, a fish hawk and one ottermaid westward bound.

In the grey half-light preceding dawn, Tiria was awakened by the high piercing call of the osprey. She looked up to the masthead to find that Pandion had gone. Making her way

279

astern, the ottermaid found Cuthbert still seated at the tiller with one eye open. She questioned him briefly.

"It's not light yet. Where's Pandion gone?"

Cuthbert scratched his ear lazily. "That ole rascal comes an' goes as he pleases, Tillie me gel. May'aps he's spotted land, I don't know."

Racing for'ard, Tiria scrambled out onto the bowsprit and scanned the sea around her. The waters were smooth, with hardly a wave of any size, blanketed by a mist that had taken on a soft golden haze as the sun began to rise. Visibility was virtually nonexistent, but from somewhere far off she could distinguish the muted cry of gulls. Hanging on to the bowline, Tiria leaned out, peering keenly into the waking day. Behind her the sail flapped idly and began to fill. The same breeze which was stirring it began to shift the mist rapidly.

Tiria stood stock-still, her eyes following the receding mists. Suddenly her fur rose from rudder to eartip as she picked out the dark blotch on the western horizon. There it was! Raising a paw to her mouth, Tiria bellowed, "Land dead ahead! Land hoooooooooo!"

The ship came alive to her cries. A babble of excited chatter broke out.

"I say, you chaps, did somebeast say land a bally head?"

"Eulalia! There 'tis, jolly old land, we made it, wot!"

"Get some blinkin' breakfast served, I ain't goin' ashore on an empty tum. I get vexatious without vittles, y'know!"

"Oh, my giddy aunt, just look, terra flippin' firma. I can't wait t'get me confounded paws on it!"

Cuthbert's shouts rang out above the clamour. "Getcher idle bottoms back on those oar benches, ye shower o' bobbin' beetles! Who gave the order for ye to stand round chattin' an' gawpin' like a gang of ole mousewives on a trip round the bay? Shape up, an' let's see a few rosy blisters on those lily white paws from rowin'! Heave an' row an' row an' pull an' push an' pull! Row! Row!"

Passing over the tiller to Rafe Granden, Cuthbert wasted

no time in retrieving his barrelhead drum. Soon it was booming as he battered away with his two ladles, still harassing the crew to action.

"Row, ye bilge-bottomed blaggards! Brekkist! Wot swab mentioned brekkist, eh? Ye don't get a single sniff o' the cook's apron until the keel hits the shallows! Row! Let's hear those backbones a-creakin', git those sweeps movin', ye misbegotten maggots, ye far-flung flotsam, ye jumped-up jetsam!"

Quartle sniggered to Portan as they pulled furiously, "Ole Blood'n'guts says the nicest things, don't he? I always wanted to be a jumped-up jetsam!"

He missed the stroke and tumbled backward. "Whoops, sorry, must've caught a crab!"

Portan whispered as he pulled his comrade upright, "Well, don't tell anybeast, old lad. They'll all want some!"

The wind stiffened, sending the vessel riding full tilt and landward. Once again, Cuthbert started berating his hapless crew. "Lay to wid those oars! D'ye want to run us onto a reef? There's rocks ahead! Ship yore sweeps, finish with those oars afore ye wreck me valuable vessel, ye cloth-eared clods! I told ye to row, not t'go bloomin' mad!"

Quite a bit of muffled laughter broke out among the oar-crew, but they gratefully shipped oars whilst Cuthbert, aided by the fat Corporal Drubblewick, frantically shortened the mainsail to decrease the vessel's speed. With Tiria at the bowsprit calling directions and Cuthbert manning the tiller skillfully, they charted a course between rocks and reefs. The *Purloined Petunia* made a stately landfall, her keel crunching into the pebbled shallows.

Even before they had dropped anchor, the main body of the crew made an eager stampede for the side, everybeast wanting to be first ashore. Cuthbert suddenly cast off his maritime coat and reverted to his role of Major Blanedale Frunk. However, it was only with the timely assistance of Captain Rafe Granden and Colour Sergeant O'Cragg that the Long Patrol were stopped from disembarking and wading ashore. The roars of the three officers froze the crew in their tracks.

"Stand fast there, ye mutinous mob. Come to attention all of ye!"

"Yew 'eard the h'offisah, stan' fast! Just twitch h'an ear, laddie buck, h'an yore h'on a bloomin' fizzer!"

"Steady in the ranks, pay 'tenshun to the Major now!"

Cuthbert strode the deck, glaring through his monocle. "Lady Tiria, Cap'n Granden, Sarn't O'Cragg an' my good-self are goin' ashore. We'll form the advance guard in case of attack. Subalterns Quartle an' Portan will drop anchor an' furl sails. Corporal Drubblewick an' the cookin' detail will follow us ashore to light a fire an' ready up some vittles. The rest of ye, form a chain from ship to shore, an' bring all supplies'n'arms to land safe'n'dry, an' in good order. Whilst you are on yonder island, you'll conduct yourselves like Long Patrol hares. Right, stan' easy, dismiss, an' attend to your duties!"

As the hares went about their tasks with military efficiency, Tiria wandered a little way up the beach. She climbed upon a rock and stared around. So this was the fabled Green Isle, she thought, the home of her distant ancestors. This was actually where the High Queen Rhulain had once ruled.

Colour Sergeant O'Cragg marched up and came smartly to attention. "Major Frunk's compliments, miss. Will ye be dinin' with the Patrol?"

Savoury odours drifting from cauldrons over the cooking fire reminded Tiria that she was hungry. "Oh yes, please, Sergeant. That would be nice!"

The burly hare saluted. "Right y'are, miss, but the major says ye don't get h'a bite 'til yore dressed properlike h'in yore regalia!"

The ottermaid looked indignantly at the tunic and kilt she had worn for the voyage. "Why, what's wrong with the way I'm dressed?"

A smile creased the sergeant's rough-hewn face. "Major

Frunk says ye look like h'a 'edgehog wot's been dragged back'ards through h'a bush, beggin' yore pardon, miss. H'accordin' to 'im, you gotta be h'attired h'as befits h'a future queen. H'either that or ye starve. Those h'are 'is words, not mine, miss!"

Fuming with the injustice of it all, Tiria was forced to go back aboard the ship and change into her regalia. She marched stiffly into camp, where she sat stone-faced amid the garrulous hare crew. Corporal Drubblewick served her with a bowl of mushroom and barley soup, some freshly baked griddle scones and a beaker of raspberry cordial.

The fat hare wiggled his ears at her. "I say, M'lady, jolly spiffy outfit, wot!"

Cuthbert strolled over, nodding his approval. "Top marks, a very smart turnout indeed! Ye really look the part now, Milady. Well done!"

Tiria treated him to a withering stare. "I'm so pleased you think so, Major."

He indicated the other hares with his swagger stick. "Oh, 'tis not just me, it's the rest o' the Patrol, doncha see? They'll be goin' into battle to regain this isle for ye. That bein' the case, some o' these buckoes may be slain defendin' your title, miss. War's war y'know, an' they'd feel much better knowin' they're riskin' life'n'limb for a queen who looks like a queen, an' not some raggedy otter gel, eh wot?"

Tiria, completely humbled by this statement, put aside her food. "Please accept my apologies, Major Frunk. I never thought of it that way. From now on I'll do my best to look and act like a queen. Forgive my foolishness."

Cuthbert tapped her paw with his swagger stick, answering kindly, "Come on now, don't get so jolly well upset. Eat up your vittles, Majesty, an' remember: Handsome is as handsome does, wot!"

Tiria cheered up, accepting the hares' compliments and putting up with their jokes. When the meal was finished, Captain Granden gave the order for everybeast to inspect arms.

"Before ye fall in t'march, look to those weapons. All lance an' spearpoints to be correctly tipped. Pay special attention to your blades, sharpen 'em blinkin' well. Bowstrings t'be waxed an' tested, you archers, check your quivers. Slingbeasts, I don't want t'see any frayed slings or half-filled stonepouches. This beach is full of bloomin' good pebbles. Make bally sure your arms ain't goin' to let ye down if push comes to shove, buckoes. Then y'can fall in, formed in three ranks. Major Frunk an' my goodself will scout ahead. Sarn't Major O'Cragg, will ye take over please?"

He murmured in Tiria's ear, "Ye'd best march with the Patrol, Lady. We don't want to risk losin' you just yet!"

The advance scouts had departed by the time the Patrol were ready and formed up. Tiria marched alongside Quartle and Portan, with Sergeant O'Cragg leading off at the front of the columns. The hares sang a marching song, though not too loudly, just to keep them in orderly stride.

"Left right, left right,
put those paws down lively now.
One two, one two,
come on chaps let's show 'em how.
'Tis on to death or glory,
for every willin' beast,
an' what'll we have to show for it,
a song a fight an' a feast!

Left right, left right,
every mother's son of ye.
One two, one two,
o'er shore'n'hill'n'vale'n'lea.
The Long Patrol are on the march,
from dawn 'til evenin' light,
as long as we can end it with
a song a feast an' a fight!

Left right, left right,
eatin' dust an' poundin' earth.
One two, one two,
'tis all a warrior's worth,
a dash o' blood'n'vinegar,
for that we'll string along,
while we're alive we'll all survive
on a fight a feast an' a song!"

Sunlight glinted brightly off Tiria's armour. Her short emerald cloak swaying jauntily, she picked up the words of the hares' tune and sang it a second time. As she marched, thoughts began to tumble through the young ottermaid's mind. She had come all the way from being an Abbeymaid who had hardly been far outside of Redwall, to a would-be warrior queen marching across Green Isle with the Long Patrol. And all in the space of one season! If only her father and all her dear friends—Brink Greyspoke, Abbess Lycian, Brinty, Girry, Tribsy, Friar Bibble and the rest—could see her now! A resolve rose within Tiria. She would not let any of them down, especially the gallant hares of Salamandastron. Squaring her shoulders and lifting her chin, she marched onward regally. Major Cuthbert Cuthbert Frunk W. Bloodpaw was right: Handsome is as handsome does!

29

Leatho Shellhound had decided on a course of action. His first job was to break out of the cage. But where then? It was far too high up for him to reach the pier below, so he planned on going upward. He would climb into the chamber above, through the window, from whence his prison was suspended. It would be a risky business, but the outlaw realised it was his only avenue of escape. Looking down through the floor bars, he checked below, lest any guards were watching. The pier and the lake beyond it lay deserted. Leatho did not stop to wonder why. Instead, he focussed on trying to loosen one of the roof timbers. Attempting to prevent the cage from hitting the side of the tower—and doing so with as little noise as possible—was no easy task. The roof bars were made of heavy wood, quite thick, and were firmly nailed in place with iron spikes. The outlaw otter attacked them with his bare paws, pulling, pushing, clawing and scrabbling, but to no avail. Clearly, it was going to be a long and painstaking chore. He began working on the iron spikes, desperately trying to budge just one. After a while his paws were skinned and bleeding from the effort, forcing him to take a rest.

As the Shellhound was licking his scratches and wishing he had some sort of tool to help, he heard the door creak in the upper chamber. Quickly he wrapped the severed rope ends around his paws and hung there limply, as though he were still bound and helpless.

Weilmark Scaut had decided to look in on the prisoner. He leaned over the windowsill and rattled the cage bars with his whipstock. "Hah, still alive, are ye, Shellhound? Wot's it feel like, hangin' up here without any vittles or water, eh?"

Determined not to rise to the bait, Leatho hung limply, head lolling forward, feigning unconsciousness.

Scaut thrust the whip through the bars, managing to tickle his victim's ears with it. He whispered scornfully, "Ain't so bold an' sprightly now, are ye? Well, you just stay there like a goodbeast 'til yore rebel friends surrender. Aye, then we'll take ye down, an' I'll give ye a proper taste o' this lash. Pleasant dreams!"

Leatho heard him retreating back into the chamber, slamming the door as he left.

A dark shadow hovered over him, and a voice nearby whispered, "Raaaark! He is gone. Ye could do with some help."

Leatho found himself looking up into the savage, golden-rimmed eyes of a mighty hawk as it hovered over the cage. He loosened his paws from the ropes.

"Who are ye, mate, an' what're ye doin' here?"

The big bird perched on the cage roof. "Kraagarr! I am the enemy of all cats. I have been watching ye trying to get out of this thing."

The otter smiled ruefully. "Ain't havin' much luck, am I?"

The hawk shook its head. "I will help ye. Push upward on this middle bar, an' I will pull. Ready!"

Leatho began pushing, grunting with exertion as he set his paws to the bar. The big bird wrapped its fearsome talons around the bar. Flapping its powerful wings, it strained upward, pulling as Leatho pushed.

Crack! The bar snapped straight through its centre. Releasing its hold on the broken bar, the hawk hovered in the air for a brief moment, its fierce unwinking eyes scanning the area. "Yeeaakkah! Pandion Piketalon must go before cats come with bows and slings!"

Leatho waved to his newfound friend. "My thanks to ye, Pandion. I am called Leatho Shellhound. I, too, am an enemy of the cats. Mayhaps we'll meet again."

The osprey circled overhead gracefully. "Hayaarr! We will make the cats weep blood, Leatho. I will bring the Rhulain and her warriors to help ye!"

Without waiting for a reply, Pandion soared off swiftly into the distance, leaving the outlaw with the name pounding through his brain: Rhulain! Rhulain! The High Queen of Green Isle was coming, just as Ould Zillo had prophesied. He repeated the word aloud like a magic spell. "Rhulain! Rhulain!"

A quick downward glance assured Leatho that all was still quiet below. There was neither sign nor presence of catguards watching. By grabbing one end of the broken roof bar and yanking it sharply downward, he managed to pull it loose. It was a jagged length of timber with an iron spike through the top—crude but nevertheless a fearsome weapon in the paws of the outlaw. Clambering out onto the roof of his former prison, Leatho shinned up the short length of rope and hauled himself over the windowsill. He went into a fighting crouch, wielding his improvised club, ready to face anybeast who stood in his way. But the room was empty, save for a table and a few benches. Leatho crept quietly to the door, holding his ear to it. The two catguards out on the stairhead were talking. Leatho eavesdropped on their conversation.

"Huh, we've been stuck here guardin' this door all day. When's Scaut goin' to send us a relief, eh? When?"

The other guard replied gruffly, "I don't know. Why don't ye stop complainin' t'me? Go an' ask him. I dare ye!"

Leatho felt the speaker lean his back against the door as he continued taunting his companion.

"Go on, mate! You go down there an' tell ole Felis you've

288

stood guard long enough. Have ye heard wot 'appened to Yund? Hah, ye'd end up bein' sliced to bits, just like him. Scaut might chop ye into smaller pieces, 'cos you ain't even a scorecat. Yore only a . . . aaaaagh!"

The door swung inward, bringing the catguard stumbling backward with it. Leatho slew him with a single blow of his club. However, before he could get to the other, the catguard was already rushing downstairs, yelling, "Help! Escape! Shellhound's on the loose! Escape!"

Leatho heard the rattle of spears and Scaut roaring like a madbeast, "Don't let him escape! Get up there an' capture him, quick!"

Footpaws thudded upon the stairs as catguards began racing upward. The outlaw seized a jug of water, together with a platter of bread and half a fish, which the two guards had been sharing. He retreated swiftly back into the chamber. Dragging the dead guard out of the way, he barred the door with the table and benches. Now nobeast could reach him, but it was a tricky situation. He was virtually being held prisoner again.

He retrieved the spear, which had fallen in with the guard, then stood swigging water and stuffing down bread and fish. The door began to shudder under blows from the guards' weapons, but it was a solid oaken door and withstood their efforts well. The banging went on for a while, then suddenly ceased.

The next thing Leatho heard was Scaut calling to him, "Shellhound, I warn ye! Open this door, or it'll go badly for ye!"

The outlaw otter laughed recklessly. "If'n ye want to see how badly things'll go, then try openin' the door an' comin' in here, ye lard barrel!"

When Riggu Felis received the news of his captive's escape from the cage, he went into a fit of rage. Bounding out onto the pier with a score of catguards, he glared up at the empty cage hanging beneath the high window. The chain mail half-mask rattled against his fangs with each sharp intake of breath as he turned to the guards.

"Archers, fire arrows through that window!"

Leatho heard the command and threw himself flat against the window wall. Three shafts made it into the chamber; two stuck into the floor, while the third thudded into the door. Other arrows did not make it that far and stuck like feathered twigs into the wooden tower walls.

The outlaw presented himself at the open window space, grinning down at the warlord. "Is that the best ye can do, skinface? Try again!"

Leatho watched the guards fire more arrows and moved swiftly out of the way. The cats were selecting their next arrows, under their leader's exhortations.

"Kill him! Wound him! Anything, but get him!"

Before they had a chance to notch arrows to strings, the carcass of the guard, whom Leatho had slain earlier, came hurtling down. Felis jumped out of the way, but the body struck two archers, stunning one and killing the other.

A booming shout rang out from the pier end. "Good shot matey, hang on, we're comin'!"

Big Kolun Galedeep and a mob of otters came thundering along the pier. Riggu Felis yelled, "Archers, fire at those otters and retreat. Back inside!" The battle had begun.

As the fortress doors slammed shut, the pier and the shore to either side of it were swarming with otterclan warriors. Rocks and stones, arrows and lances hit the fortress walls.

Leatho leaned out of the high window, roaring his warcry. "Eeeee aye eeeeeh! Forward the clans! Eeeee aye eeeeh!"

Alerted by the cries of battle, Scaut came scurrying downstairs with his guards. His voice was shrill with surprise as he met with Riggu Felis.

"Lord, are we under attack?"

It was the wrong thing to say. A butt from the wildcat's steel-helmeted head sent the weilmark sprawling.

"Of course we're under attack, you blockheaded dolt! Call the guards out of the barracks, get them here quick!"

Weilmark Scaut obeyed his master's command hastily, but his face was a picture of bewilderment as he accosted the last guard to leave the barracks. He grabbed the cat and shook him.

"There must be more'n threescore missin'. Where've the rest of 'em gone?"

The shaking guard's teeth rattled as he tried to explain. "They've gone with Commander Pitru. I thought ye knew!"

Scaut shook him harder. "Gone! Gone where?"

The hapless guard tried to salute as he replied, "Lookin' for otters. They went out the back o' the barracks. Commander Pitru said it was Lord Felis's orders."

Scaut shoved the puzzled guard away from him. "Go an' report to Lord Felis right now. Tell him wot you've just told me. Go on!"

The weilmark took his own good time getting back to the fortress doors, not wanting to be around the warlord when the catguard made his report. Riggu Felis heard the guard's report without comment. Then, spotting Scaut loitering a safe distance away, he beckoned him over. The weilmark scurried to his master's side, where he listened whilst the wildcat spoke scathingly of his son.

"You've heard, I suppose. The cowardly kitten has cut and run! I should have expected it. Hah, I don't need that traitorous idiot and his followers. At least now I won't have to watch my back while I'm facing the otters. Once those rebels are defeated, we'll hunt the bold Commander Pitru down. I'll kill him personally, just as I should have long ago, instead of letting him become a threat to me. The filthy little turncoat!"

A wild laugh nearby startled Riggu Felis. There stood Lady Kaltag. The guards had been dismissed from her chamber door to assist in defending the fortress, leaving her to wander freely. She looked manic and unkempt, her silken robes stained and tattered, her red-rimmed eyes blazing hatred at her husband. With neither the time nor the desire for a confrontation, the warlord muttered to Scaut, "Who let her out? See to it that her chamber is guarded. Get her out of my sight!"

Kaltag was hauled off by four guards, kicking and scratching, as she poured scorn on her husband. "Aye, kill your son, my lord, just as you murdered his brother! You won't find my Pitru as easy to slay, oh no! Hahaha, he's left you in a fine mess, hasn't he? Taken a band of guards and broken free of your vile schemes! How are you going to defend this fortress now, O Lord of Green Isle? Hahahahaaaa!"

The wildcat brandished his axe, shaking it at her. "Get that madbeast out of here, Scaut. Lock her up!"

The weilmark hurried to assist his guards in dragging Kaltag off, but her mocking shouts could still be heard, echoing down the passage.

"Your enemies will dance on your grave, Felis! Evil has its own reward, a long slow death. Hahahahaaaa!"

Bravely the otterclans were fighting their way along the pier outside. Arrows, spears, javelins and all manner of missiles rained through the slitted defence windows at them, with long pikes bristling from every opening. Banya Streamdog and her slingers retaliated with heavy volleys of stones. So fierce was their assault that it allowed Big Kolun to lead his comrades in a wild forward charge. Otters fell on either side of the Galedeep chieftain, but he thundered recklessly on, batting away shafts and spears with his big oar. Kolun made it to the fortress gates, where he was joined by Lorgo, who had led a party up from the shore. Both brothers raised a bloodcurdling warcry.

"Galedeep! Galedeep! Eeeeeee aye eeeeeh!"

With a hefty swipe of his oar, Kolun shattered a pike that was thrust at him through an opening. Lorgo caught a javelin. Hurling it back through a window slit, he shouted to Kolun, "This gate's well defended, mate. Wot d'we do now?"

The big otter battered at the thick double doors with his oar butt until his paws stung from the vibrations. "We need somethin' to burst the doors with. A tree trunk'd make a good batterin' ram!"

After a swift look around, Lorgo replied, "A good idea, but I don't see any big ole tree trunks lyin' about, d'you?"

Weilmark Scaut could be heard issuing orders from inside. "Cease firin'! Put up yore arms an' shutter off all openin's."

Immediately the battle halted. Kolun signalled the clans to leave off their assault on the fortress.

Banya Streamdog came in a running crouch to the doors, where Kolun stood leaning on his oar. "I don't know why, but the cats have stopped fightin'."

Banya pointed. "Look, up there!"

Fastened to a pikeshaft, a white cloth waved from an upper-storey window. A nervous catguard popped his head out. "Truce, we crave a truce! My Lord Felis would talk with ye!"

Lorgo murmured to Kolun as he eyed the catguard, "Talk? Wot d'we want to talk for, mate?"

Banya Streamdog shrugged. "May'ap ole chopface wants to invite us t'dinner. Let's find out."

Cupping both paws about his mouth, Kolun called to the guard, "Let Felis do his talkin', but no funny business, d'ye hear?"

Garbed in full war armour and cloak, the warlord appeared at the open window, two storeys up. Drawing back the chain mail half-mask, he exposed his flayed lower face and began speaking.

"I call upon you to surrender. Your lives will be spared!"

Big Kolun roared back a cheery reply. "By me rudder, that's very nice o' ye, half-gob! But wot if'n we don't feel like surrenderin'? Wot then, eh?"

The wildcat had been expecting this reaction. He leaned on the windowsill, his face set in a ghastly smile. "My fortress is secure, it won't fall to your puny attempts. If you continue to defy me, I will have Shellhound dragged from the room where he is hiding, up there at the top of the tower. Then I will return him to you, bound in a sack and flung from that window. I am not unreasonable—you have until dawn tomorrow to give me your answer."

Before Riggu Felis could speak further, Leatho was bellowing from the high chamber window, "Pay no heed to boneface, mates. His cats have already tried that once an' failed. I'll be happy to give 'em a second try! Kolun! Banya! You carry on fightin', mates. The High Rhulain's on her way!"

Big Kolun waved his oar to the clanbeasts. "Ye heard wot the Shellhound said, buckoes? Let's show these whiskery scum we're here t'finish the job!"

The warlord's grating shouts rang out. "Wait! Let me finish what I was about to say. Then, if you feel like charging, let me be the last to stop you!"

Banya replied mockingly, "Well, spit it out, skin-gums. Then stand by t'die!"

Riggu Felis continued with his ultimatum. "Whether or not Shellhound dies tomorrow does not matter. If you attack my fortress, I will start executing the slaves, family by family, the youngest first. Consider this, for their deaths will be upon your own heads!"

He vanished from the window, which was speedily shuttered. In the silence which followed, Banya stared grimly at the closed window.

"We're left without any choice, mates. We can't attack!"

30

It was midnoon. Major Cuthbert Frunk had ordered a well-deserved rest for the Long Patrol. The hares spread out along the banks of a woodland stream whose waters were clean and cold. Tiria sat with her two subalterns and Colour Sergeant O'Cragg. Sheltered by an old weeping willow, they cooled their footpaws in the shallows.

Quartle was munching on a bunch of watercress he had discovered growing near the bankside. "Rather nice, this Green Isle place. Y'could live here."

Tiria winked at him as she helped herself to his cress. "What a good idea, I may do that!"

The burly O'Cragg commandeered a pawful of Quartle's find. "Right, miss, soon h'as we rid the place o' cats h'and free yore h'otterfriends."

Quartle hastily moved his watercress out of the sergeant's reach, whereupon Portan began attacking the remainder. "Huh, that's always supposin' we run into the blighters, wot! We've been on the flippin' march all bally day an' still not spotted s'much as a cat's whisker or an otter's flamin' thingummy. I say, Sarge, how d'ye know we're goin' in the right direction, wot?"

By reaching over with his lance, the big sergeant deftly speared the last of the watercress. "Simple, laddie buck, we just keeps a-marchin' over this h'island crisscross h'until we runs into 'em."

Quartle stared ruefully at the spot where his cress had been a moment before. He sighed. "We might've worn out our bloomin' paws by then. Bit of a fair-sized island t'be crisscrossin' willy-nilly, wot?"

The high-pitched call of an osprey brought Tiria bolt upright. She saw Pandion swoop gracefully in to join Cuthbert upstream. Everybeast hurried to hear what Pandion had to report. Casting a fierce eye about, the fish hawk spread his wings dramatically.

"Yeekaharr! Pandion Piketalon has found the cats and riverdogs. They will soon battle!"

Cuthbert's ears stood up straight at the mention of a fight. "A battle ye say, sah? Where at? Out with it, at the double!"

The osprey flapped his huge wingspread. "Arreeekaaah! At the big tree fort by the long lake. The cats are well dug in there. 'Twill be a hard fight I think!"

Captain Rafe Granden drew his blade. "We're obliged to ye, goodbird, an' more'n pleased if ye can lead us t'the jolly old field of combat, wot?"

Cuthbert's eye was glinting wildly through his monocle. "Rather, I'd be distinctly ticked off if I missed a blinkin' full-scale scrap! Sarn't O'Cragg, get the Patrol formed up in skirmishin' order! C'mon, me lucky lads, off your hunkers an' on your paws. Quick's the word an' sharp's the action!"

The Patrol had to move rapidly to keep up with Cuthbert, who was already off at a swift trot, following the osprey. Quartle nudged Tiria.

"I say, miss, just look at Ole Blood'n'guts. He can't wait to get in the middle of it all!"

The ottermaid patted her sling and stonepouch. "Neither can I, friend!"

"I am thinking you will be waiting for me. I need a rest after my long journey!"

Tiria was startled to see Brantalis flying just above her head. The barnacle goose looked about ready to drop.

"Brantalis, my friend, what are you doing here?"

The big bird flopped down to earth. Captain Rafe Granden, who was running rearguard, caught up with Tiria.

"What'n the name o' seasons is a blinkin' goose doin' in the middle of a forced march?"

Tiria came straight to the defence of her friend. "I don't know, Cap'n, but he's come a long way to be with me, so it must be something important."

The barnacle goose raised his weary head from the grass. "I come from the Abbey of Redwall to see this maid."

Captain Granden twiddled his long ears in admiration. "I say, well done that, bird, wot! Right, then see her y'must, but we can't halt the march. Subalterns Quartle an' Portan, fall out! You two buckoes stay here with Lady Tiria an' this bird. We're carryin' on to the field o' battle. Afraid you'll have to catch us up later, marm!"

Tiria nodded. "Thank you, Cap'n. Don't worry, we'll find you once our business here is done."

Granden smiled and threw a hasty salute. "Oh, you'll find us, marm. Just march t'the sound o' the Eulalias, that's where the Long Patrol will be!" He sped off after the other hares.

Tiria gave Brantalis a drink from Portan's canteen and sat down by his side. "Take your time now. What news from the Abbey?"

Brantalis drank greedily before making his report. "I am thinking there is much news, but that can wait for a better time. Your father the Skipper, the Abbess and the Old Quelt beast sent me here to deliver this. I have not broken flight once since I left Redwall."

Bending his neck forward, the goose used his bill to delve among the thick downy plumage, where his neck broadened to meet his body. He had some difficulty trying to move the object which was ringed around the thick base of his throat. Brantalis grumbled, "I am thinking this was easier to put on than to get off!"

Quartle gallantly offered his help. "Straighten your neck.

297

Chin up, I mean beak up, old lad. I've got the confounded thing!"

Portan assisted him in moving the coronet from about the bird's neck. Both hares gasped in wonderment.

"Oh my giddy aunt's pinny, it's a bloomin' crown!"

"No it ain't, Porters, it's a wotsisname . . . a tiara!"

"Isn't that the confounded thing that was supposed to have gone down with the jolly old ship?"

"Well here it is, old lad, Tiria's tiara. I say, that's pretty good, ain't it? Tiria's tiara!"

The ottermaid accepted it graciously from the two subalterns. "It's called a coronet. Oh, Brantalis, how can I ever thank you? What a great friend you are!"

The barnacle goose ruffled his feathers back into place modestly. "You once helped me, I am thinking it was the least I could do to help you, Tiria Wildlough."

Quartle and Portan began rubbing their paws gleefully.

"Well, go on, miss, put it on, wot wot!"

"Aye, let's see if it fits your royal bonce, miss."

Tiria took the simple gold circlet, with its inset stone which sparkled like green fire, and placed it lightly on her head. It fitted easily about her brow.

Brantalis stood and spread his wings. "I am thinking that was made for you!"

Portan flopped his ears, always a sign of admiration in hares. "By the left right'n'centre, miss, you really look the blinkin' part now, wot!"

He was correct. With the addition of the coronet to the breastplate and cloak, Tiria looked unmistakably regal.

Quartle made an elegant, sweeping bow. "We are your most humble bloomin' servants, Queen Tiria. Your wish is our flippin' command, Majesty!"

The ottermaid struck a pose, trying to look as she imagined a queen would. Then she suddenly took a fit of the giggles. "Hahahaha, come on, you pair of duffers, stop bowing and scraping like two dithering ducks. It doesn't matter what I dress up in, I'm still me, Tiria Wildlough from

Redwall Abbey. Let's put a move on and catch up with the Patrol. That is, if you're up to it, Brantalis?"

The barnacle goose swelled out his chest. "Up to it? I am thinking I would not miss it!"

The still summer evening hung warm and dusty over the empty pier. Big Kolun Galedeep and the otterclans deemed it safer to hold a meeting in the bushes and trees of the left bank. The otters did not need a night attack by the cats to further complicate the quandary they were in. They gathered en masse, angry, puzzled and disgruntled at the ultimatum which the wildcat warlord had set upon them. The initial idea of a wild charge, and an all-out assault on the foe, had palled in the light of dire consequences—their enslaved friends, together with their families, being dragged out and executed in reprisal. The very mention of it was unthinkable. Proposals were put forth and rejected for various reasons. There seemed no answer to the problem.

Lorgo Galedeep mentioned another impractical solution. "Suppose we pretend to surrender. Then at the last moment, say, when the fortress gates are opened, we grab our weapons an' make a forced charge, straight inside?"

At that moment, any scheme sounded good to Kolun. "Aye, it might work, mate. They wouldn't be expectin' a move like that. Sounds alright t'me!"

Banya immediately poured cold water on the plan. "Do ye think the Felis cat is some kind o' fool? The instant we threw down our arms an' surrendered, he'd have us surrounded by fully armed catguards. First thing they'd do would be to confiscate our weapons or sling 'em in the lake to stop us gettin' at 'em."

Kolun patted his brother's shoulder sadly. "She's right, mate. It wouldn't work."

A voice, completely foreign to the gathering, interrupted. "You chaps sound as though yore in a spot o' bother, wot!"

Two tall hares, well armed and dressed in red tunics, emerged out of the shrubbery.

Kolun wheeled upon them, gripping his oar. "Who are ye, an' where'd ye come from?"

The leader of the two rested one paw on a long rapier hilt and threw a casual salute. "Name's Granden, old lad. Cap'n Rafe Granden o' the Long Patrol at y'service. This is my aide, Colour Sergeant O'Cragg. We're to be your allies I believe, wot!"

Banya Streamdog did not sound impressed. "Just the two of ye, huh? That won't be much help!"

The burly Sergeant O'Cragg smiled down at her. "Ho, there's h'a few more'n just the two of us, missy. Ye'll see for yoreself. Yore to follow me'n the Cap'n to a meetin' with h'our commandin' offisah, Major Frunk."

Kolun was not used to taking orders from complete strangers. He squared up in front of O'Cragg; they were both big beasts. The otter thrust out his jaw belligerently.

"We're to follow you, eh? Says who?"

The sergeant's eyes met Kolun unwaveringly. "H'I believe 'er name h'is Rhulain, sah!"

There was a stunned silence, which broke into a roaring cheer from the otterclans. Big Kolun shook O'Cragg's paw.

"Here's me paw an' here's me heart, mate! Lead on, we're with ye t'the death!"

Dusk had fallen by the time they reached the Long Patrol camp at the lake's far end. A good fire burned there, shielded in the lee of some trees and rocks. The otters filed in, packing the site with their numbers.

Cuthbert climbed upon a rock, polishing his monocle and shouldering his swagger stick. After gazing around a bit, he addressed the gathering. "Righto, me buckoes. Let's get off on the right paw, wot! I'm Regimental Major Cuthbert Blanedale Frunk. Unless I'm outranked by any o' you chaps, I think I'm in command here. Any objections?"

Receiving no reply from the otterclans, he nodded. "Good show! Reason I say this is that there's goin' t'be a bit of a skirmish, a jolly old war in fact! No offence intended, an' I'm sure you otterchaps are splendidly brave coves, but you ain't Long Patrol. Now, d'ye see these hares? There's a score'n a half of 'em, they're Long Patrol warriors. Fightin' an' soldierin' is their business. Believe you me, these laddie bucks have slain more vermin than you've had hot flippin' dinners. So take my word an' trust me, wot!"

Kolun called out. "Fair enough, Major, we believe ye, but we've come here t'see our queen. Where is she?"

A murmur of assent ran through the clanbeasts. Silencing them with a wave of his swagger stick, Cuthbert pointed dramatically to the fire.

"Friends, meet Lady Tiria Wildlough of Redwall Abbey! The High Rhulain, Queen of Green Isle!"

The ottermaid came forth from behind the fire, dressed in full regalia and flanked by her two subalterns along with Pandion and Brantalis. The otterclans fell silent, overawed. Here was their prophecy fulfilled, the living legend standing before them. Tiria strode slowly through the hushed camp. All that could be heard was the crackle of twigs from the fire. Kolun was the biggest and most impressive of the otters. She went to him first. "Are you a Wildlough, sir?"

Bowing his head, Kolun went on bended knee. "Nay, Majesty. I'm Kolun Galedeep, Skipper o' the Galedeep clan, an' I'm honoured to meet ye, yore Majesty!"

Taking his paws, Tiria raised him up immediately. "Please, Kolun, I don't want anybeast bowing and scraping to me. Don't call me Majesty, my name's Tiria."

The big otter grinned cheerfully. "Fair enough. I'll call ye Queen Tiria, how'll that do?"

She patted his huge paw. "That'll do me fine, mate. You're such a bigbeast, I thought you must be a Wildlough."

Kolun looked her up and down. "Wildloughs ain't usually yore size, Queen Tiria. How did ye get to be so tall?"

With a twinkle in her eyes, Tiria replied, "I told my dad I wouldn't be long!"

It was an old otterjoke. The clanbeasts laughed heartily, pleased that their queen was not a remote and formal presence. She was one of them.

Corporal Drubblewick and his helpers joined forces with some ottercooks. Together they set about cooking for everybeast. Cuthbert, Granden and O'Cragg convened a Council of War with Kolun, Lorgo, Banya and Tiria. They sat apart from the rest, dining on turnip and mushroom soup, fresh baked farls, fruit and burdock cordial. Banya explained to the hares what had taken place. She told them of the warlord's threat to kill Leatho and the slaves, starting at dawn. Captain Granden questioned the otters on every aspect of the fortress and the number of catguards there. Using charcoal and a piece of willow bark, Banya sketched a map of the fortress layout—pier, buildings, barracks, tower and slave compound.

Cuthbert studied it keenly. Then, moving his ears in approval, he replied, "This is splendid, just what we jolly well need, wot. Sergeant, have the Patrol ready to move out in mufti soon as ye can. Tell 'em to smoke all blades, too."

Tiria looked at him enquiringly. "You're moving the Patrol out now? But why?"

Dropping his monocle, Cuthbert winked with the air of a conspirator. "Quick tactics are best, doncha know? I've laid my plans. Ye won't see me or the Patrol again until dawn. Now, I'll tell ye what I want you otter types t'do, so pay attention, chaps. Kolun an' Lorgo, take your clans along both banks. Banya, see if ye can get some o' your creatures to knock together a raft that'll carry about twoscore. Can ye do that?"

The tough Streamdog maid nodded. "Aye, we can steal the fishin' coracles an' lay a platform of logs on 'em. Shouldn't be too much trouble, Major."

Cuthbert gazed at her admiringly. "If ye ever decide to become a hare, I'll have ye in my regiment, gel. You go with your queen on the raft, straight up the middle o' the lake. Tiria, I want you standin' front an' centre on that vessel, lookin' just like a queen, d'ye hear me? Now, all you otters, it's blinkin' well vital that ye make it to the pier at dawn, understand? Oh, an' I want ye t'be makin' as much noise as possible. Sing, shout, yell warcries, do what ye bally well like, but let's have a rousin' good din raised. So, that's about all, chaps. Good fortune be with us all. Forward the buffs, give 'em blood'n'vinegar an' all that. Wot wot!"

"Patrol ready t'march out h'in skirmish order, sah!"

Tiria looked up to see that they were surrounded by hares. Each member of the Long Patrol had shed their scarlet tunics, camouflaging themselves with twigs, grass and leaves. Every blade they carried had been blackened by fire smoke. Major Cuthbert Blanedale Frunk dropped both monocle and swagger stick and shrugged off his tunic. Tiria could tell by the wild look in his eyes that he was going into one of his many character changes. He leered villainously, squinting one eye.

"Hohoho, me beauties, the wild badgers are huntin' tonight. Lord Brockfang Frunk bids ye farewell!"

Both he and the hares were gone in a trice, swallowed up by the nighttime undergrowth.

Lorgo Galedeep shuddered. "Curl me rudder, he's madder than a mop-topped mouse!"

Tiria reassured him calmly. "Oh, I wouldn't call him mad, exactly. Let's say he's a beast of many parts. I've seen him as a shrew chieftain, a sea otter pirate and a regimental major. But one thing you may rest assured of, he's not stupid. That hare is a legend among his kind—a master of strategy and the most perilous warrior in all Salamandastron. I'd trust my life to him any day of the season!"

Kolun chuckled. "So now he's a wild huntin' badger, eh? Well, I'd hate t'be the foebeast that has to face him."

Banya tweaked the big fellow's whiskers. "But you ain't no huntin' badger, Mister Galedeep. C'mon, up with ye!

Yore a log finder now. Queen Tiria has to have a raft that won't let us down, so move yore carcass!"

Tiria squeezed Banya's paw fondly. "I like the way you dish out orders. Maybe I'd do well to appoint you my assistant-in-chief, Banya."

Kolun heaved himself up, pulling a wry face. "Wait'll ye meet my missus, Deedero. You'll make her a chief, too. She's good at givin' orders, I can tell ye!"

As the night wore steadily on, Tiria sat alone on the lakeside. She made ready for the dawn, buffing her breastplate, polishing the coronet and carefully brushing her short velvet cloak. After folding her cloak, she laid the regalia on it. Next she checked her sling and stonepouch. Rummaging about amid the pebbles, she came across something she had almost forgotten. It was the vicious star-shaped iron missile which Brother Perant had extracted from Pandion's beak. Tiria recalled the vow she had made to return it to the foebeast. She loaded it into the tongue of the sling which Lord Mandoral had made for her, thinking back to when it had all started—the day she and her three friends had rescued the osprey from the rat gang. It seemed so long ago now. A wave of nostalgia crept over the ottermaid for those she held dear: her father, Brink, Girry, Tribsy, Brinty, Friar Bibble, Sister Snowdrop and Old Quelt. She reflected on the many faithful companions she had been brought up with— the funny little Dibbuns, and Abbess Lycian, so young yet so wise. And, of course, her beautiful home, Redwall Abbey. Would she ever see it again? The ottermaid sniffed, wiping a paw across her eyes and reflecting on the destiny fate had thrust upon her: Rhulain, High Queen of Green Isle.

All those otterclans with so much faith and trust in her, and she, a single ottermaid, with the task of freeing them from the tyranny of a foebeast who revelled in cruelty and brutality. What would Martin the Warrior have done in her place?

Tiria lay down to sleep, staring up at the starstrewn skies.

She remembered Sergeant O'Cragg telling her that they were the spirits of brave warriors. Through the mists of descending sleep, Martin's voice drifted into her dreams.

"You ask what I would do in your place, Tiria. I would do the same thing you are about to do. It is called the right thing!"

31

Leatho Shellhound was bone weary for want of sleep. All
night the catguards had been trying to get inside the high
tower chamber to capture him. Luckily the stout door held,
barricaded as it was by a heavy table and thick wooden
benches wedged firmly in position. The outlaw otter stood
at the open window, breathing deeply of the cold predawn
air to keep himself awake. Below him, the pier and lake
were still in darkness. Behind him, the spears and pikes of
his enemy battered ceaselessly on the door.

Leatho threw back his head and roared at his tormentors, "Don't stand there knockin', fools, come on in! Ye
whiskery-faced, droolin', tabby-pawed cowards! Come on,
step inside an' meet the Shellhound! I'll rip the heads'n'guts
from the first ten of ye who come through that door! Ee
aye eeeeeeeeh!"

The banging ceased, as it would for a while. Leatho
laughed tiredly, turning back to the window. He knew the
cats feared him; none of them was overanxious to enter the
chamber and see him carry out his threats. But he also realised that they had their orders and would soon begin trying to break in again, driven on by thoughts of what their
warlord would do to them if they failed in their mission.

Outside the sky was still dark, though as Leatho watched

he began to distinguish the soft grey twinge which heralded a new day. This was reinforced by the first birdsong, a lark beginning its ascent, and far off, a thrush warbling throatily. Leatho's small amount of drinking water was long gone. He would have given anything for one brief, cool dip in the lake far below. During the night, he had considered a high dive from the tower window. But stretched out beneath him lay the pier; the lake was too far off for him to possibly reach. Unconsciously at first, the outlaw began humming an old otterclan warsong, thinking it had merely popped into his head. When he stopped humming, however, he could still hear the tune—distant, yes, far off maybe, but nevertheless real. Dawn's first rays seeped in from the right. Leatho leaned out over the windowsill, trying to reassure himself that the sound was somewhere present. Then the banging on the door started afresh. He howled out another challenge.

"Next one who knocks on my door, I'm comin' out t'see who he is! Ee aye eeeeeeh! If'n yore a mate of his, I'll leave his hide to make ye a cloak, an' his teeth for a necklace. Ye can do as ye please with his eyes!"

The banging stopped abruptly. In the silence which followed, Leatho heard the warsong clearly. It was coming from the banksides and the lake. He saw the long shape approaching in rising daylight—some sort of craft, headed straight for the pier. Bursting out in a great howl of joy, the outlaw otter began marching around the chamber, bellowing out the warsong of the otterclans.

"Wildloughs, Wavedogs, Streambattles, too,
Riverdogs, Streamdivers, Galedeeps true.
Death rides the wind, tell the enemy,
the clans have risen, ee aye eeeeeeeeh!

Show no quarter, stand up an' fight,
blood and steel be our birthright.
Oh Rhulain, set your children free,
the clans have risen, ee aye eeeeeeeeh!

307

Foebeast, weep for all you're worth,
curse the one that gave you birth.
Red the streams run to the sea,
the clans have risen, ee aye eeeeeeeeeh!

In the times to come I'll say,
I was one who fought that day.
Gave my family liberty,
Ee aye, ee aye, ee aye eeeeeeeeeeeeeeeeeh!"

The sound of the warsong rose to a bloodcurdling roar, echoing and reverberating around the shores and over the lake. Wakened by the eerie din, Riggu Felis burst from his chamber, donning his war armour and kicking at guards who got in his path. He arrived at the barred fortress gates. Removing his helmet and chain mail half-mask, the warlord pressed his eye to a spyhole. He could not yet see anything clearly, but the otters' warsong was getting closer, growing in volume.

Weilmark Scaut came stumbling up, his coarse features blanched with fright. "Lord, they're coming!"

He reeled sideways from the blow Riggu Felis dealt him.

"I can hear they're coming, idiot, but where exactly are they? Do you know?"

Holding his aching cheek, Scaut whimpered. "Sire, the upstairs guards say they're on both banks, an' they've got a big raft comin' up the middle o' the lake. It looks like they've come t'do battle, Lord!"

The wildcat eyed his trembling weilmark coldly. "And the Shellhound, haven't they dragged him from that chamber yet?"

Scaut tried to back off, but his shoulders were already against the wall. He shook his head fearfully. "No, Lord, he's barricaded the door with some furniture. They say it's impossible to reach the Shellhound."

The warlord licked his flayed gums, hissing savagely, "Take all the upstairs guards and go to the slave compound.

Bring me two, no, three families of otterslaves. Make sure they have young ones with them. Fetch them here to me. We'll see if those rebels feel like rushing into a fight when they witness what I'm going to do!"

As Scaut hurried off, the warlord shouted to the guards who were packed in the hallway, "Open the doors, and follow me out onto the pier!"

Lady Kaltag had her ear pressed to the door of the chamber in which she was imprisoned. Outside, she heard Scaut bellowing at the four guards who were standing sentry on her door.

"You two, follow me to the slave compound! You others, go an' get the ones who are tryin' to capture Shellhound. They ain't goin' to get him out o' there, leave him. Meet us at the compound, Move yoreselves!"

Kaltag waited until it was quiet outside before coming out of her room. Holding two blazing torches, she ascended to the antechamber at the top of the tower stairs and hid until she heard the catguards running downstairs to the slave compound. Now nobeast was outside the chamber which held Shellhound. Chuckling to herself, the demented cat crept along to it.

She tapped on the battered door, calling in a singsong voice, "Are ye coming out, murderer?"

Leatho's voice came defiantly back at her. "No! Are ye comin' in to get me?"

She cackled insanely. "Heeheehee! I can reach you without having to enter the room. Now you must pay for the death of my son Jeefra. Heeheeheehee!"

Leatho's reply sounded puzzled. "Wot Jeefra? I don't know anybeast named Jeefra!"

Kaltag screeched. "Liar! You and your otters slew him! Now you will roast before you reach Hellgates!"

More crazy laughter followed. Then something struck the door. The timbers were bone dry and heavily splintered from the guards' axes and spears. In a trice, flames were licking at the door. Kaltag was screaming like a madbeast as she tore down wall hangings and flung them on the blaze. She had dropped the other torch on the floor. Standing back from the blazing door, she went into a crazy shuffling dance, her eyes glittering in the firelight as she crooned, "Burn! Burn! You cannot escape a mother's vengeance! Ha-hahaheeeeheeee!"

The entire fortress was built of timber, mainly pine and spruce logs, all old and dry. Flames raced unchecked along the landing, ignored by Kaltag, who was screeching and dancing as tongues of flame licked greedily at her tattered cloak and gown.

On the other side of the door, Leatho felt the heat. He could see smoke billowing in under the door. A moment later, the fire broke through, making him realize that the whole place was about to go up in flames. Dashing to the window, he climbed out onto the sill. Waving his paws, he began shouting frantically to the raft on the lake, which was still a good distance away.

"Ahoy! Can somebeast help me, the place is afire!"

Both Tiria and Banya saw the figure high up on the windowledge. They could hear his shouts but were unable to hear his exact words. Banya suddenly realised what was happening when she saw smoke and a burst of flame, driven on the updraught, leap from the conical tower roof. She gripped Tiria's paw.

"It's Leatho, he's locked in up there an' the place is ablaze!"

Other otters saw Leatho and heard his shouts. They stared in horror at the outlaw, who was edging out on the high windowledge from which smoke and sparks were belching.

Banya Streamdog bit her lip, looking to Tiria. "Leatho'll be burned t'death up there. Ain't there anythin' we can do, Lady?"

Every otter aboard the raft was watching their queen. Tiria knew she had to do something—and quickly. A vision of Martin the Warrior flashed through her mind. Then she heard him say just two words: "the birds!"

She must have said the words out loud, because Banya echoed them. "The birds, marm? Wot d'ye mean?"

Tiria beckoned to the osprey and the goose, both hovering down close to her. She pointed at the figure on the ledge. "Can you get him down from there?"

Brantalis replied, "I could not do it alone, I am thinking. Mayhaps we could do it together, this one and myself. We could only lift him a short way, but far enough to drop him into the lake. I will help Shellhound, he once saved my life. Will you do it, hookbeak?"

Pandion glared at Brantalis. They had never been the closest of friends. He snapped back at the goose, "Kayarr! I have lifted many big fish in my talons. Anything a honker can do, I can also!"

Tiria's patience was wearing thin. She spoke abruptly. "Then don't just bicker and argue about it, get him away from there and drop him into the lake. Do it now!"

Both birds sped off toward the blazing tower.

32

As the fortress doors swung open, a catguard came staggering along the hallway, coughing and gasping for breath as he caught up to the warlord. "Sire, there is a fire in the upper floors!"

The wildcat seized him by the neck and shook him. "I know that, fool! We will deal with it later! Where has Scaut got to with those slaves?"

He flung the guard to the floor. Rubbing at his neck, the cat whined hoarsely, "Lord, we cannot get into the slave compound. Strange warriors have taken it. Weilmark Scaut sent me to tell you!"

The warlord tore off his helmet, throwing it at the guard. "What do you mean, strange warriors?"

The catguard scrambled backward, out of Felis's reach. "Tall ones, rabbits I think. They shout 'alaylee,' and fight like madbeasts. They are fearsome creatures!"

The wildcat stared at him in disbelief. "Tall rabbits? What are you telling me, blatherbrain?"

Loud shouting and cheering came from the lake and banks beyond the pier. Puzzled and seething with wrath, Riggu Felis shouted to the guards gathered in the hallway, "Forward, follow me!"

He marched out onto the pier, followed by his guards, who were relieved to be out of the smoky fortress. Otterclans were packing both sides of the shore and, though the raft was still some distance away, the warlord could see the creatures upon it. They were looking up toward the tower and pointing. Ignoring the enemy facing him, he, too, turned and peered upward.

Leatho Shellhound blinked against the billowing smoke which poured from the window. He could feel his fur beginning to curl and scorch in the constant blasts of heat. Hungry, flaming tongues were threatening to envelop him.

Then two great shapes swooped overhead, and he heard the hawk calling, "Karrraaaak! Seize onto our legs and hold tight!"

Pandion and Brantalis descended upon him in a noisy flapping of wings. Leatho, needing no second invitation, grabbed the hawk just above its talons, and the goose above its webbed pads. With the acrid reek of burning feathers in his nostrils, he cried out, "I've got ye, friends!"

They pulled away, dipping because of the otter's weight. It was very difficult, owing to the different flight methods of both birds, but Brantalis and Pandion flapped bravely outward. They could not keep a level path, immediately going into a descent, though they were still heading for the lake.

Riggu Felis was shouting like a beast demented as he hastened, facing backward, along the pier. It was not essentially Leatho's escape which caught the wildcat's attention, however; it was the sight of Pandion Piketalon.

"The hawk! It's the hawk! I'd know it anywhere!"

He raced ahead, reaching the pier end ahead of the trio's descent. The catguards stopped halfway along the pier, watching as the wildcat stood to intercept the two birds, who were fast losing height with Shellhound hanging from their legs.

313

As he whirled his single-bladed war axe, Riggu Felis was bellowing, "Go to Hellgates, bird!"

The osprey, within three spearlengths of the warlord when he hurled the axe, could not be missed. A cry of horror went up from the otters on the raft. They were still too far off to do anything that would prevent the fatal throw. Without thinking, Tiria began whirling her sling. Round and round it sped until it was a thrumming blur. Automatically, the old Abbey warcry ripped from her mouth. "Redwaaaaaaaaallllll!"

Never before or since had anybeast witnessed a slinging of that magnitude. The barbed iron star whistled through the hot morning air like a thunderbolt, covering the long distance in the speed of a lightning flash. Both Leatho and the two birds hit the water beyond the pier end. The warlord knew that his axe had struck home. He turned to see the hawk splash limply down. Facing the open lake, Riggu Felis laughed aloud. But no sound came from him as he stood in frozen silence for a brief moment. Then he toppled headfirst into the lake, with a hole between both eyes and an iron star embedded in his brain. Thus ended the reign of Riggu Felis, Wildcat Warlord of Green Isle, slain by a humble Abbeymaid who was now High Queen of the Otterclans.

Leatho and Brantalis reached the raft, still holding on to Pandion's body. Willing paws helped them aboard. Tiria bowed with the weight of the slain osprey as she hugged his body tearfully.

Leatho gently disengaged her from the dead hawk. "Time for grievin' later on, marm. We've got a war t'fight!"

Banya stared grimly at the pier. "Aye, an' we're goin' t'miss it if'n this thing doesn't move any faster. Lookit that!"

Before the otters on the shores could even mount the pier, the air was rent with a perilous roar. "Eulaliiiiiaaaaa!" Straight through the smokebound hallway, having entered the fortress from the rear, they burst forth onto the landing: the Long Patrol warriors, backed by a horde of yelling otterslaves whom they had freed.

Colour Sergeant O'Cragg's stentorian tones rang out over the bewildered catguards huddled on the pier. "Forward the buffs! Give 'em blood'n'vinegar! Eulaliiiaaa!"

Leatho waved the pole he was paddling the raft along with. "Let's cheer 'em on, mates! Ee aye eeeeeeeee!"

Some catguards fled; others tried to fight. But the day of reckoning had arrived. They were no match for the hares, and more especially for the freed slaves they had tyrannised and abused for long seasons. Before the day was much older, there was not a living cat left in sight. They were, as Corporal Drubblewick put it, "either bloomin' well dead or flippin' well fled, wot!"

Cuthbert had now reverted to his role as Regimental Major Frunk. He strode smartly aboard the raft, throwing a brisk salute. "All present an' correct, wot! Queen Tiria, please accept me 'pologies, marm. We must look a confounded sight!"

He wagged an ear at the two subalterns. "You chaps, get the uniforms an' dish 'em out, sharpish! My buckoes look like they've just escaped from a ragged robin's roundelay. Give Sergeant O'Cragg me compliments, an' tell him I want the Long Patrol on parade, soon as poss, washed, brushed, combed an' curried. Jump to it!"

Tiria stood gazing at the fortress, which was now an inferno. The upper storeys had burned through, collapsing into the lower ones. Tongues of flame were now crackling along the pier. She shook her head regretfully.

"It would have made a fine castle for the Clans and me."

Leatho took her to one side, speaking low. "No otter would willin'ly live there, marm. The place stunk of cats. There's too many generations o' bad memories within its walls. It's better off as a heap of ole ashes, to stay as a warnin' to foebeasts."

Tiria bowed to the outlaw's superior knowledge. "You're right, of course. It seems I have a lot to learn."

Leatho bowed gallantly. "Don't worry, yore Majesty. I'm here to help ye, all ye have t'do is ask."

Taking his advice literally, Tiria asked, "Tell me, what's this Holt Summerdell place like?"

Banya was the one who answered. " 'Tis a place fit for a queen. It's like the nicest spot ye've ever dreamed of but never believed ye'd ever see!"

That night, by the light of the burning fortress, the bodies of the slain were put to rest. Carcasses of catguards, along with that of Riggu Felis, were consigned to the flames of their stronghold. Otters who had fallen, along with the osprey Pandion Piketalon, were placed upon the flower-decked raft and floated out onto the lake's centre, where the raft was sunk, following an ancient Green Isle tradition. The clans stood on the shore, chanting a dirge in some bygone language which Tiria could not understand. She enquired of Leatho as to its meaning. He translated it for her.

"Thy memory stays midst friends,
'neath water thy body lies,
thy spirit lives, a warrior star,
set high in darkened skies.
I'll look for thee when day is done,
thou jewel in night's crown,
a fearless legend, burning brave,
forever shining down."

A hefty paw touched Tiria's shoulder. Colour Sergeant O'Cragg whispered in her ear, "We've 'eard that afore, h'ain't we, miss?"

Big Kolun Galedeep and his brother Lorgo, with lots of willing help, had managed to save loads of supplies from the catguards' barracks. Kolun waved his oar aloft, proclaiming to everybeast, "Tonight's Victory Feast Night. Sleep in late tomorrow, then we takes our queen back to Holt Summerdell. Do I hear any arguments?"

Nobeast ever argued with Kolun, with the exception of his missus. Besides, they were all more than willing to go along with his excellent plan. Temporarily shunning her role as queen, Tiria joined Corporal Drubblewick and a host of ottermums who had never seen such an array of food to cook with. They used burning pier boards as a fire and set up barrels of drink on the lakeshore sand. The otterclans were highly amused with the antics of the hares, who were always hungry and in high good humour after a battle. Little otterbabes chuckled uproariously as the hares sang barrack-room ballads.

"There's goin' to be a mutinee,
mate, I'm a-tellin' you,
if there ain't skilly'n'duff for tea,
to feed this big fat crew.
Don't dish 'em up no salad leaves,
or no burrgooly stew,
if there ain't skilly'n'duff for tea,
they might eat me'n'you!
Whoa! Skilly'n'duff, that's the stuff,
for my ole crew t'chew,
it's hot'n'thick so take your pick,
it'll do the trick if you feel sick.
So fill yore tum, by gum ole chum,
don't pant'n'wheeze'n'puff,
you'll run like a hare an' fight like a bear,
on good ole skilly'n'duff.
So don't stand lookin' silly, feed me lots o' skilly
. . . an' duff!"

They sang it twice more, each time speeding up the words. Tiria sang along with the bits she could catch; though, like the otterbabes, she mostly whooped and thumped the ground with her rudder. It was all such good fun! She looked at the happy faces around the fire, sniffed at the savoury aromas from the cooking and thanked her good fortune that the day had ended so well. The rule of the cats was finished; she had slain Riggu Felis, the tyrant. The thought of killing

317

another creature did not sit easy on her mind, but when the ottermaid saw all the freed slaves, she felt thoroughly justified by her swift action in the heat of battle.

The food, when it arrived, was a real victory feast. Tiria sat sampling the various dishes with Brantalis, Colour Sergeant O'Cragg, Banya, Leatho and her two subalterns. There was an unending supply of shrimp'n'hotroot soup for the otters, plenty of skilly'n'duff for the hares, trifles and tarts for the little ones and so many different pasties that it was hard to choose which one to try next.

Big Kolun passed a dish to the barnacle goose. "Get yore ole beak around that, mate. It's leek an' roasted parsnip in hazelnut sauce!"

Brantalis clacked his beak happily. "I am thinking this will taste as good as it looks!"

Tiria patted her friend's long neck. "I'm sure it will, mate. I wish our Redwallers were here to join in with all this. My dad, Brink and those three rascals Brinty, Tribsy and Girry."

Brantalis looked up from the dish he was about to sample. "I am thinking I should have mentioned your friend, the mouse named Brinty."

Tiria chuckled. "Why, what's that rogue been up to?"

The barnacle goose shook his head mournfully. "Alas, the young mouse is dead."

Tiria stared at him blankly. "Dead? Surely you're mistaken, Brinty can't be dead!"

Leatho placed his paw over hers, murmuring, "Hear him out, Lady. Wot happened to him, mate?"

Brantalis explained about the slaying of Brinty at the Abbey gate by the rat called Groffgut. Then he apologised. "I am sorry, but in all the excitement since I came here, I am thinking I forgot to mention this sad news."

No longer able to enjoy the feast, Tiria wandered off alone and sat weeping by the lakeside. After a while, Leatho came to comfort her.

"Brinty must have been a very good friend to ye, Lady. I have seen many of my mates slain. It's a hard thing to bear,

318

more so when yore far away in a strange place an' there ain't a thing ye can do about it."

The ottermaid nodded. "Aye, poor Brinty, and he did so want to become a warrior someday."

Leatho peered out at the lake, whilst Tiria dried her eyes. "Well, from wot the goose told us, he got his wish. Brinty went out fightin' like a real warrior. Do ye know, I think we should honour him like we did those others today. Let's do it, just me'n'you, eh?"

He pressed something in Tiria's paw, explaining, "It's a little wooden figure, Banya gave it t'me. Us clanbeasts often use it if'n the warrior gets lost in battle. It's an otter, see. But Banya carved the rudder down thin, so that it looks like a mouse."

Tiria gazed at the small object. "I see what you mean. So this is my Brinty! What do we do with him now?"

The outlaw explained. "Well, we ties him to a stone, with a few flowers bound around. Then we puts him in the lake with the others who fell today. That way he's in good company amid warriors like himself, Lady."

They gathered some meadowsweet and spearwort blossoms and bound them to a paw-sized pebble along with the figure. Together they waded out into the lake until the water was at waist height. Tiria took the package in her sling and threw it, up and out. The few golden blossoms were lost in the night sky. Then they heard a splash. Leatho watched the ripples drifting back at them.

"Yore friend Brinty is at rest now."

They held paws as the outlaw recited the verse which Tiria had heard the clanbeasts saying earlier in ancient otter tongue. Heaving a great gusty sigh, Tiria straightened her back.

"Thank you, Mr. Shellhound. I feel much better now!"

The outlaw grinned roguishly. "Aye, an' I'm still hungry. Let's get back to the vittles, Lady!"

As he turned to wade shoreward, Tiria pulled him back. "I don't think I could bear you calling me lady, queen or majesty for the rest of my life. So from now on it's Tiria to you, sir!"

She waded past him, but this time it was he who pulled her back. "Fair enough, as long as ye never calls me sir or Mr. Shellhound. Let's call each other 'mate.'"

Tiria laughed at this. "Righto, mate. Mate it is!"

Pitru stood on the highest point of the vast crater, congratulating himself. His scheme was successful: Soon he would be Ruler of Green Isle. The young cat had pitched his camp right across the narrow path which ran over the crater's rim. Behind him his followers had erected a barricade of rocks. Now nobeast could come over by this way, since he held the pass. Balur and Hinso, his confederates, listened as he outlined his plan. Pitru gazed off into the clear morning distance.

"See, the last of the smoke, I saw the glow from afar last night. The fortress has fallen. Are you not glad you came with me, eh?"

Balur bowed respectfully. "You saved our lives, Sire!"

Hinso placed a paw over her heart, affirming loyalty. "We were with ye from the first, commander."

Pitru drew himself up, leaning on his broad scimitar proudly. "Henceforth you will call me Warlord of Green Isle!"

Balur and Hinso glanced at each other, not daring to ask the question. It was Pitru who answered it for them.

"You will soon learn that Riggu Felis is dead. Look, down there in the foothills, here come the runaways."

Threading its way up the lower path, a band of catguards could be seen. Pitru smiled smugly. "That's Scaut leading the group. Take my guards and surround that lot, disarm them and bring them to me."

The mission was accomplished swiftly. By midmorning, Pitru had a dispirited bunch of catguards, refugees from the defeat of the fortress, sitting on the ground in front of him. His first act was to place his scimitar at Scaut's throat.

"Ah, the mighty weilmark, eh? You were ever my enemy, Scaut. So tell me, why should I not slay you right now?"

The weilmark gulped as the blade pressing against his throat bobbed slightly. "Spare me an' I will serve ye faithfully. I give ye my oath, Commander Pitru!"

Hinso sprang forward and kicked Scaut. "Our leader is Warlord of Green Isle now, an' ye will address him so!"

Pitru smiled thinly, enjoying his triumph. "That is, unless Riggu Felis still lives. Is he dead, Scaut? Did you see him die? How did it happen?"

Still with the blade threatening his throat, Scaut answered, "Lord, I was not there to see it, but some of these guards say that Riggu Felis was slain by an ottermaid with a sling, down on the pier."

Pitru shook his head in mock pity. "The great wildcat ruler, killed by an ottermaid. How sad! But you ran off and left him to his fate. What sort of a weilmark would you call yourself now, Scaut?"

Trying to bend his neck back from the pressure of the heavy blade, Scaut managed to gasp, "I am wot ye say I am, Lord!"

Pitru withdrew the blade, suddenly kicking Scaut flat. He grabbed the long whip, which had once been the weilmark's favourite weapon, and began beating his helpless victim with it, yelling at him, "You are no weilmark at all! From now on you will be my lackey—fetching, carrying and licking the dust from my paws!"

Breathing heavily, the young warlord turned upon the bunch of catguards who had followed Scaut. "And you, who do you serve now? A dead wildcat, or me?"

The subdued guards were only too ready to go over to Pitru. They bowed before him as he tossed the whip to Hinso. "Give them back their weapons and let them join my guards."

When this was done, he addressed his reinforced ranks. "The otters will come this way. They have a secret hideout somewhere around, but they have to pass here to get to it.

321

I can see by the signs that they have passed here more than once. I can defeat them! Now you will see how a real warlord makes his plans, not some half-faced old fool who was served by idiots like Scaut. I hold the high ground. The way forward is barricaded. To one side I have Deeplough. In front of me is a high hillside my enemies would have to scale to reach us. They have to get past me to reach their families, but they will die on the slopes below me. Then I will seek out those families and have slaves to build me a fortress of stone that will not burn, up here on the heights!"

33

The clans were crossing a stream, Tiria, Leatho and Big Kolun leading the procession, each with an otterbabe sitting upon their shoulders. The Long Patrol had a few scouts patrolling ahead, while the rest of the hares brought up the rear. Everybeast was singing as they splashed through the water. Sunrays shafted through the trees, mottling them with patches of light and shade. The babe on Tiria's shoulders kept heaving on her coronet, using it as a rein. But the ottermaid bore it stoically, singing along with the rest.

"Where are we going to? Holt Summerdell!
What'll we do there? We'll all live well!
When we get there we'll have tales to tell,
of the day that old fortress burnt an' fell!
Left right, I'll never complain,
if I never see a cat again!
Left right left right!
We had a war an' won the fight,
Left right left right!
Our queen is comin' home tonight!
Left right left right!
The clans are marchin' free!"

They halted on the far bank and sat down for a rest. Tiria heaved a sigh of relief as she lifted the babe over her head and set her down on the grass. The little one came to earth, clutching the royal coronet in her tiny paws. Tiria pretended to look shocked.

"So, a coronet robber, eh?"

Wrinkling her nose, the otterbabe returned the regalia. "H'a sorry, Kweemarm!"

Leatho bounced the babe in his lap. "Kweemarm, I like that, it fits ye well. Kweemarm!"

Tiria splashed streamwater at him. "Don't you dare start calling me Kweemarm, or I'll call you by your baby name!"

The outlaw picked up the otterbabe. Pressing his forehead against hers, he whispered, "So then, rascal, wot d'ye call me?"

The tiny otter giggled. "Heehee, Fleeko Spellbrown!"

Big Kolun sat the otterbabe on his paw. He smiled at her. "An' wot's my name, liddle cuddlerudder?"

She stared solemnly at him. "Unka Kolun!"

He planted a kiss on the top of her head. "Hoho, I'll be yore Unka Kolun anytime, darlin'!"

The cooks had packed food, which they had prepared the night before. The streambank assumed the air of a picnic lunch as everybeast sat eating and dabbling their footpaws in the shallows. Quartle and Portan shared a long loaf sliced lengthwise and filled with preserved fruit. Holding an end apiece, they bit into the long sandwich.

"I say, old lad, this is better'n haversack rations, wot!"

"Rather! Yum yum, sammies!"

The little ones thought this was hilarious. After gulping down everything they were given to eat, they splashed about in the water shouting, "Yumyum sammies! Yumyum sammies!"

Big Kolun chuckled. "Wait'll they see Summerdell—the falls, an' the waterslide, an' the swimpools. I tell ye, Lady, they won't forget ye for wot ye done for 'em!"

Tiria shook her head. "You mean for what you've done, and our brave hares. I just stood about an' looked like a queen most of the time."

Kolun winked at her. "An' ye did it very nicely, marm!"

Cuthbert came wading along. Chewing at an enormous slice of salad turnover, he waved his swagger stick at them. "Everythin' hunky dory here, wot?"

Tiria threw him a very pretty salute. "We're fine, thank you, Major. How are you?"

He squinched down on his monocle in a sort of half-wink. "Flourishin', marm, thankee. Must have a word, though."

Sitting among them, he beckoned Leatho, Kolun and Tiria close, dropping his voice. "Cap'n Rafe an' Sarn't O'Cragg have just reported back from the advance scouts. Seems there's a jolly old spot o' bother loomin' ahead."

Leatho became alert. "Wot sort o' bother, Major?"

Cuthbert explained. "Top o' that big crater over yonder. Seems a heap o' flippin' cats have built a wall, type o' barricade, right across the bloomin' path. Nerve o' the whiskery blighters, wot! Nothin' for you t'worry about, Milady. You stop here with the families. The Long Patrol an' some of our otterchums will sort 'em out, sharpish!"

Big Kolun stroked his rudder thoughtfully. "Sharpish ain't a word I'd use, Major. A few pawfuls o' foebeasts could hold that pass agin twice our numbers."

Leatho agreed with Kolun. "Right, mate. They could hold us there all season, stop us gettin' back to the families at Holt Summerdell."

Cuthbert rose in sprightly manner. "Right, then we'll just have t'shift the villains post haste, wot! You chaps comin'?"

Tiria bounded up beside Cuthbert. "Yes we are, and I'm one of the chaps. A queen's place is with her warriors. Much as I like playing with babes, that'll have to wait awhile. Raise the clans, Shellhound!"

Cuthbert was about to object when Kolun cautioned him, "Ye don't argue with a queen, Major, especially one that sounds like my missus when she's dancin' on her rudder!"

The hare took one look at the tall ottermaid unwinding her sling and coughed. "Harrumph! Very good, point taken old lad, wot!"

Balur crouched on the rimtop, holding a long pike axe by his side. Shielding his eyes against the noontide sun, he squinted down the steep, rocky, brushstrewn slope of the crater. Everything seemed unusually quiet; even the grasshoppers had stopped chirruping among the heather, and the humming of bees visiting gorseflowers was absent. He raised himself slightly higher, thinking he had detected a movement amid some rocks.

He had time for only one strangled yelp as the slingstone split his skull. Then he toppled downhill, with a few loose rocks falling behind him.

"Eulaliiiiaaaa! Ee aye eeeeeeeee!"

Slingstones whipped uphill, most of them bouncing off the barricade which stood across the path, a few finding their way over the rough stone wall but not causing much damage to the enemy.

Pitru was up and at the barricade, snapping out orders. "Archers, stand by! Spears and pikes, drop back! Slingers and boulder throwers, up front here!"

Sergeant O'Cragg shook his head at Leatho and Tiria. "Ye needs t'be further h'up to be doin' h'any good with those slings!"

Cuthbert whispered to Captain Granden, "It looks like we'll have to try a charge!"

Before Granden could reply, there was a clatter and a rumble from above. The steep crater side shook as an avalanche of rock and rubble pounded down from above.

Tiria yelled, "Find cover, quick! Get your heads down!"

She and Kolun crouched behind a rocky outcrop as boulders bounced by overhead, followed by a hurtling mass of soil, vegetation and scree. Big Kolun covered Tiria, shielding her with his powerful back. She felt the thud as several missiles rebounded from him. Then there was silence, soon broken by a cheer from the cats on the rim.

Kolun straightened up, spitting out dust and groaning as he rubbed his back. "Phew! They nearly had us that time, Lady!"

The ottermaid wiped debris from her eyes anxiously. "Are you hurt, Kolun? Did any big rocks hit you?"

The big fellow managed a rueful grin. "Oh, I think I'll live, marm. Banya, wot's goin' on?"

Banya Streamdog came scurrying on all fours, a large gash over one eye. "We lost two clanbeasts an' a hare. . . . Look out!"

The three huddled together as another load of boulders thundered down the slope. This was smaller than the first lot, and soon petered out.

Now the catguards were chanting. "Pitru! Pitru! Death to his foes!"

In the relative safety of the rocky outcrop, Cuthbert, Granden and O'Cragg joined Kolun, Leatho, Banya and Tiria for a hasty Council of War. Granden glanced grimly up at the crater top.

"Bad show all round, chaps, wot?"

Kolun looked up from pressing some dried moss to Banya's wound. "I told ye they could pin us down here, Major. There ain't no way we can get at the scum, that's a fact!"

Cuthbert polished dust from his monocle nonchalantly. "Pish-tush, old lad! I've thought of a solution already. Sarn't O'Cragg, see if y'can't get the Patrol an' a few stout otter types away off to the left flank. Quietly now, don't let the cats see what we're up to, wot! Cap'n Granden, I'll leave you in charge here. Begin advancin' slowly in ranks of three, slingin' fusillades."

The captain drew his long rapier. "I'm with ye, Major

Frunk. We keep the blighters busy while you work a flanker on 'em. Hah, we've played that game before. Remember when we whacked those vermin at the south cliffs?"

Cuthbert nodded. "Precisely! But remember, don't give the order to charge 'til ye hear me give the old war whoop."

Captain Rafe Granden threw a curt salute. "Aye, sir. The moment ye yell, we'll come runnin' like death on the wind. There'll be a lot o' cats linin' up at Hellgates by sunset!"

Major Cuthbert Blanedale Frunk began to smile. "By thunder there will, I'll see to that. G'bye, chaps!"

He stole off to the left. Tiria made as if to follow him, but Captain Granden placed a restraining paw on her. "You stay with us, Lady. The Major ain't a beast to be around today. Did ye see how wild his eyes were? Right! Kolun, Banya an' you, too, miss, follow me. I'll show ye the ropes, 'tis quite simple. You'll each be in charge of a rank. Don't worry, you'll soon pick it up!"

Pitru peered over the top of his wall, then ducked down to Hinso at his side. "Well, that soon stopped them. We'll give them another shower of rocks in a bit. Huh, they won't be so eager to charge us then, eh?"

Hinso glanced back over her shoulder. "Lord, we've used up all the stones we collected."

The young warlord replied scathingly, "Then don't argue with me! Get some more, and get them fast. Move yourself!"

There was a cry from the otters below. "Ee aye eeeee!"

Some slingstones rattled in over the walltop. One struck Pitru on the paw. He winced and sucked his paw, then scoffed, "If that's the best they can do, we've no need to fret."

Another shout came from below. "Redwaaaaallll!"

Hinso was just moving off to issue orders to the rock-gathering crew when the second wave of slingstones came over. This time they struck with more force. One hit Hinso in the mouth, knocking a fang out.

328

Crouching down behind the wall, Pitru yelled, "Archers, slingers, spearcats, up here!"

"Galedeeeeeeep!"

On this third warcry, which issued forth from Kolun, a big salvo of slingstones came whipping in, dropping several guards in their tracks. Pitru chanced a glance through a chink in the wallstones. The otters had gained ground. A long line of them stood up, whirling their slings as Banya sang out the eerie clan warcry. "Ee aye eeeeeee!"

Suddenly it was raining slingstones fast and hard. The otters dropped down low, and another long rank ran ahead of them, slinging for all they were worth. Tiria stood along-side them, shouting, "Redwaaaaaalll!"

Gritting his teeth, Pitru drew his scimitar. Anger coursed through the young cat; things were not going as he had planned. He called to his catguards, "Get to this wall, rally to me!"

As the guards ran forward, a bloodcurdling roar came from lower down the rim, past the wall. "Eulaliiiiiaaaaa!"

Using a long pike axe which he had captured, Cuthbert came vaulting over the crater rim onto the narrow path. The Long Patrol hares and some clanbeasts were hurrying behind to catch him up, but their major was gone forever. In his place was a berserk animal whom none could control or stand against. Cuthbert made straight for the silk-robed cat carrying the broad scimitar. Foebeasts fell like chaff to the scythe before his insane attack. He was roaring like a madbeast—no Eulalias or warcries, just a continuous spine-chilling screech. There were several guards, including Hinso, blocking his path. Holding the long pikestaff side-ways, Cuthbert hit them, bowling the lot backward in a heap. They struck Pitru, knocking him into the wall, which crumbled and collapsed. Cuthbert hurled himself upon them, trying to wield the pike axe, which was far too long for close combat.

Pitru scrambled from under the melee. Naked fear shone in his eyes as he gasped, "Get him away from me. Kill him!"

Hinso lashed out with a lance from behind the hare, sticking him through the side. Cuthbert turned, snapping the weapon like a twig and going for the cat's throat with bared teeth. Dust billowed up from the narrow path in the ensuing chaos. Seeing that the mad hare's back was turned to him, Pitru struck with his scimitar. Three guards fell upon Cuthbert. Hinso tried to wrest the pike axe from his paws, but nothing could stop the beast they called "Old Blood 'n'guts." He went forward, stumbling over fallen wallstones, dragging four cats with him before reaching Pitru. With one swift move, he trapped the young warlord, locking him to his chest with the pikestaff.

Colour Sergeant O'Cragg was battering his way through the guards to reach his major, when the three ranks of clanbeasts burst over the rim in a wild charge, bellowing, "Death's on the wind! Eee aye eeeeeee!"

Captain Granden, not having heard his major give the signal cry, had decided to move swiftly. The catguards battled wildly, knowing they were fighting for their lives, realising the otterclans would cede no quarter. Tiria was whipping her loaded sling right and left, watching the enemy falling before it. She saw Cuthbert besieged by Pitru and the four cats on the far rim, and began battling ahead to go to his aid. But too late!

Still making that awful sound he had last uttered on the day of his daughter's death, Cuthbert leaped over the rim, taking Pitru and the cats with him. Tiria reached the rim, along with Rafe Granden, Sergeant O'Cragg and Big Kolun, who was carrying half a shattered oar in his paw. They watched for a moment in frozen horror at the scene below, then leaped over the rim and went skidding down the steep-shaled slope toward the vast, sinister expanse of water called Deeplough.

Cuthbert could not halt his rushing descent. He hit the water holding the lifeless body of Pitru, whose back he had broken in the crushing grip of the pikestaff. The others splashed in beside him, wailing in panic and trying to pull

330

themselves out by scrabbling at the steeply banked loose scree.

Without any prior warning, the dark waters rose in a hump, and Slothunog was among them! The monster was a throwback of some primitive age, covered in jet-black scales with a humped back and a long serpentlike neck. It hissed aloud, blowing out a spray of water, its reptilian head swaying back and forth as it struck with a cavernous mouthful of glittering teeth. The body of Pitru was wrenched from Cuthbert's grasp into the creature's jaws, which snapped shut on the dead cat. Tiria and the others, having managed to stop their descent, lay on their backs in the shale, footpaws dug in tight as they gazed in disbelief at their friend.

Cuthbert had scrambled up onto the back of Slothunog, hacking at its neck with the pike axe. It sped out onto the lough, wriggling and thrashing furiously as it tried to rid itself of its berserk passenger. The hare, however, could not be shaken off. He hacked, speared, chopped and stabbed frenziedly, like some wildbeast trying to regain the prey which had been stolen by another. Then, with one massive effort, he plunged the spiked head of the weapon deep, pushing with the last of his strength as he drove it home.

Slothunog hissed loud and long before its head finally fell forward. It shuddered, sent up a crimson gout of its lifeblood and vanished beneath the unplumbed depths of Deeplough, taking with it a hare who had become, in the last of his many roles, a dragonslayer!

Colour Sergeant O'Cragg saluted, blinking through the tears which coursed down his tough face. "Perilous! I think the word was made for Major Frunk. Perilous!"

Captain Granden nodded agreement as he passed Tiria his kerchief. "Perilous indeed, Sarn't. No Badger Lord in a Bloodwrath could've done better. Dry your tears, lady. He went exactly the way he wanted to. Right, Sarn't?"

O'Cragg sniffed. "Right y'are, Cap'n. Pore ole Major weren't the same h'after 'e lost 'is lovely daughter."

331

He borrowed the captain's already tear-drenched kerchief from Tiria and dabbed at his eyes. "Tell ye wot, miss. We'll both stop weepin' an' watch the sky tonight for the Major, eh?"

The ottermaid squeezed the sergeant's big paw. "Thank you, Sergeant, I'd like us to do that. If we spot a specially big star, with a small pretty one close to it, we'll name them Cuthbert and Petunia, after the Major and his daughter."

Colour Sergeant O'Cragg gave his eyes another wipe before returning the captain's kerchief. "Bless ye, miss, that's h'a very nice thought."

Big Kolun got the situation back on an even keel with his next remark. "I'll give ye a very nice thought, Sergeant. Just 'ow in the name o' seasons do we get out o' this crater?"

Amid the laughter that followed, Kolun could be heard yelling to the watchers on the high rim, "Lorgo! Banya! See if'n ye can't knot enough ropes together to get us out of here!"

34

Deedero Galedeep was chopping leeks and scallions to add to her stewpot when an otterbabe came bursting through the waterfall curtain into the cavern. Placing his little paws either side of his mouth, he bawled at her, "Mammee, a fink our daddie's comin' 'ome!"

Deedero put aside the knife, wiping her paws on her apron. "Wot've I told ye about shoutin', Toobil? I ain't deaf!"

Toobil climbed up on her lap and whispered in her ear, "I sayed Daddie's comin' 'ome, wiv lots h'of uthers."

Picking the babe up, Deedero stowed him sideways on her hip and shuffled off through the watery curtain. "Hmph, he must've smelt my shrimp'n'hotroot soup cookin'. Come on then, let's go an' meet him."

They joined the other families heading for the ledge.

It was an odd but rousing sight. A barnacle goose, twoscore and five hares in regimental rigout, countless clanbeasts and freed slave families, and Tiria, in her full regalia, being carried at their centre, seated on a chair made of spearhafts and javelins. The situation was made more incongruous still: Everybeast was singing lustily, a barrackroom ballad which had been taught to them by Porters and Quarters, the two young subalterns. Some ottermums took the precaution of covering the ears of their babes, though a few elders marched alongside of them, chuckling aloud.

"Pick 'em up laddie buck! an' put 'em down laddie buck!
You've made it home an' now you're out of luck, out
   of luck!

Oh 'tis nice to march back home,
when there's nowhere else to go,
for home is every warrior's desire.
To see the ones you love, beat each other black'n'blue,
while your dear old granny's roastin' by the fire!

Pick 'em up laddie buck! an' put 'em down laddie buck!
You've made it home an' now you're out of luck, out
   of luck!

To taste your mother's cookin',
an' have bellyache all day,
o what a sad an' sorry tale is this.
If I could just escape, to some regimental camp,
I'd give some ugly sergeant one big kiss!

Pick 'em up laddie buck! an' put 'em down laddie buck!
You've made it home an' now you're out of luck, out
   of luck!

But I cannot run away,
'cos my sister pinched me boots,
she bit me nose an' stole me uniform.
An' Dad's nailed up the door, wot a lovely
   welcome home,
from a family so kind an' sweet an' warm!

Pick 'em up laddie buck! Put 'em down laddie buck!
You've made it home an' now you're out of luck, out
   of luck!"

Colour Sergeant O'Cragg and Big Kolun (who fancied the idea of being an officer) roared out together in fine parade-ground manner, "Regiment . . . wait for it! . . . Haaaaalt!"

334

Everybeast stamped to a perfect halt. Big Kolun swelled out his chest. "H'otterclans . . . dismiss!"

Colour Sergeant O'Cragg came next. "Long Patrol . . . dismiss!"

Clanbeasts ran to be reunited with their families. There was widespread backslapping, hugging and kissing. The freed slaves were welcomed cordially. Otters began crowding around Tiria, each wanting to shake the paw of their High Queen, the Rhulain of Green Isle.

Kolun, still struck by the thought of becoming an officer, introduced Tiria to his missus. "Milady, h'allow me to present my h'enchantin' wife, Deedero!"

The big homely ottermum stared at her husband strangely. "Why are ye talkin' like that, for goodness sakes?"

Kolun stood smartly to attention and saluted Deedero. "Because, h'o jewel h'of my 'eart, h'I'm a h'officer now."

Deedero passed him the babe to carry. "Ye great windbag, keep talkin' like that t'me, an' I'll bend a ladle round yore rudder."

She hugged Tiria and kissed her cheek. "Welcome to Holt Summerdell, Yore Majesty. 'Tis a rare pleasure to have ye here. Ye'll be stayin' to dinner I hope?"

Tiria chuckled. "I'll be staying here for lots of dinners. This is my home now."

Epilogue

To the Mother Abbess of Redwall Abbey,
From the High Rhulain of Green Isle
My Dearest Friend Lycian,

It is now eight seasons since Brantalis landed at Redwall and marked the start of my quest. What an adventure it has been—from simple Abbeymaid to Queen!

Sometimes I just sit back and enjoy the feeling of being High Rhulain.

Brantalis continues to serve us well. He is fiercely proud of his twin titles, "Queen's Courier" and "Official Messenger to Redwall Abbey," though I think our goose only takes on the tasks because he enjoys all the attention and feeding he receives at either end of his journey, carrying our letters.

Let me tell you some of what has taken place since I came to Green Isle (I am sure the Redwall Recorder will want all the details).

Holt Summerdell is now our pride and joy. What ruler ever had such good and faithful friends to serve her, with the exception of you at Redwall. My otterclans have now restored everything to its former glory. The terraces and ledges are a profusion of fruit, vegetables and flowers. Our gardeners make sure we want for nothing.

My Water Bailiffs, Whulky and Chab, tend to the ponds

and rapids, so our little ones can play there from dawn to dusk in safety. Holt Summerdell is always filled with the sounds of song and the laughter of otterbabes, which to my mind is the sweetest of all.

Big Kolun Galedeep's missus, Deedero, has supervised the restoration of our big cave. Now we have proper dormitories, a wonderful dining hall, extensive kitchens, even a wine cellar. Deedero is not so much an ottermum as a force of nature. I have never seen a creature so full of boundless energy and enthusiasm. I would be lost without Deedero and Banya Streamdog as my constant companions. We take tea together (just like you and molemum Burbee). Between us we plan and discuss everything from feasting to harvesting.

At the moment, we are designing uniform tunics for our clan warriors. Leatho Shellhound, Big Kolun and the clan leaders were so impressed by the tactics and discipline of the Long Patrol. They learned a lot from the hares before they returned to their mountain—mainly that constant vigilance and alertness will keep our isle free from foebeasts and the threat of conquering warlords. At the clan meeting, they voted unanimously to form the Green Clan Regiment.

So, I think Green Isle is now safe, with Leatho and the Green Clan Regiment to protect our shores—even though Kolun Galedeep and certain comrades of his have adopted harespeech! Banya and I have to laugh when Deedero says, "If'n that great lump and his mates come into supper wot-wotting and pip-pipping and callin' me ole gel, I'll bend a ladle over their rudders!"

Well, Lycian, that is all of my news for this season—apart from the fact that we begin planning our Autumn Pool Festival, but I'll tell you more of that in my next letter. By the way, can you ask my dad and Brink how they made those coloured water lanterns? You remember them from when we had a Harvest Feast around the Abbey pond.

Tell me, how are my dad and Brink and all my dear friends at the Abbey? Some of those Dibbuns must be growing into young ones now, Grumby, Taggle, Irgle and Ralg. Do they still remember me?

Sometimes I feel sad when I think of Redwall and poor young Brinty. I've never seen his resting place, but I'd love to visit it. How are Girry and Tribsy and Friar Bibble? I'll wager Sister Snowdrop hasn't changed a hair nor old Friar Quelt. And you, Lycian, the youngest, prettiest and wisest Abbess Redwall has ever seen. I hope you know I learned a lot from just watching you when I was an Abbeymaid. When I am facing a problem, I always ask myself, "How would Lycian have dealt with this?" Happily, I can tell you I haven't put a paw wrong thus far!

I must finish now. Queenly affairs calling me away, you know. Don't let that barnacle goose stuff himself until he can't fly. Send him back with a nice long letter to me.

Your lifelong friend,

Tiria

P.S. Don't forget about the coloured water lanterns. Tell Dad and Brink I need them soon!

P.P.S. Could you also ask Brink to send the recipe for October Ale? It's for our Brew Otter, Birl Gully. He makes something called Gullyplug Punch, and it's far too strong!

Love, Tiria

To the High Rhulain of Green Isle
From Lycian, Mother Abbess of Redwall Abbey
Dearest Tiria,

I take quill in paw to thank you for your informative letter. Well, my friend, things seem to be thriving in your Queendom. (It is Queendom, isn't it? Anyway, I like the sound of that title.)

So you'll soon have your own army, the Green Clan Regiment no less! It all sounds so exciting. I was going to add that I'd love to see it, but more of that later.

Your Banya and Deedero seem real treasures. There's nothing like having faithful friends around you, is there? Tiria, you are really fortunate in having such a wonderful life. Enjoy it, my friend, you richly deserve all the good things in your life!

Now let me tell you my news. Old Quelt has expressed a desire to retire, so his duties are to be split: Little Sister Snowdrop will be our new Librarian, and your friend Girry is to be Recorder of Redwall Abbey. I've no need to tell you he is delighted at the prospect. Who would have thought that Girry had a yearning for the scholarly life?

As for that rogue Tribsy, he doesn't know it yet but Fore-mole Grudd wants Tribsy to succeed him when he retires from being mole chieftain this winter. Molemum Burbee confided this to me over a pot of tea yesterday afternoon, requesting that I not speak of it to anybeast at Redwall. So I'm not speaking, I am writing! Besides, you're not at Redwall at the moment.

Enclosed with this scroll you'll find a letter from your dad and Brink, which includes the directions for making the coloured water lanterns that you requested.

After you told me in your first letter about poor Pandion, I relayed the sad news to your dad and Brink. They have made him a beautiful little monument, right alongside Brinty's resting place. I visit Brinty and read him your letters, you know. I also picked out a special stone for Brinty, just as you told me to. We must never forget our brave friends, ever!

So, Tiria Wildlough, on to my surprise news (I've been keeping the best for last)! Recently I met some old friends of yours—a whole group in fact of Long Patrol hares! Captain Rafe Granden, Colour Sergeant O'Cragg, Corporal Drubblewick, Quarters and Porters (Aren't those two an absolute hoot?) and more besides. They came marching up in their smart red tunics, armed to the teeth and ravenous as a horde of wild beasts. They were bearing with them a lengthy scroll from Lord Mandoral himself. Every creature at Redwall was delighted with its tidings. The Badger Lord of Salamandastron had written to inform me that he is now the owner of two ships: One is the *Purloined Petunia* (which you already told me of); the other is over twice its size, a three-masted vessel which, to use Lord Mandoral's phrase, "was liberated from certain seascum not worthy to walk its decks." It is now renamed the *Fearless Frunk!*

Next spring, both ships will anchor in the River Moss under the command of captains Quartle and Porter. From there they will sail for Salamandastron and thence, after a suitable visit, they sail for Green Isle! And guess what? I have been requested to select threescore of our Redwallers to sail with them! So, Your Majesty, be sure to have your regiments watching the coasts of Green Isle in late spring! We are coming!

Now, may I invite you and any of your friends you wish to accompany you to visit us for a full summer season? You also may bring along your brewbeast, Mr. Gully. Brink will teach him to brew fine October Ale. We will feast, we will sing, we will talk and laugh together.

Hares from Salamandastron, otters from Green Isle, and Redwallers will meet here in comradeship and peace. For you know, my dear friend, the gates of Redwall Abbey in Mossflower Country are always open to all good hearts, young and old.

Fondly yours,
Abbess Lycian